T0329449

THE WEATHERMEN
ON TRIAL

THE WEATHERMEN ON TRIAL

A BOMBSHELL STORY ABOUT BRINGING THE WAR HOME

Caleb Stewart Rossiter

Algora Publishing
New York

Library of Congress Cataloging in Publication Control Number: 2018055728

    Names: Rossiter, Caleb S., author.
      Title: The Weathermen On Trial: A Bombshell Story About Bringing the War Home
    / Caleb Stewart Rossiter.
    Description: New York: Algora Publishing, 2018.
      pages cm
    Identifiers: LCCN 2018055728 (print) | ISBN 9781628943696 (soft cover: alk. paper)
   |ISBN 9781628943702 (hard cover: alk. paper) | ISBN 9781628943719 (eBook)
    Subjects: Weather Underground Organization—Fiction | Revolutionaries—United
    States—Fiction. Historical fiction | Legal stories.
    LC classification PS3618.O8534 P38 2019 | LCCN 2018055728 | Dewey class no. 813/.6
    LC record available at https://lccn.loc.gov/2018055728

Printed in the United States

Table of Contents

My mixed feelings, my feelings of guilt and shame, these are things that I am not proud of, and I find it hard to speak about them and to tease out what was right from what was wrong... (But) I think that part of the Weatherman phenomenon that was right was our understanding of what the position of the United States is in the world. It was this knowledge that we just couldn't handle; it was too big. We didn't know what to do. In a way I still don't know what to do with this knowledge. I don't know what needs to be done now, and it's still eating away at me just as it did 30 years ago.

— Mark Rudd, as interviewed in the 2002 documentary *The Weather Underground*.

Rudd was a founding member of the Weathermen, a paramilitary group of perhaps 50 white, upper-class, under-30 American revolutionaries that emerged from the Students for a Democratic Society in 1969. The Weathermen rejected SDS's traditional support for the non-violent philosophy and tactics of the movements for Negro civil rights and against the Viet Nam War. They "brought the war home" with a five-year bombing campaign whose goals were to end U.S. imperialism and establish communist rule in the United States.

Weather bombed two types of targets: police, courts, prisons, and anti-poverty programs that the group believed repressed non-white domestic minorities; and military, diplomatic, legislative, and other government entities and their university and corporate collaborators that the group believed supported imperialist rule in Viet Nam and other formerly colonized countries.

Viet Nam drove us to mania. We decided to make the United States unlivable if the war doesn't end...If you think you have the moral high ground, you can do some really dreadful things.

— Weatherman Brian Flanagan, interviewed in the same documentary.

Experience proves that the man who obstructs a war in which his nation is engaged, whether right or wrong, occupies no enviable place in life or history... The most favorable posthumous history the stay-at-home traitor can hope for is — oblivion.

— President Ulysses S. Grant

Grant wrote this in his memoirs, commenting on his failure to oppose openly the invasion of Mexico, in which he served with distinction. After the fact, Grant bitterly condemned the war and the seizure of today's Western states as blatant, unjust imperialism.

PROLOGUE: MENDOCINO, MAY 1970

"I'm sorry, but I just can't back down like Bernie and Jeff want us to, retreating into 'armed propaganda,' all bathrooms and no casualties. We too have to destroy to save — we have to destroy American culture and the imperial will if we want to save Viet Nam, in fact save Che's two, three, many Viet Nams."

Most Americans think of themselves as patriots, and say they love our country and feel a duty to serve and protect her. Of course, all of them have their own definitions of the important words in that sentence: American, patriot, love, country, duty, serve, and protect. "Destroy to save" reveals the definitions adopted by the speaker and the six other young, white, and highly-privileged and schooled patriots lounging in the sun-room of an elegant beach house in Mendocino, California, overlooking America's western shore.

The previous decade had taught them to think of America the way a lieutenant in the invading U.S. Army had infamously thought of a Vietnamese village. The young officer had turned to a television camera as his troops applied Zippo lighters to roofs thatched with palm frond and explained, with no irony intended, "We had to destroy the village in order to save it."

"Destroying to save" was a core strategy in the final decade of America's 30-year war against Viet Nam, and the young people in the room knew it. An Army major had said the same thing about a bombing and artillery campaign to recapture the city of Ben Tre during the 1968 Tet Offensive. Political scientist Samuel Huntington of the Harvard Center for International Affairs called for free-fire zones, also in 1968, to deprive the enemy of recruits and

sanctuary. Huntington's technocratic euphemism was, "the direct application of mechanical and conventional power...on such a scale as to produce a
massive migration from countryside to city."

U.S. combat units invaded Viet Nam in 1965, adding half a million troops
to the few thousand "advisers" who had been fighting alongside South Vietnamese forces for the previous ten years of a war the United States had been
funding for ten years before that, ever since U.S. ships brought the French
colonial army back after World War II. The "direct application" of massive
industrial violence against a peasant society and a guerrilla army through the
Rolling Thunder bombing campaign against infrastructure in the North and
the free-fire zones in the South was intended to terrorize the Vietnamese —
civilians, soldiers, and their political leaders — into a settlement that left a
pro-U.S. regime in power in the South.

The young people in the room couldn't yet know it, but the strategy
continued even to the last gasp, the ten-day 1972 "Christmas" high-altitude
bombing of Hanoi and Haiphong. Unprecedented waves of B-52's based
mostly in Guam, 2,500 miles away, dropped 15,000 tons of explosive energy
— equivalent in power to the Hiroshima bomb. They would not, however,
find themselves surprised by that final act of ingenuity and ferocity.

"Look, revolution's not a pipe-dream. So we ** this first round, 'cause
we're new at making these bigger bombs. We can study, we can practice,
we can still beat them. It happens all the time! The Polish rebel, Pilsudski,
he tried to blow up the Czar with dynamite, with Lenin's brother, before
World War I. Most Poles called him crazy, even though Poland was ruled by
Russia, even though all the Poles hated that. Nobody backed him. He went
to jail in Siberia.

"But within just a few years, Pilsudski was in charge of Poland, because
he was the one with the guns after World War I left Russia weak. Everybody
loved him then! Even when Lenin took over Russia, Pilsudski never took
his foot off the throttle. He was marching toward Moscow, against Lenin,
within a year of taking power!"

Standing and pacing as he often did, speaking fast, maybe from the speed
he'd taken, maybe from the need to make his argument before his wordy
comrades interrupted and added harsh comments to their stern looks, Billy
Ayers fought against the emerging consensus of this rump meeting of the

Central Committee of the Weathermen, the violent heir to SDS, the Students for a Democratic Society.

Of course, none of these seven had been in a classroom for quite a while. As with SNCC, the Student Non-Violent Coordinating Committee of the civil rights movement, which kept its name during the 1960s even as fewer and fewer of its members were students, non-violent, or coordinated with anybody, SDS provided a useful title. Right up until the Central Committee peremptorily dissolved SDS at the end of 1969 and became the Weather Bureau, its support cadres all across the country got their offices and funds from universities.

Violence was in the air in America and in the room and, not coincidentally, so was romance. Bernardine Dohrn, who gazed lazily across the room at Billy from a barstool at a teak counter, had just started to console him in bed. Billy's long-time flame Diana Oughton had been atomized two months before along with Terry Robbins and Teddy Gold at a townhouse in Greenwich Village while amateurishly making a nail and dynamite bomb for a dance at a New Jersey Army base.

Bernardine had been born an Ohrnstein, but her businessman father had changed their name to the less-Jewish Dohrn when she was in high school in the wealthy Milwaukee suburb of Whitefish Bay. She had undergraduate and law degrees from the University of Chicago, and the verve, vocabulary, and determination to go with them. Son of the chairman of the Chicagoland energy giant Commonwealth Edison, uber-WASP Billy was a graduate of the Lake Forest prep school and the University of Michigan. Like Dohrn he had become an accomplished public speaker and often served as the voice of the Weathermen.

Billy's martyred lover Diana had come from even greater privilege: the leading family of Dwight, Illinois, outside of Chicago. Her mother's side of the family had founded the Boy Scouts of America, her father ran the family bank and served in the legislature, and the family home was on the National Historic Register. She graduated from the elite Madeira girls' prep school in Virginia and then chose Bryn Mawr from her acceptances to all the "seven sisters" women's colleges. She added a master's in teaching from Michigan to her Bryn Mawr degree while joining Billy, her colleague at an experimental elementary school, in SDS.

Across the sunny room, on a padded bench with their cups of coffee, was another pair of recent lovers, Jeff Jones and Eleanor Raskin. Jeff was the son of an artist with the Walt Disney company, and he had grown up in Hollywood and attended hip Antioch College before dropping out to organize full-time for SDS. Eleanor was in the process of reverting to her maiden name, Stein, after a divorce. Her parents were a prominent New Deal economist and a civil rights activist. After high school at elite Erasmus Hall in Brooklyn she attended Barnard College before graduating from Manchester University in England.

There were also the two survivors of the Townhouse, Cathy Wilkerson and Kathy Boudin, sitting at the dining table, as always within a few feet of each other, never smiling, seeming still to be communing with the ghosts of their friends. Cathy was the daughter of a top executive with the establishment's favorite public relations firm, Young & Rubicam. She had graduated from Abbot girls' boarding school (the sister school to then all-boys Andover, with which it later merged) and Swarthmore College.

The Townhouse was her father's: it was at the urging of her lover, Terry Robbins, that she had commandeered it while he was on vacation in the Caribbean. Boudin was the daughter of radical royalty. Her father was Leonard Boudin, National Lawyers Guild advocate for leftist stars. Paul Robeson, Dan Ellsberg, Dr. Spock, and Julian Bond were just a few of his many prominent clients. *Pour lagniappe*, Leonard's brother-in-law was radical journalist I.F. Stone.

The final person in the room, Howie Machtinger, had sunk himself firmly against a plush couch, his disinterested body language proclaiming disingenuously that he was just a good soldier, unconcerned with the discussion, and just ready to do whatever was decided. Howie had an undergraduate degree from Columbia and a graduate degree from Chicago, but came from an upwardly-mobile but far less wealthy family than the others. In this he was like John "J. J." Jacobs and Mark Rudd, his younger Central Committee compatriots who had led the path-breaking Columbia building occupation in 1968.

When Jacobs and Rudd had become too wrapped up in protest to maintain their standing and graduate from Columbia, it was an unfathomable tragedy for their parents. They were in Mendocino too, but Dohrn had excluded them from this opening meeting because they had started to demonstrate a troubling lack of fealty to her.

Ayers continued: "And Fidel, look, he was seen as crazy, nobody in Cuba backed him either, and his attack on the dictator's barracks in '53 was a disaster, and off to prison he went. But within five years he and Che and a few friends had taken over.

"And Ho, and Mao, and even ** George Washington, for Christ's sake... dare to struggle, dare to win, they all said, and they did. We can do it too! And it's always time to start, says Ho. Some bombing, some killing, we can create the chaos that unhinges everything. We know marching won't do it — the liberals march, march, march, and go back to their privileges. Voting won't do it — the system swallows up even radicals in debate and half-steps to nowhere. Those bull Progressive Labor robots and their labor organizing won't do it — most of the working class is our enemy, for sure, forever happy to have made it onto the first rung of the capitalist ladder.

"We agreed at Flint that it's time to take up the gun, like the Panthers say. We'd be immoral not to keep on. We know there's no success without violence in America. You want to stop the killing in Viet Nam, keep on killing here!

"Now, I agree with Jeff that it was bad tactics — not wrong, but the wrong time — to decide in December that Good German bystanders aren't innocent, and that pigs and imperialist troops could also be our targets. Now we know that it drives everybody away, left and right, when we hit the low man on the totem pole, or just some schmo walking by. I heard it from freaks who figured it was us who bombed the cop cars at shift changes in Berkeley and New York. Cars is one thing, but cops is clearly another. And it got worse after Townhouse.

"Even the radical press called us out for making nail bombs, almost guaranteed to take out bystanders — and they don't even know it was for an NCO dance, where sergeants and their wives and girlfriends, waiters, whatever would be killed. We were missing the point anyway: they're only pawns in the game. The hard-asses in the Army are right about one thing: get the leaders by the balls and their hearts and minds will follow, from fear.

"So no, don't retreat from bombing. Just make ** sure it gets the architects of race rule and empire, and not their worker bees and bystanders.

That's why I also like the kidnapping and assassination plan J. J.'s been pushing since he got here: it targets the right people, the top people, for once. Let's bite the bullet, no turning back, and ramp it up! Come on, Kent, Jackson, all the schools out, right now — we did bring the war home. Now let's fight it. We wanted to be Marion Delgado derailing the train, we wanted to be the 'one who fights' that the Vietnamese told us to look for — well, now we are!"

Kathy Boudin, the heroine in the room for her escape from the Townhouse explosion, tentatively raised her hand. "But the Panthers are against all of this, and we agreed after the Cuba trip to follow their lead. Our New York stuff, the car bombings and trying to burn the judge's house, that was all for the Panther 21, but it brought heat down on them instead. If we want the *lumpen* blacks to respect us as fighters, we have to be seen as obedient to their leaders. I'm fully committed to following the black lead, wherever it takes me, including killing, and I know that David and Marilyn agree with me. And on this tactical question of whether to bomb, to kill, if the Panthers say wait, how can we refuse them?"

From her perch on the barstool, Bernadine Dohrn, laughed. " ** the Panthers! Hell, I've adopted the prone position, like they say, with enough of them to earn the right to say that. We're the vanguard of our part of the revolution, the white kids. We've got to do what's necessary, go our own way, even as we praise the Panthers. And no question Billy is right on strategy, kill or be killed.

"Look where caution got Fred — he led chants about picking up the gun, but then called us Custeristic. I'll bet he wished he picked up more guns than Mark Clark's shotgun. They sure went out in a blaze of glory: 99 bullets to one! That's more Butch Cassidy than your and J. J.'s wet dream, Billy. They say I wanna stick a fork in 'em, well let's do it!"

She laughed as she made the four-finger "fork" salute the Weathermen had ironically adopted since the media had picked up her rambling complaint at the December war council in Flint about the publicity given to the murder of actress Sharon Tate by Charles Manson's "family" instead of to the police murder of Black Panther Fred Hampton: "Dig it, first they killed those pigs and they stuck a fork in pig Tate's belly!" Boudin, whose cadre had once called itself the Fork, signed back, a smile almost forming on her lips for the first time in months.

"So, yeah, we are at war now. I'm happy to make a declaration to the press. Nobody is more ready to kill or be killed than me. But Billy, you are wrong about it being OK to kill big-shots and not small fry. Any killing is gonna ruin us. We need to say, 'armed propaganda and no killing, we've never intended to kill people' or we won't just lose our lefty base, when all the Kent and Jackson demos die down, but the feds will go heavy on us and our above-ground network. Hit his pals and Nixon's gonna go unshackled, and they'll hunt us down with no regard for the rules.

"Now, let me be clear, as a revolutionary communist, as a Leninist, I have no problem doing Billy's lethal bombings or even J. J.'s assassinations, but it's too hot to do it now, unless we can somehow deny it. It's a question of survival. I want it clear that this is the public position of the Weathermen. We have to be lovable Robin Hoods, and that's final. People who disagree can find another group. Now, if there's a way to do both, kill and deny, I'm all ears."

"Isn't it a little late for denying anyway?" chimed in Howie, finally leaning forward on the couch. "When Fred was murdered and we agreed to bomb in response, we were smart, and decided to let the bombs speak for themselves, and never to claim them or issue communiqués. We ducked the whole problem. Lefties knew we were up to something, so we were respected as the vanguard, but they never had to defend a particular action.

"Think about it: the cops cars in Chicago, New York, Berkeley, the judge's house and car in New York, the firebomb at the National Guard armory in Bernardine's little town outside of Milwaukee, even the failed police bombings in Detroit and Cleveland, and the successful one at the precinct in San Francisco, where we killed one and blinded another. No claims, no hits to our reputation, no heat from the pigs.

"Thanks to that rat Grathwohl, who finally had to show himself last month when he set up Dianne and Linda, the FBI now has a lot of this. But people on the left won't believe them or him, so we can skate on that for a while. No, the real problem, the reason we're screwed, is that the cops found the roofing nails in the Townhouse. And the image of the collapsed Townhouse means that everybody, left and right, knows it's true. Billy's right about the radical press hitting us on that.

"So yes, the pigs don't know the target yet, but there was pretty loose security in New York. Lots of people knew. I notice you guys don't trust Rudd anymore; I assume that's why he's not here. Well, Mark knew all about it, and even set up an alibi to make sure he couldn't be linked to the dance — incredible, he went to see the bombing movie, *Zabriskie Point*! So someone's gonna talk, we should assume that. But even if Fort Dix doesn't get out, they've got the nails. There goes our strategy of denial."

Eleanor Stein spoke up, pretending to take on her usual role of fixer and mediator, not openly backing Jeff and Bernardine's proposal, but rather just trying to bring everyone on board. In fact, her intervention had been carefully choreographed with them during the three days of individual discussions that Dohrn had decreed should precede any group debate.

"OK, so here is how we could, I stress could, solve it: keep our Robin Hood status with the left, not give Nixon the excuse to go hard, and still step up the struggle just like Billy says. First, most important, we pin the Townhouse on J. J. and Terry, say they went rogue, we didn't know or approve, and announce that J. J.'s been expelled for his error in trying to kill. So all the cop and judge stuff, if it ever comes out, and the Townhouse bomb, which already has, it'll be all on New York, and Weather as a whole can stay pure for our base. Everybody on the left knows those two guys were hard-core; they'll believe it. Hell, like Billy said, J. J.'s been ranting about doing assassinations since he got here. We can still hold Bern's line — we never tried to hurt anyone, we were careful not to — because we say New York went off on its own.

"Now, Terry wouldn't have minded us using him for the cause, and J. J., well, let's just say he needs to be used for the cause. He hasn't accepted party discipline like the rest of us, for a while now. We know he bragged to the Panthers about fire-bombing the judge and the cop cars, and the Panthers are definitely infiltrated, so the word will get out. It's obvious there was no concern for casualties there. Hell, the papers say there were kids sleeping at the judge's house! Telling the Panthers was against orders, against all operational security. If we can't control him, let him go, and do us some good as he does — 'let nothing in his work become him like the leaving it.'

"Then, with that taken care of, we announce and carry out a major bombing campaign, as many targets as Billy can pick. It'll be true armed propa-

ganda, at least a bomb a month at targets that symbolize various compo-
nents of racism and imperialism. We do take credit, we do issue communiqués, because we are educating. So we are careful, we do it at night, we give
warnings, that becomes our M.O. That way, even if there are casualties, say
if cops come searching for the bomb, or it goes off early, we at least have our
reputation for having tried not to kill."

Ayers could sense that the fix was in. He'd set up a few pre-ordained
strategy sessions with Bernardine himself. But he wasn't going down easily,
and he fought Stein's supposed compromise.

"I get the point of expelling J. J., the whole rogue thing. I'm fine with that,
I said I don't want random casualties, or low-level pigs either. And I like the
way we can duck the whole mess. Even better, if we stick to the line that
only New York ever tried to hurt people, it throws the FBI off those earlier
actions — especially Park Station, where the collective could face murder
charges, But we can't be scared of attacks on pig leaders. That's the real war.
Stop with the caution.

"Kids want us to be the vanguard, the engine, not the caboose. There's
four dead in Ohio, but the people who plan the wars are walking around free
as birds: the think-tank professors, the generals, the congressmen, the corporation presidents. Killing them won't hurt us with the left anymore, not
after Kent and Jackson, after kids are gunned down for protesting. They're
on our side now.

"And in some ways even before. I mean, did you hear Phil Ochs on stage
after the Townhouse? 'If they bombed this concert I wouldn't object. It'd
be great. Bomb my concert.' And Dustin Hoffman, who lived next door, we
almost kill his kid, and he goes on TV and says he's not angry at us, but
scared for our country! And as for the feds, look how easily we've moved
around — the money we get from people who don't agree with violence, but
hate the government more.

"Look, nobody from our families and friends, or any lefty, is gonna turn us
in, no matter what the heat. We're better than Robin Hood — we're Pretty
Boy Floyd the outlaw! H. Rap is right: violence is as American as cherry pie,
and we're the all-American heroes. Those Snick brothers, Ralph and Che,
they knew it when they went to back him up, and you guys know it. You're

just scared to take the final step, to really commit to the revolution. In revolutions, you kill the enemy. Period."

Cathy Wilkerson interrupted: "Billy, just stop with the cheerleading. My bomb went off too early, but your latest one didn't go off at all! I can still smell the dynamite, and the death. Ralph and Che are as dead as Teddy and Terry and Diana, and for the same reason: incompetence with violence. And what makes any of you think we can outfight the federal government? The Vietnamese told us to march, not bomb, as I recall. You're the only ones who seemed to hear them say 'bring the war home.' I've seen enough death — no more killing." She suddenly dissolved into sobs.

It was clear to all during the embarrassing silence that followed that Cathy, always a weak reed, always under the sway of her latest lover, was still physically shell-shocked from the explosion in the Townhouse and emotionally drained from its grim tally.

Jeff took an almost paternal tone as he softly talked Cathy down: "Sugar, I'm sorry for them too, but if we stop now, their deaths will be for nothing. They were on the right track, and you were part of it. We'll get better on the bombing. In fact, you should study up on it, you're the math and science geek. Work with Fliegelman, now that he has the new design. We have to keep going. I'm with Eleanor. It's the smart road. And yes, J. J. has to go." Jeff was in on the fix, too.

"Damn straight on that," interjected Howie again deep in his lair on the couch. "He's gone. Expel him, but make him see that he needs to be the goat, and say that he accepts it, that he admits he was wrong to be the violent rogue. I actually think it will appeal to his sense of history. He'll see it as a true *Darkness at Noon* contribution. Then just let him go off and do those assassinations he's been railing about."

For a few moments, everyone caught their breath. Cathy's melt-down had brought a lot of tension into the room, and Bernardine's ultimatum made it clear that there was only one way to resolve it, unless people wanted another split like the one she'd forced a year before that tossed the PL out of SDS.

Dohrn iced the deal by offering Ayers a way out. "Well, thanks to Eleanor for seeing a way to get J. J. and armed propaganda sorted out. And as I sit here and think about it, it actually opens up a way, Billy, to go your route, but keep it off us. Why not form our own little assassination group, bring

J. J. into the loop, and have him roam on his own, doing all the research and the hits. We'll make all the final decisions, and nobody outside this room will know. It'll be seen as completely separate from Weather, completely different crazies, like the Madison bombers. Even more removed than what Mandela did when he ran Spear of the Nation, MK, for the ANC.

"J. J. can pretend to be on his own, angry with us for being wimps — you know he loves dramatic plots, and the FBI loves splits and would believe it. Or maybe not J. J., maybe we'd need somebody farther away from us to run the actual hits and spread the fear among the elites. That's a detail, but what do you think of the main idea? Since we're so into Dylan songs, we can just call it our own *Lay Lady Lay* strategy. 'We can have our cake and eat it too' by killing these ** pigs on the sly! No full-court press from the feds and no ** from the lefties — then we're heroes, no different from Sam Goodman, what's his name now, Melville? **, he and Janie Alpert were cheered by the lefties — they shut down Wall Street with bomb threats after those bombings! But we still get our real message out: lead the empire, die for the empire."

"OK," Ayers said, "I can see where this might work. My only problem is how we do it. It's too risky for any of us to be the hitters, and if J. J. gets caught on the job, it definitely gets back to us. J. J. can plan, and talk to us for a 'go,' but I agree it's better to have someone else do the hits, preferably someone who doesn't connect with us, and maybe doesn't even need to know it is us, someone we can capture under a false flag.

"So who can we use who isn't known already? We have about 30 committed in Weather — but the FBI probably knows them all. And while they're loyal, for now, and won't rat on each other or us over armed propaganda and short sentences, if they get snagged for murder, anybody might turn. It's one thing to tickle the dragon with little bombs in bathrooms, but I can see that if we poke him too hard, he'll get really pissed off."

Dohrn jumped in, eager to close the deal. "Well, how about Kathy Power or Susie Saxe — what the hell are they up to these days? They left protest behind a long time ago, and I hear they're getting into some deeply weird **, planning to raid an armory for weapons, robbing banks. We could see if they wanted to do it — it's right up their alley."

Jeff Jones spoke up. "I don't know — they're close to us, not now, but they have been. That doesn't insulate us if they get caught. But wait, I'm just thinking: do you remember that kid at U of C that our above-ground guy there, Thad, reported on? The Nathan Hale fan who said he wanted to kill the Joint Chiefs? 'Don't bomb bathrooms — just shoot the highest-ranking guy to use them'? This sounds just like him, especially because if the FBI gets him, he'll have that trail of being against us.

"We approach him indirectly, with a cut-out. Maybe, like Billy says, we make a false flag for other radicals. Hey, it could be J. J., as our expelled, pissed-off martyr, definitely another role he'd love. He'd have the perfect credentials to look down on us as cowards, so then he and the kid can be pals."

Bernardine put her seal of approval on it: "You know, as I recall this kid, he'd like that. Remember what he said about us? 'SDS would put me up against the wall. I'm not a joiner.' Fine, let him tug on Superman's cape by himself. Better yet, we truly can have our cake and eat it too — we bomb a symbolic place, issue our communiqué, and he comes along later and kills someone from the same place, saying we weren't tough enough.

"We'll be in the news all the time, but with no cost either way: we say it's not us, so we don't lose the liberals or call down the feds, but we don't denounce anybody fighting imperialism, so we don't lose the radicals. By the time he's done, we'll still be Robin Hood but Billy's point will be made, too: nobody will want to take charge of imperial policy. They'll all be scared off. They're good at sending other people's kids to die — not so good at facing it themselves! So, do we agree? Then let's keep this just to ourselves, and now go see if we can't find young Nathan."

* * *

PART 1: THE KILLINGS

CHAPTER 1: OCTOBER 1969 — THE DECISION

A chilling crosswind pushed the white teenager across the quad at the University of Chicago as he walked from his calculus class toward his dorm on 55th, shivering inside jeans and a light Army jacket. At five feet, seven inches and so slight that he had to eat heartily rather than cut weight to wrestle at the lowest class, 118 pounds, Val Shaw didn't have much fat for protection from the lake city's vaunted wind. "Christ," he thought, "only October and the Hawk they warned us about is out already!"

As Val came out of the quad his eye caught the headline from the bright orange Chicago Tribune box: *Thousands Resist Draft, Overwhelming System.* Val stopped short, and peered into the box, his eyes moving quickly past the pro-war, anti-hippie Trib's "Flag of the Day" picture to read the first few paragraphs above the fold. The article concerned the very matter that had been on his mind, day and night, for the two months he had been in college. What was the right thing, the moral thing, the patriotic thing, to do about the draft, when he turned 18 in November?

Should he just ignore it, and wait to get caught? Or would the university require him to show registration to stay in school? But even holding a draft card, and not burning it, because he was scared of prison, that would be cowardly anyway, and nothing to be proud of when people asked years from now, "What did you do to oppose the U.S. invasion of Viet Nam?"

"No," he thought, "I have to stand up. I'm not going to hide. I'm going to throw my body into the gears of the machine, like the people stopping troop trains in Oakland. 'The pump won't work 'cause the vandals took the handles'."

Smiling now, and humming the Dylan song that had been revived in anti-war circles a few months before because of another line in it that had been appropriated by SDS's action faction — "You don't need a weatherman to know which way the wind blows" — Val turned the corner and continued on up Ellis, now straight into the nasty wind, finally resolved to resist the draft like the thousands in the newspaper, no matter what came of it.

But once he had made it to the sanctuary of his room, Val realized that this decision only raised more, equally thorny, moral questions. "Resisting the draft" was a broad cloth. Should he take the student deferment that was offered to undergraduates, giving him four years of safety, during which the war might well end? Or become a conscientious objector, scrubbing floors in a hospital? But maybe either would be an unacceptable compromise with the immoral system, recognizing its authority, and its cynical sacrifice of working-class kids to mollify anti-war students. And why should he even register anyway, since he'd be recognizing the government's right to sort, select, and decide who to kill? God said to Abraham, kill me a son, indeed, Mr. Dylan! It would be more admirable to announce to the draft board that he was refusing to have anything to do with it, and get prosecuted now rather than after a charade of deferments and applications for the C.O.

* * *

"Jesus, my head hurts from all this. I'm paralyzed. Whatever I do, I'll always think maybe it was the wrong decision, the coward's way out," Val said a few days later in his still-unbroken voice, after running through the possibilities for the hundredth time with his roommate. "Man, you are so out your ** mind," exclaimed Art Thomas, slipping into the dialect he liked to affect with his peers but would never dare use at home with his parents, who were teachers and proud members of the Negro middle class.

Val leaned back on a massive, bright blue beanbag chair in the bay window between the two beds, staring down from the sixth floor at 55th Street stretching west and out of sight. Art was crooked up on his elbow on his bed, his gravelly voice emanating from the haze of smells of hair products and creams on his night-stand that so mystified Val — although never enough to cause to him to ask Art about them.

"This ain't complex. Ain't but one thing to do, Slim, and that is take the four years of life so the war can end without you. Just take the deferment, just like me and everybody else in this dorm, in this college. You think we's all cowards? And don't give me that ** about you makin' someone else go in your place — that's on the system, not on us.

"And, hell, you're not going to go anyway. I know you — you can't. And if you're in prison, they're not gonna have one less warrior — they're just gonna grab another one from your town, or mine. You wanna save a life, keep marching against the war. All that's gonna happen from you going to prison is you getting ** the ass, day and night. Is that what you really want, you secret ally of the Gay Liberation Front?"

Later that week, after tossing and turning many nights in worry, Val knocked on the door of Max, the dorm advisor, a jolly, chubby, white graduate student in Divinity. "Hey, can we rap about the draft?" he asked. With his constant, cherubic smile the advisor welcomed Val inside. After shutting and bolting the door, Max said, "Hold that thought. I was about to groove on some opium-tainted hash. Join me and then we'll be in the mood to figure it all out."

A few hits later, as the Beatles bashed about and screamed, "Look out! Helter skelter, helter skelter...," Val asked Max, "Please, please, turn that crap off — got to be Yoko's madness got to them all! How can the same people who did *Lucy in the Sky with Diamonds* put out ** like that? Jesus, I'm glad this wasn't playing instead of *Can't Buy Me Love* when I told my parents the Beatles were better than Beethoven! Well, at least I'm still right for telling them that Dylan was as good as Shakespeare! He just gets better and better — a Nobel Prize someday I'm sure! Now just put on the new album, side two, please..."

Laughing, Max lifted the needle, and replaced the disk with Abbey Road. The soft guitars led into "Here Comes the Sun," and Max tumbled back onto his water-bed, holding his ocean-in-a-bottle over his head and dreamily rotating it up and down so the glittering goo languidly slid back and forth. "Well, that's some image — Dylan in a tux like Faulkner, 'Man will not only endure — he will prevail.' OK, young blood, so what's it to be?"

Val answered: "Max, I've decided — I can't in good conscience take a student deferment. I have to act in solidarity with the working class kids, in my home town and everywhere. It's just not right. But I don't want to go to jail right away, not 'til I get set. So I'm gonna register — but no student deferment, no medical deferment, no marriage deferment when Sally and I hitch up next summer. What I want to know is, can you find out if I can take my courses at U of C in prison, by correspondence, so when I get out I have my degree?"

Max, as always, smiled as he talked, seeming to enjoy the simple sensation of rolling each word carefully in his mouth. "Now, that is a question that has never, ever crossed my mind. Really, Val, how am I gonna look when I ask the dean about that? He's gonna say, what? We should make all our professors redo their syllabus and teach an extra, prison-writer section so you can say you were pure? Look, if you want to be in college, that happily comes with the deferment. If you don't want to be in college, it doesn't. Why the hell do you think I'm here? Divinity school is one of the few deferments left for graduate students outside of the sciences. I'm 4-D my man, and don't believe in any God but ocean-in-a-bottle!

"But, if you want me to, I'll talk to the dean. I just can't imagine it will make any sense to him. The administration is actually showing a bit of guts by refusing to send in a list of failing grades during the year, like the Selective Service demanded, and it took some heat for resisting Hershey on the class rank and test nonsense back in '66, too. Why should I pick a new fight helping someone who refuses to help me protect him? That's gonna be his attitude, I bet. You know, Why can't he be like everybody else, and take the damn deferment?"

"Yeah, you're right — it seems I'm always the 'one in every crowd' — it's my *modus operandi*, and always has been. It's my fate to never go quietly, to never leave a room with somebody thinking I've bought into whatever bull is going down. It got me kicked out of a couple of high schools when I'd just say no to whatever nonsense they were puttin' down. But don't worry, I'm used to it. 'Here I stand and can do no more.' Now pass over the pipe."

Max complied, but then went on: "If I'm going to talk to the dean, I need a bit of meat. Now that you are properly mellow, run it down for me. Why? Where does this come from, this need to take a stand without balancing the consequences? Why are you so sure you can't take the deferment, and just express your opposition in marching and writing?"

"Man, I don't know. It's a mood, a feeling, something that just rises up in me when I hear lies, and I don't want to think that I just let them go. I guess I was trained to it, especially when it comes to being a patriot, and protecting my country and making it do right. My mother's a history professor at Swarthmore, and almost my first memory as a kid is of the posters she hung in her office. They were big rectangles, paintings of the founding heroes she lectured and wrote about. Not the old guard like Jefferson, Washington, and Franklin. These were the crazy brave, the Weathermen of the day, the front-liners who didn't have to be there, like Lafayette, Hamilton, and especially young Nathan Hale: 'I only regret that I have but one life to give for my country.' My own name, Valerius, that's the second name of Publius, the pen name Hamilton used for the Federalist Papers.

"In elementary school I read every one of the kid hagiographies of those guys, and talked over each prescient incident with my mother, the little ways you could see when they were kids that they would be brave patriots when they grew up. I dreamed, literally dreamed as I fell off to sleep each night, of being them, as kids and as adults, in the situations I read about. And then, every Memorial Day for as far back as I can remember, both my parents did special things with us that made us yearn to serve America.

"My mom would scrub the four of us up to decorate the grave of the son of a neighbor, an old widow we didn't even know well. Kenneth Reed, a navigator on a bomber in World War II, lost over the English Channel after hitting Berlin, when he was 24. We'd walk down to the cemetery and leave the flowers by the fresh flag. I still remember the inscription on his stone. At five years old I knew what *dulce et decorum est pro patria mori* meant.

"And my father, he would get out his swords. One was a gorgeous, gold-braided ceremonial sword, awarded for him being the top officer in his Navy training class, all of them college graduates who volunteered the day after Pearl Harbor. The other was a blunt, nasty-looking curved scimitar sort of thing, a Japanese officer's sword he had traded for in the Pacific.

"We'd line up and march, taking turns carrying the swords, as he played the only song he could on the piano, the Navy Hymn. You know it? 'Eternal father, strong to save, whose arm hath bound the restless wave?' We'd beg him for war stories, for details of what his ship did, who it sank or shot down, but he wasn't into that, wasn't a VFW kind of guy."

"Wait, with that back-story, you should be enlisting then," said Max. "How did your patriotism become a refusal to serve?"

"Well, as we got older, there was a lot of political talk at the table. We did get my father to talk about Germany, because he'd visited it in college, on a bicycle trip with a friend, just as Hitler was coming to power. He'd seen Hitler speak, and he helped us imagine the way the crowds were whipped up, thinking with the blood despite Germany beings the most sophisticated country in the world. Hell, he told us that he had to learn German as part of his law degree, because that was the international language of learning, like English is today.

"And he would say, 'Don't be a Good German. Don't be like the people I saw who thought Hitler and his Nazi gangs in their silly suits were buffoons, and ignored them and just waited for them to go away.' He'd quote his hero Edmund Burke: 'All that is necessary for the triumph of evil is for good men to do nothing.' So now, for me, the evil is Viet Nam, and the good patriot resists it!"

"Well," said Max, "that's all well and good, but I'll bet you a hundred bucks your father wants you to take a student deferment!"

"True enough," laughed Val, "but don't you see? That just makes my point. True courage means standing up against everybody, him too, if it's the right thing, the patriotic thing."

* * *

November 22, 1969

Dear Members of the Delaware County Draft Board:

I am writing in response to the pamphlet you sent me, titled "Claiming Conscientious Objection." I am hereby officially submitting this request to be determined a Conscientious Objector. I have a "deeply-held" objection, as required by your pamphlet, to participating in an organization whose purpose is, at present, killing Vietnamese who are resisting our illegal, unconstitutional, and immoral invasion. I am an atheist, so my objection is moral rather than "religious" as your pamphlet requires. However, my understanding of recent court decisions is that it is unconstitutional for you to distinguish between these two types of objections.

Like Martin Luther King and Albert Einstein, I see myself as a Gandhian. I have studied and absorbed Gandhi's works on the philosophy of political non-violence, or Satyagraha, and I am committed to non-violent means of ending this war, such as my refusal to fight in it. However, also like King and Einstein when it came to the evil being done by the Nazis and the Japanese imperialists in World War II, I do acknowledge that my conscientious objection falls short of the "all wars" standard in the pamphlet. My objection relates both to the invasion of Viet Nam and our general "Viet Nam foreign policy," in which our armed forces, covert agencies, and State Department-approved arms supplies and foreign aid are used to maintain "friendly" dictators like South Viet Nam's in power all over the formerly colonized world.

My government, which King accurately called "the greatest purveyor of violence in the world today," is fighting an imperialistic war to gain control over Asia. I find this policy a horrific repudiation of American values. It is consistent, though, with many of the imperialistic wars and racist policies we have undertaken while, like today, claiming to be defending freedom and democracy: the genocide of American Indians, slavery and abandoning Negroes at the end of Reconstruction, and backing "our bastard" dictators in Latin America, Asia, the Middle East, and Africa who let our corporations make profits.

As to your categories, I am applying as an absolutist: I refuse to take non-combatant service as a medic, or to take alternative service as a hospital worker. Just as I refused to take a student deferment, I will not cooperate in any way with a system that claims the right to categorize young Americans into death and life for an immoral war.

My father volunteered to serve in the Navy in World War II, and could well have died in any number of combat operations against the Japanese. I respect his service — and in fact I would have volunteered too, just as he did, because our country was attacked.

I would definitely kill in self-defense, and in defense of my family, and in defense of my fellow citizens, and even in the armed forces in defense of my country. But this war is none of those. We are simply on the wrong side, and have no business being there. If I were Vietnamese, I would be killing right now, killing American invaders.

I ask you to consider whether you are part of a polite, respectable murder machine, along with the other Good Germans around me: the statisticians and test-markers at the College Board (both for its creation of the Qualifying exam that took student deferments away from people who scored low and for giving colleges SAT scores to determine admission and life or rejection and death), the mayor who holds the farewell pancake breakfast for draftees, the university that submits to you the grades of failing students. Even Burke Marshall, my hero from his civil rights work for Presidents Kennedy and Johnson, is trying to kill me, by running Johnson's policy review for the draft. God said to Abraham, kill me a son. Shirley Jackson's "Lottery" lives, and you are running it next month.

I await your invitation to the interview. Since I am in college in Chicago, I would appreciate the interview being scheduled between December 10 and January 10, during our break.

Sincerely, Valerius Shaw

* * *

CHAPTER 2: DECEMBER 1969 — THE RAGE

"Gentlemen," implored the diminutive professor in his thick East European accent, "gentlemen, won't you come up front and take these good seats so you can hear and I don't have to shout?" The five black students in the freshman calculus class, all boys, sat stone-faced at the back of the room, separated by five empty rows of chairs from the ten white and Asian-featured students in the front. From the very first class they had pointedly occupied the rear, asking no questions, responding to no prompts, and usually talking and giggling among themselves rather than watching the blackboard.

"Really, I don't understand. Don't you want to learn? Isn't it harder without hearing and without interacting? You know, I come from a very oppressed minority myself. My family is Jewish, and we fled the war in Poland. When I was exactly your age I was living in a displaced persons camp in Germany. I most certainly sat in the front row when I finally got to college in America, and took advantage of my good fortune! Why won't you?"

"What you mean, minority? We are the majority in the world, racist dog!" The young men laughed, and exchanged hand-slaps. The professor stood sadly, thinking for a moment, then shrugged his shoulders as if to say, "I tried," and continued with the lecture. "So, looking at the picture of the secant line, whose slope is the average rate of change of the function, what happens to it as the change in x in our equation of the derivative gets smaller and smaller?" A slight Asian girl raised her hand, and in a classic Bronx accent said, "It gets closer and closer to the tangent line, whose slope is the exact rate of change at that moment."

"Precisely," replied the professor, now rejuvenated by her close attention and eager to hammer home his point. "And that is what Newton wrote, word for word, although of course in Latin, when he was the first one to see this happening. You, young lady, have just cracked the secret of calculus, the mathematics of the infinitely small motion. Without it, we'd have no industrial revolution, no increased income, no science, no medicines to double our lifespan from the 35 years expected in Newton's England three hundred years ago to the 70 years expected in America today...or, on the other hand, no nuclear bombs to reduce our life expectancy. Science, as Einstein reminded us, is morally neutral. Now, let's practice with a few examples. Calculate the y-values for x-squared, with x as 0, 1, 2, and 3, and sketch the curve on your graph paper..."

Val followed along, enjoying the math and feeling sorry for the professor's confusion. The answer to his question to the black students, Val thought, was obvious to anybody white under the age of 25, and non-existent to anybody white over that age. Just the day before he had been standing in Chicago's downtown "Loop" area with thousands of the former, probably all college students, as Fred Hampton, the chairman of the Illinois Black Panthers, led the usual Panther chant of:

"Revolution has co-ome — Off the pig. Time to pick up the gu-un — Off the pig."

In the judicial building soaring above the protestors another white man, Jewish like the professor, had recently ordered Panther national chairman Bobby Seale shackled to his chair with chains and gagged because he kept speaking up, acting as his own lawyer. Judge Julius Hoffman had refused to delay Seale's trial until long-time Panther lawyer Charles Garry had recovered from gall bladder surgery, and Seale had refused to accept the lawyer Hoffman appointed for him.

Tom Hayden, one of Seale's co-defendants in this "Chicago Eight" trial for conspiracy to disrupt the 1968 Democratic Convention, had spoken just before Hampton, describing in detail the way court marshals had punched Seale and held him down with knees in his back as they tightened his gag after each muffled outburst. Hayden and the other defendants had tried to intervene until the Judge, in his fury and frustration, ordered Seale frog-marched out of the courtroom. The whole explosive spectacle had been recorded in drawings by newspaper artists, which were now plastered on posters all over the U of C campus. After seeing one old white man order a black main chained, Val knew, no self-respecting black student would let his pals see him let another one tell him what to do, even in a math class.

* * *

Black rage was all the rage in Chicago that fall. Val had gone to an anti-war lecture in a packed university hall where the featured speakers were noted white political scientist Ted Lowi and a black alderman who was an undertaker. The professor, after stating to great applause his opposition to the war, had patiently explained to catcalls and hoots why the United States sometimes looked, waddled, and quacked like an empire but was really just an accidental Asian traveler. The undertaker said he had no idea why he had been invited to speak alongside a brilliant professor to brilliant students, since his only academic experience was attending the Simmons School of Mortuary Science and Embalming in Syracuse, New York. Still, he said, he had to speak up because he was sick and tired of burying black Chicago boys who had died in Viet Nam for no reason.

White rage was burning hot, too. "Fire burns, and does its duty," intoned Jules, Joyce Carol Oates' white revolutionary anti-hero in *them*, and Val felt exactly what she meant. The white rage was stoked by watching the radicals blow up mansions in *Zabriskie Point*, or listening to Bob Dylan drawl "You ask why I don't live here — honey, how come you don't move?," or watching Lyndon Johnson or Richard Nixon or Henry Kissinger or anybody in the Establishment talking on TV about bringing "democracy" to Viet Nam as they bombed it back to the stone age, the dour ones who wouldn't know democracy if it smashed them in the face, and who proved it by buying or stealing not just Vietnamese and Guatemalan elections, but their own. "No, no, no to you and your way," was Jules' message, just like that of the black students in the calculus class.

them was one of just three books Val had actually read that fall. The other two were *Intervention and Revolution: America's Confrontation with Insurgent Movements Around the World*, by Richard Barnet, the founder of the anti-war Institute for Policy Studies, and *Satyagraha: On Non-violent Resistance*, by Indian independence leader and philosopher Mohandas Gandhi. The latter two had been confiscated as subversive by a Pennsylvania state trooper, in lieu of

Val's arrest for hitch-hiking on the interstate to visit Sally, his bride-to-be, at her college back home near Swarthmore.

None of these books were from Val's own freshman seminar in "Ideas and Methods," where he ignored Thucydides, Heller, Kierkegaard, and Emerson in favor of working full-time filing x-rays in the university hospital to put money aside for his upcoming marriage. His well-meaning, radical professor had sat in stunned horror as Val explained to the class that while he had only read the description on the book jacket, he wanted to "rap" about how the Peloponnesian War was "just like Viet Nam."

The irony of wasting his parents' tuition money while saving his own was lost on Val. Outside of calculus, which was just plain fun, it was impossible to generate interest for studying when his country was murdering peasants from the sky, when Bobby Seale was shackled and gagged, when he and his friends all woke up every day asking just one question: How can I help stop the war?

Val had wanted no part of the SDS "Days of Rage" in October, where a few hundred young, wealthy, white radicals donned motorcycle helmets, picked up iron bars and baseball bats, and attacked shop windows and the Chicago police. He had liked Fred Hampton's historical reference to the tactic as "Custeristic," and noted that only a handful of even the most radical U of C students went the seven miles north to take part in the suicidal demonstrations. The net result, as far he could see, was the enrichment of the Chicago police when the SDS gang all got arrested and skipped out on millions of dollars in parental bail. But Val did want in on the November anti-war mobilization in Washington and, purely for defensive purposes, he brought his motorcycle helmet for that.

Arriving early in the morning in one of the thousands of busses that kept pouring down the interstate to Washington, Val and his fellow students stepped groggily out onto the national Mall, right onto the march route. He was momentarily stunned by the number of people streaming off the rise by the Washington Monument to join the march. The crowd was later estimated at over half a million, but to Val it just looked like the entire country had decided to come out against the war. He and Thad Leslie, an SDS member from the Pierce Tower dorm, put on their helmets and wandered down into the street.

Thad was a smallish, slightly misshapen, stringy-haired white sopho-more. He looked like a child in his over-sized jeans and Army coat, incon-gruously set off by his steel-toe hob-nailed boots, the footwear of choice for serious street-fighters, and the full-sized motorcycle helmet that wobbled on his head. Thad's light touch of cerebral palsy made him an unlikely street fighter, but he had actually marched on the first night of the Days of Rage. Somehow, he had escaped injury or arrest, despite rushing about in the heart of the action. Val figured Thad had been untouched because none of the cops could take him seriously as a combatant.

"Ho, Ho, Ho Chi Minh — NLF is gonna win...One side right, one side wrong, we support the Viet Cong." So went the chants echoing in booms off the tall government buildings as Val and Thad came west along Pennsylvania Avenue, heading toward the defensive ring of busses and bayonets surround-ing the White House. Turning to look at the crowds marching behind him, Val saw a banner reading, "Yale SDS Smashes Imperialism."

"Hey. My older brother's in Yale SDS. I wonder if he's here." And sure enough, he was. "The ** you doin' here, bro'?" Val yelled out happily. "Well, where else would I be, little bro'?" replied Jonah.

"Well, now that I think about it, of course! This is Thad, from U of C SDS, my riding partner. Thad, this is my revolutionary brother Jonah."

"Well, revolutionary, yes, in fact so revolutionary that this is my last semester at Yale. I'm dropping out to go full-time with YWLL, first to Cuba, where I'm signed, sealed, and delivered of my $500 to cut cane, and then to Youngstown, organizing in a factory."

"Bro'," said Val, "I have no idea what you're talking about. What's Y-what-ever and what's this about Cuba?" As the boys walked along the parade route, Jonah brought him up to date on radical politics. Thad shook his head in bemusement at Val's willful ignorance about the left's dogma and faction.

"YWLL is the Young Workers Liberation League, a soft landing spot for SDS-ers who want neither side of the split. Wait, do you even know about the SDS split last summer, that led to the crazies declaring the Days of Rage? Good God, Thad, I apologize for my retard of a hippie brother, who'd rather write a revolutionary song than act it out!

"Well, there's a few people in SDS, the RYM, Revolutionary Youth Move-ment, that's the Weathermen, who want urban war, and then there's most of us who just want to stop the war in Viet Nam. We both want to stop even more wars from happening, get the troops home not just from Viet Nam but from everywhere, but the crazy Weathers think you can only do that with bombs and lead pipes. I'm with the group that wants to use demos and strikes, although we're falling apart because a lot of those SDS people aren't even students, but PL moles and trolls — that's the Progressive Labor Party, actual living, breathing communists who follow their party line; don't you know any of this stuff?"

"No man, none of it," said Val. "You know me, I just read Gandhi, play gigs, and fantasize about derailing troop trains!"

Jonah laughed. "Well, all right with that! I'll do the reading of Marx and Engels, and Chairman Kim Il Sung, and all his skulking, low-rider pilot-fish of revisionism for us both! Just don't go near the Weathermen or the PLs — they're both nuts, and when they say 'Up against the wall, mother **,' they mean you too. Just like the femi-Nazis who go after the men in the movement because nobody wants them!

"Now, I agree with every inch of their analysis about the empire, and how it's backed by our corporate, conformist culture that we have to smash, but 'come the revolution,' as they say, if these good guys and gals take power, you and I, and anybody on the left who deviates one inch from their bull, we'll be the first up against the wall. The only people they even think about compromising with are the blacks. Whatever the Panthers say, or actually whatever any thug with a revolutionary rap says, they do. And the Panthers are stone cold killers. Erica Huggins tortured Alex Rackley and Bobby Seale ordered him offed — we at Yale SDS know that even if the Yale president doesn't. He's such a wimp with the Panthers. Hell, I danced on Brewster's desk in a demo once — no punishment: he always backs down."

"Well," said Thad, "I think you're too harsh on the Weathermen. I'm not one, but I went to their fight with the pigs, and I gotta say, I help them out whenever I can, with anything they need, like student I.D.s or a place to crash. They're our vanguard, they push the contradictions of this racist, fascist, imperialist society out into the open, and you agree that their analysis is right-on. Crazies? Yeah, I can see that. And brook no dissent? Ditto for that. But I wouldn't worry about them being around after the revolution. They'll be dead long before that!

"Anyway, that's great about getting picked for Venceremos. You must have signed up early, because I just tried and was told they were all full for whites at 300. Now they have to give that many slots to blacks and other third-worlders — and that's what your $500 will support, radical scholarships!"

Later in the afternoon, at the rally, the boys got to see the Weathermen in action. First 50 Weathermen tried to storm up onto the stage when an anti-war Senator started speaking. Viet Cong and Red Star flags trailed behind them in the wind as they chanted, "Smash liberal imperialism! Smash liberal imperialism!"

"They're definitely right about that," said Jonah, "but they're politically insane, pissing off the very politicians we need to vote to end the war, whatever their reasons." The patient, well-trained march marshals locked arms and pushed the Weathermen back down the stairs. "Hey, the marshals are as efficient as Pete Townsend," said Val. The brothers had seen the Who's guitar player use his instrument as a weapon against an attempt by Yippie and Chicago Eight defendant Abby Hoffman to take over the microphone in August at the "Woodstock" music festival.

As the speeches ended the brothers and Thad followed the noise of the chanting Weathermen as they headed off toward the Justice Department. Clouds of tear gas floated about them as they joined the now-hundreds of motorcycle helmets, all turned upwards toward a balcony on the corner of the top floor, looking out over Constitution Avenue. " ** you, Mitchell! ** you, Mitchell!" came the chants, amidst the explosion of cherry bombs and the smashing of bottles thrown against the building. Sure enough, there on a top-floor balcony was the recognizable stout form and slicked back hair of the esteemed Attorney General of the United States. He slowly extended his hand, middle finger raised, back down toward the scene below that his wife, to the protestors' delight, famously described as something out of the Russian Revolution.

Val returned to Chicago as sympathetic as ever to the Weathermen's analysis and as opposed as his brother to their violent tactics. But he was about to see something that would change him forever, and make him think their tactics were in fact too tame.

* * *

"Let's go, let's go, come on with us." Thad stood at the door of Val and Art's room at eight o'clock on the morning of December 6, in his usual street-fighting outfit, absent the helmet. Art stumbled to the door: "Cuz, cuz, what the ** is your problem?"

"Art, sleep is for the weak. You and Val get up and get dressed. I just got word from the SDS president — the Panthers are opening up Fred Hampton's apartment, to show what the pigs did. We're going to hold a mass march down to there in solidarity."

"Fool, you can't march down to there — I know the street, and it's west of the Loop, at least ten miles away! And I've got a chemistry final, so thanks but no thanks. Maybe Mr. Ideas and Methods and pass-fail grades can go with you." Art tried to close the door, but Thad pushed through and started shaking Val awake.

The solidarity march never happened, but two hours later, Val, Thad, and ten other white students hopped off the "L" and walked a few blocks to Monroe Street, where over a thousand black people, young, old, some dressed for work or church, some dressed for the street, stood silently in line on the sidewalk. The line moved slowly, but by noon Val had made it up the stairs and past the bullet-pocked door of the apartment, and was actually standing at the spot where Hampton had been gunned down in his bed. Blood covered the mattresses, and the wall behind it had been fractured into chunks by a hailstorm of shotgun pellets.

A phalanx of Panther men, boys mostly, ringed the room silently and solemnly, in the full uniform of black pants, black shoes, black leather jacket, black beret, and dark glasses. A woman in nurse's scrubs broke down, sobbing. Two of the Panthers comforted her, and helped walk her out of the room, repeating calmly, "strength, Sister." The tears startled Val, rousing him from a sort of trance, and he felt his body tremble with a surge of fear and anger.

None of the normally loquacious students said a word on the long train ride back to the South Side. Back in his room Val sat, still stunned, in the beanbag chair, looking as he often did due west down 55th. "What a coward I am," he thought. "I'm a new version of the Good German, thinking I'm moral, a draft resister, trying to be a conscientious objector — but I'm just scared, trying to find excuses to delay prison. There was no reason to go through this circus, no reason even to sign up for the draft and acknowledge America's right to decide to make me fight and die. Fred Hampton knew what would happen if he rose in opposition, and so do I — that's why I've been delaying it."

As he sometimes did when trying to imagine his future, Val closed his eyes and began to daydream. Usually these daydreams made him the hero, loved by all the pretty girls and befriended by all the cool boys, and revolved around him being called up on stage to help out a rock star with a guitar solo, or scoring the winning goal in a soccer game. This one was different — violent, hopeless, without the acclaim of the masses.

Val saw himself in uniform, a private in the Army, carrying a tray of coffees into the meeting room of the Joint Chiefs of Staff in the Pentagon, keeping his eyes up and away so as not to rock and slosh the hot liquid out of the cups, a trick he had learned ferrying drinks to the luncheon tables of the summer school on the Swarthmore campus for the wealthy children of suburban New York. Generals, admirals, and their attendant officers, all white, all men, all adorned with their fruit salad of decorations, sat around a long oval table. There were maps on the walls, charts on easels, and a giant television screen hovering at one end of the room. "Thanks, private," said one of the junior officers, as he reached out for the tray.

Val suddenly flipped the tray at the officer, staining him with the steaming coffees. As the officer froze in amazement, Val reached behind his back and pulled out the Army Colt .45 he'd tucked inside his belt. As a qualified marksmen from years of hunting with his father, even before being rated expert in both basic and advanced training, he knew he had one round in the chamber and seven in the magazine, and he started to use them, one careful shot at a time, two-hand grip, staying smooth, completing each shot before turning to the next. First the junior officer, a straight heart shot, then he started on the Chiefs, who sat stunned at the unplanned violence in their inner sanctum of planned violence.

As he'd been trained to, Val didn't look at their faces, just at the target area. After two seconds and two more heart shots, the three remaining Chiefs tried to push their chairs away from the table and dive under it. Val got those three in the back, the right spot, through the heart that way, sitting ducks. Boom, Boom, Boom. He could smell the nitro in the air, before he felt and then heard the shots from the guards rushing in from the anteroom. A newspaper headline pulsated in his dream: "Chiefs Assassinated; Copy-cat Killings on Bases; Nixon Pulls Out."

Val sat in the beanbag chair, trembling, mesmerized by the images in his mind. Later that night he explained his vision to Art and Thad. "That's it," he told them. "That's the way to do it. To hell with going to jail — don't take yourself off the board. To hell with people burning themselves — if you're gonna go, take 'em with you. And who's the target? The top dogs. I'm gonna be for the Joint Chiefs what Eartha Kitt was for LBJ's White House, upsetting their little 'meet and greets.' 'You send the best of this country off to be shot and maimed? No, you're the ones getting shot and maimed!' That'll get the point across. And then the others will always wonder, is it about to happen again?"

"Now little brother," said Art, "Murder and suicide, that's a big jump from 'I'm a pacifist.' What happened to debate, to winning people over with marches, to all those things you always tell me about Martin Luther King at Riverside Church, opposing even your Satyagraha sit-ins, let alone anti-war violence? I can quote you, I've heard it so often: 'It's not the point for that. The preliminaries are to rouse the nation's conscience, inform with massive teach-ins and preach-ins.' If anything, it's easier to get people to think about opposing the war now than then, just two years ago. After Riverside, the *Washington Post* called him a discredit to his race who should stick to civil rights like a good boy. Last week, after your Mobe march, they took his exact position! Get out!"

"Art, I've been wrong — there comes a time, and Hampton's murder is my time." Val spoke calmly, carefully, now. "I wasn't a big Hampton fan, I never took part in the Panther chants about killing cops, but straight out murder can only be met with straight out war. I don't have the heart to sign any more petitions, march in any more demos, write any more letters to the newspaper. I physically can't do it.

"Look, I didn't bring the war home — they did. I didn't kill pacifism — they did. "For me, it's on, and like my old friend Nathan Hale, I'll give the one life I have to my country. I just gotta figure out how to give it. It's like King told the angry parents of the children marching in Birmingham, when they said he was setting the kids up to be attacked by police dogs. 'If I'm gonna be bit, let me be dog-bit for justice!' I could die in prison for draft resistance and achieve nothing, so I'd rather die in combat and start a wave of attacks. You know how we hear about soldiers rolling grenades into the tent of the officer who keeps calling up patrols? Think of me as Super-Fragger!"

Thad looked on, thoughtful and quiet for once. Finally he spoke. "Val, there's lots of ways to fight the war, really fight it like you want, without being Nathan Hale, without committing suicide. You know I know some of the Weathermen. Well, it's no secret they've decided to leave behind all the street-fighting and the arrests and the bail, and go to war, really get it on, like Fidel, like Fanon in Algeria, like Sam Melville and Jane Alpert in New York, bombing buildings. Like some of the Panthers, they're ready to take out cops; even like the VC, they say they're gonna take out army barracks and officers' clubs.

"But whatever they do, they're gonna stay alive to keep doing it. The last time you're gonna see them above ground will be at a meeting in Flint in a couple of weeks. If you want, I can set you up to talk with them, maybe join up."

"Thad, I appreciate it, but I'm not a joiner," laughed Val. "Hell, I wouldn't even talk to the draft counselors, 'cause I was scared the decision wouldn't be my own. And remember what my brother said — the Weathers will put me up against the wall if we disagree on something. Jonah told me they've actually announced, publicly, that they've given up their founding principle — Port Huron, 'participatory democracy' — in favor of efficient, war-time dictatorship, lockstep with whatever Dohrn and Rudd and their pals say.

"My mother always tells me she named me after a republican ruler, Publius Valerius, and not the selfless, temporary dictator Cincinnatus, for a reason. I have my own opinions, and I make my own decisions, and I sure don't take orders well. I question everything, and if I survive the war I'm sure I'll keep getting fired from jobs just as fast as I got thrown out of high schools. Man, I heard Ayers and Dohrn speak when they came here to try to talk us into coming to the Days of Rage. I'd last about as long with them as I would at IBM. The only difference would be that 'come the revolution,' IBM wouldn't put me up against the wall, mother, and you guys too if you peeped against them.

"Besides, I don't get those Weather-tactics: bombing bathrooms like Melville? What's that? If you're at war you don't kill toilets, you kill the highest-ranking person who uses them! And killing cops and soldiers? I got nothing against them. The VC can and should do what they want — but in my war, no way. Hey, I know cops and soldiers, I went to school with them, I played in bands with them: they're working class guys, they follow orders, they're not the enemy. The killers are the ones telling them what to do: congressmen, generals, corporations! That's who I'm gonna get."

* * *

CHAPTER 3: FEBRUARY 2017 — COLD CASE

After wrapping up his taped interview with Fox commentator Sean Hannity, President Donald Trump headed upstairs from the oval office. "Amazing stuff, outrageous," he said to his top strategist, Steve Bannon, as they climbed the staircase. "Sean says he's been onto these killers, these pals of Obama's, for ten years, and nobody does anything about it. It's perfect for us. I'm gonna raise it. Hey, I'll see you on the plane for Florida this afternoon."

As always, Bannon knew what "raise it" meant, and knew better than to ask the president if he could, just once, take a look at and maybe edit a Trump "tweet" before it entered the political arena. "What the hell," he thought, "this is what got us here, and it usually works out."

Sure enough, by the time they met on Air Force One it had been out for hours, sent by probably the first president since Lincoln to write final drafts with his own hand, or in this case, thumbs:

> FBI has hundreds of agents to chase fake news on my @realTrump campaign and Russia. How many chase Obama's terrorist pals, Ayers and Dohrn? #Goldennonsense

That hashtag was Trump's favorite one recently, a dig at the "Clinton News Network" and the rest of the mainstream media, which had reported allegations that he'd hired prostitutes to urinate on him in a Moscow hotel, and then had been unable to back up their story. Whenever Trump was challenged on his alleged ties to Russia, or on his own cascade of undocumented claims, he hammered on the "Golden Shower" story until the hostile reporters acknowledged that their outlets had indeed published that one with no basis. Bannon loved the story for two reasons. First, it was absurd, because Trump was so obsessively fastidious that he used disinfectant as soon as possible after shaking hands. Second, because Trump could keep trotting out the media's admission of error whenever they had him cornered for something else.

That evening recently-confirmed Attorney General Jefferson Sessions called his FBI director, James Comey. "Jim, did you see this tweet about Obama's pals, what is it, Ayers and Dohrn? Who are they and what the hell is that all about? I know he's going to ask me about it when he gets back from Florida. I wish for once he would just ask me about the facts before shooting off his iPhone!"

"Tell me about it," replied the director. "Look, those are '60s radicals, anti-war bombers, and if we ever developed a case on them, what do you think is the first thing those bastards' lawyers would do? Use Trump's statement to get it dropped! Does he even know the history of presidential prejudice? Does he even know the concept? Somebody's got to explain it to him, and I hope you'll be the one. I've been to that fair, and I'd like to avoid going again.

"You may not remember, but back in 2004, when I was deputy A.G. and had to stop Bush from getting Ashcroft's approval, when he was passed out in a hospital bed, for that surveillance plan? I took so much ** for that! I sure wish this time somebody else could explain to a president why he just can't do some things, just because he wants to. How about you?"

Sessions laughed. "Now, Jim, you know damn well that in the end you were lionized by the Democrats, and that's probably why Obama picked you for FBI! But, all right, I'll do my best to educate him on this, and beg him to let us look into it, without tweets!"

"Anyway," Comey went on, "as soon as I saw this, I had the historians pull the internal reports. Here's the deal. As usual, the president has an underlying point. These two people ran a tiny underground anti-war group that was, for some reason, called the Weathermen. They carried out maybe 20 bombings. That sounds like a crime wave today, but it was actually a small share of hundreds of political bombings the FBI was investigating back then — anti-war, black revolution, and especially Puerto Rican independence.

"So, we indicted them and had good cases, but couldn't make any of them stick, because our agents, with top approval, had gone black bag on them and their families. That all came out, sort of a pre-electronic version of Snowden and Wikileaks: stolen files, news stories, hearings, and leaks. The courts were in no mood after Watergate to let anything with black bag in it go to trial. Hell, the number two guy here, Felt, Deep Throat from Watergate, was the one who was convicted, for the black bags, not these Weather-bombers."

"Well, what can we get them for now? It's been over 40 years."

"Well, time itself isn't the issue. No statute of limitations on federal capital cases, like murder, treason, terrorism — we can always make a case. But the easiest by far is murder — and the only dead bodies we could link to the Weather-people were their own, incompetent ones: they blew themselves up in 1970 making bombs at a fancy New York townhouse to use at an NCO dance at Fort Dix, in New Jersey. A couple of days later, a black student group blew themselves up too, on their way to a courthouse. Good thing the radicals were studying political science and not electrical engineering!

"Lord knows these Weather-people tried, over and over again, to kill — and mostly cops and judges at that! Almost all those were because of jailed black radicals, even though these Weathers were all rich white kids. These files show there were at least ten times, both before and after the townhouse in 1970, where the bombs could have killed cops or judges, plus families and bystanders, but were found, or failed, or the timing was just off for people being around when they exploded. Jesus, one, at the Berkeley police station, was a bunch of bombs in cop cars, set for a shift change, and the fuses went off just a few seconds too early.

"After the townhouse, though, the Weathermen backed off and stuck to property damage — bombs in bathrooms at the Pentagon, back when you could just walk right in, things like that. When the war ended in '75 almost all of them came in from the cold, like the two the president mentioned. A few stayed out, revolutionaries without a revolution, and funded themselves with bank robbery. Those we got, clean, and some are still inside, and always will be, for murder during robbery."

" 'Weatherman' still doesn't ring a bell," said the attorney general, "but I do remember something about Weather-cat killings — of a congressman, right? Is that the same group?"

"No, that was a separate case, a group that thought Weatherman had gone soft, calling in warnings after the townhouse. After a Weather-bombing of a building they would swoop in and murder some top official who worked there, and issue a statement criticizing the Weathermen from the left, if that's possible. They assassinated six people, including that congressman, and we got nowhere with it. The press started calling these copy-cat killings, and someone came up with Weather-cat. Not related to this."

"OK, Jim, thanks for the info. Now at least I know what it's all about. But look, I need something. I want to respond to the president, have an answer to why we can or can't go after these people. When he sends these tweets, it's his way of sending me a memo."

"Well," said the director, "I did have one thought. There's one case where someone died, and we thought it was their work, but the Weather-people never took credit. We looked at it again, right at the start of Obama, after the local police union made a stink and got a grand jury on it. We found some usable DNA on a bomb fragment, but there were no matches in anybody's databases.

"I'm thinking that you can tell the president that we plan to send it to the Cold Case unit that Congress set up to handle old civil rights murders. They help with any cold case, actually, so it'll be fine to use them. Now, if they do find Ayers or Dohrn or any other names from the Weathermen around the scene, and maybe a few other hints of probable cause, Justice could try to get a court to approve a DNA test for them. A match wouldn't be enough for conviction, of course, but it'd be plenty to start a full-scale murder investigation. I'll warn you, though, Court rulings on seizing DNA on suspicion have been pretty messy, which leads to lengthy appeals. I think that's why Justice decided not to pursue that route on this case in 2009."

Sessions laughed: "I remember the Emmitt Till bill — and I voted for it! Nothing would give me greater pleasure than to tell my Democrat colleagues — you know, the ones who called me an unrepentant racist and opposed my confirmation — that we plan to use that unit against anti-war activists! And once Gorsuch is on the Supreme Court, we'd be in a good position to clear up the DNA mess anyway. This could be the test case, lots of publicity. That ought to make the president happy!"

"Fine," Comey replied, "I'll kick it down to the unit. No guarantees, but if you're willing to take on the DNA subpoena fight, we just might get something done. And please make sure the president knows I'm on it. I'm right in the middle of leaning on OMB for the 2018 staffing request. If ICE can get 15,000 new agents to chase border-jumpers, I deserve a few thousand myself, so I can do wonderful things like bring his Weather-folks to justice!"

* * *

Clad in her never-varying black pantsuit, 30-year-old Mar'Shae "Black" McGurk eased through the narrow entrance to her cubicle at Cold Case, a Starbucks in one hand and an iPad in the other. "Black" had been her nickname since she was a baby. Like Smokey Robinson, she no longer even thought about the racial implications of everybody, white, black, or whatever, calling her by her color. It was just her name, and Lord knows she was indeed purple-black, black as night, and straight outa Simple City. That was the legendary Benning Terrace war zone "east of the river" in DC's all-poor, all-black third that had long since been abandoned by the black middle-class, which had fled over the line to Prince George's Country, Maryland. Lots of kids there went by color nicknames, like Chink or Congo, or were routinely identified by friends and teachers as "that light-skinned girl" or "that African boy" without a hint of joning. And anyway, and here again Mar'Shae was like the Motown star, it wasn't even clear that her nickname first came from color anyway.

Black appreciated every day at work, because she knew how unlikely it was that she'd gone from gang-banging drop-out to the Army, to college, and finally to the FBI in less than a decade. Still, she didn't really look forward to another quiet day in the Cold Case office, and she was counting the months until the new postings came out. When she'd joined Cold Case 18 months before as her first assignment, fresh out of the academy, it had been a plum posting, clearly a bit of politically-correct affirmative action that was just fine with her. It was her own personal reparations, she thought at the time: a great salary to chase aging Crackers!

Black had been excited about the chance to track down the Klan and White Citizen Council killers while her friends from the academy followed brain-dead bank robbers around the Midwest. One of the few things she had gotten out of high school was an interest in civil rights cold cases, from a film the teacher had shown in AP U.S. history. Whoopi Goldberg, as black as her, had played the supporting role of Medgar Evers' wife, while the lead role was the redeemed white Southern prosecutor, played by Alec Baldwin. Together, they took down James Woods, a.k.a. Byron de la Beckwith.

Of course, Black had failed the Advanced Placement class, which was part of the school district's "AP for all" publicity campaign, in which all students at her segregated, high-poverty school (not a low-income, but a no-income school, the teachers liked to say) had to take a college-level class, even though few would ever attend a college. As in all her classes, she and the other students rarely attended and never did the homework. Then they would be automatically signed up for, but rarely attend, "credit recovery" sessions or summer school, and magically move on to the next course in the sequence the next year. The district signed Black up to take regular senior history and a few other missing credits over the summer so she could be recorded as a fall graduate, but once out the door she never came back.

High school had been fun for Black: warm in the winter, cool in the summer, free breakfast and lunch and even a packed dinner to go, and safe. Even in the neighborhood, though, she had never felt in danger. She'd always been a hard-ass tomboy, and known she was a lesbian from the get-go. She was too humorous always to be showing a hard face, but she could fight when she needed to, and from 9th grade on never had to rely on her mother for money or even for a place to stay. That was good, because her mother, who had her when she was a 14-year-old drop-out, was a mess, mostly drugged out and living with her own mother, who had her when she too was a teenage drop-out. Being a lesbian was all that kept Black from the maternal fate of her friends, half of whom had babies by 16 and all of whom had them by 18, despite the line-up for DP shots at school every three months.

After kicking around for a year, cutting and packing drugs for a local corner gang, and enforcing payment from female customers, Black and one of her main squeezes decided on a lark to enlist. It was a slow month east of the river for the recruiter in the government building at the metro stop. She was way behind on a quota, so she worked creatively on a plan to enroll the girls in Army base high schools, and get their degrees while they completed their basic and advanced training.

Black turned out to love the Army, where everything was on time, and there were no choices to make. She easily handled her remaining five courses, and after a hairy one-year tour escorting trucks to and from Bagram Air Base in Afghanistan she applied to become a military policeman. After four years of that, in four different parts of the world, Sergeant McGurk was ready for an Army-funded college degree in criminology. After figuring out in one semester that the on-line college where some of her high school teachers had taken their degrees was no ticket to the mainstream, she transferred to George Mason University. She finished there in just three years, while working nights in security. The girlfriend was long-gone, and she felt no need to choose now-legal marriage over dating.

Black's freedom to work long hours came in handy when the Mason career office got her into the FBI through its affirmative action program. Since the day she entered the academy, she had not had a day off, and that was fine with her. She just wanted more action, since everybody she'd helped track down was either dead or in a nursing home. No chance of drawing a weapon there!

* * *

Tapping her computer to life, Black was surprised to see an alert on her electronic schedule, placed there by her boss, as always into the office ahead of her, telling her that ASAP was the time to come on down and be briefed on a new assignment.

"Black in a black suit, what's goin' down? Close the door." Jerry Cummings, the lawyer in charge of the Cold Case unit, leaned back in his chair — a special one he'd brought in himself after three years of sitting through case meetings with worse and worse back pain, which he was determined to clear up before he retired in three more at 55. "S'up boss? Do I finally get to jack somebody up?" Black, replied.

"What's up is your hair, girl. Straight up. Enough with the process: when you goin' natural? That latest sugar tell you the James Brown look is still tight?" Jerry's status conferences with Black usually started with a few minutes of joning on clothes, hair, and love life. As the only two African-Americans in a 15-agent office, they enjoyed having a brief time to reconnect with their own culture. It was funny, she thought, that a prep-school educated doctor's son could bring it as well as her old girls in Simple City.

"I got two words for you, O.G. — 'not yet' — as in 'The Afro is not yet back in style.' You best be puttin' that stocking cap back on, and get your own stack low, bro'. And that vest! Blood, ain't nobody at the FBI wore a vest since *The Untouchables!*"

"OK, I know enough to stop when I been kirked," laughed Jerry. "Now, let's get down to business. You just might get to go after somebody under the age of 80 — but barely." He handed Black a copy of the short memo he had received from the deputy director the night before. Cold Case was to detach an agent to investigate the 1970 bombing of the police station in San Francisco's Golden Gate Park in which an officer had been killed. The agent was to study the case files from a 2009 review, review all visual and printed media mentioning the case, and propose an investigative plan, preferably within one week. The plan should be based on the assumption that subpoenas would be issued to any person of "reasonable suspicion" for matches to the DNA from a hair that in 2009 had been found embedded in a bomb fragment.

"Now, here's what's off the record about 'reasonable suspicion,' and is actually the key to the case. They're using that term because it popped up in a recent appeals court decision expanding the usual 'probable cause.' Justice is committed to accepting any, and I mean any, reason you can think of to subpoena for testing people who have any connection to anybody who themselves have simply been rumored, in print or on tape, to have anything to do with this bombing. Is that enough 'any's' to make myself clear about where this is going?"

"I get it, boss," replied Black. "I'll find a reason for a deep grab. But before I start reading, do you mind telling me what the hell is going on? In my year and a half here I've never seen us pulled off civil rights and onto another cold case. And the last few times we had cases come down to us from the deputy, it was because a senator pushed it from their state. Is that what's going on here? I mean, even then, we had six months to make the proposal. One week? Something's cooking."

"You're right about that, Black. ** runs downhill, and this, for your information and only your information, runs all the way from President Trump. Look up his "tweet" from yesterday afternoon, about 2 p.m., and you'll get your answer. Now hit it. I gotta finish up this first cut at the annual Till report." Jerry turned his chair back to the computer and tilted it into reading mode.

* * *

CHAPTER 4: FEBRUARY 2017 — FIRST CUT

Black spent the first two days reading, just reading, every word in the 2009 case file, and every word in any book or magazine or on-line that the techs could find with a mention of the Park Station bombing, or of any political bombing, from the beginning of the Weatherman offensive in January 1970 until mid-March, when the "own-goal" explosion at the Townhouse brought an end to their attempts to kill people. She also watched clip after clip from movies, documentaries, and television interviews that the techs had helpfully compiled for her. The techs were all hers, first in line, and all on overtime, something rarely decreed by the deputy, and they were generating a lot of material.

For a secret, underground group, she thought, these people never learned to shut up. All the 70-year-olds seemed to have a memoir, a website, and a speaking tour, and most of them broadcast the same message, which was repeated in interviews for the books and documentaries: "We were right then and we are right now: America is an evil empire, with a culture that cynically talks about freedom while enslaving other countries, and both the empire and the culture have to be attacked. And unlike the government that made war in Viet Nam and Central America, and still does in the Middle East today, we never killed anybody. We used 'armed propaganda' and blew up a few symbolic targets, but we weren't terrorists like our government is, then and today."

Black's weakest subject in college had been history. Coming from a seg-regated, day-to-day culture, she simply had never absorbed historical references even when she briefly encountered them in school or on TV. The words, words, words of the Weathermen rolled off her brain, but her FBI training attuned her to pick up the many connections between various sus-pects and the bombings. She had been loaned two other Cold Case agents for the week, and together they built a spider web on the wall, consisting of bombings, both completed and failed, and the Weathermen who talked about, or were talked about, having a connection.

Noted on the web were the dates that each suspect first admitted, or was said to show, knowledge of particular bombings. While nobody in the Bay Area cadre had admitted to the Park Station bombing, a number had copped to the Berkeley police bombing just three days before. They had been staying at a safe house just a mile from Park Station, and most of them bombed other police or court targets over the next five years. Black's DNA subpoenas were going to be heavier on suspicion than proof, and a pattern of behavior was an accepted way of establishing suspicion for federal warrants.

The FBI historians had found a ten-year-old Ph.D. dissertation by Vanessa LeBlanc, who was now a professor of political science at the University of California at Berkeley. LeBlanc had read everything any former Weather-man had written, and had also interviewed a number of them. When Black was making her list of subpoenas and the reasons for them, she found her-self folding back pages of the dissertation again and again at discussions of which Weathermen were in the vicinity of various bombings. With this information, she had the FBI historians pull the suspects' surveillance files from the '70s, which saved her team thousands of hours of cross-referencing.

After five days Black was reading over her final draft, just about ready to hit Send on an email to Jerry titled "Done." But in conversations with the two other agents who had made the web with her, she had found that they were as confused as she was about a crucial point. She felt she needed to clear it up before going forward. So Black looked up the political science department at Berkeley and found an email address for LeBlanc. She sent her a request to call her as soon as possible and then called the department office and asked the secretary who answered to call LeBlanc and tell her that an FBI agent working on Weatherman had just sent her an email, and was in a bit of rush to speak with her. Within minutes LeBlanc was on the phone. After Black's first few questions the professor asked her, "So, which one are you chasing?"

"Good try, Professor, but you know I can't answer that question in detail. Let's just say I've been through your dissertation on the Weathermen lately, back and forth, and since I was born in 1987, I'll admit that I'd never heard anything about these people and their bombings. What I need is, I hope, quite simple. As I try to I understand them to see their motives, as I wade through their river of words, there's one key thing I just don't get.

"I get that they declared war on the United States because it attacked Viet Nam, although you argue that most people were turning against the war anyway and it was about to end. I get that they were angry about racism, and so they backed black radicals, which led them to bomb the cops who arrested them and the judges who tried them. Frankly, as a black woman, I'm impressed that white people cared enough back then to do anything — but as part of law enforcement myself I don't know what else the Black Panther types thought was going to happen when they started walking around with guns.

"But what I don't get is why all these Weathermen, at that time in their underground press releases and after they surfaced, in their memoirs and interviews, keep saying that they just bombed buildings and never tried to harm anyone. What difference does that make? If you're at war, of course you're going to kill people. And blowing up buildings, you can't control who's coming by, even if you set it for the middle of the night. Calling in a bomb threat to clear the building can actually bring cops in to try to find the bomb. There's just no thing as safe 'armed propaganda,' this sort of bombing that won't hurt anybody they keep talking about."

LeBlanc thought for a moment, then responded: "Well, for me the key is at Mendocino, where they decide not just to stop targeting people, like the Townhouse group, but to claim that they never really had. Do you remember that part of the dissertation?"

Black replied, "Yes, that's when they pinned it all on a rogue operation, as if the Townhouse group existed on its own and never talked with the rest of the leadership — and after seeing how much they love to talk over every little thing, back in their endless '70s political publications and in their memoirs today, I doubt that. I've been looking through a number of recent books, one by Burrough, one by Eckstein, that rip all that up, by going over the bombings of police in Berkeley, Detroit, Cleveland, and maybe the Golden Gate

Park case, but my question is still, why? Why make the change to armed propaganda? And I guess, now that I think about it, why claim Townhouse was rogue? I just can't see either one, and it's clearly crucial to understanding how they were thinking, to motive."

"Well, I think there are two reasons for the switch itself," said the professor. "First, at Mendocino it is clear that they want to stay relevant — nobody came to their Days of Rage, they missed the big Kent State demonstrations, they just don't matter. It's important for them to be the vanguard of the revolution, but nobody's following them. Attacking cops, either in the streets or with bombs, is just not what the anti-war movement is all about.

"The movement was actually very main-stream. One book on it, *The Chimes of Freedom Flashing*, breaks it down into Marchers, Sitters, and Trashers: Marchers obeyed all laws, and just wanted to convince voters and the government to change, call Viet Nam a mistake, and simply get out; Sitters did non-violent sit-ins and civil disobedience, and wanted not just to force the government out of Viet Nam, but to question our relations with other 'friendly' dictators; but the violent Trashers, like the Weathermen, saw Viet Nam as no mistake at all, but the inevitable tip of the iceberg of an evil empire, if there's any other kind, and took up arms to destroy it, fighting alongside all the rebels in the Third World.

"Just look at the people on the stage when Weatherman tries to storm it at the November 1969 Mobe: famous folk-singers leading the crowd in "Give Peace a Chance" with no thought to the reasons for the war, when Weather believes in Che Guevara's 'two, three, many Viet Nams' in rebellion against the American empire; and Senators, including a Republican, the father of today's NFL commissioner, who turns football games into celebrations of our sainted troops. From the Weather perspective those troops are still enforcing neo-colonialism on the countries that were supposedly freed in the '50s, '60s, and '70s."

"'70s?" Black interjected, confused. "There were still colonies in the 1970s?"

"Oh yes. Portugal was fighting off liberation movements in its many African colonies, with U.S. support, because Portugal was a member in good standing of NATO and we had a big air base there. One of the Weathermen's bombings, in Pittsburgh, against the Gulf Oil headquarters, was related to that. But back to your question.

"By the time of Mendocino, Bernardine Dohrn and Jeff Jones had decided they had to stay in touch with the mainstream of the movement but not lose support from its more radical side. Their solution? Armed propaganda. It really was a brilliant piece of politics, you know. Suddenly Weather was Robin Hood to all the strains of the movement, because they were tweaking, pricking, but not bloodily killing the Sheriff of Nottingham, just like in the movies. You and I might not think bombing can be non-lethal, but a lot of people in the anti-war movement clearly did.

"This 'New Morning — Changing Weather,' as they called it in a communiqué that December, probably made people in the movement more willing to read their position papers, and also to hide them underground, give them expense money, and never tell the FBI anything. And in later years, when they came back above-ground, the notion that they were careful not to hurt anybody probably helped them get and keep their jobs as teachers, professors, advisers on various boards, and even as lawyers — or rather law professors and legal aides, since they usually can't get their bar licenses back. The rogue narrative was crucial to that."

Black jotted down a few notes, and said, "OK, professor, thanks. I can see when I can't see — it still makes no sense to me, and politics rarely does! But now, you said there was a second reason you think they did it, pushed this rogue narrative?"

"This one in more conjecture on my part," replied LeBlanc, "but I think they were worried that Nixon would get fixated on them if they killed people, and would 'take the gloves off' the FBI so it could track them down. Now, recent releases of FBI files show that the gloves were already off, with a huge task force, top priority, and black bag jobs everywhere the Weathers might have been, and also against parents, siblings, and friends. But once rumors of kidnappings and assassinations of government officials died down, and the Weather Underground started a fairly predictable pattern of infrequent bathroom bombings, I do think there was less of a sense of urgency, and some reductions in staffing.

"And I do want to point out that on the 'rogue' claim you have one thing wrong: you're not right when you say they all claim, 'we never tried to harm anybody.' No, what most of them claim is, 'we never killed anybody.' Only a very few still keep up the fiction about the rogue operation. Go back and check: Rudd, Machtinger, Wilkerson, Flanagan, people from all three loose collectives in the Bay Area, the Midwest, and New York, and in fact nearly everyone in Weatherman admits that from January to March of 1970 they were trying to kill enemy warriors — troops, cops, judges, whoever was enforcing order for the empire. The New York group saw the Ft. Dix NCO's like the V.C. saw American troops in the barracks at Pleiku, as combatants, as legitimate targets. And all three collectives clearly saw cops the same way."

"Stop, professor, what's a Pleiku? What's V.C.? I told you history isn't my strong suit."

"Well," said LeBlanc, "I'm sorry to say that much of 'motive' won't make sense to you if you're not as steeped in Viet Nam as the Weathermen were. Their predecessors, the people who founded SDS in 1961 and led it until the explosion of anti-war protests in 1965, people like Tom Hayden, had civil rights and the system of racism behind it as their common history, and knew every Klan murder and every creative, non-violent campaign in the South, because they had all gone there to take part. But this next generation of SDS, who came on after the first march on the Pentagon in 1965, were there because of Viet Nam and the imperialism they saw behind it. That's what they studied, that's what they knew.

"Pleiku refers to an attack by the National Liberation Front, known in slang as the V.C. for Vietnamese Communists, Viet Cong. They killed a lot of American troops sleeping in their barracks on a base in Pleiku, and it was denounced as criminal and terroristic, proof of the wickedness of the enemy, by Johnson, the president at the time. He used it as an excuse to start bombing the V.C.'s allies and suppliers in North Viet Nam, the campaign the million idiotic motorcyclists don't know they're celebrating in DC every year in their 'Rolling Thunder' parade. The Weathermen would know the reference: 'Pleikus are like street cars.' Meaning, you wait for a while and one comes along to justify the supposed retaliation you actually had planned all along. That's what Johnson's top aide, Mac Bundy, openly and cynically said at the time they started Rolling Thunder.

"But back to your mistake about the 'we never tried to harm' story from Mendocino. Nobody stuck to that except two. Any guesses?"

"I get it, professor. I was being sloppy in the way I said it," answered Black. "That would be Dohrn and Ayers, the happy couple ever since Oughton died in the Townhouse. They keep up the story because it takes the Midwest operation, which Ayers ran, and the Bay Area operation, which Dohrn ran, out of the loop."

"Bingo, and now that I've had time to think about it, I bet that's exactly why you're calling me. Not only did the jobs they held for decades at universities depend a lot on this narrative, but there's also one unclaimed blue body out there, with no statute of limitations on murder, and there's some evidence pointing Weather's way. Might you, Ms. McGurk, be planning a little trip out my way, to take a stroll in Golden Gate Park, down by Haight-Ashbury and the original Panhandle?"

Uh-oh, thought Black, she's not a professor for nothing. "Professor LeBlanc, you of course can speak your mind whenever you want, and it's possible that soon everybody will be speaking their mind about what I'm working on. I can't confirm or deny, as they tell us to say, and I hope that you'll wait on talking about any of this. If you don't, I guarantee you and I will never speak again. But if you can just wait a bit I promise you'll be the very first person I fill in if this matter is about to become public. I think you'll be happier hearing about it from me, as opposed to waiting another few decades for some more files to be released."

Later that day, Black finished putting LeBlanc's conjectures into the motives section of the report, and sent it off to Jerry. Half an hour later he showed up at her cubicle, smiling: "Way to get on it, Black. I skimmed it, it looks good. I'll read it tonight and send you some edits for final," said Jerry. "But give me the bottom line. Are we gonna solve this one? Is it hot, or not?"

"Well, it's certainly an easy one to start," said Black. "We've got 10 Weathermen still alive we can place, usually by their own admission, in meetings to plan bombings during these three months, and five of them are from the Bay Area collective that carried out the Berkeley cop attack. Of course the issue is, can we even indict without DNA? And I think the 2009 review was right: we can't. So, we've got to have their DNA, these ten, and I've made the case for each one.

"I've proposed we speed up the process, even before we subpoena, and increase our leverage by dumpster diving on them, and getting our own tests done. Most of the rulings on using 'surreptitious collection' as evidence have gone our way recently, but just to be safe, if we get a hit we should still serve all ten, and just use those results for our case. Of course we'll already know who we're looking for, but the courts have backed Justice on that in all the big mafia and terror cases.

"Black, I think the suits are gonna like this, and given the interest up top, they're gonna have you going within days. I see your first proposed move is to the crime scene. Do you think that's necessary? Shouldn't you be supervising the DNA grabs?"

"Boss, I really need to be in San Francisco for a week or so, get a feel for the bombing, for the case. Local agents can be tasked for the grabs for our top ten. They're spread out all over the country anyway: Chicago, New York City, Hudson Valley, Albuquerque. I can write the instructions just as well from there as from here. I'll have them track 'em down, and swipe their coffee cups and gum out on the town, whatever, and check their home garbage if that doesn't work. Don't you worry. Whoever did Park Station thought they had it all figured out back then, how to put this behind them with the tale of rogue operations — but they'd never heard of DNA."

* * *

Jerry was right: within days Black got her approval, her budget, and her staff. Local FBI teams were sent out to grab DNA, and she flew to the Bay Area. She brought two interns with her to read and copy the files from the local efforts in 1999 and 2009, and go over them with any investigators they could track down. What she wanted to do herself was walk the scene and interview the retired cops who had survived the blast.

Jerry had contacted the chief, Tony Tritt, to explain the visit and the new commitment of the Justice Department to push the case. Tritt had just come on the job after 20 years in Portland, where he had risen from patrolman to chief of detectives. He was black, and the previous chief, a white, 35-year veteran of the San Francisco force, had been pushed out after an officer killed an unarmed black woman. Then the Justice Department issued a report on police profiling of African-Americans, nixing the mayor's plans to appoint the black acting chief, another local veteran, as the permanent one.

So Tritt was an outsider, just starting to wade through the complicated racial tensions on the force, and his instincts told him that showing an interest in the Park case, or the McDonnell murder, as the police union called it after the officer eviscerated by the pipe bomb, was a good way to start. When Black came out of the gate a little after noon, she was momentarily taken aback by the unexpected sight of the chief, in his formal gold braid and tie, as he stepped forward from the huddle of his security detail to greet her.

"Agent McGurk? Tony Tritt. I'm the Chief. We're grateful that you've come to take on this case. Let me give you a lift into town so we can talk about it. Your boss filled me in a bit, but I want to make sure you get everything you need from us."

The two agents who had come to pick up Black stood by quietly. Protocol was always an issue with local police, and if the chief wanted to give her a ride, they weren't going to say otherwise. "Thanks, Chief, let's do it. And, please, call me Black," she answered. "Yeah, I know," she said as he raised his eyebrows and smiled, "it is what it is, and it's my name." She greeted the agents and sent the interns and her carry-on with them.

In the chief's SUV she compared notes with him on their backgrounds, the unspoken theme being how unlikely it still seemed to them that black people would be in charge of anything. Back in the chief's palatial office with his top planners, Black politely demurred when they asked her what she needed and offered to call in the lead detective from the 2009 cold case review right away.

"Thanks, but not right now. Of course we'll get there. But what I need today is just your safe conduct pass to wander the Park Station scene by myself. Please apologize to the detective, and tell her I can't work this case, just like I can't work my Klan cases and I bet she can't work her other cold cases, without first standing in the middle of the crime, and starting to smell it. That's how I need to spend today.

"Now, if you have the staffing, there's one thing that would save me a lot of time. Can somebody track down any retired cops or staff who were there when the bomb went off, and ask them to meet me at the scene for a walk-through tomorrow morning, say O-seven hundred?"

One of the chief's deputies laughed, "O-seven hundred? McGurk, these folks would have to be over 70, maybe 80 years old. Can't you let them sleep in a bit? I bet a bunch will still be in the Bay Area, but probably not in the city — it's too damned expensive for retirees! So there's travel time too. I suggest 10."

* * *

The week passed quickly. The interns pored over the case files, and checked them with the mostly retired deputies who had worked them. They confirmed the previous interest in the five still-living leads the techs had identified from the historical record. Black herself spent much of the time in Park Station and the area around it. She decided that the dead officer,

Brian McDonnell, and the one badly-wounded and eight lightly-wounded ones weren't specifically targeted for some alleged racist act on their part like some police had been in the Detroit and Cleveland cases, and had probably never even been seen by the bombers. They just happened to be in the area near the window on a busy staircase between two sets of offices. The bomb had been placed on a ledge from outside the building.

The department had purposely left the station and its grounds as unmodified as possible, so as not to change the crime scene. The inside of the station had been modernized without changing the lay-out. The outside had pretty much been left alone, and looked its age. The terrain had made it possible to lay the bomb by stretching up, without a ladder, so the approach of the bombers wouldn't have appeared remarkable to any witnesses.

On the first day Black had walked east along the Panhandle, a sliver of park that jutted out into residential streets. A hundred years before, its shape had given a moniker to the drifters who congregated there and asked passers-by for hand-outs. Then she cut south on Ashbury Street to Haight, to the site of what had been a Weathermen safe-house in the epicenter of the youth culture in the late 1960s. The journey took her no more than ten minutes, and she began to imagine the route the bombers might have taken to scout the station and place the bomb.

On the last day she opened her email, and her heart jumped when saw the title of one from her boss: it just read, "Hit!" Five of the ten DNA teams had succeeded, and the lab said that one had a certain match, of the one in a million variety. It came off a Robust Coffee Lounge cup discarded after a meeting of friends at that Southside Chicago café, the drinking and the discard captured on an agent's video. The cup had been only in the hands, and mouth, of one Bernardine Dohrn, 75 years old, retired Northwestern University law professor and former member of the Central Committee of the Weather Underground.

Black thought about the two claims from the '70s that prosecutors had decided were too weak to make a case on: one from an FBI informant recalling that Bill Ayers complained that the Bay Area cadre was so unmotivated that Dohrn had to build and place the bomb herself, and one from a Weatherman in the cadre, a woman actually, who had been born-again. She had peppered her statement about Dohrn planning the bombing with memories of her conversations with Jesus. Well, enough with claims: it was Dohrn's hair that was embedded in the bomb fragment from Park Station.

"Jerry, it's too sweet," crowed Black when she called him. "Northwestern wins its first NCAA game ever last night and loses its killer-prof today! I hope you had them in your bracket."

"Yes, I had them, and I'm still ahead of you in the pool. Look, come on back, girl. We'll work on the subpoenas over the weekend, and the fireworks will begin. Now, this'll probably be prosecuted as a state crime, and we don't want to get into strategy directly with the D.A.'s office there. Leave that to Justice. But our suits want you to let the chief know we have a hit; just say protocol means you can't tell him who yet. Let him know we don't mind if that word gets out and around, as long as it's all no-attribution, no-source. Old-school, not tweeting, got it, Black?"

"I got it," Black replied. "But I don't follow the high-jingo here. Why warn Dohrn's lawyers that a test will sink their client?"

"You're in the wrong California city for high-jingo," laughed Jerry. They were both fans of a series of novels about Hieronymus "Harry" Bosch, an intense, anti-bureaucracy Los Angeles detective who often found his cases enmeshed in police department and city politics. "Don't you see? If she thinks we've got her, she's more likely to take a plea and finger her co-conspirators while the subpoenas are being argued in court, which could take months, maybe years. The hair is the start of the investigation, not the end of it. We're looking to take down as many as possible, and her hair on the bomb is no guarantee of her conviction anyway, certainly not of murder. It's the smart move for her, and as I read your memo I see her as the smartest of that crowd."

* * *

Black and her team prepared the ten DNA subpoenas, throwing into the supporting memo for Dohrn's everything they could think of, from her own statements advocating "killing pigs" to her documented presence in the Bay Area at the time of the crime, along with a list of all bombings admitted to by the organization she essentially ran. They also fanned out for interviews with the other nine bombing veterans, hoping that somebody, after all these years, would be willing to break ranks on a murder. Dohrn would hear about the inquiries quickly, they assumed, and that might increase pressure on her to start cooperating.

A week later, all ten subpoenas were served. Dohrn got hers outside of her house in Chicago, where she was walking two visiting grand-children to a Hyde Park playground. Her lawyer rapidly filed such a detailed appeal of the order that it was clear this was an issue he'd been researching fever-ishly since Tritt's leak. Justice agreed to stay the other nine subpoenas while Dohrn's appeal wound through the courts.

An Obama appointee at the first level of federal courts, the district court for Chicago, decided to stay the subpoena pending the final outcome of the appeal, finding no urgency in a cold case that could outweigh the irreversible harm Dohrn's lawyer asserted a successful test would do to her presump-tion of innocence if the subpoena were eventually invalidated. The stay was applauded by a number of commentators in the liberal and radical media, who had spent the past week attacking an unsourced San Francisco Chron-icle column saying the FBI had already used informally-collected DNA to place someone in Weatherman at the Park Station scene. A number of the commentators cited the FBI's history of fake stories planted in the '60s to discredit Martin Luther King and Malcolm X.

A week later, though, a Bush-dominated seventh circuit panel reversed the stay, saying that the government was likely to prevail on the appeal because of the plausible suspicions the Justice Department had taken straight from Black's memo. The previous finding on irreversible harm was acknowledged, but deemed moot because of the government's admission in court that without DNA, the case would likely be too weak to prosecute. Dohrn was ordered to appear for testing in one week.

As Dohrn's lawyer rushed the issue of the stay to the Supreme Court, Harold Middles, a prominent criminal attorney who had developed a pro bono side-line in Guantanamo prisoners, made an immediate appointment with Salvatore Imaglio, a law-school friend and frequent prosecuting opponent whose nomination by President Trump to be assistant attorney general for the criminal division had just been confirmed by the Senate.

"OK, Harry, what's the rush that brings you down from New York?" The two men sat in Imaglio's regal office high over Constitution Avenue. "I hav-en't seen you since the moot court we juried, what was it, three years ago?

You're usually too busy playing Bill Kunstler for drone-dead sheiks. You're not here about the guy whose brother started bombing again as soon as you got him out of Guantanamo, are you? You know I can't get into that without bringing in the Pentagon."

"Hey, one out of ten gone wrong's not bad, Sal — but no, it's something else entirely, and I need someone I trust to walk it through the system. It's a bombshell, but we have to work fast. My client is William Ayers. His wife is Bernardine Dohrn, the Weatherman you're trying to test for a 1970 bombing."

"Ah, we've been expecting such a visit, but from her attorney," said Sal. "What does Ayers want to offer us? Is he gonna do the right thing, and take the fall for her? Do what Julius should have done for Ethel? You know, he probably threw rocks at this window right here when he was screaming up at John Mitchell, what is it, 50 years ago? I should throw you out right now," he joked.

"Sal, it's about his wife, for sure. Ayers told me last night that he's ready to make a deal, a stunning deal, actually, one I'm still reeling over. Do you remember the Weather-cat murders, six officials in government and business assassinated in five years, including a Louisiana congressman and a general, each time right after a Weatherman bombing of where they worked? What if he and Dohrn knew who did it, and could give 'em to you, on a plate? Could you decide the San Francisco case is just too weak, and pull the subpoena? Even if you win the subpoena, you know that's just the beginning of a real mess anyway, what with Trump fingering them and all.

"I mean, let's assume that it really is Dohrn's hair on the bomb. That's still gonna be too many steps away from a murder. You know the defense will have a field day with her visiting a house where maybe later somebody made a bomb. In fact, a judge may not even allow that in, too many possible gaps to charge murder."

"Harry, what I am going to say now, I want you to know it's not an insult," started Imaglio. "We've been on opposite sides of a lot of cases during my time as a prosecutor, and we've always played it straight. But you have to tell me, face to face, right now, that this conversation is just between us. Not your client, not Dohrn's lawyer, not anybody at any stage of this case. The politics are too intense on this for me to be characterized in any way, by anybody. Deal?"

Middles laughed, and gave him the line from the Godfather: "What have I ever done to make you treat me so disrespectfully?"

"OK, then, here's what I'm thinking," said Imaglio. "On the face of it, of course I'd probably take some kind of deal for her, with the subpoena held in abeyance but not dismissed, as usual, until all guarantees of cooperation, from both of them, are met. Of course, if they were somehow in on the Weather-cat murders themselves, in any way, no deal, or at least a heavy plea.

"But you know the president started all this because of Hannity's attacks on Ayers and Dohrn, so Sessions would have to make the final call. If he wants to, he can find out how it would play at the White House. I'm not gonna get into that. I'll lay it out for him, and implement what he decides. And I'll tell you, when I talk with Sessions, I have to give him what Trump would need, even if he never talks to Trump. He'll need closure on San Francisco, on the police officer. Dohrn will have to plead to something, do some time."

"That's gonna be a problem, Sal," said Middles. "No way on Dohrn and prison. Now, my client actually says no nothing on Dohrn and San Francisco, but I could go back to him on that, if there's no felony, no prison, something like full allocution and a misdemeanor for failing to report."

"No promises. That'll have to be bargained after I talk to Sessions. But if you want me even to go to him and stop the subpoena, you've gotta give me what Ayers has, now. Then he can make an informed decision."

"Sal, that's fine, but let's keep that between us too, so I can tell Ayers we just dealt in hypotheticals," replied Middles, blithely ignoring his promise to walk out without providing details if Dohrn wasn't free and clear, completely and immediately. Clients could be their own worst enemies, and it wasn't the first time he'd disregarded their instructions, in their own best interests.

"Have your agents look back at the files for Weather-cat," said Middles, "and they'll see that the six communiqués jumped all over the Weathermen for being too soft on war criminals, so they had to be killed, and they were all signed by the Nathan Hale brigade. Well, there ain't no brigade, because as my client will testify, 'Nathan Hale' told SDS he 'wasn't a joiner' when they tried to recruit him in 1969. It's one guy, a killer on his own crazy mission, and they've known who he is since just after the killing stopped in 1975.

They've kept tabs on him all these years, sort of as an insurance policy for this very situation. Look, she walks, this Nathan goes down. Guaranteed you can build a case when some rookie goes all over the east coast to assassinate six people in five years. Aren't six sure things, including a congressman and a general, worth one 'maybe'?"

* * *

CHAPTER 6: MARCH 2017 — THE DEAL

Attorney General Sessions and FBI Director Comey sat to their weekly breakfast, in a closed-off corner of the Justice Department cafeteria. The room was a SCIF inside a SCIF-like building — an especially secure compartmented information facility where complex jammers and composite walls scrambled or absorbed every possible type of electronic or sound waves. There were lots of these double-SCIF's in the building, at least one for each division. However, most employees rarely took the trouble to walk into them to discuss classified information — because literally everything was marked "classified," no matter how mundane.

Thousands of potential felonies were committed every day as top staff whispered through cupped hands rather than take yet another pain-in-the-ass stroll down the hall to see if the SCIF was free, or brought their phones and laptops into a briefing rather than go to the trouble of having to keep going out to email yet another requested file to the secure computer in the room. In the context of continuing, massive Wiki-leaks of entire secret programs by contractors and the frequent hacking of supposedly secure computers, government and commercial, it all seemed pointless to most staff. The system knew it too, and largely just winked at the violations.

But that was impossible for Sessions or Comey: given their political profile, sooner or later they would be asked in a hearing if they had ever discussed classified material outside of a SCIF, so they had to have all their briefings in their offices or other SCIFs. Before coming into the breakfast nook they'd turned all electronics, even their top-grade secure phones, over to the two-person teams that traveled with them just to handle cyber-security

"Jim, I've got some interesting news for you," Sessions said. "Your Park Station subpoena has turned up an offer, but it's not the one you expected. Dohrn's husband, Ayers, the one whose connection to Obama got Hannity all hopped up, and started the president down this path, sent his lawyer in to make a deal: leave her alone, no DNA test, and Ayers offers up the 1970s 'Weather-cat' killer who took out six of what he called the 'imperialist enemies of the people' — a congressman, a general, a State Department official, a professor, and two business executives.

"It's a stand-off right now: Trump's people like it, getting six murders done, but insist on Dohrn copping to the Park bombing and doing a little time. But the husband's lawyer, old Harry Middles, he's hanging tough on it. As of yesterday he wouldn't go farther than her taking a misdemeanor plea, something in state law like failure to report, but fully describing the plot and her bull claim that she had only a tangential role in it. Of course, we haven't talked with Dohrn's lawyer yet, but we assume she and Ayers are coordinated on this. The Supreme Court will take up the stay in two days, and neither we nor Middles can predict their move, because it's not a classic liberal-conservative choice. That's what's driving us both to make a deal: most of the Justices swing both ways on subpoena cases, depending on detail."

"Amazing. Look what a little presidential "tweet" can do in under two weeks: maybe take our biggest political murders since the Kennedys and King off the board!" Comey thought for a few seconds. "Well, thanks for keeping me up to date, but obviously it's your call. Personally, of course I'd like jail time for her, but I'd take the offer in a heartbeat without it, and not lose a second of sleep.

"It may be tough for a politician to say, but you and I know that this is our business. Hell, we'll make deals like this about 40 times before sundown tonight with the first one to talk in murder, extortion, kidnapping, you name it. The locals, and in this case the police union, will scream, of course, but they know it won't be the first or the last time, and they do it every day, too. And Weather-cat, these are huge cases, much more important to the national interest."

* * *

Unlike Comey, Black had never been through it before, and she was pissed. "Are you kidding me? We're gonna just ** that chief who gave us everything we wanted, to chase another case? You're the one who told me to say to him, 'The president is determined that McDonnell's children will have justice.' And now you want me to tell him, 'Sorry, I lied: we found a more important case. Be satisfied with a bull misdemeanor?' On top of that, I'm supposed to start again, like now, putting a team together to make the Weather-cat cases? Why, so we can later trade those for a missing nuclear weapon, a drug king-pin, or some such ** ?"

Jerry Cummings leaned back in his chair, trying but failing to stifle a smile. "Black, Black, I thought you'd be happy. You're gonna be agent-in-charge of an even bigger cold case. Look, I know it hurts, but it had to happen. We call this the 'welcome to Washington' moment, but of course, you've been here your whole life. I'll bet you knew lots of kids in high school who got off by being the first to rat out their drug-dealing pals; 90 percent of the time, that's how cases are made! But it's not just police work, it's everything in your young life. Higher-ups will always smile, lie, and throw you overboard if they need to. I'm sorry you had to learn it on this one, a tough one, but you had to learn it sometime.

"Look, let me tell you about when I learned the lesson, on my first job, at 22, and it wasn't a cop job. I was a teacher, right out of college, teaching social studies, working at a Catholic high school in the Newark ghetto that promised 'no excuses,' so our black kids would know they had to work and not play. And the principal was there to back me up, make sure, as she said, I would be king in my classroom. 'You're the teacher,' she said. 'I'll never interfere in how you teach. That's your job. You let me worry about the parents and the board of directors. That's my job.'

"And everything was fine, the principal was happy, we joked around and she praised me to the skies, right up until the end of the first semester, when I turned down a request from a girl who hadn't done much work and now wanted to retake the final exam after she scored a 20. This brought her grade below failing, and she'd have to take the semester over again. I remember her there with tears in her eyes, saying, 'Mr. Cummings, I thought we was homeys!' I told her indeed we was, and I was holding her to the rules because

I was trying to teach her the most important lesson she could ever learn: do your work the first time!

"About a day later, there was the principal with the parent in tow, right up in my grill. Now it was 'Mr. Cummings,' and not 'Jerry,' and she told me, with the parent right there, that this sort of attitude harmed children, and I needed to offer the exam again.

"Even worse, the parent complained that some of the questions on the exam contained new material, asking students about how they would decide a court case I summarized in the exam book, a different case from those we'd studied. I explained to the mom that this was an announced purpose of the course, right there on the syllabus she had, to help students learn how to apply their knowledge to new situations. But the principal took her side, and told me to write a new exam for the student, based just on cases in the text-book. I knew if I backed down, the kids in the class would never do another stitch of work, so I refused: no retest, she'd learn from the experience, and I could still be 'king in my classroom.'

"I was young, I was bold, what did I know? Within a week, my evaluation file was littered with low assessments of my 'classroom management,' records of my kids' 'low' scores on standardized tests, fantasy claims that other, magically anonymous, teachers had said I wasn't a 'team player' because I wouldn't cover their classes when they had meetings during my planning period, and even a warning that I had been observed hugging girls in the hall — well, that one was true. You know there's a lot of hugging in our culture, and I never turned any child away who came to me with open arms!

"Anyway, I found out later that the principal had a contract based on the percentage of kids passing courses. And I never took it personally when I wasn't offered a new contract that spring. I was better off going to law school anyway. I'm sure the principal had administrators over her who were lying, spying, and willing to kick her to the curb just like she'd done to me. I mean, really, do black people need to learn that nobody can be trusted? Wasn't last hired, first fired invented just for us? You know, the OJ's? 'Smile in your face, all the time they wanna take your place'..."

Black finally smiled, and sang out, "'The back-stabbers'....OK, I get it, but it just isn't right — you have to keep your promises."

"Look, two things, girl. First, no you don't, not if you have a mortgage. The only people who can walk away from the daily ** of any office are those who've already paid it off, and that's not most of us. Even Harry Bosch gives in to the high-jingo sometimes! I never refused an order at work again in my life. That's why I'm sitting here, looking at that sweet retirement package!

"And second, to be fair to Justice in this case, what would you do? The color of truth is gray, here, not black and white. Can't you make a case for solving six murders over one? Look, it's over. They made the deal. If you want, I'll be the one to make the call to Chief Tritt, but I tell you, he won't be surprised, or take it personally either. And then let's get on with our new assignment, roping up this Weather-cat. Now, I don't want you to take any bull from Ayers and Dohrn when you interview them. Read through the confidential agreement Ayers and Dohrn signed: if they lie, if they even short you on leads and testimony, it's all off. The subpoena's on ice, not dismissed, until we dispose of the six assassinations."

"OK," said Black, "I'm Army, I can take orders like the best of them, but before I do, I'm certainly going to send my disagreement up through the dissent channel, like they told us to in training."

"Oh no you won't, not if you have half a brain." Jerry put his hand on Black's quadriceps muscle and squeezed until she jumped in pain. "What the ** , Jerry?"

"That's to make you slow down and listen to me. Every time in your career that you take a mind to dissent with the suits, in a meeting or on some bull dissent channel, you pretend I'm grabbing your quad and squeezing 'til you scream. I'm serious now. 'Things without all remedy should be without regard. What's done is done.' That's brilliant Bill Shakespeare, sugar.

"See, everybody loves freedom of speech 'til they disagree with what's being said. I remember my uncle, one of the first black finance guys on Wall Street, telling me about an 'off the record, listening' meeting that Chase Manhattan Bank had in the '70s for him and the rest of its fresh class of analysts. The president, David Rockefeller himself, ran the session, and asked for any questions, any at all, about working at Chase.

"And this rookie, he popped up in his little mini-businessman suit and said that his college classmates were asking him why Chase was loaning money to brutal dictators, like the white government in South Africa, or Idi

Amin in Uganda. Long silence, Rockefeller straining his jaw to stay polite himself, some bull about not getting involved in other nations' politics, this from a guy whose entire business model was getting a lot more than involved in picking governments."

"Hold on, I've heard that name, like Rockefeller Plaza, the Rockettes," cut in Black. "There was a Weather plot to kidnap a Rockefeller in 1970. Machtinger ran it, but they never could find him. And the summaries on the Weather-bombings had a reference to David Rockefeller in the bio on William Bundy, the guy whose office in Cambridge was hit. I remember now, I went to the book in the reference pretty much just for fun, because it had something to do with football.

"I think the author was named Bird, something like that. Turns out there was a whole family of these Bundys in government. Anyway, Rockefeller chaired a foreign policy council of some kind in New York, and he took this Bundy to the Harvard-Yale game and offered him the job of president, no application necessary. Guess those were the days before affirmative action. Being it was a football game, you'd think they might have used the Rooney rule: at least interview one brother or sister! So, yeah, he was deep into foreign policy."

"Right," said Jerry. "So, Rockefeller allowed to the inconvenient questioner, 'Of course we'd draw a line at something like a Hitler,' he said, and lo and behold, the kid didn't back down. He just said, still very polite, that he'd heard that Chase in fact had done business with Hitler. My uncle said the kid was gone within a week. And don't think it's not the same at every organization you're ever going to be in — you want to change things, talking about it is the last way to do it, because you'll be pushed out before you get to the level where you might, might, be able to change things."

* * *

"Mr. Ayers, Ms. Dohrn, I'm FBI Special Agent Mar'Shae McGurk, one of the Cold Case investigators, and I'm taping this interview so my colleagues can get all the information too. As you are aware, the terms of your agreement with the Justice Department require, and I quote, 'complete and truthful cooperation in solving the so-called Weather-cat murders of 1971 to 1975, with the agreed-upon plea and immunities contingent on an indictment of those responsible.' So, let's get started. Tell me who and where the Weather-cat is, and how you know this is the killer. Use as much detail as possible, please.

"And I caution your attorneys, this isn't a deposition, to be used in court. That will come later, with the prosecutors. Let me quote, again, from the agreement: 'This is a confidential federal investigation, and restrictions in answers for legal reasons will not be accepted.' You may consult with your attorneys, but not answer through them, and if I judge that your answers are not complete and truthful, I'll report that to my superiors. I don't want to waste a lot of time poking around for the truth. You made this deal, you have to live with it."

Bill Ayers spoke up first. He was determined, as he had been from the beginning of the negotiations, to minimize Bernardine's risk. Weatherman had declared chivalry sexist, but his protective instincts were too strong, after 45 years together, to care. "There was no Nathan Hale brigade like the six communiqués claimed, just one guy, just one Nathan Hale. It took us a while to figure out what was happening, because we were moving around, and didn't always get national news, just like national news didn't always find out about our actions.

"Weather had a lot of actions, as you know, in the 'armed propaganda' phase, and we didn't claim them all, either. Maybe every fourth or fifth one, though, something like this would happen, a murder of a person related to the bombed building — and only in a case when we had issued a communiqué. That meant this person was copying us, a copy-cat, so the press began to label these the 'Weather-cat' killings.

"After the first few killings, maybe by 1973, somebody remembered that an SDS guy at the University of Chicago had told us about a student in 1969, a draft resister who was anti-imperialist, stridently moralistic, but a little confused — he wouldn't take his student deferment. This kid told the SDS guy he wouldn't join the Weathermen because they just bomb bathrooms, and he was planning to just shoot the highest-ranking people who used them.

"The kid kept calling himself a 'new Nathan Hale' — the American spy, a kid himself, really, a patriot during the Revolution, the British caught and hanged him. And that Nathan Hale fan is now 65, and a professor at Vanderbilt, in Nashville. His name is Valerius, goes by Val, Shaw. That's your killer."

"Mr. Ayers," said Black, "That's a little weak, a 50-year-old conversation with someone using a name that maybe other people who studied American history could have associated with revolution. There were more than a couple 'John Brown' bombing collectives that had nothing to do with Weathermen, and the record shows they weren't even aware of each other. I sure hope you have more than this, because this would be laughed out of court. And as you agreed, no indictment on Weather-cat, no deal on San Francisco."

"Oh, I can explain that," interjected Dohrn. "We made it our business to find out about Val Shaw, since he was attacking us by name. By 1974 we'd tracked him down through the SDS member at U of C. He was living in Swarthmore, Pennsylvania, had just finished college there, was working a bit and playing folk music in bars for a living. We put the word out to our network, with surveillance pictures we took of him, and described him and all his details, his history, to see if anybody could link him to any actions. And after a few months, early 1975, right after the State Department bombing and the final Weather-cat killing, I got a call from somebody who had been in our all-women's group in Boston, the Proud Eagle Collective. It was a match, just like with your DNA computers, but a bit slower.

"She placed him at a meeting in October 1970, traveling there with John Jacobs. We'd told all the collectives that Jacobs had been expelled in May, but some people were apparently still using him as a resource, not a member, to get dynamite and build bombs. Their target was a Harvard professor at the CFIA, Center for International Affairs, who worked with the Pentagon, who'd openly advocated 'free-fire' zones to drive peasants in Viet Nam into the cities, into 'modernity,' to deprive the NLF of their base."

"Yes, we have that one, Ms. Dohrn," said Black, "but there was no assassination there, and no Nathan Hale communiqué. What is the relevance of this to Weather-cat?"

"Ah, but there was an assassination attempt, much to the collective's surprise, and apparently to yours. One of the women was close, shall we say, to J. J., Jacobs, that is. They were together, had sex that night on the high of building the bomb, and he let it slip, sort of showing off. He said his pal was off taking out Samuel Huntington, the professor, right then. When the kid came back later, maybe 11, he and J. J. left immediately, so they'd be well out of town when the bomb went off at 2 a.m.

"The woman sort of didn't believe it, but she decided to look up Huntington's address and went by there the next afternoon. There was a glass company truck out front, and three guys were replacing a window. The inside panel was lying in fragments on the ground, but the storm window they had taken off to replace, which was made of a hard sort of plastic, had a two separate holes in it, clearly from bullets.

"It was definitely a hit: Val Shaw must never have read the Warren report, about Oswald failing to kill the right-wing general a few months before Kennedy, because his shots were deflected by the glass. We think there was no communiqué for the Harvard hit because Shaw had failed. We think the professor had some *huevos*, too. He took his own tough-guy advice, having written about not helping radicals get publicity. We think he never told the police, maybe never told his family, just decided whatever it was would be unlikely to happen again."

"So, we know it's Shaw, and now you know it's Shaw," said Ayers, "and you can build a case from that. We'll give you the U of C student and the Proud Eagle woman. Unfortunately, we can't give you Jacobs, because he's dead, 1997, after years on the run in Canada, his ashes, appropriately, spread on Che Guevara's grave in Havana. Remember, we told our people in May and announced publicly in December in 'New Morning - Changing Weather' that we'd expelled him for his violence against people, instead of armed propaganda. We had nothing to do with all this shooting, or the six murders that followed, and with J. J. involved, it just shows we were right to announce his expulsion. Now, none of the people involved in the other bombings, the ones before the six killings, ever saw Valerius Shaw, but that's probably because he and J.J. changed their tactics, and carried out the hits weeks later. "

Black questioned the two Weather leaders for a few hours, squeezing every detail possible out of them. She felt something was wrong, that the neat story was just too neat, but Jerry had told her to expect that. "These people are too practiced as liars to even think about telling the truth," he had said, "but your job is get as much of it as you can, so we can follow the leads." Well, she had gotten a lot, and she thought that the Harvard incident would be sufficient to get an indictment, just on pattern alone, for the successful assassinations. It would take something else, like placing Shaw at the scenes, to get a conviction, but Black and Jerry agreed that the deal could stand for now. She went off to work with the field teams, first in Nashville, and then in Swarthmore.

* * *

CHAPTER 7: JUNE 1970 — THE CONTACT

Val unfolded the legs of his father-in-law's aluminum card table on the sidewalk in front of the draft board in Swarthmore, Pennsylvania. He taped a hand-drawn poster over the front of the table and placed a pile of flyers on the table, under a rock to keep them from blowing away. And then, as he had for the past week, from when the draft board opened at nine in the morning until it closed at five at night, he sat down in one of the two folding chairs.

On the first day he had gone inside and sat by the door inside the draft board, telling the ladies he was there to counsel people against the draft. It was a small enough town, and he was a rare enough case, that they all knew him from his unsuccessful application to be a conscientious objector. The head secretary had said, "Val, I understand your point of view, and all I can say is that my father had to go in World War II, just like yours, but mine died in it. And my son enlisted for this war. It's just the price of patriotism. Now, you can't be in here, but I am sure you can hang around outside to talk to people."

So Val had taken his place on the sidewalk, only to find that few people actually came to a draft board. His father had been the first person to stop by, on the first morning, on the way to his law firm a block away. He had brought Val a box of Spaulding white-powdered Krullers, shaken his hand, and said he was proud of him for standing up for his beliefs, but would he please just take the student deferment so he could keep on expressing them. Of the ten other people who had stopped to talk to him during the week on his sidewalk, four blocks from the main shopping street, only one had been a kid coming in to register. He took the flyer, which was a reprint of an advertisement Val had put in the local paper for $75, and walked in to do his business.

"Sons of America, don't accept their lies!" read the headline (only because the editor had refused to accept 'Amerika'), which was followed by five paragraphs of tiny type of Val's beliefs about America's imperialist role in the world. When it had come out in the paper only one person had called the listed number, "to talk or to act," and it had been a conservative acquaintance from high school who told him he respected him but he was "nuts."

On this bright and breezy June day, after Val had been sitting and reading for an hour, thinking that maybe he needed to find some other way to protest the war, a slender young man walked up to him. "Val, I'm Pete, and I've come a long way to find you," he said. "Can I sit down and talk about it?" Surprised, Val simply nodded, and pointed to the empty folding chair next to him.

Pete was hard for Val to peg. He had a beard, but it was neatly trimmed, hair that was neither short nor long, and clothes that were somehow halfway between conservative and hippie: neatly-pressed jeans and a button-down shirt, and soft Wallabee boots. In an era when clothes revealed the man, or at least the man's politics, Pete was a cipher.

"First of all, Pete's not my real name. I'm underground, used to be in the Weathermen but now I'm out, thrown out, and I came looking for you because of something you said to Thad Leslie in Chicago last year. I don't like public talk, even in my dull disguise. Can we meet at your place on Cornell later today, to 'talk and act'? I have some ideas for anti-war actions."

Val considered this apparition, arriving just as he was thinking about a new way to protest the war. "That is so strange." he said. "How do you even know our apartment is on Cornell?"

"Man, when you live underground, you're gonna have to take chances," Pete replied, "so you minimize them. I've been here for a week, checking you out, staying with one of the friends the underground has, seems like in every city. Once I learned you'd moved back home from Chicago, it was easy finding you. I actually can move around easily, with half the FBI looking for me, despite being tossed from Weather, since people in the network don't care too much about Weather politics. I guess that's why they're above ground. Anyway, gotta go. What do you say?"

"Well, I guess I say noon at my place," said Val, "since the draft board closes up at lunch anyway."

Two hours later, as they shared steaming cups of Campbell's chicken noodle soup, Pete told Val that Thad had reported his reaction to Fred Hampton's murder to the Weathermen. "You wanted to make the killers pay a price, and that's exactly why I went to war, and that's exactly why I pushed the military option in New York," Pete was saying.

"What's that?" asked Val.

"You know, the job we were planning when the Townhouse exploded," said Pete. "Wait, you don't know about the Townhouse?" As often happened, even when he talked to radicals who, like him, woke up each morning with the first, painful, guilty thought in their mind being how to help end the war, Pete sensed that Val had no idea about the Weathermen and their campaign. The internecine splits of SDS were of interest only to those involved, and the national newspapers and TV carried little coverage of the dozens of seemingly random bombings acts across the country. The local newspapers and radio carried none at all.

All Pete had heard on the local stations about foreign policy while he had been in Swarthmore had come at noon each day, when right-wing commentator Paul Harvey would intone "Stand by for news!" and spew nonsense about the war being heroically won. Pete and his contact had laughed almost until they cried when Harvey described the Venceremos brigade in Cuba receiving weapons training for insurrection in the United States. That was a fantasy his old girlfriend Bernardine had spread, he thought, and here it gets picked up by this racist dog. His friends who had gone had certainly asked for training in weapons and tactics, but all they'd gotten in Cuba were blisters from cutting cane and advice to build the size of the protests, and leave the armed rebellions to Latin America.

"Well, forget the Townhouse, we'll talk about it some other time," continued Pete. "The bottom line is that I'm here because I read your ad, and I know we're on the same page. We want to, we have to, do our part to turn our country around, to do what the Declaration of Independence wanted. I've been thrown out of Weather because they are too scared to fight, scared to take the risks that war means. They want to put bombs in bathrooms in places like the Pentagon, and call it 'armed propaganda,' but I want to go to war for real, and do whatever it takes to drive us out of Viet Nam.

"I know you agree — you said the same thing to Thad after Fred was murdered: kill the highest-ranking person to use the bathroom. ** the Weathermen and all their rules, the queen and her princes. I know what I want to do and I don't need anybody's permission. I want to team up with you.

"I'm not suicidal — I don't want to get caught, like we did during the Days of Rage last year. But I'm a soldier, a patriot like you, and I'm willing to risk combat to win. Now, I want to tell you what I have in mind, and see what you have to say."

Val was mesmerized, as if in a dream. He had been waiting for allies, he didn't know what to do, and here was an ally who'd already done it, and was here in the flesh, asking for his help, as an equal partner, showing respect. Throughout the long afternoon, Pete laid out his vision: surreptitious assassination of not the troops, but the guilty leaders, the top of the conspiracy, the people who planned the crime of Viet Nam. Smart planning, and they'd never get caught, but if they did, it was the price of patriotism, exactly the phrase the secretary at the draft board had said.

"Now, I don't need you to say anything today, maybe not even this week. I want you to think about it, and write me a letter at this post office box, in this name, if you are ready to, as you say in your ad, act. Then we'll start our partnership. But as you think about it, let me make clear there will be two rules, for operational security. First, never tell a soul about me or this, not your wife when she comes home from waitressing at five — trust me, I know and I have someone watching in case she leaves early so I can get out of here. Not your best friend, not your professor mom or your lawyer dad, I mean nobody, ever. This can only work if it's you and me.

"I've got a contact here, Melissa, the woman I'm staying with. Even if I communicate with you through her, she's a cut-out, so assume she knows nothing, she's not part of *cosa nostra*. Once we're a go, she can exchange our letters, set up our meetings and calls, you can trust her for that, but you give her nothing more, make no comments on me or our plans.

"Second, enough with the draft resistance. You've made your point, now all you're doing is drawing attention to yourself. You can't help stop the war in prison anyway — you need to take that student deferment and use your time outside. But you can wait on that. Stay in school, no change to draw attention, just play it out 'til the very end. When they send you an induction notice, and only then, with no space left, then you go 2-S.

"After all, you might get a high number, or break your leg on your motor-cycle, or they might just run out of want-to, since most resisters don't actu-ally get arrested. Hell, the secret is they don't have enough lawyers to try them all or enough jails to hold them all. But for God's sakes, why would you take yourself off the board? That's just what they want! Look at Bruce Dancis, the head of Cornell SDS, I know him well. First guy to burn his draft card, first guy into prison, and he's still there. When he gets out it'll be with years of parole, so he can't organize with anybody who was in SDS or he'll be violated right back inside. What the hell good does that do? We are at war with this murderous government; don't surrender to them!"

* * *

Val went for a walk by himself later that night, after his wife had come home and they'd gone to his parents' house for dinner. His folks were get-ting nicer about accepting the marriage, after fighting it for six months, even surprisingly, hilariously, taking the hippie side and asking him and Sally to just go on and live together. That had stopped after they said they wanted to have children, right away, so they could raise them in a revolutionary way. His parents, like Sally's, had even come with them to the courthouse for the ceremony, which was all the wedding that revolutionaries needed.

But things weren't working out like he'd thought they would when he and Sally had decided he should transfer back from U of C to Swarthmore. His mother taught American history there, and her dean had gotten him in along with Sally, who had spent her first year at a nearby state teachers' col-lege. He had no real grades to show after the Kent and Jackson State strikes had forced U of C, and nearly every other college in the country, to go "Pass-fail," so Swarthmore had no idea he'd wasted the entire year of classes.

Val thought that he'd be part of an anti-war clan, busy every day with planning demonstrations, getting arrested chaining themselves to the doors of various war symbols, like the draft board, and maybe banks, corporations, and even the university. He'd day-dreamed about them being attacked by cops and veterans, and fighting back until he was heroically bloodied. Well, he had gone up to talk to the anti-war students at their offices on campus, and even to the radical priest who was their faculty adviser, but summer lethargy seemed to have set in after the wild action of the Cambodia spring, and they were all waiting for the students to arrive again in the fall before planning anything.

So none of what he had dreamed about was happening, and it felt like none of it would. Unlike all his previous summers, during high school, he hadn't taken a summer day job to supplement his three regular weekly gigs at nearby folk music clubs, so he could do his thing outside the draft board. And just as it was coming clear that it was a waste of time, from out of nowhere, because he had committed in a U of C dorm room to fighting and dying, somebody had shown up to collect the debt!

Well, he could keep a secret, and he could live up to his promises. Nothing was more important to him than doing the right thing about the war, doing all he could to be on the side that stopped it. He'd think about it some more, but he was already drafting in his mind his letter to Pete, who with a little research at the library he had figured out was J. J., the John Jacobs of Columbia SDS fame, the street-fighter and bomber who was too radical even for the Weathermen. "Come on by," it would say.

* * *

CHAPTER 8: MARCH 1971 — THE CAPITOL AND FELIX HÉBERT

At two on a Thursday afternoon Val kissed Sally and went in to take a last look at four-month old Nat, who was napping in his Dr. Denton "ones-ie" like a tiny alligator, lying on his belly in the crib with his legs splayed out behind him. Since Nat's birth they couldn't seem to take their eyes off him. It made for dangerous times when they went out driving, since they just couldn't help turning around to gaze at him as he lay on the mini-mattress they had wedged in behind the front, and only, seats of their Triumph fast-back. This was long before car-seats for babies had become standard practice.

"Gotta run, Sugar," he yelled to Sally as he banged through the door of their apartment on Cornell, one of Swarthmore's many college-named avenues, with his four cases — acoustic guitar, electric guitar, banjo, mandolin — and knapsack. "Mañana!" He put everything in the limousine's trunk, took a book and a magazine out of his knapsack — *War and Peace*, an annual addiction, and *Sports Illustrated*, a weekly one — and hopped into the back seat. "Motor, motor," he told the driver.

Things were going well in Val's new life. He and Sally married in June and had Nat in December — a revolutionary baby, they joked, conceived when Val had come home during the Kent State strike in May. The baby had been two months early, time he had spent in the hospital for safety, but he seemed no worse the wear now. Val and Sally were in good standing at the college; he had actually started doing a little bit of studying.

The only real cloud on their horizon had been the draft. All of Val's conflicting emotions about it — fear of prison, fear of being cowardly about prison, fear of shirking what he saw as his patriotic duty to correct his country, fear of shirking his new parental duties — collided in the hundreds of soul-defining decisions he had to make during that long day in January when he finally was called to the draft board in Swarthmore for the bus ride to the induction center in Philly.

Show up? Show up and openly refuse to get on the bus? Hand out leaflets on the bus to his fellow draftees, of whom he was the only one from the city rather than the rural county around it, because most city kids had college deferments? Wade into and stay with the dozens of chanting protestors outside the induction center? Refuse to answer the security questionnaire, which listed over 100 organizations you had to deny or confirm membership in? Refuse to try hard on the armed forces intelligence test — one part easy and quick for him, like an SAT, so he was the first one done, drawing angry looks from his rural peers, and one part indecipherable, pictures of gears and electrical wires — which could place you in specialized assignments rather than combat? The one thing he knew, which he'd known from that first day looking at the news box on the South Side of Chicago, was that he wouldn't step across the line when it came down to that.

At the last minute, Val was pulled out of the group standing on the white induction line. They told him he needed one more check-up. In a side room, a doctor yet again looked in his chronically-infected ear, wrote some notes on his file, and Val was magically given a six-month medical pass, 1-Y status. He was mystified, and could only guess that they just didn't want to bother prosecuting yet another hippie, with all the American troops coming home anyway.

The very next day Val had gone down to the draft board and finally taken the 2-S under the smirking eyes of the ladies he had harangued the previous summer, ending the tragicomic charade and making everybody happy, from his parents to his secret friend Pete. Only Sally had seen how much it hurt to do that, and only Sally hadn't pressured him, saying she was fine with going to Canada, or with the Joan Baez life while he was in prison, if that was what he needed to do. He found her unquestioning support endearing, but more than a little scary, as if she had no preferences of her own.

He still woke up, every day, just like he had in Chicago, aching with the knowledge of his country at war, just with all Asian bodies now, Vietnamese dying just as fast under the 'Nixon Doctrine' of using U.S. bombs and weapons but paying for South Vietnamese soldiers to do the fighting. It still made him feel powerless, a little man, unable to stop it. But now he knew he had too much to do on the outside to let himself go in, or to Canada, now.

"So, where're we going today?" Val asked the driver.

"DC, the Cellar Door. Three hour drive — we'll be there by five. Back when you want, of course. I'll just be sleeping at the club, waiting for your call. Here's the note from Mr. LoPinto. The address and house phone where I'll be are on the envelope."

"Good morning, Mr. Phelps," the note read as always, which was Dom's homage to the Mission Impossible TV show. The show was imperialist propaganda, but Val had always liked it as a kid, so he'd even written a song to honor Dom's joke, a simple mandolin shuffle with big chords, sorts of like Dylan's Buick Six, "I ride a mail train, babe, ain't that a thrill?" It wasn't good enough for a record, but good enough to include in most shows, especially in Swarthmore, since it was full of with local references:

> I was sittin' by the bank on the co-op wall, waitin' for some angel to fall.
> All of a sudden, the angel walked by, and she told me with a wink in her eye:
> 'Good morning, Mr. Phelps, here's your assignment for today.
> Should you accept, it's our time to play.
> Rutgers Ave., 3-2-3.
> Come on by, you'll find me free.

The rest of the song was, like "G-l-o-r-i-a" by Shadows of Knight, a step-by-step stroll through downtown landmarks on the approach to the nirvana of 323 Rutgers, laced with mandolin chord solos stolen from Bill Monroe's *Rawhide*. It ended with a monotone statement mimicking the TV show: "This song will self-destruct in five seconds."

Dom's note continued: "7 p.m. first show, then 9, 11. 30-minute opener, Aztec Two-Step, Boston folk duo."

Val read and slept as they hammered down I-95, the toll road to Washington. He'd been taking opening act gigs from Dom for a few months now, good pay, if time-consuming because of the drives. Anywhere on the east coast, almost always one-nighters, the limousine would take him there, he'd do his thing, maybe get lucky with a girl in the crowd, then head home. Dom took the limo out of his own cut, which of course Val never asked about, and

Val paid the union dues, which were only $40 a year, and came back with $150 a night.

Hell, $150 was as much as he made, total, for the four nights a week he was now playing in the Swarthmore and Philly clubs and as a solo and in rural roadhouses and small-town American Legions as a sideman in a country-rock band. Along with Sally's waitressing and their parents picking up the tuition — reduced, thank God, because each family had one person employed at the college — and the way they coordinated classes and spent not a penny on babysitters, they were doing just fine.

It was a Thursday night, but the Cellar Door in the busy Georgetown section of DC was packed, with fresh patrons for all three shows, which was what Val usually found on these road trips to folk clubs in bigger cities. The Aztecs, Rex and Neil, were clearly already well-known, despite not having an album yet. At $8 a pop, 200 seats a show, with drinks and some food, and three shows, Val could see why business was good. The marquee over the door on M Street, the main shopping drag, listed big names Val recognized from folk, folk rock, jazz, even bluegrass music. It wasn't every day, he thought, you got to take the same stage where Miles Davis, Joan Baez, Linda Ronstadt, and Ralph Stanley were coming soon!

Val pointed this out to the stars of the show as they sat chatting in the tiny dressing room, after the sound-check. "*Sin duda*, dude," Rex, the tall, skinny, and taciturn one said, and then lapsed into a stoned silence. Neal, the short, chubby, chatty one laughed, saying, "Don't mind him: his favorite activity on the road is getting stoned and reading Ferlinghetti so he can write more songs. Me, I'm just the hot licks man!

"Actually, that's where he got our name, from a line in Poem Number 9. You know it?" Val replied that he only had some vague recollection of the poet's name, maybe in relation to Jack Kerouac, whose travelogue he had read while on the road himself, hitch-hiking back and forth from Chicago to Swarthmore. "Well, then you'll like our new song, *The Persecution of Dean Moriarity*. He was one of Kerouac's riding partners too, of course," said Neil. "Listen to it tonight, then you'll know 'Why society lies.'" He sang out that last phrase, and then bundled his partner out to the bar: "Gotta deal with his munchies now, and not on stage!"

Val started his sets, as always, loud and fast, with his electric guitar, to grab everybody's attention and stop the talking at the tables. Nobody was there because of the opening act, but he knew by now how to make sure they at least paid attention. It was a Buddy Holly song, *Not Fade Away*, that he'd learned in his junior high school band off a Rolling Stones album, which they did with a Bo Diddley beat: "I'm gonna tell you how it's gonna be!" bum-bum-bum....BUM-BUM "You're gonna give your love to me." Bum-bum-bum.... BUM-BUM

Then he did a big-chorded, Byrds-style song he'd recently written with a woman, a 30-year-old fan of sorts who always popped up at his regular Wednesday gig. Not too many people came to that, so he had begun to sit with her during the breaks, one thing had led to another, and she had penned the lyrics that he set to a country-rock beat:

> My friend Big Mary used to say
> "Just give me a truck stop, out on the high-way
> Where the great big semis and the Mack trucks rest
> Make me a truck stop honey, servin' coffee, takin' money
> And honey I'll be feelin' my best."
>
> But me I never had any plans to serve greasy eggs to no truck-drivin' man
> And while I sang White Line Fever along with the Hag
> I never dreamed of the big trucks and the drivers in their cabs
> But, oh, sweet truck drivin' man, that's before I met you.
>
> Now Big Mary's gone and got funny
> And she laughs at the old talk of truck stop honeys
> But me, I've felt a change
> Aw, don't time do some awful strange things?
>
> 'Cause ever since the day you ran over my heart
> Like a Peterbilt, clickin' time
> Honey, I don't care who you're drivin' for
> I just want a little of your down time.
>
> And now you come to me, while I'm still flat on my back
> You say you're heart's been broke and crushed, and as a matter of fact
> You feel like you been run over by a big Mack truck
> Your lyin' down in the high-way, and down on your luck
> And if that's the way she makes you feel, sweet truck-drivin' man,
> Can't you see what you're doin to me?

So pick yourself up off the road
And I'll direct you to the nearest white line
'Cause ever since the day you ran over my heart
Like a White Freightliner, doin' time

Oh, honey, sweet truck drivin' man, I don't care who you're drivin' for
But when you pop a gear at the top of the hill
Just remember that you've got the key to my back door!

Val always wove a few of his own songs, like that *Truck Stop, Honey*, in with Jackson Browne, Bob Dylan, Merle Haggard, and the Beatles. There were hundreds of good songs out there, and he found new ones he could adapt from random albums virtually every day. A few repetitions and, to his constant surprise, the lyrics, verse after verse if it was Dylan, stayed right on the tip of his tongue, even if he hadn't played the song in a year. That came in handy in bars where guys yelled requests drunkenly to impress their dates, and he always answered, "Send your requests up on the back a 20-dollar bill, unless it's by the Monkees, who are a corporate fraud, not a real band," before giving it a try.

The 30-minute set moved quickly, as Val cycled through all his instruments before ending, as he had started, with a high-volume electric guitar. He even got an encore in one set, which was always a slow, quiet song, and he used a new one he'd written about his infant son.

There were a lot of teenage girls in groups at the tables, as usual a lot of them looking younger than 18, the drinking age. Val was only19 himself, but he'd learned, even at the clubs in Swarthmore, that he was best off trading glances with women who were clearly late in or maybe done with college. No drama, just fun. He started scanning for locked-on faces during the last set, at 11, as he opened with, "You're gonna give your love to me."

Val ended up going to late breakfast with a graduate student who had been sitting with two girlfriends during his last set. Her swaying, long brown hair had caught his eye from the stage as he sang and she winked back at him. He went out to the tables and they talked briefly as Aztec came on, and agreed it was time to leave. Breakfast was humorous, as they compared anti-war protests they'd been to in DC. After all the talk, it was clear that he was going back to her apartment and there, as he loved to say, paraphrasing

Dante on the illicit lovers Paolo and Francesca, they would talk no more. By four a.m., he was back at the Cellar Door, shaking the driver from sleep.

"What, you didn't want me to come pick you up?"

"Nah, I felt like a walk. She didn't live far. You ready to roll? I'd love to make a noon class. Well, let me rephrase that, I probably should go to that class once in a while! And remember Ray Charles' famous saying, right?"

"Got it: what happens on the road, stays on the road. Here, let me help you with the instruments."

* * *

The assassin struck at three in the morning, after expertly cutting a half-moon in the kitchen window of the Georgetown townhouse, turning the clasp, raising the window, and climbing through. After pulling out a pistol with the silencer already screwed on, the killer stepped quietly up the stairs to the second floor, went directly to the second door on the right, opened it, walked through without hesitation, and put two bullets in the temple of the man sleeping alone there. Almost without breaking stride, the assassin moved out of the room, down the stairs, and out the kitchen door.

The body was found by the housekeeper the next morning when she came in to make breakfast. The broken glass scared her, and she bravely walked up the stairs to check on the congressman. Seeing the blood on the bed she screamed, and ran downstairs to call her husband.

Thirty minutes later a gaggle of DC detectives, FBI agents, and Capitol Police stood over the body of Felix Hébert, 69, a 30-year congressman from New Orleans who had recently taken over the chair of the powerful Armed Services Committee. They agreed it was a probably a professional hit because of the clean entry, the silencer, and no apparent theft. The techs had dusted the window and doorknob, and found nothing, and no wiping either, so that probably meant gloves, a professional sign, too.

"Now, I don't like to speak ill of the dead," said one agent, "but I did my time in Louisiana, during the JFK case, looking into all of Garrison's bull, and I think we have to think Mob on this, right away. One thing I learned down there, where there's blood in politics, there's usually money, a government favor that was supposed to be done for it and wasn't, and an angry Marcello."

But before the agents had much time to get going in that direction, a bombshell changed everything. At three p.m. the next day the editor of the

Washington Star notified DC police that they had received, and in the next afternoon's paper were going to reprint, a letter postmarked the day before in Washington, written in block letters:

War Report, Nathan Hale Brigade

The Weather Underground bombed a bathroom in the Capitol two weeks ago to protest the U.S. invasion of Laos. Well, that's fair enough, because Congress votes the money to bomb other countries all the time. But we think it's pathetic, and counter-revolutionary. Why bomb a bathroom when what we really have to worry about is all the big shots who use it? So we have punished the racist war-dog Massa "segregation forever" Felix, the chairman of the committee of Congress that funds illegal invasions, not just in Laos, but in Viet Nam, Cambodia, and many other countries that were officially declared to be freed from colonialism, but are now ruled neo-colonially by Amerika.

Beware, you other war-dogs, we are coming for you. Fair warning: this is just the beginning of our spring offensive, in honor of the National Liberation Front's spring offensive. Stop backing the empire. The war has come home, and will stay home until:

● all the troops are back and set free, along with the draft prisoners and exiles

● all the bombing stops

● Congress stops sending the puppet government the money that simply substitutes yellow bodies for white and disproportionately Black ones for the same evil cause

● all the Black freedom fighters are out of jail

The FBI jumped in with a vengeance, and across the country agents spent the rest of the day and night squeezing its informants from the fringes of the old SDS. But not a hint emerged. Nobody had heard of the Nathan Hale Brigade, and nobody had any reason to think it had a connection to the Weathermen. The next morning FBI director Hoover called the paper's publisher to ask that it hold off on the letter and not reveal the name of the brigade, or even that it was an anti-war killing, or any details from the ranting statement. His argument was that publicity was precisely what the radicals wanted, and that making the link would encourage others to do the same sort of thing. The conservative leadership of the *Star* agreed to wait a bit, but a day later, when student and underground newspapers in a number of cities began to publish copies they had received of the War Report, the *Star* published the full story.

* * *

New driver, same limo, Val was off on the six-hour trip to Boston, the Passim club near Harvard Square, to open Friday and Saturday nights for Aztec. The duo had told Dom they liked having him open, and had especially asked for what they called the "Bo Diddley song," even though Val had told them it was Buddy Holly's. Val and Sally were separated now, filed for divorce and sharing the baby, so he'd had to lean on his mother for the weekend, since it was his turn. The lawyers insisted that the road to happiness in divorce lay in never, never, changing the agreement and its clear dates of custody.

The break-up hadn't occasioned much drama, on either side. Married at 18, divorced by 19, that's what his father had predicted, and it sure came true. They just had nothing to talk about anymore, just seemed to have grown into completely different people from each other. It certainly hadn't helped that barely after Nat had been born, they'd both tentatively brought up the idea of other attractions, which ended not in any open agreement, but rather in a tacit acceptance of the ideology of the day, emblazoned on a poster they'd ripped off its backing and stolen from a discount store:

> You do your thing, and I do mine
> I am not in this world to live up to your expectations,
> And you are not in this world to live up to mine
> And if by chance we find each other, it's beautiful.

That sentiment of non-commitment and defiance of rules seemed to go well with the Kahlil Gibran poem they'd already put on the wall by Nat's crib, the one that started, "Your children are not your children; they are the sons and daughters of Life's longing for itself," and ended with the image of parent as bow and children as arrows: "Let your bending in the archer's hand be for gladness." No question, Val thought, they hadn't figured it all out yet. He cringed when he thought of their parents, sneaking in the back door of the apartment to bring Nat some presents because he and Sally had threatened to throw out such bounty of materialism.

So it wasn't quite cheating when Val had decided to keep it to himself when he started to range on Sally, right after she had, with his agreement, spent a weekend rekindling an old flame. It started with the stunning girl who ran the underground press that printed his anti-draft pamphlets, whom Pete had been staying with when he first contacted Val.

Melissa Laurel was 25, six years older than him, and had led the Swarthmore SDS chapter before Weatherman shut them all down. He was literally addicted to her political and sexual sophistication, both of which were way past his meager experiences. Even better, she liked to call herself his French-style mistress, because she had no problem with, and in fact preferred, their clandestine visits to an above-ground romance.

The only thing that troubled Val about her was her taste in movies. Melissa would often ask him to watch radical films with her at the press, where she pre-screened them to decide which one to use in a regular slot she had bargained for at the campus theater, through the religious studies department where she had taken her degree. The more violent, the more graphic the depiction of Brazilian, Chilean, or other South American urban revolutionaries garroting, stabbing, or beating policemen to death, the happier she was. Once, after watching *The Battle of Algiers* together, she had demanded that he literally rape her while she struggled against it, leaving him troubled and her smiling like Scarlett O'Hara in *Gone with the Wind*.

That particular fantasy was never repeated, however, so Melissa's apartment over the underground press became his refuge where Val could fully relax. There was none of the lying, silent misleading, and juggling that often came with the musical affairs he had started the very first time Truck Stop

Honey flirted with him. Almost immediately, he had begun to spend each and every gig trying to find the one for the night. He told himself he was an artist who was simply full of the need for connection, and that he was far nobler in that pursuit than his low-life country-rock colleagues, the Don Giovannis of the late-night diners who crudely compared the numeric "totals" of their conquests.

Feeling conflicted, Val once tried to have a heart-to-heart talk with his brother, but had only received a laugh and an adaptation of a favorite line of theirs from *War and Peace*, "Never, never pass it up, my dear fellow, until you are too old to be good for anything else!" Now that he was getting divorced, the issue was moot. He sometimes found that he, rather than the ladies, wanted more than one-night fun and games, and those heart-aches gave him a whole new repertoire of original songs.

At Passim he tried out one of those he'd just written, using a Caribbean beat he'd lifted from Otis Redding's *Champagne and Wine*, along with bits of *Dancing in the Moonlight* by Boffalongo, a fantastic upstate New York band whose records he'd snatched up in high school when he'd seen them play at a fraternity party at Swarthmore. He called it *October Snow*.

> Sometimes your eyes they promise to me a hot daybreak on Jamaica's shore
> But deep down it seems you cloud and freeze, like
> the winds that blow the October snows
>
> I know it's not as cold as a day in December
> But it's only your warmth that I care to remember
> Oh your eyes may shine like champagne and wine,
> but your heart's an October snow
>
> Out on the street we happen to meet, I wish I was living an ocean away
> You'd never find me, and no one would remind me.
> Do you feel in my touch what I can't say?
>
> I would not complain if I lived by degrees
> But the first taste of winter bites deep into me.
> Oh what a day to see you on, a day of October snow.
>
> October wind, here you come again, look at the
> leaves, you make them dance and play
> I run for cover, yes I love her, but I'm not ready to be blown away.

I know it's not as a cold as a day in December
But it's only your warmth I care to remember
Yes your eyes may shine from champagne and wine
But your heart's an October snow.

After the first set, a group of Harvard–Radcliffe students asked Val to join them to watch Aztec's set, but he demurred, saying he saved his college degree by reading during his breaks. That led to a discussion of MIT's Noam Chomsky, and his latest book on imperialism, *American Power and the New Mandarins*, and lots of talk about the Weatherman bombing of the office of William Bundy, a professor and one-time State Department architect of the war, at MIT's Center for International Studies the previous weekend. It also led to a midnight date with a biblical Rachel, tall, curved dark hair, full-bodied, dripping life, openly born to boogie, her arms downed with T.S. Eliot's light brown hair.

Val woke in her bed and smiled as he recalled his favorite phrase from a demo Dom had been sent of a new West Cost singer, Tom Waits: "As I pulled away slowly, feelin' so holy, God knows I was feeling alive." He did the ritual meeting of the roommates at the breakfast table, and after a brief stroll to leave a fan note on the door at Chomsky's office down Massachusetts Avenue at MIT, just past the building where the bombing had taken place, he met Rachel at the Radcliffe library, where they each did their own readings. She asked him, as he gathered up his things to head back to Passim that evening, "Will you come back tonight, when you're done?" Val thought, then said, "Ah, no, the limo driver wants to leave after my last one — has something he needs to do Sunday in Philly. But why don't you come down to see me next weekend? I don't have any travel gigs for at least a month."

* * *

It was midnight. The assassin waited in an alley off Berkeley Street, a mile north of Harvard Square, in Somerset. Scouting had revealed a routine: some time during the next half hour, Lucy Van Oss, a sociologist of Latin America and one of the few female MIT professors, would bring her unleashed Scottie out of the brick townhouse, turn right on the street and right down the alley, and continue the "last walk before bed" loop on Oxford Street. She lived alone, since her boyfriend taught at the Berkeley on the left coast, and there was nobody else to walk the dog. Lucy actually took the bus home and back in the middle of the day to do that, down Columbia to Summer, but at irregular times, based on her meetings.

Peering out from behind a large, machine-lifted, rectangular garbage bin, the killer saw Van Oss turn the corner into the alley, the Scottie skittering ahead. Not a loud dog, not aggressive, but feisty. The Scottie missed the human smell in the swirl of stale garbage aromas in the bin. Good. As the woman's shadow crossed the line of the bin, the assassin stepped out from the side and swung, Ted Williams-style, full contact of the bat a maximum speed to her temple, crushing the entire side of her face. There was no sound other than the cracking "thwack." One step, hands crushing the throat, and she was dead before the dog even turned around, came back to lick the wound, and lie down quietly next to her.

At noon on Sunday, the manager of the underground *Boston Phoenix*, a somewhat-weekly progeny of New York's *Village Voice*, found this block-letter communiqué in the mail slot when she came to open the office:

War Report, Nathan Hale Brigade

Tonight the brigade punished the acting director of the imperialist Center for International Studies. Lucy Van Oss paid the price only because our real target, war-monger William Bundy, is hiding, supposedly on sabbatical. The Weather Underground righteously destroyed his office a week ago, and we applaud that. But that won't win the war. Dare to struggle, Dare to win, said Uncle Ho. No minion of the war state is safe now. Being part of an oppressed group, Woman or Black or Chicano, doesn't protect you from justice if you are serving the Pig. Remember that.

CIS was founded to serve the war state, 20 years ago, and will continue to do so until all professors refuse to work for it. A year ago the Weather-women bombed Harvard and its fascist Center for Intenational Affairs, led by free-fire murderer Huntington and nuclear war planner Kaysen. But the CFIA is an amateur in empire, compared to CIS.

CIA agent and CIS founder Millikan took the lead in turning campuses into servants of the empire they have become today, helping it plan its strategies, build its weapons, and dominate the supposedly former colonies; Viet Nam invader Rostow created economic neo-colonialism for Eisenhower, so Amerika could keep its friendly dictators in the corporations' economic orbit; war-planners Bloomfield from the State Department and Kaufmann from RAND came to CIS to make empire and war more efficient and successful. CIS brags of bringing in Daniel Ellsberg as a fellow, but even that won't wash away its sin: before he got religion and stole the Pentagon Papers, Ellsberg was planning nuclear war and helping the great "Pacifier" Landsdale kill revolutionaries and herd peasants into strategic hamlets in Viet Nam! Venceremos.

The manager immediately called the Liberation News Service, which provided most of the political copy the Phoenix used, and within a week the story was being carried by dozens of underground papers and radical radio stations. Outside of Boston, though, no mainstream media picked up the story. Of course the FBI read the underground papers. But it still couldn't find any link to the Weathermen, and indeed, any leads at all.

* * *

CHAPTER 10: APRIL 2017 — THE TARGET

The hardest thing to do as an FBI investigator is keep the target unaware. As soon as people are approached with questions about someone, even someone they don't know personally but who just appears in their files, their first instinct is to go out of their way to contact that person and say, "Hey, the FBI was asking about you."

Black wanted Val Shaw unaware of being a target for as long as possible, so that he wouldn't interfere with potential witnesses or evidence, or even run. She decided to start with a completely passive approach with both sets of resident agents, Nashville for the present and Philadelphia, which covered Swarthmore, for the past. This meant no mention or identification of Shaw as a person of interest. The agents would build a subject profile and timeline through media reports and public records, and interview people at Shaw's various locations, but never ask a question that would highlight his identity. She would go back to Jerry if she felt she needed to move to a moderately passive approach, in which investigators use the subject's name, but also warn the people they interview against discussing the interview with anyone else, particularly the subject.

Most people don't know about their right, whether after an informal interview or even grand jury testimony, to talk about the experience, the questions and their answers, and police and prosecutors do all they can to keep it that way. Black knew that when she moved to moderately passive, her agents would show why the FBI is the master of the technique, by sternly intimating punishment for even revealing that the FBI had come around.

Of the two teams, Nashville had it easiest. Shaw was a political science professor, and he seemed to profess constantly, filling his faculty and personal web pages with blogs, links to his articles, and information on his career. The first thing Black noticed from summaries the agents submitted was that he held the same view as the Weathermen about America being an evil empire, both during the Viet Nam war and in the present. He actually had an article posted that he'd written in the *Wall Street Journal* that was titled, "Evil Empire is Redundant." Like Rudd, Ayers, Dohrn, Wilkerson, and the rest of the current Weather-writers, he could list off the oppressed countries then and now. One of his recent links was to a piece in the *Los Angeles Times* in which he decried then-President Obama's bombing of six countries in a single day without a shred of the congressional authorization Shaw said the Constitution required.

Shaw also showed up sporadically in local news stories and opinion columns or letters to the editor, usually in the Vanderbilt student newspaper, *The Hustler*, but at times in the city newspaper, the *Tennessean*. His name also appeared a few times each year on the logs of talk-show and news-show guests for local radio and TV stations. And the story was always the same: Shaw was a gadfly, moved to question a local policy or opinion and link it to a global evil, American imperialism.

He went after Vanderbilt professors by name, even in his own department, who had taken a government contract to run girls' schools in Afghanistan, which he called a component of an illegal invasion and occupation. He went after Vanderbilt students, although not by name, who called on the university to divest its stocks in energy companies because of what he called disproven claims of carbon-fueled climate catastrophe that were restricting home and industrial electrification rates in Africa to 25 percent, or its stocks in running shoe companies because they failed to correct what Shaw called unproven labor crimes. Both of those criticisms ended up with an attack on the students' "neo-colonial" acceptance of the West's dominance of international trade that kept the formerly colonial countries from refining and manufacturing rather than just selling raw commodities.

Surprisingly, to Black, the on-line summaries the university published of Shaw's teaching evaluations by students contained no mention of his strident positions. Students focused on his questioning of everybody and every claim, on all sides in class discussions, and seemed to be largely unaware of his contentious public side. "If you want a good grade, in class participation but especially in the final paper," said a typical comment, "never just cite a study's finding to support your position. You have to analyze it, as fully as if you disagreed with it." His on-line syllabi were full of the same sort of exhortations. The one for "Research Methods in Social Science" started with:

> Why do we believe what we believe? Why do our opponents believe what they believe? Answer these two questions with an open mind and you will start to be a political scientist. That means you test, rather than try to prove, your hypotheses. You appeal to logic and data, not to authority. You think with the mind, not with the blood. After all, to paraphrase *The Godfather*, we are not in law school.

Black almost liked Shaw for that dig at lawyers, although she could see it was another example of his insensitivity to the feelings of his academic colleagues. The insensitivity had finally caught up with him in the fall of 2014, she noted, when environmentally-active students had protested his opposition to divestment from fossil fuel companies, disrupting a campus debate in which he had faced off with the professor who headed the Climate Change Media major. Then they sent his dean, and published in the student newspaper, a petition against Shaw's rehiring that was signed by 300 students and even five professional staff, although not professors: "It is an embarrassment and a contradiction for Vanderbilt, which has committed to reducing carbon pollution and spends students' tuition money in the Green Fund to do so with renewable energy, to also pay a professor who denies what is agreed to by 97 percent of all scientists."

It didn't help that during the same semester Shaw and a Black Studies professor had exchanged four increasingly bitter opinion pieces in *The Hustler* about a sign that students had carried at a Black Lives Matter protest: "Assata taught us." Shaw began his original piece with, "And just what did you learn from Joanne Chesimard, admitted cop-hunter and convicted cop-killer, esteemed guest in the paradise of Stalinist Cuba?"

The Black Studies professor claimed in her response that Shaw was a racist and had reduced black students to tears by teaching them that blacks were genetically less intelligent than whites. One of Shaw's black students then wrote in to dispute her, stating that the class had indeed studied a controversial 1969 article by Arthur Jensen making that claim, but that Dr. Shaw had called in the two black students beforehand to explain the purpose of the exercise and had promised them it would come out well, when a key component of Jensen's argument — British scholar Cyril Burt's twin studies, which found strongly correlated I.Q.s in 53 pairs of identical twins put up for adoption and raised in lower and upper class homes — was discovered to be a fraud. There were no 53 pairs of such twins with similar I.Q.s, despite their disparate environments: Burt had just made them up, and Jensen had speculated that this fake finding on the irrelevance of culture and environment to intelligence could be extended from class to race.

The professor then shifted her attack and focused on another study Shaw's syllabus listed as a class reading, which reported that poor black mothers used millions less words in interacting with their babies than middle-class white ones, hampering their intellectual development. She accused Shaw of promoting racist stereotypes, and he in turn accused her of ignoring class and racial realities. Black could just imagine the pounding headaches the administration and its office of minority recruitment were experiencing as the dispute escalated.

In a virtual retelling of Jerry's story about his high school principal, *The Hustler* revealed the next year that the climate change petition was written by a student who had received an F on a final research paper, and so a C for the research course, for pointedly refusing to analyze claims and evidence for and against climate catastrophe, on the principled grounds that "the debate is over." After Shaw refused the dean's request to allow the student to submit a new paper, the dean had not renewed Shaw's third five-year contract when it came due the next year "for a variety of reasons, which as they involve a personnel matter remain confidential." Since then he had been only a part-time, adjunct professor.

Black learned that this had not posed much of a financial hardship for Shaw. From court and municipal records and news stories, Black's team had been able to reconstruct Shaw's family life. His wife had always been the primary earner. Selam Dibaba was a surgeon, and for the past ten years a top hospital administrator. She was the daughter of an Ethiopian doctor, her last name being his first name, as in the manner of her national group, the

Amhara. He had sent her to college in the United States, and she had met Val in a graduate-level statistics class she took as an advanced pre-med and he took for his Ph.D. Their wedding announcement in the *Tennessean* revealed that they had both felt "an immediate and unexpected thunder bolt" and been inseparable ever since. They married after living together for 10 years, and now had two grown children.

In one of the on-line newspaper comments about Shaw's alleged racism, a contributor had said, "How can a black woman live with such a racist, who looks down on black culture in America?" Black chuckled at that, having had friends who had served at U.S. bases in Ethiopia, and told her stories about ethnic groups there that were as deeply racist as the Klan, and saw themselves as superior to the "Wagas" — the sort of rural Africans who might live in Burkina Faso's capital of Ouagadougou. In her college days, too, she had tried to befriend some Amhara, only to be driven away by their open contempt of black Americans as shiftless, violent welfare cases.

Black noticed that there was nothing in the public record to indicate Shaw's membership in any radical organization, although until the carbon fuel controversy he often appeared on the list of speakers for rallies sponsored by campus and Nashville anti-war groups. That seemed to fit what Ayers had said about his 1969 statement, that he "wasn't a joiner." In fact, thought Black, Shaw didn't seem to have changed at all, in any way, in 48 years. He was still argumentative and difficult, whether as a student or employee, automatically questioning every claim he heard, not just in the political arena but over simple administrative routines at the university, and he quickly submitted these arguments to print. A review of a book Shaw had written about his years as a staffer in the Tennessee legislature included this bit of praise: "Refreshingly for readers, Shaw doesn't use anonymous sources, even when professional courtesy and discretion would imply that he should. He simply names names. Fearless, but foolish."

Above all, Shaw was openly and bitterly opposed to American foreign policy. Black was simply baffled by one controversy he had brought on himself by writing a piece for the *Tennessean* in 2010 about why he yelled "bring them home" rather than stand up and cheer when the Predators hockey team did its traditional salute to American troops during the Zamboni break between periods. He attacked such public pro-military displays, including the Predators dressing in camouflage uniforms, as "a cultural pump spewing out imperialist propaganda," and actually referenced the Weathermen: "The same Dylan song that said 'You don't need a Weatherman to know which way the wind blows' also contained 'the pump won't work 'cause the vandals took the handle,' and I call on all anti-imperialists not to miss a chance to vandalize this pump." Shaw wrote that he wore a black armband during the Gulf War in 1991 when the rest of America was wearing a yellow ribbon to support the troops. The paper was inundated with angry letters from veterans, and the local Fox News channel paired one of them and Shaw in a phone-in debate.

As a veteran, Black was deeply offended and could not see how Shaw's nasty behavior squared with his claim in the article that he was a true patriot, motivated by his affection for both the troops and the people they were killing in his name. She looked again at his 1970 newspaper ad about the draft and American imperialism. Not a softening, not one bit of change in his thinking or language. Motive wasn't going to be a problem on this one, she thought. But what about the other parts of the indictable trio, means and opportunity? That was up to the Philadelphia team.

* * *

There was a lot less to go on in the public record and the media files for Shaw's nearly five years in Swarthmore, from May 1970 through December 1974: no arrests, a few letters to the editor about, of course, American imperialism, his name in some newspaper ads by folk-music clubs and festivals, a release party for an album he had recorded, and a B.A. degree in political science. And then he was gone, first to North Carolina for a Ph.D. and then to Nashville, to work for 20 years as a staffer in the legislature, playing a little music on the side, and then teaching as an assistant professor at Vanderbilt on non-tenure, five-year contracts until he became an adjunct professor in 2015.

There was some gold in the records the team got from the Selective Service, and in the FBI file that had been started as a result of Shaw's letters to the draft board. There was a newspaper ad titled "Sons of America, Don't Accept Their Lies," with a note that it had been distributed at the draft board, at some rallies, and on the bus to the Philadelphia induction center. There also was a time-line of his draft resistance, starting with an application for

Conscientious Objector status that had been denied on grounds that he was admittedly not a pacifist opposed to all wars, just this one, and ending with him finally taking a student deferment right after receiving a six-month, 1-Y deferment for illness in January 1971.

An agent's entry on the time-line a few months later noted that, due to troop withdrawals, draft calls in 1971 were just a third of those in 1969, and that few draftees were still being sent to Viet Nam. It ended with the statement that, "Subject refused to discuss with agents why he had switched to 2-S when he was not currently subject to draft call, and unlikely to be so after the 1-Y." Can't focus on planning murders if the draft board is always checking up on you, thought Black.

"We've gone as far as we can under the radar," Black told Jerry one morning. "We've been completely passive in both cities, and we used secrecy agreements to take statements from Ayers, Dohrn, the Chicago college friend Thad Leslie, and the Cambridge bomb lady Alice Truxton — a sweet little retired high school math teacher in Texas, if you can believe it. Boston identified the storm and inside windows on the professor's house as being from 1970 manufacture, but failed to identify the company that put them there, just too long ago, too many links in the chain broken. The professor, Huntington, is dead, his wife remembers nothing about it, and their kids were just too young then to recall anything now. Maybe we can find some of his colleagues alive who he talked to about it, but that will take some time.

"Still, with what we have, it all ties together like Ayers and Dohrn said, not that I trust them at all. That happy couple of criminals is just soooo smart, so perfect in their stories, so used to lying like they breathe, when they were underground and since, that I know they're playing us somehow. But, that's what we've got to work with, and I think it's time to get to work."

"Agreed," said Jerry. "On my end, we've got both Dohrn's subpoena and her plea on ice. Her statement's fairly weak, and she held out for a misdemeanor to preclude jail time, but she admits to hearing discussions of plans to bomb some police station. It's the best Justice could do." He grimaced, and threw up his hands. "Once her lawyers knew Sessions had approved a deal, they refused to budge. It went all the way to Trump, is what I hear. Jesus, I hope he can keep from tweeting all this to his friend Hannity until we're done!

"Apparently Trump stared her down for a week, had Justice threaten to dump the whole deal and go back to the subpoena. That was after Sessions told him that she went to jail for seven months in 1982, after she came out of the underground. Contempt of court for not testifying in a Brink's robbery and cop-killing by some pal of hers who had used ID Dohrn stole from one of her underground jobs. That really pissed Trump off, all the more, but in the end, the great deal-maker blinked, and he bought the six for one line.

"Anyway, the plea will be filed after she and Ayers testify throughout all the Weather-cat cases. Three will be put in a single federal case — Congressman Hébert, General Hemmings, and the State Department aid administrator. And three will be state murders: the MIT director and the two business executives, New York and Pittsburgh, but I doubt the states will bother to run with them if Shaw goes down for the federal cases. So, what do you have in mind?"

"Look," replied Black, "sooner or later we have to talk to somebody who can place him at these six scenes. We have him near the Harvard professor, but there's no murder there, so it can't be a count, just evidence of similar attempts. We have to go moderately passive, and use his name if we need to, of course control it as much as we can.

"What I want to do is drop Nashville, there's nothing more we need there. I'll move to Philly and make the time-line with the local team, try to match Shaw's life up with the six murders. If we're lucky, nobody really has reason to track down Shaw and warn him we're poking around. I think I'll stay away from the college, because we'd certainly bump into friends of his mother.

"I want to try to get his movements around town: landlords, the bars he played at, old girlfriends, the ex-wife, although the records show it didn't last long, just a year before they filed. They shared the kid, so they may still talk, but odds are we can encourage her to keep quiet, since she may have guilty knowledge about 1970 and 1971, the years he got started. If she does, we can encourage her to get a lawyer, who will certainly agree to secrecy for the interview."

"OK, go," said Jerry. "Let's get this thug. Rip his past apart, and don't call me 'til you've nailed him."

* * *

"McGurk, the ex-wife is a bust, but the music clubs, that's panning out. We found out from three of the old owners that Shaw needed replacements on some weekends, because he traveled to other jobs, like to New York or DC." The Philadelphia agents were reporting back to Black on their first foray into Swarthmore under the new rules. "They couldn't remember exactly when he went, but they all said there was only one booker in town then who handled out-of-town gigs, a guy they only remember as LoPinto. Unfortunately, they say he died in the '90s. We told them not to disrupt an on-going investigation. We've also tracked down an address for the widow of this LoPinto, first name Dominic, but have not made contact."

"Well, all right, let's go talk to her," said Black. "Maybe we'll get lucky, find someone who worked with him, someone who knows about the old days."

Later that day LoPinto's widow pointed them toward the son of her husband's partner, who ran a local recording studio and concert sound company. "The father ran the booking business for a while after Dominic died, kept the same name because it was well known, and the son had to handle shutting it down when he started fading," she said.

Finding the man, Bill Coles, at his studio, Black put on her good cop mien when the rotund, classic aging hippy, maybe 70, bald but with a walrus of a mustache, seemed to welcome her with open arms. "Hah, the FBI cold case squad, just like on TV. What can I do to help, Agent, what did you say, Mary McCain? Maybe I'll get on a reality re-enactment," he laughed. In Black's experience most people were less than cooperative when the FBI came calling, assuming nothing good and lots of bad could come from talking, so she was relieved to have this response for once.

"It's Mar'Shae McGurk, just Mar'Shae to you." Black decided to get as chummy as possible, and keep Coles in his open-book mode. "We think that files from the old business could really help us recreate a terrible crime, a murder, maybe solve it."

"Well, who's the evil picker? I was already running sound in Swarthmore back then. Maybe I knew him...or her?"

"Nice try, Bill," laughed Black. "I can't tell you that yet. Now, can you think back to when you closed up your father's affairs? What did you do with the records? I assume you had to save some for tax purposes."

"Hah, I certainly did," said Coles. "Matter of fact, the lawyers told me to hold on to them in storage for at least seven years, and I did."

"Uh-oh," replied Black. "I don't like the sound of that, because that would have ended, what, ten years ago? What did you do then?"

"Hah, never fear, because I am a careful son-of-a-bitch with my money. I never rented a separate space like they wanted. Simply put them in the corner of my own storage here, you know, for my sound stuff, and never gave it a second thought — except, of course, when I deduct some of the cost directly from my dad's expenses each year. And I doubt you're here to lock me up for saving the old man a little bit of dough! He needs it for the nursing home where he sits, 90 years old, healthy as an ox but totally spaced out."

"Bill, no need to worry about that. I do murder, not taxes," answered a relieved Black. "And just where is this storage space?"

"Hah, Agent McGurk, you're sitting in the right spot. Come through this door with me and you shall see! No need for warrants, like on TV, you can dig through them all you want. All I gotta do is figure out who should play me on the streaming show. Denzel Washington, maybe, or Kevin Costner? Nah, too old, maybe a cameo by Keanu Reeves?"

Black had the happy hippie sign a consent form and called her team to come take away the boxes, over 50 of them, that had all the billings and contracts for LoPinto Artist Booking for 1965 to 1999. She decided not to do a simple search for every mention of Shaw's name. Her time in civil rights cases had convinced her that there was a lot of rich information to gain by getting a full picture of the files. Local police go small, she thought, not the FBI. We just bring in more staff and find everything that's in there.

It took a solid week for the five-person forensic team sent up from Washington: annotating each piece of paper with its original artist, making four copies, and then distributing them into separate chronological piles by city, artist, year, and related acts before anything logical emerged. And then, suddenly, cross-checking Shaw's travels with the dates of the six murders, it was obvious: they had their opportunity. Only means remained.

Black went back to Coles' sound company, and found him out in the storage room, wrapping cables for a campus concert that night. "OK, Mr. Coles, Bill, we need to talk, and I need you to keep it confidential. I am trusting you to wait to tell anybody, including your wife, or your girlfriend, if you're cheating on your wife. Are you OK with that?" She was his best friend now, joking around, hoping that this bond would keep him on board. Coles agreed, and Black used the Bureau trick of warning him about the legal consequences of making false statements to federal investigators. This was a bluff; she was implying that talking to Shaw would turn his promise into a lie, and hence a crime, when the statute actually had nothing to do breaking promises.

"Do you remember a singer your father booked, named Val Shaw?"

"Hah, are you kidding? Val? Professionally, he went by Valerius, no last name. Thought it sounded more mysterious." Coles stopped, laughed, and shook his head: "Val, a wanted murderer? No way, José — You are barking way, way up the wrong tree. Guaranteed."

Black was taken aback for a moment. She'd heard vehement denials turn out wrong, but this laughter was somehow more worrisome. "Bill, what makes you so sure Val Shaw couldn't be a killer?"

"Look, I know this guy, deep inside. In fact for about two months once I was more intimate with him than with any wife or girlfriend." When Black looked at him quizzically he laughed, "No, it's not like that! I'm straight as an arrow, and Valerius played his C and W with a notorious pussy band. But when you record an album with somebody, they're on your mind 24/7, and you're on theirs, and the two of you had better be in love, for as long as it takes to mix, remix, and re-remix every track. You know, I always keep a copy of the tapes and the actual album, once it's pressed — then into vinyl, today into CD's. You want it? You listen to it, you'll hear a nice, young kid, sad about his love life, devoted to his kid. No anger, no meanness."

An hour later, after interviewing Coles on what he remembered of his father's travel arrangements for his musicians, Black left with the record album *Valerius*, recorded in 1974. On the front cover was a drawing of Shaw strumming his guitar on stage in a dark, smoky club. On the back was a large photograph of him, hair down to his waist, holding on his lap a smiling little boy, maybe three or four years old. The caption said it was his son, Nathan Hale Shaw.

***

"Val, please, help me out. I know it's last minute, but Bobby Edwards has been great for me over the years. When his regular band dumps him for a festival, I'd love to be able to repay. And he did ask for you, in particular, said the booker at the Cellar Door thought of you when he called." Dom and Val were arguing over the phone on a Monday, about a two-night stand the coming weekend in Washington, the first weekend in June.

"And look, you say you want to make a record, well, this is perfect. The main acts filling in for the Seldom Scene at the Red Fox are both people who are making records! Great connections: a local girl named Emmy Harris is taking the slot Saturday, she already has an album, and is going to record a duet album with Gram Parsons, for Christ's sake, starting next month. And for the Friday main Bobby just scored an L.A. group that's coming east any-way to finish some mixing for their first album, on David Geffen's new label, Asylum. Guess who produced it? Glyn Johns, the Stones and Beatles man. Good enough for you? They're called 'Eagles,' no 'the,' apparently. Just say 'Eagles' when you promo them during your sets, if you don't want to piss them off."

Val knew exactly what Dom was doing, with his rapid-fire details and the pleasant, but insistent, hidden affirmation that Val was already on board. He'd heard Dom do it over the phone dozens of times to promoters and bookers; it was just funny to see it done to him! And indeed, his resolve was already crumbling. "Man, I don't know. Of course I want it, but it's not exactly the best time to ask my soon-to-be officially first ex-wife to switch

Nat's weeks. I don't even know if she's gonna be in town." Dom could almost hear Val grimacing over the phone, but he knew he had his man. "But I'll try. I'll call you later if I reach her."

Sally had, in fact, already left on a trip to New York with her new guy, but, surprisingly, a few hours after he mentioned the problem to Melissa when he skipped a class to visit her on the way to getting Nat from the babysitter, she called and offered to come over for the weekend and take care of Nat. "After all, it's not like Sally's gonna care anymore," she laughed. "And it'll be good practice for when I start following Curtis Mayfield's instructions: 'Every brother is a leader, every sister is a breeder!'"

"Eagles, no the" turned out to be the best folk-rock band Val had ever heard. All four guys sang like angels, and their harmonies created a physical surge of sympathetic tones that overwhelmed the sound system and the crowd that had packed into the smallish club. They had a hot picker, Bernie Leadon, whose guitar, banjo, and steel work Val knew from an album by the Flying Burrito Brothers. His instruments provided the only bright sounds in the mellow, low-volume set — the drummer and singer, Don Henley tapped rather than struck his set, and the other lead singer, Glen Frey, mostly played an acoustic guitar mic'ed fat through the sound system.

The effect was soft and warm, creating an intimate vibe. When Eagles, by now accepting that people called them The Eagles, morphed into a nasty, powerful rock band a year or so later by adding Leadon's old friend, electric slide guitarist and Duane Allman protégé Don Felder, the vibe was more intimidating than intimate. Val loved and would do songs from both eras, though, joking that the "peaceful, easy feeling" was "already gone."

Unlike the rest of the band-members, who were clearly tired from the flight east and grumpy about their manager signing them up for a three-month, cross-country tour as the opening act for Yes, Leadon was hyperactive and social. During the sound check Friday afternoon he was happy to show Val the magical "B-bender" guitar lever attached to the hook for his guitar strap: with a jerk of his shoulder, the strap pulled the lever, which stretched notes up, like a pedal steel guitar.

"It's a new version of Scruggs banjo pegs," Leadon explained excitedly, which then led him to teach Val a duel banjo part to play together on Paul

Craft's *Midnight Flyer* during Eagles' last set. Val had heard the Osborne Brothers play their bluegrass version of it earlier that year, and was happy to oblige, but he was wary of the tension between the talkative Leadon and his uncommunicative colleagues. It didn't seem to bode well for Eagles' longevity. "You sure it's all right if I come on and join you? Don't we have to check with the other guys, maybe practice a take?"

"Nah," said Leadon, "listen, it's obvious we don't always get along, but we're all pro's. We make stuff like this work, all the time, at our club in L.A., the Troubadour. Typical evening, Linda, Jackson, Neil, Joni, no telling who will wander up on stage. Hey, we're California, man, go with the flow, life in the fast lane. Like the song says, take it easy!"

That actually was the name of the song they started every set with, which Leadon said was going to be the single from the album. The band went out of their way to credit it every time to Jackson Browne, whom they said was a friend and flat-mate of theirs, so in the sets after that Val sang the two songs he knew off of Browne's *Saturate before Using* album: *Doctor, My Eyes* and *Rock Me on the Water*. He'd asked the guys to come to sing harmony if they wanted, but all he got was stone faces. When it came time for Val to join them on stage in their last set, though, Leadon was right: they were perfect gentlemen and perfect showmen, bringing him into the music and crediting him to the crowd. After the set, though, they returned to their aloof ways and, since they had roadies to handle their gear, were quickly gone.

In each set Val tried a couple of new songs he written recently, *Bookstore Clerk* and *Cornfields and Cobwebs*. He was so addicted to pick-ups now that even as he wrote them he was imagining how his target would look back with sparkling eyes and assenting smile as he held out the last, inviting lines. He felt fraudulent singing them, because their melancholy was studied, forced, and untrue. He knew he wasn't really portraying his anxious fears, but rather pretending to, like Boris and Julie in their transactional courtship in *War and Peace*.

The "bookstore" song, with mood and finger-picking stolen from folk-singer Ralph McTell's FM favorite, *Streets of London*, pined for a peace of mind that was illusory, because Val already knew that the everyday people he referenced weren't any happier than him:

There is a man and he wants to love, a man and he wants to dance
But he can only laugh at his foolish body, when the mirror shows his stance.
If only once he wouldn't look, and if he gave back more than he took
Maybe she'd come to see, the man that he might be.

He loves to listen to beautiful women, who speak with smoky eyes.
They tear your heart out, the way they move,
and when you look at them, you cry.
And quiet men who drink after work, carpen-
ters, painters, and book store clerks.
They seem to know the plot, and he does not.

He'd like to stop it all, and take a little time.
Finding the woman to make him love, the woman to make him mind.
But there's so many women every day, and so many smiles to take him away.
His life would be much sweeter, if she could only make him need her...

"Cornfields," based on the lovely major seventh chords from Gerry and the Pacemakers' Liverpool hit, *Don't Let the Sun Catch You Cryin'*, whined about unhappiness and also asked for a magical woman to ease it:

The corn stands by my window, and I stand by the door.
No one's looking for me, but that don't bother me no more.
I make a fool of myself, about once a God-damn day.
So it don't surprise me at all, that I ended up this way.

I dreamed you were with me last night, as I lay wide awake.
Listening to the wind in the shade trees, and the sounds they make.
We were done lovin', and could listen again.
As they rustled and parted, like women and men.

Cobwebs on the telephone speak of quiet days.
I lose myself in songs, and I vanish in the haze.
That washes over the cornfield, leaving it fresh and clean
I just wish you were here, someone to share my dreams.

But the melancholy songs didn't even work! Some smiles, but no winks and no date. Too cloying, maybe. After a stop at the nearby diner the driver dropped Val at the hotel the Red Fox used for pickers. As he drifted off to sleep, he decided he'd never play those two songs again. He woke just after noon, and took the express bus down Wisconsin Ave to the National Mall. He spent a few hours down there, remembering the 1969 march and eating oysters on the cheap at the waterfront, and got back to the Red Fox around six, with an hour to spare before the first show.

Opening the door to the dressing room Val stumbled into a gorgeous girl, maybe 25, dark hair cascading around her face like two question marks and falling all the way down in back to her waist. She was wearing a sort of poncho with Santa Fe motifs and holding an oversized acoustic guitar.

"Hey," she smiled, "I'm Emmy Harris. And I know who you are — my opener! What kind of stuff do you play?" Val was taken aback by her beauty and her warmth, and soon by her clear, pealing voice as she ran through a song she was learning, Tompall Glaser's *(My Baby Walks) The Streets of Baltimore*.

Harris was talkative, and a bit combative about her relations with the manager of the Red Fox. "This rascal and I have been fighting for weeks, since I found out he was paying the Seldom Scene twice as much as me. I don't care if there aren't just five of them but 20! An act is an act, and I told him I'm not playing 'til there's equal pay for equal sets! He finally came around this weekend, but that's probably because the Scene left him high and dry. We'll see about next time."

Val and Emmy compared notes on being single parents, and then he played a few of his original songs for her, including the new one about his son. She asked him to back her with his banjo on "Green Pastures" and a couple other of her hard-core Ralph Stanley mountain songs. Val happily agreed, but told Emmy after her second show that he wouldn't be able to stick around for her last one. "Problems with the drivers' schedule, you know. But, have your hated Bobby ask for me as an opener when you make up with him, and I'll be down soon — maybe bring my son, the kids can play!"

* * *

Major General George Hemmings threw a moving salute at the two tall corporals from the ceremonial Old Guard who were standing post at the gate to Fort McNair. They didn't bat an eye, holding their rigid salutes on this warm Saturday afternoon. *Haec Protegimus*, read the patch on the corporals' right shoulders, under the two swords crossing the American flag — "This, we guard" — but there was no need to guard the commander of the United States Army Military District of Washington, off on his regular four o'clock run, or jog, as the newspapers had begun to call it. He'd be back, as always, in precisely 30 minutes, after running along the Potomac River, up to the Washington monument and back.

Hemmings was 46, and thinking about retiring with his two stars. He was pondering his dilemma this afternoon, as he often did while on his runs. It had been hard to get to major general, but it was a hell of a lot harder to get past it. He'd fought as a teenaged private in Italy against fascists, as a captain, after college, in Korea against communists, and as a colonel in Viet Nam, but there he wasn't quite sure against whom. Within the Pentagon, he was certainly respected as reliable in command, but was he just too controversial a figure for the personnel board to put at the top, with three and then four stars, and a seat at the JCS table?

He knew that he'd been right in the fall of 1968 when he started pushing his superiors at the time, Army Chief of Staff William Westmoreland and Vice Chief Bruce Palmer, to accelerate the planned withdrawals from Viet Nam. But had he been right too early, in terms of his career? Nixon didn't formally recognize the reality of withdrawal until his "Vietnamization" speech in November 1969, but as the J-5, the officer in charge of strategic plans for the JCS, Hemmings knew that the plans had been set in March 1968, although not the timing. That was when Johnson turned down the request of Westmoreland, then the commander in Viet Nam, for more troops in response to the Tet Offensive. Typical of LBJ, Hemmings had thought at the time: against the advice of the chiefs, he hadn't told the country that he was going to war in 1965, and now he wasn't telling the country that he was giving up.

Palmer had said that he agreed with Hemmings' conclusion that fighting while withdrawing wouldn't only incur losses with no prospect of South Vietnamese victory, but also continue to devastate the Army's core discipline. It was Palmer, indeed, who had compiled his own, rapidly growing list of combat units that fired off their weapons before heading out on patrol, warning the NVA they were coming, making an implicit deal: leave us alone and we'll leave you alone. That wasn't an army, his Army, that was a mob! And there were just too many such incidents to even contemplate prosecution. On top of that, since Tet that January there were even a dozen outright refusals to patrol, and over a hundred "fraggings" and other attacks on officers or NCO's who ordered patrols. The troops knew the war was over and they were determined not to be the last to die during the withdrawal.

Hemmings had ended one of his memos to Palmer with a nod to Bismarck's famous declaration: "Since withdrawal has been decided upon, delaying it is not worth the life of a single American grenadier. The ARVN will never attain the commitment of the NVA, the commanders or the soldiers, like the tanker we captured last year who had chained himself to his gun, and had 'Born in the North to die in the South' tattooed on his chest. They will sell off all our equipment, steal all our cash, and lose the battle, whether we leave this year or in five years."

As he came closer to the end of his term as Washington commander, with none of the usual hints from people close to the personnel board, Hemmings had to assume he was suspect goods, and that the promotion might not happen. He knew Palmer was truly pushing for him; Westmoreland, not so sure, despite his promises. The dilemma was that if he resigned, to avoid the stigma of being denied promotion because it might hurt his chances with the defense contractors, he would miss the last few weeks of behind-the-scenes lobbying that just might get him the big break. It was getting toward crunch time. He had to decide.

With these thoughts on his mind, Hemmings never even heard the Buick Estate Wagon that had been idling at the southern end of the waterfront plaza, 50 yards behind him, as it accelerated until it topped 60 miles an hour and ran him over from behind. He was driven under the front bumper, smashed unconscious by the concrete plaza, and killed by the undercarriage of the car raking his body as it spat him out the back.

The Buick continued on, not stopping to assess the damage, and in fact not hesitating for an instant as it veered from the plaza back toward the street, jumped the curb onto Maine Avenue, and drove, carefully at the speed limit, north toward the Tidal Basin and Ohio Drive. Four miles farther on the assassin pulled the stolen station wagon off the access road from Rock Creek Drive and parked on residential Woodley Road. With hands still gloved, the killer locked the door, rubbed some mud on the Virginia plates, and started walking, quickly but not too quickly, out to the bus stop on Connecticut Avenue. With any luck, the car would sit without notice until parking inspectors checked for out-of-zone stickers on Monday afternoon.

WAMU was American University's FM radio station, featuring bluegrass music and news programs. It was located in Tenleytown, a neighborhood

half-way from Georgetown to Bethesda. When its staff checked the mailbox
on Monday morning for weekend drops, they found this communiqué:

War Report: Nathan Hale Brigade

When Weatherman said they'd bring the war home until it stopped in
Viet Nam, we applauded them. But then they backed off, calling off the war
in favor of "armed propaganda." The latest charade is them hypocritically
choosing Ho Chi Minh's birthday two weeks ago to put a bomb in a Pentagon
bathroom to protest Nixon and Kissinger's carpet-bombing of Hanoi. What
would Uncle Ho say to that, destroying toilets when the American officers
who use the toilets order B-52s to level cities? Don't the Vietnamese patriots
deserve all of our support, and not just 99 and a half, like the Wicked Pickett
says? Don't the Weathermen remember chanting in the 1969 Mobe march,
"Ho, Ho, Ho Chi Minh: Dare to Struggle, Dare to Win"?

The war is not only an illegal invasion, but is now being fought illegally:
ever since the carnage of World War II, international law has prohibited the
bombing of cities. As long as the laws of war are violated, then people who
violate them will be legitimate targets of the people's war. General Hemmings
invaded Viet Nam, and in fact won his rank by killing patriots and civilians
there. Since then he's been a top planner of the war, advising the killer and
liar Westmoreland. He just found out that Washington is a tough place for a
Hemmings. Just ask Sally! Fair warning: he won't be the last to pay the price
for invasion and war crimes.

* * *

CHAPTER 12: SEPTEMBER 1973 — IT&T AND VICTOR IGLESIAS

"Dom, I want to do a record. It just feels like it's time: I've been play-ing two years around here, hitting one of the travel gigs every few months, I'm about to graduate, and maybe could put more time into it. I know you bought a piece of the recording for Orleans, that great Woodstock band, and look what happened! I'm not saying I'm gonna get picked up by a national label and get whisked down to the Swampers in Muscle Shoals to record like them, but even if it doesn't go national I can easily pay you back and more by selling them at gigs."

Val and his booker were having sandwiches at a picnic table outside the agency at Chester and Park, at the angle of Swarthmore's main business strip, on the first real day of spring. A light rain that morning had left the fresh smell of a new season in the air. SEPTA Commuter trains hummed into the nearby station, exchanging comers and goers, each with their own directions and dreams. It all created a mood for Val in which anything seemed possible.

"Well," said Dom, "why not you, eh? Your original songs are better than half the crap on the radio; then again, that's not sayin' much. But if we're gonna do it, the best way may be to cut it here, with Billy Coles, and then pitch that product to the labels in New York. They're overwhelmed with tapes, and some groups use test records, fully packaged, to catch their eye."

And so it was that a month later Val sat down, put on his headphones, and began playing the guitar tracks in a sound-baffled room, a closet, really, as Bill worked his magic behind the glass window. And magic it was: one morning Val came in, still frustrated from a five-hour session the night before in which nothing seemed to sound right, and heard a gorgeous version of his *Collegetown Deck* flowing out of the control room speakers.

"Who did that? Has somebody else cut my song? But wait, that's my lick on the piano!" Val was confused, since recording had changed his way of listening and he automatically picked out individual instruments from the mix. That was certainly his piano line, but he'd never done the song like that, like a for-real rock and roll hit.

"That's you, little brother, better living through technology," crowed Bill. "See what a little sleep, a lot of fresh coffee, and 16 tracks can do?" Val was stunned. By raising and lowering the volume and timbres on each track Val had laid down, Bill's mix had removed all the weak moments and powered up the ones where good pickin' and singin' overlapped. Drums, bass, piano, lots of different guitar pieces, fiddle and banjo, harmonies, even a bite of simple pedal steel guitar chords, lifts and drops, once in a while. It was unbelievable.

"Holy ** ," said Val. "I sound good! And I know my voice isn't that big, or that on pitch. How do you do that?"

"Oh, you never want to hear any band, from the Beatles to the Eagles, until someone's played with the voice — I can modulate the voice an entire note, make it fat, make it spare, until it's just right. Now, let's get to work — I want to patch in a couple of better notes on the guitar solo, where you don't bend it quite far enough to get the pitch you need."

Val thought for a moment, clearly troubled at the thought of tricking the listener. "Wait, put in a new note to cover a bad one, you can do that? Isn't that sort of cheating, because I didn't play it right? Shouldn't I just redo the whole solo, so it's truly me? I'm not going down the Monkees' path here, am I, putting out a fake record?"

"Monkees? Hey, the same pickers that play their stuff, the Wrecking Crew, do all the Beach Boys, all the Byrds, like Mr. Tambourine Man. Hell, by the end, the Beatles had entire orchestras to hit their notes, and it was all remixed like this by George Martin, plugging in notes and harmonies. My standard is, how do you want it to sound? Not, how did it sound?"

It sounded so great that Val, for all his scruples about honesty, just gave in. The cut was a tribute to specific Swarthmore characters. Anybody who knew him could figure out right away who was the drunken Jack, the black Queen, the uncommitted King, and the saving Ace. Tolstoy said to write about what you know, and the specific will become universal. For once, at least, the tune itself was all his own. The beat, he sensed, was clearly derived from his growing appreciation of the ** -it, so-what mood of country rebels Waylon Jennings and Merle Haggard. And as for the words, they were about real people he knew, but the chorus he'd stolen from a drummer from one of his earlier bands, who'd written lyrics about a "travel tree" that watched him go by, going nowhere.

> There's Jack of Diamonds, the old drinking man
> Working on a double of gin.
> Sitting at the bar, dreaming his plans
> That depend on the woman who will never walk in.
>
> He's seen her in the dark of the long and lonely skies
> She reaches down and brushes the years from his eyes.
>
> Hey Ace of Cups, don't forget me, as you travel 'round, don't regret me
> Stay all night, don't you let me live my life alone.
>
> The Queen of Spades is out and desiring a man
> She's tired of her strength, she's done all that she can.
> She tours the town, flaunting her freedom
> Looking for the man who can make her need him...
>
> She thinks she's got it made, 'cause my heart's on my sleeve
> But she don't see me put my coat on, when I go to leave.
>
> Hey Ace of Cups, don't forget me, as you travel 'round, don't regret me
> Stay all night, don't you let me live my life alone.
>
> The King of Hearts, he made "a wise choice"
> But now his woman pales, a crack creeps through her voice.
> He wants to get out, but you can only get in
> He wishes that he could choose again.
>
> I hold them all right here where I stand
> But it takes so long to play out the hand.
> If the Ace of Cups could only be the draw
> I'd lay her right down, and beat you all.
>
> Hey Ace of Cups, don't forget me, as you travel 'round, don't regret me
> Stay all night, don't you let me live my life alone.

Here Val was, again, like in so many of his songs, talking about people who were too weak to choose on their own and wanted somebody with stronger character, here the mysterious Ace of Cups, the love card in the Tarot, to demand loyalty from them. Taking a break during a mixing session, Bill had remarked on this theme showing up in other songs on the album: "if she could only make him need her," from the revived version of *Bookstore Clerk*, and this, from *White and Picket Fence*:

> I painted that fence, and I fixed it up strong
> But I never could stay on one side too long.
> She would not use her lock, what else could I do?
>
> And if time could tell, would she say that I'm
> Just another man who never really tried?
> Did I always have the choice, but never dare choose?

"I see that everywhere in your songs. Since it's always on your mind, can I ask why you don't just choose? What's so bad about committing?"

"Well," responded Val, "it's not really always on my mind. There's only one thing always on my mind, and has been since I was in junior high in '65, writing 'U.S. out of Viet Nam' on the blackboard next to my math problems, instead of my name, and that's 'what can I do today to stop the genocide in Viet Nam?' Romance? I only realize I should commit when I sit down to write — but day to day, that doesn't compete with the next darling face I see...or hair, eyes, smile, frown, legs, indentations under a shirt, frankly anything that smacks of female, and I'm lost!"

"Very funny...but, hey, genocide?" wondered Bill. "Not to support the war or anything, but exaggerating sounds kooky. Genocide is, like, Hitler killing six million Jews in a gas chamber, right?"

"Indeed my misinformed friend: and in the 30 years since we brought the French back to take over their Indochina colonies in 1945, and funded their war until 1954, and then took it over ourselves, you bet we've caused at least six million deaths — maybe two million soldiers and civilians directly, bombs from the air, artillery from the ground, but many more people by all this violence destroying the economies of all three countries, Laos, Cambodia, and Viet Nam. That's what sends millions of people out wandering as penniless refugees, drinking dirty water that kills kids and old folks in droves. That's why I ache when I wake up each morning — I only ache for true love late at night, and only those nights that I'm alone!"

"Well all righty then, thanks for letting me see that side," said Bill. "We've been working together for two months now, literally day and night, and that's the first time I've heard your politics. The only hint is in 'American Girl, American Man,' the one we decided we didn't have space for, and I mean hint. If you hadn't told me, I wouldn't have known it was about a murderous Black Panther. If it's so important to you, and you sing to crowds all the time, why don't you have anti-war songs?

Val thought for a moment. "You know, I've never figured that out. Maybe because political songs sound so trite, so cheap, so 'preach to the choir and no propers to everybody else.' Anyway, look at Dylan, his cryptic poems, like *Highway 61*, 'God said to Abraham, kill me a son,' or *Like a Rolling Stone*, 'How does it feel?," turn more people against the war culture than his hit-you-over-the-head explicit folk songs, *Masters of War* or *Blowin' in the Wind*. Just the big rock beat of those electric songs, just Bobby Greg popping the snare and kicking the bass to start *Like a Rolling Stone*, man, that's why I knew I couldn't fight for the American way.

"But I think it's more because I just don't like it when people put politics in their personal life, and ask you as a friend, or even a stranger, to agree with them, and then become distant if you don't. I mean, I'll tell people where I've written stuff on the war, on the empire, and they can look at it if they want, but I don't even like handing out leaflets on the streets — it seems like intruding in their lives, like bull military tributes when vets come back to the high school football game. Leave politics out of sports, leave it out of our daily lives, so we can live.

"That's why I could never stick with the anti-war groups in college, here or in Chicago. I'd go to a meeting against the war, take on an assignment, like knocking on dorm doors to get people to buy a bus ticket to go protest Nixon appearing at a rally in Philly, and I'd do it, but I just hated it, bothering people, repeating the same line over and over again. I'd rather just write it out once and put it in the student paper, and they can decide if they want to go."

"Well," laughed the engineer, "for someone who gets up on stage all the time, you sure are shy one-on-one! Let's hope Dom isn't counting on you going table to table, selling this album. You just set them in a pile by the stage and see how many people come up and buy! I know music has to be marketed, up into people's faces, and I bet politics is the same thing! But, hey, let's get back to it — we're close on this mix, and then there's only one more song to go."

A couple of months later, his record in hand, the high hopes Val had developed for stardom based on Bill's magic mixing came crashing down in a dingy back-room office on Manhattan's music row. Dom had prevailed on a friend at a smallish label to go over the recently-released album with Val, and the executive sat politely, listening carefully to the first few cuts before lifting the needle.

"Done — we always need the lean and hungry who can put words together and then go out and flog them. We can do this for East Coast distribution, then you join our packages, Dom will release you for a bit of the take, and you tour about 200 nights a year, Florida to Maine, some first act on weekends at larger clubs, main act on weekdays and at smaller clubs, we've got enough clubs you won't even repeat 'til the next year! Regular one dollar cut for each record, we'll re-master and release, and send the songs around to all the labels. Best case? You're the Beatles! Second best case, somebody takes some of the songs: royalties beat the road! But until then, you gotta push it, make your name mean something to the industry. It's show-time!"

"Wait," said Val, for the first time thinking through what this long-hoped-for response implied. "You mean that you'll only distribute the record if I go on the road all year to promote it? But I can't go on the road like that. I only go out of town every couple of months for a few nights! I'm a single parent with a three-year-old kid, I have a teaching job I'm about to start, I can't be in Maine on a Tuesday night. I have a life!"

The executive looked at Val as if he had fallen from the sky. "Good Lord, Jackson, how do you think we make our money? This is the business: musicians travel to push the records. How did you think it worked? There's no day job, no home life, for anybody you ever hear on the radio! Any kind of music. B.B. King? 300 dates a year. Ralph Stanley, the same. Merle Haggard, the Eagles, it's all the same. The road, baby, is where you live.

"Now, you go home to Swarthmore, and you think about it. Pack up the kid, like Jackson Browne, or get a live-in babysitter among your many fans, find a way and give me a call. The songs are good, the voice, not so much, but that never stopped Dylan! It might go somewhere, but only if you do. This is no business for amateurs — there's no home life for road warriors. This is all day, every day."

And that was that, the end of Val's excellent dreams. He would never become an absent father. It was simply not going to happen. He'd actually made that pledge, happily, not long after Nat was born, of course in a song, the one he used for encores, *Roman Times*:

> Nothing they can do can make me run away
> I'd die like a Gaul in Roman times, that's what I used to say
> But then you came into my life, or rather unto this earth
> And the feeling died within me, the moment of your birth.
>
> And it's not 'cause I love you, and you're my deepest joy
> It's just that you need me more than I need you, little boy.
>
> I know you need a lot more than just my love and time
> The world owes you something, and I guess the burden's mine
> Once I met a poet, and this is what I was told:
> Give a woman your heart, boy, but give a child your soul.
>
> And it's not 'cause I love you, and you're my deepest joy
> It's just that you need me more than I need you, little boy.

Val kept playing, of course, while he kept house and started his job prepping high school dropouts for the equivalency exam, and still traveled for Dom once in a while. And indeed he did make both of them a decent chunk of change, selling his album after his sets. And life was still good: he kept loving the truck stop honeys, as he called all his musical affairs, whether they were college dance students and their professors, whom his brother called the "flexible flyers" after their childhood sleds, or the waitresses he got to know so well over the five hours of set-up and break-down it took to play a three-hour job.

And Val kept on spending some of the nights Nat went to his mother with Melissa at his refuge over the radical press. She understood his disappointment, but also his decision. "You are still gonna keep your October dates at the Bottom Line, though, right? I was thinking of riding up with you for that weekend, if you don't mind bringing your groupie in the limo rather than eyeing her out of the crowd, for once...and I'll never chew you out for eating meat, like the last one you told me about. Is that OK? I'm really eager to be there for this one."

* * *

The assassin read over the scouting report one last time, and then ceremoniously burned it with a lighter and left the ashes in the gutter. Harold Geneen, the big man, was untouchable. After his tough bargaining with Brazil over expropriation, and then International Telephone and Telegraph's widely-reported support for the CIA coup there in 1964, the president had been one of the first top executives to add full-time bodyguards to his perquisites. Just like Kissinger, the killer thought — nobody's gonna get a chance to pull a McNamara on him, try to throw him off the boat when he vacations in Martha's Vineyard.

So, it had to be this top aide, to send the message that even being near an imperialist corporate leader was suicidal. Victor Iglesias lived on the upper east side with his wife. By chance they were both Chileans who'd attended the Harvard Business School, which made it all the sweeter. Well, they'd become a case study, all right.

For three hours that afternoon the assassin stalked Iglesias and his wife, following them from their apartment over to the Lexington Avenue subway, and then downtown to Soho, where they window-shopped in the art galleries and then walked over a few blocks to Little Italy for lunch. This was their Saturday routine, and it usually led them to the little-used Spring Street station for the ride home. The killer walked ahead, and when the couple came down the stairs he was already sitting on a bench halfway down the platform, apparently raptly reading a New York Times that was held high to block eye-contact with the few passers-by.

As the uptown train shrieked into the station, the assassin moved smoothly behind Iglesias, who stood arm-in-arm with his wife, just a foot behind the standing line. Fortunately for her, the link wasn't tight, and as her husband was suddenly driven forward, over the edge, she was merely knocked sideways and to the ground. From there she never caught more than a glimpse of the figure striding quickly, but not too quickly, back up the stairs.

A block-letter communiqué made its way to the desk of Pentagon Papers reporter Neil Sheehan at the *New York Times'* Washington bureau a few days later. Sheehan was actually on leave, writing a book on Viet Nam, but an assistant opened his mail, at which point the *Times*, true to its Pentagon Papers approach, published first and handed to the FBI second:

War Report: Nathan Hale Brigade

We applaud the New York Times for defying Nixon, publishing the Pentagon Papers, and revealing the lies about the invasion of Viet Nam that our imperialist government has told since bringing the French back to colonial glory in 1945. The study admits we were never there to win freedom for the South Vietnamese, like we said, but to maintain imperial "credibility." But what the Times won't say is that this invasion is no mistake, no unique error in judgment applying just to Viet Nam. Imperialism, as Lenin said, is the highest stage of capitalism, coming after monopoly capitalism pushes aside free competition capitalism. As a victim of U.S. imperialism, Viet Nam is no different from Laos, from Cambodia, from Indonesia, from Congo, from El Salvador, and yes, from Brazil and Chile, where IT&T was the monopoly capitalist that conspired with the CIA to drive democratically-elected governments from power.

As you might guess by now, this being our fourth action, we applaud the Weatherman bombing of IT&T's headquarters two weeks ago. And as you might also guess, we still think that Weather needs to step up the struggle, to live up to their support for Malcolm's "by any means necessary," and for their own words, "we are going to do whatever we have to do" to stop the violence not just in Viet Nam but everywhere the imperialist flag is planted. The pigs have to pay, not just their bulidings!

What happened to the promise in the SDS declaration of war? "All over the world, people fighting Amerikan imperialism look to Amerika's youth to use our strategic position behind enemy lines to join forces in the destruction of the empire...Revolutionary violence is the only way."

We still hope to bring justice to Harold Geneen, who personally helped the CIA bring down João Goulart in Brazil in 1964 and Salvador Allende in Chile a month ago. But any executive who serves imperialism, who carries out its strategies, is equally guilty. That is why we executed Victor Iglesias in the Spring Street station, after judging Geneen guilty of the four-count indictment in the Weather Underground statement.

To all executives of imperialist corporations who meddle in other countries' affairs, to all bureaucrats at Defense, State, AID, National Security Council, we warn you: We are at war with you. To the public we say: Yes, war means violence, but war reduces violence when it stops a greater threat. Our parents defeated Hitler and Tojo, with violence, to end the worse violence of Nazi Germany and Imperial Japan. We, their successors, will use violence until not just the war in Viet Nam but all the wars and subversions, the choosing of friendly bastards to run other countries, come to an end, and America's claimed values are regained. *La lucha continua*, for Chile. *A luta continua*, for Brazil.

* * *

CHAPTER 13: APRIL 2017 — THE CONFUSION

"So those are the just the details for the first two cases, sir. The others are in the memo, but it's the same M.O.: travel for music jobs at the time of the murder, within a month of the bombing, in and out of the city in question by limousine. We have the limousine records, we have the appearance contracts." Black had sensed from the flagging interest around the table that this was a good time to finish up her presentation at the conference table in Cold Case, a calm, straight-faced review of what she had crowed so happily and loudly about in her one-on-one meeting with Jerry the day before.

The case memo they had then sent around was the reason the room was filled, with the proud Philadelphia team joined by top techies and senior FBI officials, even the assistant attorney general, Salvatore Imaglio, a level so high she doubted more than a dozen FBI officials had ever even met him. It was all a sure sign, Black realized with frustration, that she was probably about to lose the case to the big shots.

"Agent McGurk, you and your teams have done great work," said one of the dour senior officials in Imaglio's entourage, clearly handling the details on this case for the man himself, who simply peered intently at Black. "The case is powerful and probably winnable on circumstance, even before your investigators dig up the corroboration. Unfortunately, while you've solved one of the mysteries — why just Weather's east coast bombings led to murders — I count three more mysteries that Shaw's lawyers will certainly attack if we can't solve them.

"First, Shaw isn't traveling with the LoPinto booker until 1971, so the failed hit on Professor Huntington, which is our only eye-witness account, doesn't fit the M.O. What about that?"

Black breathed a sigh of relief. This was gonna be easier than she'd feared. "Ma'am, we think it makes our case stronger: without the limousine method, Shaw probably traveled to Cambridge and back with J. J. Jacobs, the Townhouse rogue who'd been expelled in May because he refused to accept the Weather Bureau's change to bombing just property, to minimize casualties. Jacobs seems to have been helping the Boston collective with their bomb-making, on his own.

"He's a strange guy, seems out of control. The fact that he let these Weather women meet Shaw, let alone him bragging about a hit, shows that the leadership was right to expel him — a loose cannon, impetuous, poor discipline. We think he helped with all the hits, and was sticking it to the Weathermen who'd canned him, hoping they'd take the heat for the killings.

"Shaw had never traveled to play music before he signed on with LoPinto in 1971. We think Shaw and Jacobs dreamed up his new interest in road trips and he went to LoPinto with the assassinations already in mind, or maybe that they just took advantage of it when LoPinto made the offer. Other than Shaw, there's nobody else who can answer that: Jacobs is dead, LoPinto is dead, his partner has dementia. However they set it up, though, it was a great M.O., in and out by limo, and the attempts were all well-planned after Boston. Probably, Jacobs did the scouting and planning, and clearly made the one bomb they used, and Shaw did the hitting from Jacobs' reports."

"OK," replied Imaglio's aide, "we thought about that. The prosecutors can spin that in, address the problem of the new M.O. before the defense does. But that's the easy one. Try this one on for size: how about the other east coast Weather bombs, the ones where there's no assassination? Why these bombings and not the others, some in the same cities that Shaw played in regularly, and in fact killed in?

"From your memo I've pulled out this list: New York, police offices, June 1970; New York, two Bank of America branches, late night, July 1970; Queens and Long Island courts, October 1970; Albany, the Department of Corrections after Attica, September 1971; New York, the Puerto Rican Bank, maybe to catch up with the busy Puerto Rican bombers, June 1975. Why no murders related to those bombings?"

"Let me address that, ma'am," said Jerry, continuing the polite fiction that they were talking to the aide and not Imaglio. "First of all, we don't think Shaw got started until October, at Harvard. But even if he got started in June, right after meeting Jacobs, all those bombings have one thing in common: no connection to Viet Nam. Our historians have classified all of Shaw's books, articles, letters to the editor, since he first shows up in 1968 as a teenager, and it's all war and imperialism, all the time. Nothing on courts, nothing on cops, nothing on Black Panthers.

"In fact, outside of his decidedly non-left wing views on climate change, which come from him happening to teach statistics, he never writes anything on U.S. domestic issues, period. It may have been the Hampton and Clark murders that allegedly set him off, away from being Mr. Gandhi, but they seem to have set him off just in foreign policy."

"Marie, let me take it from here," interjected the assistant attorney general, finally dispensing with the fiction that he was just there to listen. Black sat up straight, realizing that the whole point of Imaglio's attendance was now going to be revealed, and that she wasn't going to like it. The assistant attorney general turned to address the whole group — apparently it was beneath his pay grade to question individual agents.

"I agree that the foreign focus is a solid point for the prosecutors, Agent Cummings, but you've got a bigger problem, our third question. Don't get me wrong, this team has done great work, and Agent Black got as close to this as a soul can be. But I fear she got too close. Reading it over cold, pardon the pun, it hit me right away. Now I don't doubt that Val Shaw is our killer, our trigger-puller, bat-basher, car-driver and all that. But we're being played, and I'm thinking of blowing this all up and certifying to the court that the deal has been broken — by Ayers.

"It only dawned on me when Marie made that list of bombings — Albany? Even if he'd wanted to, how could Shaw arrange to play in Albany on a few weeks' notice? Just by chance, because an Assemblyman I know kept bugging me to come watch him when he'd get a slot to play the harmonica there with some of his colleagues, I know that Albany only has one music club, and bookings are made months in advance."

Imaglio paused, to let the implication sink in. "Think about it — if the business works that way, if bookings are made well in advance, how did Shaw manage to get booked into all his cities within a few weeks of a Weather bombing? Isn't it more likely that he first knew when he would be in those cities, and then Jacobs started looking for targets? But all the hits came after bombings, so Jacobs had to know when those would happen.

"I mean, I can see a lucky coincidence once in a while, but six times in five years? Get it? Once Jacobs found a target for Shaw's window, maybe the chain went the other direction, not from the bombing to the murder, as a supposed response, but from the murder to the planning of the bombing that would supposedly trigger it."

Black's head was spinning, as she saw the logic of the timing, but not the logic of the chain of command. "Yes, sir," she said, "I clearly missed that possibility, that the gigs were there before the bomb plans, but Jacobs was an openly expelled Weatherman, not only with no authority, but positively somebody not to listen to. The Boston group, Proud Eagle, the women, they only used him in 1970 to help make a bomb, as a mechanic. What you're implying, I think, sir, is that Jacobs' expulsion was phony, and everybody in Weather knew it. But that's never, never, emerged from all the memoirs of these talkative folks."

"Don't jump so fast and so far, Agent McGurk," said Imaglio, for the first time focusing his eyes, laser-like, just on her. "I'm really not ready, nor should you be, to make up a new story line. I just know that the old one has big problems, and if we go with it, Shaw's attorney will see that too." He smiled coldly at her, and she felt the deserved zing — she was out of her league with him, just like with that professor, not enough seasoning yet, and she knew it.

Imaglio slowly turned back to survey the group, looking each person in the eye before he said: "You want to make this right, focus on the one thing we know. And that is that our star witnesses are lying sacks of ** ." The room erupted in laughter, letting out the tension about whether Jerry, Black, and her team was going to get hammered for missing what Imaglio had so quickly found. "Go see them, threaten the end of the deal, and see what pops out. Meanwhile, Art Middles and I have a little personal reckoning to do."

* * *

The call to Middles brought rapid action. As soon as he heard the story from Imaglio he promised to get to the bottom of it. If there was an iota of truth in it, Middles promised, he would resign as counsel to Ayers immediately. Minutes later he was on the phone to Ayers.

"Give it all to me, Bill, or I'm quitting. The way it looks now, you lied to me about not being connected to Weather-cat. I set up the deal, so I was lying to the feds. God damn it, the only reason I'm worth anything as a lawyer is that they know I'd never do that. They know I don't have to give them anything, I don't have to correct their misimpressions, but I can't lie, I can't deliver the misimpressions myself. Why do you think Imaglio took my meeting?

"Oh, right! That's exactly why you hired me, because you knew they'd trust me, because Bernardine walks in legal circles, and she knows that I'm no radical, I don't agree with my clients, I play it straight — that's why I'm the go-to guy when you really want protection, and not publicity! That's why people come to me when they want to be Kathy Boudin, and take a plea to get out of jail someday, and not David Gilbert, and make a point of being a captured soldier who stays in for life. Now, lay it on me, or I'm gone."

Ayers answered, "Slow down, Arthur, what are you talking about?"

"Oh, really? No idea? Don't you slow-roll me, God damn it. Justice just told me that the killer didn't follow Weather bombings — he led them, since he had the hits arranged before they occurred, based on his preplanned travel schedule as a folk-singer. Imaglio told me so I'd understand his certainty, and he'd have to produce it eventually after an indictment: Shaw was driven in and out of these cities by a limousine service to play concerts the night of the murder, but his schedule was set before the bombings. Pre-planned! That means the Central Committee had the murder dates in mind when it planned the bombings. And you, pal, and your wife, you pretty much were the Central Committee."

His decades of experience kept Art from asking the obvious question, "What did you two know about the murders?" Instead, he just let it hang in the air.

"OK, OK, I'm sorry. Just wanted to hear what happened. In fact, we've been expecting this call, from the beginning," responded Ayers. "I know the timing looks bad, and it's true that we ordered bombings for those particular dates, but we can show we were played, that we had nothing to do with the killings. Yes, we misled Justice in the statement, but only because we were worried that the whole truth would right away have put us, more than Nathan Hale, in their sights. We decided that once they got on to him, built a case on him, they'd be more likely to understand that we were clean on the killings. The problem was always our relationship with J.J. — John Jacobs."

"John Jacobs? You expelled him in 1970. What has that got to do with anything? Well, I doubt that my contacts at Justice are going to like excuses, but let's hear it, all of it, or I swear I am gone, immediately," replied Art.

"OK, this is all John Jacobs' doing, pure and simple, but we had no knowledge of his link to the killings until March 1975, when the woman from the Cambridge bombing, the Harvard CFIA, Huntington's office, put the finger on him and Nathan Hale, together. We purposely did not lie, to you or to the FBI. Look at our statements, word for word, because Bernardine's not a law professor for nothing: 'it was reported that J.J. was expelled,' or 'we told the collectives he had been expelled.'

"Just because her reputation keeps her from getting a law license doesn't mean she can't write a legally accurate statement! Now, what was reported and what was told to the collectives, you're right, it wasn't accurate. We've hidden that from everyone, in the movement, in the media, our families, our friends, for almost 50 years now, saying that he was expelled. But we never said that in our FBI interviews, because he never was. It was all a dodge, so he could move around the country and do what he did best: plan bombings that would be educational, based on ideology and opportunity. He was sacrificed to make our case against the Townhouse collective, all right, but only publicly, not in reality.

"At first J. J. wasn't happy about being labeled a rogue, but since he'd lost the fight over armed propaganda anyway he accepted that his expulsion would be the clearest statement of a 'New Morning.' A real team player, as always. For five years we never saw him: he'd travel the country, sometimes taking our suggestions for places to scout, sometimes sending his own suggested targets, the best time frames, and operational data, his own scouting report on the target, to the Central Committee, which we began to call the Weather Bureau. After much back and forth by phone, in code, we'd decide on a target and pass on the scouting reports and orders to the cadres. Of course, as you know, after a while we were the cadres ourselves, since so few people stayed underground as long as we did."

Ayers continued: "But at their core our FBI statements are still true: we had nothing to do with the killings. Of course we noticed that sometimes after a bombing there'd be a killing and a communiqué, but not very often, not most of the time, never often enough to think the Nathan Hale folks had advance knowledge. So we figured the brigade members had traveled there afterwards, responding to the bombing and making their case that we were weak and cowardly.

"J. J. was never supposed to interact with the cadres. Like I said, the only people who knew of his role, who knew he wasn't really expelled, were on the Central Committee. Everybody else? We never told them — no need to know, right? And once he was in play, only Bernardine and I ever dealt with him, and we didn't brief the others, so it was a circle of three.

"The plan was for him to be a lone wolf, to case the various cities himself. Only once did we ask him to help with an operation, that one at Harvard. At the last minute they told us they weren't sure how to ground the bomb. We didn't want another Townhouse, Fliegelman was away, his pupil Cathy Wilkerson was still unsure, so we sent J. J. to handle it. We had no idea about the Nathan Hale connection until the woman from the collective told us in 1975, responding to Shaw's picture, just like Bernardine said. That's when we finally figured it out. J. J. had played us like we played the FBI: he was still on his assassination mission. Well, there wasn't much of group to really expel him from then, so we just broke off all contact. We knew we could count on him, of all people, to maintain secrecy, whatever the circumstances.

"We knew Nathan Hale was a folk-singer before he was a professor, because we kept up on him, just in case we needed to trade him — which, obviously with the subpoena for the DNA, we eventually did. But I don't remember anything about this traveling limousine business, although I can see that it really fits: that's why J. J. would give us about a month's notice for what he would say was the best window of opportunity for a planned bombing. Some bombings we would just decide on ourselves, but he was usually in the loop for most of those as a scout, too, not just for the ones he suggested, so it's possible some of those dates lined up for his singer, too. Some of his bombings we rejected as too risky or too soon, so it's possible there would've been more hits if we'd taken those on."

"But Art, don't quit — we didn't lie to you. We just wanted to make sure that the FBI took the bait. We'd decided that was our play when we gamed it out, years ago. Now that they have Shaw, with this travel stuff as a bonus, we can tell them the whole story. But don't say we lied: they, and you, just never asked us if the reports about J. J.'s expulsion were true."

"Bull, Billy," yelled Middles. Now that he had the explanation, he didn't have to hold back. "You can try that nonsense on your gullible book tour groupies, but not on me. You misled me, so I misled Justice into thinking it was a true story, and misleading is just lying by omission. My next call is to Justice, to tell them I'm resigning. I'll understand if they never play it open with me again, because there's a price to doing what you've done. If it hurts my other clients, it's on your lying head. Good luck explaining yourself to them and keeping your deal."

But Billy was still the smartest kid in the room. Well, Bernardine, actually. As usual, the idea had been hers, she'd convinced him, and indeed she had figured it right. When they told their new story to Black she was irritated, and threatened an end to the deal. But after she took it back to Justice, to her surprise, the deal stuck. Working now through Dohrn's lawyer, Ayers and Dohrn had to submit to new interviews, and explain in them in detail why they misled the FBI in the first ones, since Shaw's defense attorneys would have access to both the original and the new interviews. But the case would go on, with teams of agents gathering as much of the background as they could in their moderately passive mode, minimizing mention of Val Shaw and hurrying to an indictment. At that point, they could go for it, ripping his life apart, piece by piece, adding to the already damning evidence.

* * *

CHAPTER 14: JUNE 1974 — GULF TOWER AND ROOSEVELT AND MARY GRAY

The limo cruised along the Pennsylvania turnpike toward Pittsburgh; the driver pulled into the truck-stop town of Breezewood so he and Val could get coffee. Val pulled out Dom's note to see what was in store. It still started, "Good Morning, Mr. Phelps," and then went on: "Pittsburgh, top jazz club, the Encore, Will Shiner is adding an early folk lineup to get the nearby college crowd in. You open for Chris Smither. Two nights, 6 and 8. But stick around for the 10 and 12 — nobody blows a bone like Harold Betters. Guaranteed. Like you, a family man — he won't leave home, or you'd have heard of him!"

Chris Smither, now that'll be fun, Val thought. A great open-tuning guitar player — he'd heard him backing Bonnie Raitt at a Swarthmore concert after Smither had written her hit, "Love Me Like a Man," but never on his own.

Val had been out of college for a year, and was really doing nothing but being a father. In addition to playing four nights a week at local clubs, either as a solo or a sideman with country-rock bands, he had the half-time job at a state high-school equivalency center, helping drop-outs from 16 to 60 get ready for the General Educational Development test for a high school diploma. It was rewarding work, but rarely successful, since the GED was an SAT-style exam, the same type of learning that had helped drive these folks from high school in the first place. He and Sally had settled in to being the parent a week at a time, Sunday dinner being the trade time, so Nat could go off to Head Start each Monday under a new regime. No switching, the plan known months in advance, so Dom knew which weeks not to book travel gigs.

As predicted by the New York record executive, nobody had wanted to produce a first album of somebody who wouldn't tour on it, so Val and Dom found an independent presser, and just split all the sales from the road. After the thousand from the first run were down to a hundred, Dom suggested they run another set, but Val asked him to hold off. He wasn't sure how much longer he wanted to perform, even how much longer he wanted to stay in sleepy Swarthmore. A thirst for growth was stirring in him, the sense he'd had during high school, when he just had to get out of the one-horse town, and go somewhere bigger, somewhere more important, somewhere he'd be his own man, and not his parents' son.

Like nearly all his anti-war friends, during college Val had pointedly not prepared for a career, thinking that marching straight into law, medicine, or science, and car payments and a mortgage would be a surrender, an acceptance that life could go on normally as your country burned Viet Nam to a crisp. With no thought for the next step, he took the minimum number of political science courses needed to get a major, and then grazed on whatever sounded interesting in the catalogue: American Indian culture, advanced calculus, intro to engineering, Riemannian geometry, history of migration, the Russian novel, the politics and music of Mozart's era, even consortium courses on dairy cattle and farm math from a nearby Penn State outpost. "Where there's a will, there's a waiver," was his oft-stated motto.

The only course he did much work for was his mother's History of American Political Thought, since she had refused to bend with the times, and still crisply asked students to leave the class and do the readings if they showed in response to her rapid-fire questions that they hadn't. Forced to read carefully, Val started to worship Madison and Hamilton for their constitutional battles the way he'd worshipped Nathan Hale and Lafayette as a boy for their actual battlefield heroics.

The fact that the two key framers disagreed so deeply on the very first constitutional dispute just four years after the convention — whether the words "necessary and proper" were to be read finely to prohibit a national bank or broadly to permit it — made him skeptical of the certainty he heard in the constant debates around town, in the papers, and of course in Congress over the constitutionality of Nixon's actions in the Indochina bombing campaigns, the Watergate break-in and cover-up, and his extended refusal to release the tapes of his White House conversations.

Now Dom's push to press more records had forced Val to consider what he wanted to be doing for the next few years, and he found that it probably wasn't more music and limo trips. The war was ending, that was clear. Nixon's air bombardment had barely contained the North Vietnamese tank offensive in South Viet Nam's northern sector in 1972, and Congress was finally constraining funding for the South's troops. With the end of draft and the sense of an inevitable U.S. defeat, the anti-war movement had collapsed. He hadn't heard of any demonstrations being planned for 1974, despite the actual escalation in combat deaths — mostly South Vietnamese, no longer G.I.'s, under Vietnamization. There was really nothing to do. Maybe it was time to move on, focus on something other than the war.

The limo got in at about five. The Encore was on the east side of Pittsburgh, on Walnut, the entertainment strip near the old Shadyside train station. A poster over the front door proclaimed, "The House that Betters Built," the words emblazoned over a picture of a trim, smiling, elegantly-suited black man with his hands resting on his trombone. Coming from a pretty much all-white town, the first thing Val noticed was that all the staff in the Encore, from kitchen to front door, were black, while all the people in line out front were white. The owner, an elegantly-suited white man named Will Shiner, explained it to him:

"My wife and I were jazz fans, and we just got tired of the long lines at the black and tans, the mixed-race clubs, like the Crawford Grill, Gus Greenlee's old place at Crawford and Wylie. There was more demand than seats, I figured, and here we are, 15 years later! Anyway, my wife and I are the exception: jazz is still mostly a Negro thing in Pittsburgh. We have a big colored middle-class, and they do love their jazz. So my patrons and staff are pretty much all colored, and that's actually why I'm starting these early folk shows: two big universities nearby, full of white kids who love music, but jazz isn't their thing.

"First I tried to mix the shows, put a folksinger on as an opener for Harold, but that was a disaster. Not as bad as the time I booked Smokey Robinson and Donovan for a show at U. Pitt, and the colored kids started screaming "Where the ** is Smokey?" as soon as Donovan took the stage in a white robe, walking through paths of rose-petals, which I had to provide by contract. He walked off in tears...But still, it just didn't work here: when one act would finish, half the crowd would just walk out. So now we've started separate shows, move 'em out after the two white shows. You'll see the effect when Harold comes on for his 10 o'clock."

Val made his own stab at racial tolerance, ending his sets with *American Girl, American Man*, a song he'd written the year before, but didn't have room for on the album. It referred to the mayhem caused by 17-year-old Jonathan Jackson when he took hostages at the Marin County courthouse in 1970 to exchange for his brother, literary lion and famed "Soledad brother" George Jackson. George had gone to prison at 20 for armed robbery, and his sentence had been extended indefinitely for violence against guards and other inmates. Earlier in that year he had been charged with a capital crime in the killing of a guard as retaliation for the shooting deaths of three inmates during a riot.

Jonathan's raid left four dead — the boy himself, two conspiring Black Panther prisoners, and a judge to whose neck the kidnappers had affixed a shotgun — and an assistant district attorney paralyzed by a police ricochet after he grabbed one of Jackson's other guns and shot some of the kidnappers. Angela Davis, a Communist Party revolutionary who had bought the guns for Jonathan and was rumored to have been his lover, was later acquitted of all charges in the kidnapping before resuming her career as a professor.

> American woman, American girl,
> Dishes in the sink, now what do you think, has happened to your world?
> You gave all your love to just one man, and he loved someone else.
> Don't you think it's finally time you learned to love yourself?
>
> And to them you are, just one more, armed black punk and teenage whore.
> But all of you is a part of me, cloud to rain and river to the sea.
>
> American boy, American man,
> Standing in the courtroom, with your gun in your hand.
> You only loved your brother, and you had to set him free.
> Now he's gone and so are you, never more to be.
>
> And to them you are, just one more, armed black punk and teenage whore.
> But all of you is a part of me, cloud to rain and river to the sea.

Val had written the song with the attitude that Jackson was a hero. He hadn't felt a need even to read the details of the escape attempt. Taking up the gun for the Black Panthers was reason enough to be considered a hero, and family loyalty just added to the aura. And as he jokingly told Melissa when he first played her the song, "At least he died happy: what other 17-year-old got to live out the fantasy we all had, ** Angela Davis?" Val's automatic affection for Jackson was typical in that time of Kent and Jackson State of the radical left and even liberals: supporters of Angela Davis' defense included hundreds of local committees around the world, Beatle John and Beatles-wrecker Yoko, the California Federation of Teachers, and the United Presbyterian Church.

A year later, when George Jackson was also gunned down while trying to escape, Val started to sing Bob Dylan's popular paean to him, along with "American Girl." There too he never bothered to read the horrific details about the three guards and two white inmates who were slaughtered when Jackson used a smuggled gun to take over a wing of San Quentin prison. It was enough that Jackson was supposed to have said, "The dragon has come," when he first drew the gun, referencing a poem of Ho Chi Minh's from his incarceration by the French colonialists: "When the prison doors are opened, the real dragons will fly out."

Val's attitude was instinctive, of a piece with the songs he sang about Jesse James and Pretty Boy Floyd, and with his belief that John Brown was the greatest white person who ever lived. The hundreds of non-violent white liberals who refused to tell the FBI the whereabouts of the Weathermen shared the same instinct.

After his opener, Val watched the first set of the white main act. Chris Smither had brought his own top picker, another tall guy named John Bailey, and the two lanky figures seemed to fill the whole stage. As soon as they started on the Stones' "No Expectations" with booming twin open-tuned guitars, Val was unconsciously stealing the tunings and riffs so he could play the song the next week in Swarthmore.

But then the barmaid who brought him his 12-ounce strip steak, the claimed house specialty, occupied all of his attention. Her mini-Afro implied a lack of interest in anybody but brothers. After six hours of intermittent chats as she kept him fresh in his "working-man's screwdrivers" of orange juice and ginger ale while he watched Harold Betters almost literally blow the crowd away with his trademark, "Blow Your Horn," it was clear that she would be willing to make an exception this night. Her name was Julia, and she was a pre-med student at Carnegie-Mellon who had transferred back home to the Hill District after two years at all-black Cheney State. She didn't shy away from talking about the elephant in the room of America, of the bar, and of her and Val's flirting: race.

Julia brought it up as they talked under crisp sheets in her dorm room: "It's everything, it's everywhere, it bonds me to every so-called Negro, and I like to say African-American, because Negro means black, and color is the least of it. We're a tribe, and we're treated that way not just by ourselves but by every white person. You can never be in the tribe — tonight was fine fun, but we're just visiting, we can never understand each other. It'd be like a Vietnamese girl really falling for a G.I. — your people killed my people and took my freedom for no good reason and there's too much bad blood to make a life together.

"You know, I went to an integrated school, Schenley High, on the white down-slope after Sugar Top, the peak that separates the black Hill District in the west from the white parts of town to the east. That was my school because my family was part of the lighter and wealthier crowd that lived up near Sugar Top, while the darker and poorer you were, the farther west and down the hill you lived. I had lots of white girlfriends, but the guys, forget it — I wasn't givin' nothin' up to them.

"You notice the Saigon girls aren't coming home with the troops, white or black, like the German and Italian girls did after World War II. They knew their government had been wrong, but the Vietnamese know that Ho was right. And I know that even the liberal whites sold us out at the convention in 1787 as the price of the nation, and again in 1876 when the Republicans gave up Reconstruction in a bargain for the presidency. Can't trust y'all, that's the fact."

"You damn skippy," Val laughed, in his best ghetto accent. "Anyway, you're just channeling my hero Alexander Hamilton: he knew he did it, he hated to do it, he always tried to make up for it with manumission societies...but he did it, all right! Still, you know I'll ache for you, probably write a whole new album about how much! But what about John Brown, could he have been your true love, a man who laid it all on the line for Negroes, I mean African-Americans?"

"Funny," replied Julia. "And Negroes was indeed the polite term back then. Maybe someone like that, yeah, he's an honorary brother. Look, there are even some of them out there now, you know. The Weathermen are white, but they bombed prison offices after Attica, and tried to kill the judge in the Panther 21 case. You sang about Jonathan Jackson tonight, that was when I first cottoned to you. The Weathermen bombed that courthouse after he was murdered, and other courts after George was murdered the next year. Hey, earlier this year they bombed a welfare office in San Francisco over the sterilization of black women.

"And now they're local heroes, too: did you hear about their Gulf Tower bombing two weeks ago? That's our famous building that has different lights for different weather forecasts? 'You have 17 minutes to clear the building... the bomb is in the cavernous underground' — but the cops and firemen went in, couldn't find anything in the basement, and then had just gone past the 29th floor when the bomb, which had been there all the time, destroyed the entire floor. The Weathermen's communiqué was all about African freedom fighters, and Gulf giving oil revenues to the Portuguese colonial army. Me going to Carnegie-Mellon, you know I'm down with that: Gulf is part of the Andrew Mellon fortune. Now, any little white Weatherman who pulled that off, maybe I could throw in with him!"

Val pulled her lithe body closer: "Good, Angela Davis, but for now, throw in with me again!"

* * *

The two assassins met at 2 o'clock Sunday morning at the fringe of a darkened parking lot at the Three Rivers baseball stadium. The Pirates were off on a two-week road trip to the west coast, so the site was deserted. The other killings had all been solo acts in the deed, although not in scouting and planning, but placing and arming a bomb under a car was definitely a two-person task.

Roosevelt Gray had been easy to track as he drove his sports car each day from his home in suburban Homestead, across the Monongahela, and eight miles north-west to the Gulf Tower and back — always under the speed limit. It was actually the regularity of his schedule, and his limited deviations from it, that led to the decision to use a bomb. The design was completely different from that of the Gulf Tower dynamite charge, which had used an alarm clock. This one was a hair-trigger weapon, with a wooden block breaking the circuit. The block would be replaced with a spring after the bomb was planted and activated under the front seat of Gray's car. The first big pothole, and boom!

Gray was the director of exploration for Gulf Oil, and without a doubt the highest-ranking African-American in any Fortune 500 company that didn't sell music or hair products. His parents, share-croppers in Mississippi, had sent him to live with an uncle in New York at ten so he could pursue the obvious academic talents that his teachers at the Rosenwald school in nearby Pass Christian admitted they could no longer challenge. Roosevelt aced the exam from junior high to high school, and graduated from the Bronx High School of Science in 1950.

He took a North Carolina A and T degree in math, and then a Cornell degree in engineering physics brought him into Gulf's world through the recommendation of a friendly professor. Dale Corson was white, like the rest of the department and indeed the entire faculty, but had gone out of his way to make sure Gray and the smattering of African and Asian foreign students got the same fellowships, summer positions, and job placements through alumni as the white ones. When he became Cornell's president 20 years later, Corson made more formal affirmative action his hallmark. Gray had risen swiftly, working mostly in Africa and Latin America, until he was brought back to headquarters in 1970.

Gray returned to America with his much younger wife Halim, an English language graduate from the British-copy University of Khartoum who had been his translator on a Sudanese exploration, and they now had twin five-year-old girls. The marriage had been arranged in the African way, as a contract between families, with lengthy meetings and negotiations between his uncle, whom he had flown over to represent him, and the eldest men in her extended family. During the month of negotiations, Halim had stayed with the women of her family, and she and Roosevelt had not seen each other until the marriage documents had been signed by his uncle and her elders, and sanctioned by an Imam. That, rather than a public pledge by the couple, had constituted the wedding.

Some of the conditions in the contract Roosevelt intended to meet, such as converting to Islam, not divorcing unless every signatory or their heirs approved, and paying a broker $2,000 to deliver 20 acceptable dairy cows to Halim's family. Other conditions he and Halim secretly agreed to ignore after they arrived in America, including that Halim and the girls, when they became teenagers, go covered with at least a half-hijab, that the couple accept any Sharia court's death penalty if either renounced Islam for another religion, and that they send their children to an Islamic school if they moved to America.

Halim had argued strongly against the condition on schooling, since it was actually contrary to her Sudanese experience, but the elders had insisted on it as a way to maintain their faith in a country where only one percent of the people practiced Islam — the converse of the percentage in the Sudan. After Lord Kitchener had led an expedition to Khartoum in 1898 to avenge the Mahdi Muhammad's defeat and execution of General Gordon and his 7,000-man Egyptian army in 1885, he established one of the few benefits of British rule in Sudan, which otherwise focused on extracting cotton, oil seeds, and gum Arabic, the key to Coca-Cola, from farmers at the lowest possible prices: non-religious, coeducational schools and colleges in the major cities, with admission to each succeeding level based on Oxbridge-style admission tests. Only the top few percent on the college test, like Halim, were admitted to the U of K, and it was a point of national pride that being a woman there was neither a rarity nor a handicap.

While they wanted their daughters to experience a full American education and life, the Grays did keep the faith by attending mosque in Pittsburgh every Friday evening at al-Masjid al-Awwal, the self-titled "first Muslim mosque." The mosque had been founded in the early 20th century by descendants of the quarter of all American slaves who were Muslim when they had been seized in West Africa. It was largely Salafi in orientation, while Halim, like most Sudanese, was Sufi, but it was still mainstream enough for her, especially compared to the first mosque they had sampled, Mosque 22 of the black separatist sect, the Nation of Islam.

Halim had been stunned to see Louis Farrakhan emerge onto the stage of Mosque 22, since she had been taught in Khartoum that he was the murderer of Malcolm X, who had visited Sudan in 1959 and was venerated there because of his later conversion to mainstream Islam. It was well-known in Sudan that Malcolm's burial after his assassination had been guided by the Sudanese sheik Ahmed, his spiritual advisor and one of the first teachers in Malcolm's post-NOI mosque. Seeing Farrakhan, Halim had immediately risen from the women's seats and caught Roosevelt's eye in the men's section. They met in the aisle and pointedly walked out together.

Homestead had a black, largely middle-class residential area, stretching back to the days of its famed Negro League baseball team, the Grays. The team had actually started in 1912 as a collection of black steel-workers from that neighborhood. By 1920, though, the Grays were fully professional and playing their "home" games at the Pirates' stadium in Pittsburgh or, for about half of the games after1940, in Washington, DC.

This Gray had chosen Homestead over Andover Terrace, the elite black neighborhood in the Hill district in Pittsburgh proper, on a whim: the shoeshine man who was snapping outside the Gulf Tower the day Roosevelt started his new job raved about the long-defunct Grays, and castigated the other Negro League team, the Pittsburgh Crawfords. Apparently the Crawfords, owned by legendary black numbers man, informal banker, and Crawford Grill proprietor Gus Greenlee, had abandoned the city for Toledo in 1940.

Homestead's population of 20,000 during U.S. Steel's heyday had fallen to 6,000 by 1970, and most of the flight had been white. The Grays purchased and lovingly restored a declining mansion on still-white East 11th Avenue, near one of the first of the thousands of public libraries Andrew Carnegie had built with tax-free profits from the empire he started at the steel mill in Homestead. Their grounds stretched half a city block, and this June night the house was hidden from street view by a forest of azalea bushes in full flower.

The two-seat Mercedes Benz W-113 convertible on the left side of the large garage was Roosevelt's pride and joy, a souvenir of his time in Caracas. The scout had watched him wash and wax the Benz with his two daughters each of the previous four Saturday mornings, before taking them, in turn, for a spin around the neighborhood. On Sundays, it sat idle, because the family only fit in his wife's staid Ford station wagon when they went out for their weekly diner breakfast and walk. The diner was always the same, as was the walk, through the informal park that had sprung up between the rail lines and the river near the now single-shifting steel mill.

The killers parked a mile away from the house on 11th, a block down the street from a still-busy all-night diner, and took turns carrying the suitcase containing the 30-pound bomb frame. They never started down a block unless it was empty of all traffic, and twice they ducked behind a hedge when a car turned onto the street. The garage was open in the mild summer night, and they quickly reversed their coats and slipped under the side and the front of the Mercedes. One assassin held up the bomb frame while the other, the bomb-maker, affixed its four epoxy pads and then carefully removed the block and replaced it with the spring. The final step was to switch on the current, sending the bomb live.

The two assassins retraced their steps to their car and headed back towards Pittsburgh. They had no way of knowing that Halim Gray was developing a cold, and would ask if she could stay in bed Sunday morning, or that Roosevelt would be in an uncharacteristically spontaneous mood, and decide to leave the Ford, and strap the twins together into the front seat of the Benz when he took them to the diner.

War Report: Nathan Hale Brigade

Yesterday we served justice on Roosevelt Gray, Gulf Oil's director of exploitation, just like the Weather Underground served justice on his employer three weeks ago. As Chairman Huey P. Newton has often said, the uncle tomming house nigger has existed since slavery, and pork-chop cultural nationalism does not protect boot-lickers any more than the pigs whose boots they lick.

What is it about Pittsburgh that attracts anti-imperialist attacks? First the Weather-women launched their "jail-break" at the high schools in 1969 because of imperialist indoctrination, then the Weatherman Gulf Tower bombing in May, and now we have imposed justice for Gray's and Gulf's repression and exploitation of the colonial peoples.

Is it Pittsburgh's history as the center of the first revolt against the Amerikan project of continental and then Pacific and then global domination? Founding racist, capitalist imperialists — oh, sorry, we forgot that Lenin teaches us that these are redundant terms, that one requires the others — Washington and Hamilton had to bring overwhelming force, all the American militias, to Pittsburgh to put down the righteous Whiskey rebellion, a protest against regressive taxation. Or is it Pittsburgh's history as the first center of revolt against capitalist monopoly, the Homestead steel strike in

1892,which again took an Army to break after the Amalgamated Association union defeated Andrew Carnegie's Pinkerton guards in pitched combat?

Actually, the point for all of Amerika is that there's nothing special about Pittsburgh — you could pick any city, even any crossroads in America, and find a deep connection to imperialism. Here it is Gulf Oil's millions for the Portuguese colonial army, to back their slaughter of the Angolan freedom fighters.

But every Amerikan is guilty of the same crime, because our government funds this repressive war too, with arms and aircraft for our charming Portuguese NATO ally. Gotta hold onto that airbase in the Azores, so we can move troops everywhere we want! Be warned! Think through what your city or county does to promote empire, and stop it, or we are coming to find the criminal masterminds there.

Carnegie tried to cover his sins by building all sorts of libraries and centers for international peace, but he and his heirs are still imperialist enemies of the people. His henchman in the Homestead massacre, Frick, build all sorts of fancy museums, but his heirs too are still on our Emma Goldman list — she almost got him, but we won't fail.

The Pittsburgh Press claims that "Nobody with any sense is listening" to the Weatherman — well, for your own sakes, we hope that's wrong. It's time to choose a side. There are no good Germans!

We do regret the change in Gray's plans that put his daughters in his fancy sports car. Obviously we did not intend to kill one five-year-old and wound another. Of course, that makes us sound like U.S. pilots, who dropped three times more tons of bombs on the peasant societies of Indochina than were dropped on industrialized Germany and Japan in all of World War II. So now collateral damage is a problem, because of young Mary Gray? It always was, for the five million Indochinese, mostly civilians, who have died since we started the war in 1945 by bringing back the French imperialist troops as part of our drive for global domination. Maybe now you'll think of your communities as potential "free-fire" zones like the Vietnamese must.

* * *

Dom and Val sat over coffee in the booking office in December of 1974. "Well, I guess this is it, then," said Dom. "You're sure about this?"

"Yeah," Val replied, "it's time. I've got the assistantship for as long as the degree takes, and I don't feel any need to wait. Starting in January is as easy as starting next September — the core courses are offered each semester, so why not head down now and get it going?"

Val's mother had reached out to one of her former students, now a professor at the University of North Carolina, and he'd guided Val into a Ph.D. program in political science. There was a housing allowance, full tuition, and $5,000 in stipends for being a teaching and then research assistant about 20 hours a week. Altogether, it was probably more than he was making in the music business, and the hours were a lot nicer. The only issue had been Nat, but Sally was remarried with another child, and she hadn't argued against him spending school years with Val and Christmas and summers with her.

"But look, do me a favor, as you leave music behind: I have one last gig, perfect, just came in, for a Louisiana party in DC. February, the Friday after Mardi Gras. My pal Gary at the Birchmere there, great folk place, musician's dream, no talking, no TVs on during sets, he's put out a general call for an opening act with Louisiana themes — and I know you play some Cajun accordion, since you saw that documentary and sent down to Marc Savoy for one."

"Let me think on that. Is it a long way from Chapel Hill?"

"Come on, can't you handle one time without a limo? Hop on the bus, Gus, or just drive straight up through Richmond. Hell, your hero Ralph Stanley goes twice as far just to get home to the Clinch Mountains every night!"

And so it was that on Friday morning, February 14, Val was driving his Ford Pinto north to DC, the small back seat filled with instrument cases, on the way to his last gig.

* * *

Just two weeks earlier Daniel Parker, the Administrator of the Agency for International Development, the U.S. government's "foreign aid" program, was taking a meeting in the State Department with Clarence Kelly, the director of the FBI, and a grim-faced aide. The smell of burned plastic was still in the air from a bombing two floors below his office the day before.

Parker was 48 years old and had no particular expertise in international development outside of running his grandfather's Parker Pen corporation, which had some overseas sales. He had been appointed by Nixon to the AID job two years before as a reward for his fund-raising stint as vice president of the finance committee of the Committee to Re-Elect the President, the infamous CREEP of the Watergate scandal.

"Dan, we have to talk about security plans for you and your people. There's too strong a pattern of east coast bombings by these Weathermen being followed by an even more radical group coming along a few weeks later and targeting, and indeed succeeding in killing, what they call 'the highest-ranking person to use the bathroom' that Weatherman blows up. For this bombing, that's probably you. Now, I assume you read through the bombers' statement to the press? AID's no charity, just a counter-insurgency arm of Kissinger's, training South Vietnam's brutal police, putting people in concentration camps, Food for Peace sold by the army so it's Food for War, AID paying the government's entire non-military budget so it can use all its taxes to pay the army, on and on?"

Parker smiled and sighed. "Yes, I did, Clarence, and it was pathetic. Twelve pages to say we're all imperialists, and the North Vietnamese and Fidel Castro and some guy who blew off a judge's head with a shotgun are all angels. These people, when they were students for a democratic society, do you think they ever went to class? They ought to come to our earthquake meetings for emergency aid in Central America or our planning sessions for power plants in Africa that can clean water to bring down disease and death rates.

"Those are the offices they destroyed! Wait, I wrote down their key line for a speech I'm going to give to our staff: 'Our intention is to disrupt the empire...to make it hard to carry out its bloody functioning against the people of the world.' Housing and electricity, that's the bloody functioning of an empire? Listen, writing a check to the South Vietnamese government, a check our democratic government tells me to write, that's just about the smallest part of my workday. If it's wrong, if they're so right, it should be easy for them to convince voters, and then I won't be writing the check.

"As a matter of fact, the irony here is that democracy already worked. It's clear from newspaper tallies already: no thanks to these bozos, Congress isn't going to give Ford the $500 million in extra aid for Viet Nam they're complaining about anyway, and they probably know it! My son Geoff called to tell me what this is about, a Bob Dylan song that says, 'The pump won't work 'cause the vandals took the handle.' Well, vandals is right. It's not the war, the war's virtually over. It's our way of governing, majority rule, that they're after. They want to rule, and they can't stand that people disagree."

Parker took a breath and stopped. "Ah, well, sorry about going off like that, just working out my speech, apparently. Look, Clarence, back to the point of your visit: as a company president I've had my own security, and as corporate entertainer-in-chief Sally has had her own house staff, with its own security, for 20 years. I doubt people who are stupid enough to write this crap are going to penetrate our world, especially with my State Department security stuck on top of it all."

"Well, that raises two possibilities," said Kelly. "First, you're right, so the Nathan Hale Brigade, as the killers call themselves, does what it has done three times before: they recognize your security profile, give up, and pick out a subordinate who doesn't have protection. That's happened now to Gulf Oil, IT &T, and a general here in DC. Second, you're wrong, and despite your security they have a plan to come calling. That's what happened to Congressman Hébert in 1971 — they left him alone at work or on his social rounds, where he had Capitol police, and got him in his house, at night.

"Now the first case, I think it's the most likely, so I want you to notify your top staff, the appointed assistant administrators, for sure, but go a level deeper than that. They need to know the threat, they need to come in for a group briefing with us on protective measures and what we can offer. Certainly we'll work with the local police to watch them and their houses at night for the next month. Agent Grier here will handle all the logistics with your staff.

"But let's not dismiss the second case so quickly. Grier will arrange for our protection team to review routines with your private and State Department folks, and I want their full cooperation, and yours. Just between us, we really have no workable leads on either the bombings or the assassinations. Fortunately, our analysts think that this is probably a last gasp.

"Despite the claims of the Weathers in an endless manifesto last year called *Prairie Fire*, they're not gearing up for an expansion. The draft is over, now the war is pretty much over, Ford's not going to get his request from this Congress, and South Vietnam will go the way of history. And so will the Weathers with their dream of inspiring a popular revolt. It's clear to us that they are down to a handful, maybe less than ten, maybe even five people from the thirty they started bombing with in 1970.

"And these folks, for all their education, never even learned how to blow things up properly. You know the Oakland Defense Department office they talked about in the 12-page manifesto? It was a federal building with a recruiting office — and the bomb never went off — they had to call back in the morning and give its location. The bomb squad carried it ticking to the street and blew it up with a rifle shot. Dumb ** ! There's another ten people these 'we never harm people' ** could have killed. Unfortunately, this Nathan Hale group doesn't seem to have the same level of incompetence. Assume the worst, Dan. Be careful, OK?"

* * *

Val got confused by some construction at the Capital beltway as he drove north from Richmond and ended up coming into town from the west, on the George Washington Parkway. He chuckled when he recalled how easy it all had been when he'd had a driver. Across the Potomac River Val saw the Georgetown Waterfront where he'd played the Bayou with Aztec, the Kennedy Center, and the Lincoln Memorial, where he'd gone during the '69 Mobe and where Nixon had bizarrely gone early one morning the next year during the Kent State protests to try to connect with sleepy protestors. He drove past the hated Pentagon and looked across the river to the DC Waterfront and Fort McNair, where he'd gone during his last DC gig.

Val finally came to Four Mile Drive, and after a few miles heading into the sun he pulled up in a shopping center parking lot, in front of a rundown storefront that looked altogether too small to be the famed Birchmere. Apparently angry Emmy Harris had worked out her equal pay issues with the Seldom Scene, because the marquee read: "Special Mardi Gras Show: The Seldom Scene, Featuring Emmy Lou Harris!!" In smaller letters underneath: "With Valerius — Cajun Accordian." Well, he wasn't gonna do two 30-minute sets just with the accordion, but it was nice to get a plug with that gang.

Emmy Lou was a much bigger deal now, a national country-rock star known for recording and touring with Gram Parsons, right before he overdosed. She told Val that she had an album coming out that month, *Pieces of the Sky*, and that the *Scene* would be backing her on one track from it that had a Cajun beat, *Queen of the Silver Dollar*. She was about to go on a national tour with her "hot band" of top country pickers like guitarist James Burton that her label had put together. Then she and the band would record another album from their road material before the end of the year. "So, you still want to trade paychecks with the *Seldom Scene*?" Val laughed.

"Ah, good memory!" Emmy Lou shook her head. "When was that, '72? Man, I was pissed at the owner, really, not them! But that's all forgotten now. We're pals, still, and when they asked me to help out with this little party, I was glad I was gonna be in town anyway, visiting my mom and daughter. But tell me, are you really done, this is it?"

"Yeah, I found out you all-stars' nasty little secret when I tried to pitch my record. I realized I'm a stay-at-home dad, not a road dog, and that's it. So, I'm off to graduate school, political science. Lots of fine pickers down in the Carolinas, though. Some even called Earl! I'm not worried about having fun playing once in a while, but never for a living again."

The Birchmere looked small, but somehow it fit in the couple hundred people who had found it hidden in the suburbs. It was a great night to end on. Val started his first set with a few Cajun accordian songs, from an old Amédé Ardoin record from the 1920s, the *Eunice Two-Step* and *Allons à Lafayette*:

Eh, quoi faire, jolie? Comment je va se faire, tu m'abandonné!
Comment je va se faire, 'tite fille jolie?
Toi, tu fais du mal.
(Hey, what'd you do, sugar? What am I gonna do, you abandoned me!
What am I gonna do, sweet little girl?
You, you done me wrong.)

Allons à Lafayette, c'est pour changer ton nom
On va t'appeler madam, madam canaille comme moi.
Petit t'es trop mignone pour faire ta criminelle
Comment tu crois mais moi, je peux faire moi tout seul.

(Let's go to Lafayette, just to change your name
You'll become Mrs. Rascal, taking my name.
Little one, you're too sweet to play such a criminal toward me.
How do you think it will be for me, what will I do all alone?)

The Scene then put on a great first set, including a bluegrass version of *Sweet Georgia Brown* featuring dobro master Mike Auldridge, by day a graphic artist for the *Washington Star*, by night a countrified magician in his legendary cut-creased blue jeans and can't-be-too-pointy boots, and creative banjoist Ben Eldridge, who looked every bit the frumpy mathematician at a dam-designing firm he was by day. In addition to Shel Silverstein's *Queen of the Silver Dollar* they helped Harris try out a few other Cajun-tinged songs her new-found acquaintances in the country and rock pantheons had been writing for her: Rodney Crowell's *Leavin' Louisiana in the Broad Daylight*, Willie Nelson's *Sister's Comin' Home*, and Robbie Robertson's *Evangeline*.

Val closed his second set by telling the audience that this was his last performance, and by playing a song he'd written showing that he'd had amateur status all along. He told them how he'd once asked a woman he was trying to romance how she liked a song he'd written about her. She'd shrugged, unimpressed, and said it was "just another country-western, rock n' roll love song," so he'd immediately sat down and written on a cocktail napkin another song based on that line:

Here comes just another country-western, rock n' roll love song
From just another country-western, rock n' roll man
It may be slightly out of tune, but you can't miss the 4/4 time
And you won't have to strain your brain to read between the lines

Smooth and simple, just like I thought it would be
If you would bring heaven to hell and fall for me
   But just when I thought I was being saved by you
   You said, hey boy, there's a woman over here,
can't you see that she needs it too?
   (That's when I opened my eyes)

Now I'm thinking of you, the way I should, for the very first time
But you still think you can guess all the words, half-way through the line
   So if I happen to lose a beat, somewhere in
the bar [here, Val did drop a beat]
   Keep on clappin' like you know what you're
doin' til we figure out where we are
   (Keep on tryin')

So that was just another country-western, rock n' rollin'
Sharin', tryin', reachin', hidin', carin', lyin' love song
To my surprise you knew the ending, all along
   Now must my voice always ring out alone, echoing the man?
   Don't close the door on me just when I'm startin' to understand
   (At least I think I am...)

When Val left the stage after the second set, Harris hugged him and said, "Well, I hope it worked on her — it sure worked on me! Stick around?" Val, stunned at this turn of events, stood in place for a few seconds, but finally worked up the courage to look her in the eye and say, "Well, ain't this a test of my emergency broadcasting system! Bad timing, bad timing, ma chère, but 'I have promises to keep, and miles to go before I sleep.' Gotta head home to my son — I think I've finally met the one, her name's Selam, and she's with him."

Harris laughed: "Well, thanks for that level of detail! You really are done with this business, aren't you? I'll have to put you down in my book of regrets, with Gram. Well, here we go." She strode out onto the stage, to the wild cheers of the crowd, and out of Val's life forever.

* * *

It was 11 o'clock that night, 30 minutes after Val had come off stage at the Birchmere and briefly disappointed Emmy Harris. The assassin parked on a dark side-street off of Connecticut Avenue in northwest Washington, took the rifle bag from the trunk, walked through shadowed sidewalks to the Howard Law School, and then went carefully down the steep open field behind it, reducing the imprint by walking softly in crusted sledding tracks.

Fifty yards into the woods was the spot with a perfect view down onto the back of the Parker mansion on the road that ran along Broad Branch creek. The range read 550 yards, and the slight wind registered on the gauge at eight miles per hour, 45 degrees left of zero, so it was an easy calculation: just 5 clicks on the scope. Focusing in on the back porch, the killer waited. Ten minutes later, just as predicted, out came the men for their cigars. Probably Cuban, an extra, ironic pleasure for the above-the-law imperialists, thought the shooter.

But it wasn't a group of men, as predicted — it was clearly an intimate dinner for two couples, not the regular Saturday night production that had been Sally Parker's trademark for two decades of corporate and now government entertaining. What? Looking into the scope, the killer was shocked, actually feeling a physical jolt. Standing there in the floodlight, right where the scout said Parker liked to take his evening cigar during the Saturday parties, wasn't just Parker, but, incredibly, the number one devil himself, Secretary of State (or was it National Security Advisor, or both?) Henry Kissinger. And now it got worse: after them, contrary to all the scouting, bundled in their coats against the February chill, out came their elegantly dressed and coiffed wives. Nancy Kissinger, his recent bride but decade-long acquaintance through her foreign policy job with his patron, Nelson Rockefeller, was easy to recognize from pictures in the newspapers. At six feet she stood out over the others on the porch.

Holy ** ! Abort because of the extra security that would be there for Kissinger? Take them both? Unlikely — the first shot would make the other one move. Complete the mission with just Parker, to go with the communiqué, all written and ready to be mailed to the *New York Times'* Washington bureau? ** , this was to be the last mission. Think, think!

Never wait once you have the shot — that's the hunter's rule. So there wasn't any time to think. Rote took over: Parker was the shot. Just like a listening deer, no movement, no need to lead. A gentle squeeze, a firm hand on the stock, and it was done. Run, run, to the car — screw the footprints in the snow. By design, they were two sizes too big anyway, stuffed with socks like Mick Jagger's show pants. The time to the car had been timed at 2:30 for the shooter by foot and four minutes for bodyguards by car, but in the snow it was slower going. Run!

War Report: Nathan Hale Brigade

Again our Weather brothers and sisters have shied away from true combat, true revolution. AID was the right target, a central part of imperialism, masquerading as American goodness, playing cynically on humanitarian emotion while running the same old wars, the same old counter-insurgencies. AID is to the Pentagon what the Peace Corps is to the Green Berets: a soft face for the same hard repression. Remember, JFK founded the Peace Corps and the Green Berets on the same day, for the same purpose: imperialist rule in the Third World.

And so was Daniel Parker the right target. He's the head running dog at AID, whose only credentials for the job were being born rich, raising money for Nixon's dirty tricks team, and being a skulking pilot-fish of the low-roading National Association of Manufacturers and the outrageously-named Better Business Bureaus, lobbyists for imperialist trade agreements.

As an hereditary capitalist, picked for leadership by the affirmative action of lineage, not talent, Parker claimed that the "enlightened self-interest" of corporations is "greater than pure altruism." Greater for whom? Not the working people of the Third World. To everybody in management at imperialist corporations, to everybody on Wall Street who trades their stocks, to every banker who holds their cash, and to all the worker bees at AID, the State Department, the Defense Department, the White House, the Congress, the captive universities, or any other place backing the empire in opposition to the world's liberation movements, we say: remember the dogs Daniel Parker and Lucy Van Oss, the pigs Congressman Hébert and General Hemmings, the ethnic traitors Victor Iglesias and Roosevelt Gray. This is just the beginning. If you want to avoid revolutionary justice, tell your bosses to get out of the business of empire. Learn what those six no longer have the chance to learn: live by the sword, die by the sword.

* * *

CHAPTER 16: MAY 2017 — THE INDICTMENT

"*Prima facie*, this is a mess," James Purpose, the federal prosecutor for the District of Columbia, said as he started the conference call with his peers in Pittsburgh, Boston, and New York. "But there's a simple solution: the local D.A.'s agree to wait on indicting on their three cases until we've finished with the three federal ones.

"You see, the easiest way to handle it is to simply drag the facts for the three state murders into our DC federal case, but not charge for them, since they aren't under our purview. We'd have to walk a fine line, working with the judge and bending over backwards, to avoid creative appeals on prejudice, double jeopardy, whatever. But I can't see any Supreme Court, for the assassination of a congressman and a general, ruling that the travel evidence and the three private deaths aren't relevant to the conspiracy element. That means you have to ask the local D.A.'s to hold up, and not charge for now.

"I know they're not going to like it, hell, they never do. But if they balk, tell them that we would have problems anyway providing them with our evidence until the appeals end, which is essentially never. So they'd have to build their own cases. No need to point out the financial commitment to do that. They'll know that already. My guess is that if we get convictions, they'll just let it go. Let them know we'd appreciate them saying that in advance. It'll make our argument for detailing the private cases even stronger. And for God's sake remind them to keep this to themselves until the arrest."

Purpose and the other three men on the line had recently been appointed by President Trump after Sessions had asked for the blanket resignations of federal prosecutors. They had been successful Republican county D.A.'s, and they had all unhappily been on the losing side of such spats with Justice. But where you stand depends on where you sit, was the Washington saying, and their background actually made them better ambassadors for the deal than federal careerists.

A week later, the local D.A.'s submitted their written intentions not to seek indictments if the federal case resulted in a sentence of life or the death penalty, with guarantees of prior notice of parole hearings in sufficient time to allow intervention. That way they could promise their voters: he's never getting out of prison alive. Purpose then convened a grand jury in the E. Barrett Prettyman courthouse a few blocks away from his office.

All 23 members showed up for the five days it took to take testimony from Val's SDS friend Thad Leslie, who had heard and reported Shaw's assassination promise to the Weathermen, Bill Ayers and Bernardine Dohrn, who described John Jacobs' advocacy of assassination, and Alice Truxton, the member of the Boston collective who had identified Shaw to Dohrn in 1975 as Jacob's partner from the 1970 bombing and assassination attempt. Tying it all together was the lead FBI investigator, Mar'Shae McGurk. Director Comey had been fired by Trump earlier in the month, but the case he'd built for the president soldiered on.

Art Thomas, Shaw's roommate from Chicago, had told Black he remembered nothing of 47-year-old conversations, and so wasn't called to testify. She was sure he was lying, but she respected, and indeed had expected, an African-American's refusal to put any sort of finger on his old friend. With him it probably wasn't the "snitches get stitches and wind up in ditches" survival skills from her 'hood she was seeing, but rather a deep middle-class skepticism that whites would be pursuing justice, the pro-O.J. phenomenon.

Purpose went easy on Ayers and Dohrn, since with no defense attorney present there was no need to explain the whole mess of the initially misleading statements to the FBI about expelling John Jacobs. Credibility was going to be a problem with them, given their years of living underground with false identities, and their self-serving tales after surfacing of always having been humanitarian bombers, in contrast to wicked J. J. and the Townhouse collective. Purpose preferred to wait until trial to rough them up, and defuse dramatic defense "discoveries" of their brazen falsehoods. In contrast, he treated

Black's testimony as he would in the jury trial, to get her used to the way he would anticipate the defense attack, and explain away possible inconsistencies with her before turning her over for cross-examination.

"Now Agent McGurk, other than at an initial meeting described by Ms. Laurel, the only testified sighting of Mr. Shaw in the company of Mr. Jacobs, the publicly-expelled but privately operational bomb-planner for the Weathermen, was at a failed assassination attempt of a Professor Huntington in Cambridge, Massachusetts, in October 1970. Yet that act isn't requested to be part of the indictment, there being a statute of limitations for such non-lethal crimes. Further, at that time Mr. Shaw had not traveled outside of the Swarthmore area as a musician, while such travels form the entire basis of the proposed indictment.

"So why are you so sure that Mr. Shaw is the murderer of the congressman, the general, and the foreign aid director, as well as the three private citizens, when you have no fingerprints or other physical evidence tying him to the crimes? Isn't this all just circumstantial evidence?"

"Sir, your question misstates our approach to solving crimes," Black responded. She had memorized this answer after Purpose wrote it with her. He expected this line of reasoning to be the core of the defense case, and he needed her to practice defusing it. "It's not like on TV or in the movies. When I investigate cold cases of murders of civil rights workers in the 1960s South, I rarely have surviving witnesses to them. Indeed, for very few murder charges of any type that go to trial is there an open and shut case, with all the evidence, all the witnesses, and all the weaponry available to the authorities. Cases like that usually end in a plea by the defendant, and not a trial.

"No, in most cases in court, juries are asked to decide beyond a reasonable doubt whether what you call circumstantial evidence, like motive, means, opportunity, and previous tendencies, can be explained any other way than by guilt. I've helped bring successful cases for politically and hate-driven murders like these with far less evidence. Here we have motive: the anti-imperialist beliefs that Shaw held then and holds now, the anger at the killing of Fred Hampton, whose bloodied apartment he saw, the pledge to kill instead of protest the Viet Nam war, the reporting of that pledge to the Weathermen.

And we have means and opportunity: in all six murders, Shaw was in the city the very day of the murder, transported by limousine, and he wasn't on stage at the time of death officially established by the coroner. Now, what are the odds of all that happening at random? Far, far less than the standard of five percent chance that courts use in statistical evidence. It's not reasonable to doubt the connection.

"And finally, previous tendencies: we have him working with John Jacobs to try to kill a professor during another Weather bombing, before they worked out the musical appearance and limo ride arrangement. Jacobs continued to set up Weather bombings, by the admission of its leaders, and he planned them around Shaw's schedule. At the same time as Jacobs scouted the bombings he could scout the assassinations — the very crimes that he first advocated to his leadership in 1970."

Purpose's work was more than sufficient for the grand jury, which far exceeded the 12-vote requirement as 20 of the 23 jurors judged that the standard of "probable" guilt had been met, and voted to return the following "true bill" of indictment:

● Conspiracy to murder a Member of Congress, Felix Hébert.

● First degree murder of a Member of Congress, Felix Hébert.

● First degree murder of a federal official, Major General George Hemmings.

● First degree murder of a federal official, Agency for International Development Administrator Daniel Parker.

All of the charges carried the death penalty, and that is precisely what Purpose would seek. He sent the file over to Jerry Cummings, as the lead agent listed for the case, and instructed him to arrange the arrest. Purpose would have loved to put Shaw in the general population in DC Jail for the duration of the trial, as he knew the U.S. Marshalls did under contract for about half of his cases. But he also didn't want to lose his defendant. Too many petty criminals, by definition contemptuous of government, bizarrely also had a savage patriotic hatred of people who criticized it.

So Purpose added to the file an instruction of "BOP pre-trial cell, Isolation, No Bail." That would put Shaw in a monitored individual cell managed by the Bureau of Prisons, 24 hours a day, either in the basement of Prettyman itself or at the federal courthouse in Alexandria, across the river, where the Al-Qaeda "shoe-bomber" had been held during his trial. Purpose's top aide went off to arrange Shaw's removal from Nashville to the FBI holding facility at Fort Myer in Arlington.

* * *

Bill Coles' email had made its way to Val a few weeks before, just as he finished up his daily writing stint, his four hours, as he liked to tell students asking for advice on writing, chained to his desk like a North Vietnamese tanker chained to his gun. Val was at home, since in his adjunct status, or as he told his friends without admitting to not getting renewed, in his retirement at 65, he no longer had an office on campus.

> Greetings from Swarthmore, Bro: I'm sure the FBI is reading this, but, hey, it's still a free country. Haven't seen you since I bumped into you and your mom at the reunion concert I was working, what, 10 years ago? Well, I found you easy enough on the web, although I see you, like me, don't go for Facebook! Your website stuff looks interesting, and it reminds me of our conversations about politics when we were recording. First time I ever heard the word "imperialism"!

> Anyway, you aren't gonna believe this, because I didn't, but some cute little FBI honey (yeah, that's you if you're listening!) sweet-talked me into showing her Dom's old travel records, and then announced that you, that's you, Val, Valerius, were her target: she was pinning a murder on somebody who traveled there by the limo service.

> I know she's cracked, and told her so, but thought you should know whassup! So good luck with that bizarritude. Drop by next time you come, and bring me another copy of your album: she took mine!

> Blast from the past, Bill Coles

Sitting at his computer, reading this email from his old recording buddy in Swarthmore, Val was stunned. The FBI was looking at him for a murder on a road trip for Dom? What? Impossible! He forwarded the email to Selam at work, and texted her: "Sugar, take a look at your email. You are not gonna believe this!"

Selam called Val after reading the email. "What in the world is this about? Did you get in some trouble back in the crazy days of Swarthmore?" They rarely talked about his Viet Nam politics, both because they'd met the year the war ended and because current politics seemed to give them enough to chew on. Also, although their two children were finally grown, they were somehow not quite gone, a condition they shared with many friends whose college graduates lived in their basement apartments or in "tiny houses" out back, placed on wheeled flat-beds to duck zoning bans on permanent construction. Around the kids, Ho Chi Minh and Viet Nam were 50-year-old words, literally from another century, as if Val's parents in 1969 had tried to have an animated dinner table talk about Clemenceau and the Versailles treaty.

"No, no, no, it's just crazy. I don't get it. Must be a mistake, but what should I do? Leave it, or get a lawyer and show it to them?" After a few days' consideration, they decided to wait, figuring that Nashville wouldn't even have the kind of lawyer they'd need if there actually was something to Bill's rumor. They'd cross that bridge in the unlikely event they ever came to it.

But as another long-time resident of Nashville, Harold Jenkins, as Conway Twitty, had sung to Loretta Lynn — when she told him that "The talk is around that we're through. Oh darling, tell me what to do. I knew you'd tell me they were wrong, as soon as I picked up the phone." — "Ah, but it is true, they're not wrong."

A month later Val was sitting at the rear of a classroom, unobtrusively taking notes as two five-person teams of his summer-school undergraduates faced off on Donald Trump's famous, or for most of the students, infamous plan to build a "wall" facing Mexico. He and the rest of the class were grading the three-minute presentation by each team member, using a form that listed the areas to grade: accurately describe the plan (under this heading were these warnings: give the devil his due, no commentary, no gilding the lily, no leading the witness!); fairly imagine the points for and against it (no straw men!); set up your argument (but acknowledge its weaknesses); provide accurate and relevant data (but report limitations of data and methodology).

Val was optimistic after the first few presentations. The trick in the assignment was that he had asked for a show of hands of students who opposed the Wall, and then assigned them to the pro-wall position. The pro-wall students, in like fashion, would argue the anti-wall case. After the usual protests, particularly by Hispanic students in this case, but women when his classes analyzed politicians' claims that one out of five women are sexually assaulted in college, or African-Americans for the claim that being black increases the chances of being shot by police, the students had given in when he asked them to trust him on the exercise, and now were enjoying the novel experience of making good arguments for a cause they detested.

The door opened, and four well-dressed people walked in, incongruous on campus in their dark suits. Val stood, immediately thinking FBI, and trembling a bit with anticipation. Still, he managed to say calmly: "Can we help you?"

"Valerius Shaw, I am Special Agent Mar'Shae McGurk of the FBI. I have here a federal warrant here for your arrest for the murders of Congressman Felix Hébert, General George Hemmings, and AID Administrator Daniel Parker. Kindly turn around to be hand-cuffed."

"That's crazy. What are you saying? I've never killed anybody, I've never even heard of those people — well, I have heard of Parker, I've written about him. I think I even went to summer camp in Wisconsin with his son, Geoff..." Val's voice trailed off, as he realized he was in a state of shock, and caught himself before he babbled on. He turned to his students and laughed, "Well, this is one day of class you won't forget!"

"Sir, let me advise you not to say anything," said Black. She hooked him up as another agent read from a card listing his rights to silence and to counsel. The students sat in silence, all right, completely stunned, hoping this was one of the professor's tricks to stimulate discussion. But a minute or so after the party left the room, it became clear to them that this was the real thing. The group ran out of the building and over to the department office, where it became clear that the FBI had operated alone: nobody there had been approached to set up the arrest, indeed nobody on the entire campus. Subpoenas for all of Val's personnel files would be coming, though.

* * *

PART 2: THE TRIAL

CHAPTER 17: FEBRUARY 2018— THE OPENING

There are many ways to seek the truth, Val always told his statistics classes in the opening lecture, using a rhyming list he'd stolen from his Ph.D. advisor, who had probably stolen it in turn from his Ph.D. advisor: Meditation, inspiration, hallucination...

"Let's try the first...meditation. Everybody close your eyes, take deep breaths, and intone OOOOOOOOOOM like the Maharishi says...repeat it, breathe deeply...good. And now that you are in touch with the universe, let me know which is the most effective program out there to convince South Africans to use condoms to avoid HIV, and snap the transmission epidemic. Is it the bus stop posters, the plays in schools, the cartoon books for itinerant grape-pickers, or the one-on-one contacts with prostitutes on the truck routes? We need to know, so we can put our limited funds into the most effective method.

"Oh, you can't say? Meditation didn't give you the answer? That's bad — or 'shame,' as they say in South Africa. Well, then we can try...inspiration. After all, as the bumper stickers say around here, 'The Bible says it, I believe it, that settles it!' So, if God speaks to you from a burning bush and tells you that the one degree rise in global temperature over the past 150 years comes from there being four carbon dioxide molecules out of every 10,000 in the atmosphere rather than the three that were there before we invented the SUV, and that the one degree rise is gutting crop production and flooding coastal cities, then let's start taxing coal plants to death. I said God, now, not the United Nations! They're not the same thing.

"Oh, you say divine inspiration won't visit you? Well then, how about... hallucination? Back at the Woodstock music festival, in 1969, the announcer told us that 'the purple acid is not particularly good, so stick to the orange,' as if the orange goop some chem major bubbled up in their basement had FDA studies saying it was a safe way to scramble your brain. But hey, our brains were already scrambled by definition if we were even thinking of taking acid, so let's try that: LSD, peyote, magic mushrooms, anything hallucinogenic, because I hear you can see the truth when you're tripping...although I'm not sure if you can remember it later.

"Oh, you don't want to try that? And so you're no closer to the truth on HIV methods and on the causes and effects of global warming? Well then you are ready for the secret, the magic method that created modern societies and has kept people in them living longer and longer: the scientific method, known as the testable hypothesis. A results in B because of C. That's a measurable independent variable, a measurable dependent variable, and the causal mechanism between them. Make a claim, account for possible intervening variables that might affect the result, and then you'll see if correlation is indeed causation.

"For HIV education programs, we compare the HIV rates from small random samples of people using various methods. The famed 'bell curve' will tell us how often such differences in rates would happen just by chance. If there's a low possibility of that, then it must be that the best-scoring method probably works, so we choose it and use it with groups similar to those tested, and see if the impact is replicated. For attributing temperature changes to carbon dioxide changes, same thing: test the hypothesis, look at the data. The only problem here is that we have a tough time with the intervening variables, given both random changes and long-term cycles in the complex climate system, not to mention only having a sample of one earth, so we are faced with a 'modeling problem from hell.' But if we can do it, that's how we do it: the hypothesis beats all. When they say 'the data show,' you say 'show me the data,' and you subject it to the hypothesis test with an open mind."

But Val's professional commitment to the truth, an unstoppable force in his academic world, met an immovable object in his new legal world: a lawyer who didn't believe in it, and wanted no part of it.

"I have no interest in finding out the truth, and neither does anybody else in that courtroom," were the first words Val heard from his new, very expensive DC lawyer, Sharia Denby, pronounced as in "they call the wind Maria," not as in Sharia, or Islamic law: long before America knew that word, her very Christian father Josiah had given names to all of his children to rhyme with his: Zacariah, Qua'ria, Leniah, and Sharia.

"In law school they showed us a series of quick clips of surrogates in the 'spin room' after candidate debates, intoning to credulous reporters: the truth of the matter is, the truth is, truly, she was the true victor. The point was that truth is not the currency of the realm in public contests. Another great one they showed was from the Senate Judiciary Committee, when Joe Biden says, looking over his glasses at Clarence Thomas during his confirmation hearing, which had long since degenerated from judicial philosophy to pubic hairs on Coke cans and a film called *Long Dong Silver*, 'You have nothing to worry about, Judge. We're just here to find out the truth.' There was a pause, and then the entire hearing room, including all the senators, broke into laughter, because the last place you look for the truth is in a congressional hearing.

"Well, a trial is another place where the truth is thought to be the goal, but is really the enemy. Lawyers get this. We routinely engage in presentations that violate the fundamental rules of logic: *ad hominem* experts whose word you are supposed to just accept; correlation being suspicious so you can assume, *post hoc ergo propter hoc*, it's causation; and the *non sequitur* introduction of irrelevant facts and arguments...anything to cloud the mind, to appeal to emotion, and win, win, win! And that, my scholarly friend, is what we are going to do: confuse, create many reasonable doubts, and get you out of here in once piece.

"Just remember that the truth will not, in fact, make you free. Nobody wants a truth-telling, because everybody in the room, from judges to jurors, with bailiffs and witnesses in between, has broken the law when nobody was looking, has been scandalous in private morality, and has lied to protect themselves, so the system is actually tightly constrained, purposely designed to protect the truth from full exposure. It's like getting *solo el puntito* — fun, but not fully satisfying. So get over it!

"Look, the very fact that Greg Craig passed up the half million you've raised and kicked you over to me after he saw the government's case makes my point. Greg doesn't think I'm somehow a magically better lawyer than him. He's defended an impeached president, he's been a president's White House counsel, and look at how slickly he got you out, no bail, because the FBI wouldn't release its files without redaction. But he knows a DC jury doesn't want to see a big-shot white guy beating up on the FBI's heroic black female lead witness.

"Two black women going after each other is fine for a DC jury. But think about silver-maned Greg, from a mansion west of the park, straight out of the Brooks Brothers catalogue, might as well have 'easy five bucks' written on his forehead when the pan-handlers on K Street see him coming up from the metro. You want the jury to see him attacking home girl Agent McGurk, the Klan fighter who came up on Benning Terrace, probably takin' off the 'homeless' when they got home that night, so she could buy dinner at the Chinese take-out? That's definitely not fine. Greg telling you to take the case to my firm and specifically to me, that's really an insult to the jury, saying they aren't smart enough to avoid taking sides based on the irrelevant race and gender of the witnesses and lawyers, but that's how we roll, and we roll to win."

Val was bowled over by Denby's energy, fully-formed spontaneous paragraphs, and particularly the aura she exuded in her tone of certainty. He could see how a jury would think that anything she said was...the truth.

"Wow, I'm impressed," he laughed. "You're so convincing, I bet you win a lot! So, let's get down to it, how will this go, what's our strategy?"

As Sharia explained it, she would first hammer the credibility of Ayers and Dohrn, based on their lifetime of lying and Dohrn's self-interest in avoiding a murder charge for San Francisco. Then she would have to address the motivational evidence of Val's agreement with the Weather Underground's goals and the circumstantial evidence of his presence in the cities where the murders took place. It would be best to do all that during cross-examinations, and perhaps not even put on a formal defense. Having a defense would raise the idea in the jury's mind that Val should take the stand to deny it all. Sharia said she had never let a defendant take the stand, and she said she was not about to start now.

"Defendants often think they can explain things away, that the jury wants them to. Look, it's just not true. One of the strongest instructions of the judge, which I'll get her to say at the outset, in the middle, and right before the jury deliberates, is that failure to testify may not be considered by the jury. You see, the Supreme Court figured out a few decades back that if it's a constitutional right, the Fifth Amendment, not to testify, then invoking that right shouldn't be able to hurt you — then it wouldn't be much of a right! I'll have that instruction hammered so far into the jury's head that if anyone peeps about "well, why didn't he testify?" during deliberations, the others will be programmed to jump on them right away.

"Of course, the decision will always be yours, and there may be cases where it's needed, but I don't think this is going to be one of them. You see, you tell me that you're completely innocent of the charges, so you think there's no downside to telling that to the jury. But unlike Dohrn and Ayers, who are witnesses, you have no claim to selectively invoking the right against self-incrimination. Once they waive the Fifth, defendants have to answer every question the prosecutors put. They can delve into your mind, your thinking now and at the time, into other alleged misdeed and statements that could make you look bad. It will be a ** mess, if you'll excuse my language. I just want to make it clear that our strategy does not involve you testifying, and may not even involve a defense portion if I think we've bloodied their witnesses enough."

* * *

The largest trial room in the Prettyman federal courthouse, right off Constitution Avenue at the foot of Capitol Hill, was packed, as was an overflow room outfitted with a big screen. The feed was purely internal though: Judge Anne Brittain, with the blessing of both sides, had rejected requests from various outlets to broadcast the case.

"I like to think sometimes you can learn from history," she told Court TV's lawyer at the end of the hearing. "Life's too short for me to be another Judge Ito, driven crazy for your ratings. And defense counsel should note that I'm not going to be Julius Hoffman to your Chicago Seven, either. This is going to be a murder trial, not a political seminar."

Val whispered something to Denby, and she laughed and told the judge, "Yes, Your Honor — although my client wishes to give you just a mini-seminar, and remind you that for him, it will always be the Chicago Eight, in honor of Bobby Seale and his chains."

The jury had been picked in just two days, and most of the dismissals had been by the judge, and not the lawyers. Neither Denby nor U.S. Attorney Purpose, who had decided to take this big case himself, had bothered with jury background checks beyond courtroom questions. Both had come to believe that there was no science to selecting a favorable jury, and both knew that checks could lead to messy legal challenges and even sanctions if they even appeared to be targeted at specific classes of jurors.

The same held for a pattern of dismissals requested by a lawyer, if it coincided with ethnicity, gender, or even education level. The risks of micro-managing jury selection were usually not worth the supposed benefits. The mood of a jury was a living beast, with its own logic, and individual prejudices were quickly subsumed in the group experience and by the group's level of commitment to the task. Simple categories were often so wrong as predictors anyway that it was best just to find the first 12 people who seemed intellectually able to handle the chore, and get to it.

As a result, the jury was a classic DC stew, roughly appropriate for a city in which much of the black middle class had fled to suburbs in surrounding states and there were no white lower or working classes, only professionals. The city was about 50 percent black, and despite the dramatically higher share of blacks than whites incarcerated or ineligible as "returning citizens (from jail or prison)" so was the jury. Half the jury was women: four black, one of Chinese heritage, and one white. Of the men, two were black, one was Mexican-American, and three were white.

Ages ranged from 22 to 65, and occupations from student to lawyer, with most jurors working for the federal government or its contractors. Two were related to police from the plethora of forces in the District — but of course had assured the court that they wouldn't automatically credit police testimony over that of civilians. Almost all had attended at least a two-year college, and eight of the 12 had a bachelor's degree, twice the national rate.

In his opening statement, Purpose outlined his case succinctly, putting it in the context of recent terrorism cases, like the Boston Marathon bombing. "These are strange cases, for prosecutors and for jurors. The law does not recognize a difference in motives, purely criminal versus purely political.

The law only asks if the defendant is guilty, beyond a reasonable doubt, of the charge — in this case, conspiracy and murder. But we all know these are different sorts of cases, we know it takes a certain set of political beliefs for the accused to plot and carry out the crime.

"So I'll concede to you that the defendant had none of the motives I've seen in prosecuting other murder cases: financial gain, passion about love gone wrong, anger at an insult that could not be ignored, fear of an attack on a relative, fear of a witness' testimony. And I'll concede that from the perspective of the defendant, a perspective he seems to share with some of the government's own witnesses, the crimes might be seen as justified, perhaps even noble. I'm not trying Mr. Shaw's politics, as much as he'd like me to. I'm trying his murderous actions.

"You'll hear again and again from the witnesses for the prosecution, my witnesses, that they, like the defendant, were at war, they had declared war, against the United States of America. They did this because they believed our 'system' was killing, robbing, and exploiting people around the world. They called that, and they call it today, both the witnesses and the defendant, imperialism. And I say again to you, the jury, I don't care how they justified it. It's not relevant, it's not a defense. We're not revisiting the history of the Viet Nam war or holding a teach-in on U.S. policy in the Middle East today. We're deciding guilt or innocence on three cases of murder."

Denby rose slowly, and in a polite tone, interrupted. "Pardon me, Your Honor, I truly did not intend to argue with the prosecution's opening statement, but I must object to that slick trick right there." She did not continue, and the planned silence, like the pleasant tone, focused the courtroom's attention far more than an angry complaint would have.

Purpose quickly put an end to the theatrical moment. "Your Honor, could counsel kindly explain herself? I'm not sure what she's talking about."

"Oh yes you do, Mr. Purpose. You know very well that while millions of Americans, like Mr. Shaw, marched and voted against what they considered imperialist policies, it was only your witnesses, admitted bombers, who formally declared war and then waged war on our country with dynamite, fire bombs, pipe bombs, and nail bombs.

"Your Honor, the rules of evidence are generally suspended for opening statements, but the U.S. Attorney's claim that my client declared war should be stricken and the jury instructed to ignore it as without foundation. There's nothing, nothing in any historical record that indicates that my client took any violent action against anything or anybody, unlike his witnesses, who openly declared war and have admitted to bombing over 20 buildings. And the star witness, Bernardine Dohrn, recently admitted after nearly 50 years of denial that it was a bombing by her collective that killed a police officer and blinded another."

"That will do, counselor," interjected the judge. "An objection is one thing, and I will sustain it, but you may not hijack the prosecution's opening statement to make your own. The jury will disregard both any of the defense counsel's claims about Ms. Dohrn and as well any implication by the prosecution that the defendant, Mr. Shaw, declared war or carried out a war on the United States, unless evidence is presented to the contrary."

"Thank you, Your Honor," said Purpose, happy that the judge's slap at Denby's over-reach had given him a way out: "And indeed, ladies and gentlemen of the jury, we will show, well beyond a reasonable doubt, that while the defendant did not formally declare war on the United States, he carried one out, in the form of one failed and six successful assassinations."

When Sharia got her turn, she started with the words she would end with, before the final jury instruction from the judge: "Reasonable doubt. That is the standard that our country, our Constitution, holds dear in this courtroom. It's the basis for our democracy. Other countries have judges, elected or appointed experts in the law, to listen to testimony and decide who they think is probably guilty. In America, we trust you, citizens, ourselves, and the standard is: did the government prove its case beyond a reasonable doubt? And there's so much doubt in this case that I believe it should never have been brought.

"What the prosecution didn't tell you is that this is indeed a strange case, but not because it has political overtones from the Viet Nam era. This case arises from a 'tweet' by our president, Donald J. Trump — it has political overtones today! President Trump wanted a murder conviction for the death in 1970 of someone the prosecution forgot to mention. Sergeant Brian V. McDonnell was a father of two, a World War II veteran whose only crime was to be a cop, and he was killed in a cowardly pipe-bombing at a San Francisco police station that also blinded Officer Robert Fogarty.

"President Trump started the ball rolling, and it rolled right onto Ms. Dohrn. To avoid a murder charge for the death of Brian McDonnell, indeed to avoid any felony charge or jail time, she and her husband William "Billy" Ayers, self-named Jesse James, self-named Sundance Kid for his desire to kill policemen, concocted a tall tale 48 years ago, a tale you will hear shortly during the prosecution's case. That tall tale is that my client, Professor Shaw, a person, unlike those witnesses, whom nobody has ever witnessed undertaking a single violent act in his life, killed six so-called imperialists, three of whom were federal officials and so are the subject of this trial.

"I will show you, beyond a reasonable doubt, that there's no evidence, not one shred, that places Mr. Shaw at the actual scene of these crimes, that ties him to these crimes in any way. Oh, indeed, he was in these cities at the right times, and that wasn't by chance. When you get to know the devious minds of these witnesses, you'll see that the far more reasonable explanation for Professor Shaw's presence in those cities was that they, people who have admitted to violent acts, got ahold of his travel schedule and then planned these murders so that he could be their fall-guy, their ace in the hole, their get out of jail free card. And it's worked out for them so far: the government took the bait, again under pressure from the president. But you, you won't let them get away with this, the last lie in their cynical career of lies.

"I do agree on one thing with U.S. Attorney Purpose: let's forget any type of justifications, and just focus on the crime. That's all we can do in a court of law. And at this trial's conclusion, using the regular standards for the crime of murder, not confused by any political justifications, you will see that the evidence is not there, that the prosecution cannot make its case. Maybe someday the government will find enough evidence to prosecute the real killers of the congressman, the general, and the foreign aid official. But they certainly don't have the evidence, or the right guy, in this trial."

* * *

CHAPTER 18: FEBRUARY 2018 — MOTIVE, MEANS, AND OPPORTUNITY

Over the next two weeks James Purpose carefully built an edifice of circumstantial evidence that he believed would remove any reasonable doubt. He started with Black, whose personal observations during the investigation allowed her not just to enter necessary documents, but also pretty much to make his entire case in a coherent fashion before he called on his balky and somewhat unpredictable Weather-witnesses. Had she not been present at the unearthing of motive, means, and evidence, and had just read about them in other agents' reports, he would have been more constrained by defense objections.

"Agent McGurk, let's start with the most basic of facts, the actual attacks by Mr. Shaw, in chronological order. Then we can move on to the classic requirements for conviction: motive, means, and opportunity, backed by evidence. I am going to hand you seven crime scene photographs, each with their corresponding two-page FBI case summary, labeled exhibits one through seven, that have been approved by the judge. Would you please start with a description of the first case as I project the photo on the screen for the jury? This first one is the picture of the bullet holes in the wall at the home of the late Samuel Huntington. Now, what led you to search that house last year?"

"Objection for the record, Your Honor," interjected Sharia Denby. "I know you have ruled on these in chambers, but I would like the record to reflect my objection to the exhibits labeled one, three, five, and six, and to any discussion of the alleged crimes they reflect in this trial. They are clearly outside the scope of this trial, and so are prejudicial to my client and clearly inadmissible under the numerous precedents cited in my motion on this issue."

"Thank you, counselor," said Judge Brittain, continuing for the jury's benefit an exchange that had been carefully scripted in her chambers. "Let the record reflect that the defense objects to any consideration of alleged crimes other than those in the indictment, including a failed assassination attempt at Harvard University in 1970 and successful assassination attempts in Cambridge, Massachusetts, in 1971, in New York in 1973, and in Pittsburgh in 1974. I have ruled in the prosecution's favor that these other cases may be used to reveal patterns of behavior that the jury may decide are relevant to this trial. I caution the jury that to consider these disputed cases relevant, they must use the same standard of guilt as in the cases at trial: beyond a reasonable doubt."

"Thank you, your honor," replied Denby. She added a parting shot, so the jury could infer unfairness from her sarcasm: "And the attorneys of the world ought to thank you, too, because the appeals that will flow from this ruling will make it truly the Lawyers' Full Employment Act of 2018...through 2028."

Starting with a snapshot of Professor Huntington's wall and moving through the crime scene pictures and descriptions of what he called, with his own sarcasm, the six murdered "imperialists," Purpose led Black through the identification of each of the assassin's targets and had her discuss the specifics of each crime scene. After each murder summary he displayed, and she briefly explained, its Nathan Hale communiqué. After a lunch break, he asked Black if there had come a time when she became aware of a suspect in the one failed and six successful assassinations.

"Yes, sir. In the course of investigating a 47-year-old murder in San Francisco, I was called upon to take statements from Bernardine Dohrn, someone who was of interest in that case, and William Ayers, her husband. They had been terrorists in the 1970s in an organization known as the Weather Underground, which declared war on the United States over various foreign and domestic policy issues. Their statements as former members of that organization's leadership, which they called the Weather Bureau, provided us with leads, which we then corroborated with evidence that the seven assassination attempts had been the work of one Valerius Shaw and one John Jacobs, also known as J. J., now deceased."

Black continued on for three long days, first on motive, screening blow-ups of flyers and letters from Val's draft files, and then on means and opportunity, walking the jury through the records of limousine services and artist contracts for his travels to the cities at the time of the murders. Denby regularly disrupted Black's flow with objections that she was simply previewing witnesses' testimony to give it the government's interpretation, but Purpose had been careful to limit his questions to interviews she had conducted and documents she had obtained. He saved the highlight for the end, so the jury would remember the drama the most.

"Agent McGurk, you usually work on civil rights cold cases, chasing down Klan killers who got off the first time because of racist juries. Do you often have physical evidence to make your case after a period of some 40 plus years, as in these murders?"

Black was primed, eager to show off the diligent work of the Boston office. "That is rare, sir. We usually achieve our convictions based on means, motive, and so-called circumstantial evidence, which we have in spades in these Weather-cat assassinations. However, in this case we have also succeeded in gathering relevant physical evidence. Our Boston office sent a team last year to the house where Professor Huntington was the target of the failed assassination in 1970, his home study, and extracted two bullets from behind a refurbished wall.

"Now, there are striations on all bullets, spiraling markings, just like fingerprints, unique. They result from the way the inside of its barrel is 'rifled' or grooved to improve accuracy. The striations were still intact on the two bullets, and our lab states with a 99 percent certainty that the rifle was a Remington 700, a top-grade deer-hunting weapon with a telescopic sight, and that it was manufactured during a particular production run, the first major revamping of the 700 since its introduction in 1962, that lasted from 1969 to 1971. And the lab is 95 percent certain that this was the same, fairly rare model of the weapon that ejected the used shell recovered in the 1975 murder of Daniel Parker."

Val could see that the jury was eating this up. It was all the fault of John Grisham and *Law and Order*, he thought. Everybody's read about something like this or seen it on TV, so they think it's got to be real. Like a mobster who took on an attitude from watching *The Godfather*, Agent McGurk was playing the part of the brilliant FBI agent.

Purpose let Black's last statement settle for a minute, then said: "So, the same rifle was used in both shootings?"

"Possibly, sir, but we can't reach that conclusion definitively. Just the same model. Unfortunately, the bullet that killed Daniel Parker in 1975 has disappeared. Again, this isn't unusual in my experience with cold cases. Perhaps after autopsy it was discarded, because of damage or fragmentation upon hitting bone in his body, perhaps it was taken to be compared to other bullets and not returned, we simply don't know.

"But as I testified, the lab can say, to about 95 percent certainty, that the murder weapon in 1975 was also a 1969 to 1971 Remington 700 because of markings on the cartridge case from which the bullet was ejected by the explosion, what people often call the 'shell.' The original investigators found the shell by making some calculations about velocity and trajectory, and tracing their way back to the stand of trees above the house, where the shooter had been standing. The only reason we can't match the shell and the bullet to the identical rifle is because we don't have the gun for the necessary test-firings to get a pattern for both."

When it finally came time for Denby's cross-examination, she stayed away from the bullets. Whatever she needed to do for reasonable doubt, she could do in her closing arguments, after researching the number of revamped-run Remington 700s in circulation by 1970. But even the potential match required her to attack vigorously the idea that Val had been in Cambridge during the 1970 bombing and shooting. Denby forced Black to concede that she had no limousine or appearance records for Val's presence at the Harvard attempt, and then hammered Black with the same question for the six murders: "Did you find any physical evidence that the defendant was present at the scene of the crime?" Black had been coached not to argue, and to simply say "no."

As the trial moved into its second week, Purpose called witnesses who could, unlike Black, give direct testimony to Val's motive and means. First Thad Leslie, a retired investment banker who kept stressing his membership in SDS and not Weatherman, recounted Val's fall of draft resistance and rage, ending with his pledge to "kill the highest-ranking person to use" a Weatherman-bombed bathroom. Then came Alice Truxton, who had taught middle school math for 30 years after serving a short felony sentence for possession of bomb-making materials, which had been found in her apartment during one of the FBI's rare, properly-warranted raids. She testified that Val had come with John Jacobs to Cambridge when Jacobs had helped with construction of the Harvard bomb, and that J. J. had said Val was going to kill Professor Huntington. She recounted her visit to the professor's house when the bullet-scarred windows were being replaced.

Denby airily dismissed Leslie without a question, drawing an objection from Purpose for her editorializing as the jury listened: "Your Honor, I have no need to review what 18-year-olds on drugs said to each other 50 years ago." At Purpose's objection, the jury was instructed to disregard that argumentative statement, but her point was made as well as a cross-examination would have. But then Denby spent a long time on Truxton, frequently reminding the jury that she had tried strenuously, but unsuccessfully, to exclude the Harvard incident because it did not relate directly to the charges at trial.

Denby forced Truxton to admit, repeatedly, that she had lied, repeatedly, about not being involved in the Harvard bombing for decades, planting the question with the jury as to why they should believe an admitted liar now. However, she couldn't shake Truxton's claim that Bernardine Dohrn had sent her a photograph in 1975 of a person, whom she now recognized in the courtroom as Shaw, who had come with J. J. in 1970. Denby did wound her by asking if she had told anyone else about the picture at the time, or about the murder attempt in 1970, so that that person could be called as a witness to verify her claim. "No, I kept all that communication to myself," replied Truxton.

"Wait, are you telling me that you found out in 1970 that you were all implicated in an attempted murder, and you never told the other women in your collective? And that you all looked at his picture together in 1975, and you didn't tell them that you recognized him, so they could prepare to protect themselves legally? You only told Bernardine Dohrn?"

Denby could not believe her luck when Truxton came out with: "Revolutionary discipline: there was no need to know. We were well-trained, like the cadre in the Battle of Algiers. That was the best protection for the Weather Bureau, the central committee. We cadre were expendable, the leadership wasn't. We were taught to say nothing, to reduce the circle of knowledge."

"So, you were a revolutionary communist, well-disciplined to protect your superiors. And you still think of yourself that way, don't you?"

Truxton angrily fought back, which was exactly what Denby wanted. "I'm not in any organization, there's no more Weatherman, but yes, I am a revolutionary communist, opposed to American imperialism and the capitalism that creates it and uses it."

Denby closed in for the kill. "And isn't that why, comrade, you agreed to lie about all this when Bill Ayers called you last year, to go along with this story, to protect his wife, to give her a way to trade out for her murder in San Francisco, because you still think of her as your superior on the Weather Bureau?"

Denby happily accepted the Judge sustaining the objection she'd known Purpose would make to her unfounded question. It was the best she could do to cast some doubt on Truxton's story.

* * *

"Your Honor, the government calls Bernardine Dohrn, born Bernardine Rae Ohrnstein, also known by her aliases Christine Louise Douglas, Marion Delgado, H. T. Smith, and Rose Bridges."

A primly-dressed, well-maintained 76-year-old white woman with long, curly hair and sensible shoes took the stand. The jury was openly staring at the infamous revolutionary they had heard described by Agent McGurk as a bomber and fugitive who had made the FBI's "Ten Most Wanted" list. Purpose led her through the necessary identification, in which he asked her to make it clear, right off the bat, that she had indeed declared and carried out war on the United States because of what she called its genocide in Indochina and against black Americans, and that she was still, as she had first claimed in 1968, a revolutionary communist. Purpose had decided to get all the negatives out of the way himself, rather than let the defense enjoy the benefit of dramatic revelations. Then he turned to her tale about Shaw.

"Professor Dohrn, I am going to ask a series of 'yes or no' questions, so we can proceed quickly to the matter at hand. First, did you know of plans to plant a bomb in 1970 at the Park Station of the San Francisco police, which killed Sergeant Brian McDonnell and wounded nine other officers? Yes or no?"

Dohrn ignored Purpose's direction, and said, "As I have acknowledged in my FBI statement, I recall being part of a single discussion about a possible bombing at Park Station, but I never heard of any planning meetings after that, and in fact I don't know if our collective actually did it. Some historians think that it was actually another group, not the Weathermen but black revolutionaries.

"In any case, the bomb has been described in FBI reports as having been placed on a window ledge outside the station, so it clearly wasn't targeted at an individual. It was a tragic accident that it harmed anyone who by chance was nearby the window, inside. I am deeply sorry for Sergeant McDonnell's death. If any actual plans and actions developed from the discussion I attended, I apologize to his family and to all the wounded officers and their families. In all the bombings I was a part of in our campaign of armed propaganda against the war on the Vietnamese and on black, brown, and red Americans, we were always careful, and never hurt anyone."

"I'll take that for a 'yes,'" laughed Purpose, trying to mask from the jury his anger that Dohrn had immediately departed from their prepared dance. But in his own mind, he sadly shook his head and said, "These people: they always have a plan, and they always have an excuse!"

"And did you recently plead guilty to a misdemeanor for taking part in planning that bombing, in return for your agreement to testify truthfully and fully at this trial of Valerius Shaw for conspiracy and murder? Just yes or no, please."

"Yes," said Dohrn, "I pleaded guilty, but not to planning but rather being aware of discussions and not reporting them to police."

"Good, we're getting closer to 'yes or no'! Now, let's start with the first bombing. Did you participate in any way in planning or carrying out a bombing at the Harvard Center for International Affairs, in 1970? Yes or no?"

Dohrn paused, then looked up at Brittain and said, "On the advice of counsel I invoke my fifth amendment right against self-incrimination. My agreement was only for the San Francisco incident and the contact with Valerius Shaw." Purpose was stunned into silence, unsure how to proceed. The notion of immunity had never been raised, either in the lengthy negotiation of the agreement or in the hundreds of hours of pre-trial interviews. Finally, Purpose rallied, and proposed to the judge that the attorneys discuss the matter with Dohrn in her chambers. Dohrn interjected: "Not without my own lawyer, we won't." Brittain angrily reached for her gavel and pounded it down. "That is the last time you speak up during this trial without authorization, Professor, without serving a sentence for contempt. I run this courtroom, is that clear?"

In the end, after a two-day recess for negotiations involving assistant attorney general Imaglio, Dohrn's lawyer got her what she wanted: a blanket immunity for the seven bombings the prosecution planned to ask her about in court. Imaglio had been initially perplexed by the demand. The criminal statute of limitations on destruction of property had long run out, and there were no known injuries from those bombings that could provide the basis for civil suits, should they survive their own complex statutes of limitations. He concluded that her lawyer was, reasonably, dotting the i's and crossing the t's just in case some future prosecutor creatively interpreted anti-terrorism laws from that era, which like murder have no time limitations.

Dohrn's lawyer raised the idea of offering a similar deal to Ayers, but Purpose pocketed the suggestion. Having been played, jumped really, by Dohrn he was unwilling to follow her script. He'd deal with Ayers when he needed to — and for now he was questioning whether Ayers would even add anything worth the trouble he was bound to bring. Purpose would use Dohrn to establish the link to Truxton, and that was really all he needed beyond the powerful circumstantial evidence of the travel records, which were the make or break of the case anyway.

Imaglio did right by Purpose, taking responsibility for giving Dohrn immunity and openly admitting his error in ever going down the path of treating Dohrn and Ayers like typical defendants, who tended to want to please the Department after a deal because they feared the consequences of not doing so. "Jesus, these people are as much sociopaths today as they were when they were cleansing the world of their enemies," he told Purpose. "We're just pawns in their game. Anything is justified if it helps them and their cause, so they plot and lie until even they don't know where they started."

"Welcome to my world," said Purpose. "I was thinking the other night, after working with her on her explanation for the bombings, they're the Tom and Daisy Buchanan of the radical left, Scott Fitzgerald's careless people. I remember the line, a beautiful one, from *The Great Gatsby*: 'They smashed up things and creatures and then retreated back into their money or their vast carelessness or whatever it was that kept them together, and let other people clean up the mess they had made.' Well, what can we do? It was a success-ful hustle on their part, but I don't think it'll hurt our case. Now I can take Dohrn back in there to sink Shaw."

And sink him she did. When court reconvened, Dohrn was compliant, indeed eager, to provide information, because every incident she threw in was immediately immunized. After describing each of the seven bombings and the Weather Bureau's growing concern about the Weather-cat killings, she described the successful search for Nathan Hale and Truxton's identifi-cation of him. Purpose decided to end her testimony with some more immu-nization — of his case against the confusion he knew Denby would generate about Dohrn and Ayers' initial failure to mention John Jacobs' work with the Weathermen after his supposed expulsion.

"Now Professor Dohrn, you went to great lengths in your technically accurate but less than forthcoming initial statement to the FBI to cover up your continuing collaboration with the Weatherman whose expulsion from the group you announced in 1970, John Jacobs. Why was that?"

"Well, we decided not to tell the FBI about J. J., as everybody called him, in that first interview, because it's a messy, unclear story that would only have confused the issues about Val Shaw. After the FBI found Shaw, we were happy to fill in the blanks."

"I'm not sure I follow you, professor, so let's clear it up with a specific question." Purpose had practiced this exchange repeatedly with Dohrn, and he prayed she would stick to the script. "Alice Truxton testified that the Weather Bureau sent Jacobs to help her collective make the bomb in Cam-bridge. How could that be, when he had publicly, as well as in your messages to the operatives you had in different cities, been expelled from the group?"

"OK, our central committee decided at the May 1970 meeting that J. J. could no longer be part of the leadership, because he kept insisting on full war, on attacking people. I was shocked when we learned that there were roofing nails, clearly for an anti-personnel bomb, found in the Townhouse when it blew up. We asked him to renounce that strategy and only bomb property when no people were around, but he kept refusing, lobbying for lethal actions. So we told him he would be publicly expelled, but could keep working as the central committee's personal bombing scout, non-lethal only. For the good of the organization, he accepted the conditions.

"We couldn't have him interacting with various cadre, because they might lean toward his leadership, so we told him to work alone in the field, to keep up the fiction of expulsion, and interact by phone, through code, just with me and Bill. We only put him together with the collective in Cambridge because they called us to say they were worried about their construction. We didn't want to lose more comrades in another Townhouse accident, so we sent him, just that once.

"For the rest of our time, for five years of bombing, J. J. roamed alone, carefully casing sites and recommending timing. Everything was centralized then in the Weather Bureau, as opposed to the early months of 1970, when J. J. and Terry Robbins decided on their own to go lethal with roofing nails at Fort Dix with the Townhouse bomb, as opposed to the accidentally lethal Park Station bomb. So after reviewing J. J.'s ideas, Bill and I would present them to the others. Having unnamed sources was typical for our discipline, nothing unusual there. Then if we all agreed on a target, we'd send his scouting reports and the dates to the cadre in the relevant city — although after a while there really were no cadre, just the Weather Bureau, about ten of us, who did it all."

"Just one last question, Professor," said Purpose, "and it really cuts to the core of the contentions Ms. Denby raised in her opening statement, the convenient claim by Mr. Shaw that he's a patsy, a set-up for somebody else's murderous rampage. The question is this: J. J. recommended 'windows' for the six bombings, and then there were murders within a few weeks after each one. Didn't you think then that J. J. was involved in the murders?"

"Not at all," said Dohrn. "We just assumed that this Nathan Hale brigade was going to each city, it wasn't even half of them that we bombed, and taking someone out after our action. We didn't think it was J. J. He was complying perfectly with our agreement. His scouting was good: nobody was ever hurt in our armed propaganda. And he wanted to continue, even after we stopped in 1975."

"But how about now, now that you know about Mr. Shaw's travel arrangements, about how he first would have the contract to play in a city, and J. J. would give you a window for each one ending about two weeks before Shaw's trip there?"

"Well, it's obvious to me," said Dohrn. She paused, and the jury sat up straighter in obvious attention to this key point. "J. J. played us, just like we played the other cadres in the Weather Underground. We had a secret from them, and he had a secret from us. The only way for me to interpret the facts here is that J. J. was conspiring with Shaw to make the hits, and he used us. We had no idea about Shaw or his connection to J. J. until 1975, and knew nothing about his limousine trips, which were only discovered recently by Agent McGurk. J. J. had it his way to the end. He wanted to bring the war home, to kill the enemy, and he did. Why did he want to link the killings and the communiqués to us, calling us out for being weak? Well, why not? I can't explain J. J.'s thinking. It might've been the only way he could motivate Shaw. But maybe, just maybe, it was pay-back: the world thought we'd expelled him, but he sort of expelled us."

"Your witness, counselor," said Purpose, relieved to be done with the contentious professor without any more disruptive bombshells being dropped.

* * *

"Ms. Dohrn, are you an accomplished liar?" Sharia Denby was going to be damned if she would refer to the witness, whom she considered a socio-pathic thug, with the esteemed title of professor, especially since she had noticed Purpose always denying that title to her client.

"Well, as I just testified, for operational security we had to say that J. J. had been expelled, when he was secretly still working with us. And in my years in the underground, of course I had to adopt new identities and main-tain them, if that's what you mean."

"That's not at all what I mean. I mean now, you lie about everything." Denby left her notepad on the lectern, and went up to Dohrn, like a boxer leaving her corner. "For example, your academic work focuses on children's legal rights, on the protection of children, does it not?"

"It did. I'm retired now."

"Isn't that entire enterprise, this concern for children, a lie? Didn't you tell two pregnant women at the 1970 Flint conference that they should kill, and I quote, 'their honky pig babies' and fetuses? And didn't you use your friends' children as 'beards,' asking their parents if you could take them out for a fun day, which included using them to reduce suspicion about you by the police, the 'pigs' you repeatedly exhorted your colleagues to 'off,' while you cased sites to plant bombs? What about the legal rights, the protection, of those children?"

Dohrn shook her head: "That is a hodge-podge of statements taken out of context and outright lies. I don't even know what a 'beard' means."

"Oh really? So when I bring in Delia Mellis and her father Dennis Cunningham for the defense, and they testify that when she was nine years old you and Mr. Ayers repeatedly traipsed her around San Francisco as you did reconnaissance for what she remembers you calling 'great actions,' they will be lying?"

"Objection, Your Honor," said Purpose. "This is ridiculous. Counsel's asking the witness to assess statements that haven't been entered."

"Sustained," responded Brittain. "Counsel will stick to questions with a basis."

"Yes, Your Honor. So here's a direct question, Ms. Dohrn. Agent McGurk read out testimony by FBI informer Larry Grathwohl before a congressional committee to the effect that Billy Ayers complained to him, in 1970, that so few West Coast Weathermen were really committed to your 'struggle' that you, a member of the central committee, had to plan the Park Station bombing, build the bomb, and put it in place yourself. Is that true? Did you, Bernardine Dohrn, place the bomb on the window ledge with your own hands?"

Before Dohrn could respond Denby plowed ahead: "Come on, now you have immunity from prosecution, so let's have the truth. You don't need an FBI report to tell you that the bomb 'was placed on a window ledge,' like you said this morning, do you? You weren't just 'part of discussions' about the bombing, like you said, right? You put the bomb there yourself, didn't you?"

Black, who because of her encyclopedic knowledge of the case had remained in the gallery after her testimony to assist the prosecution team, leaned forward in her seat. Maybe Dohrn would fall for Denby's rapid-fire badgering, and lose her cool. But Dohrn had clearly prepared herself for the battle, and calmly responded: "Absolutely not. As I said in my plea, after the initial discussion, I never heard anything more about any plans to bomb Park Station."

"Oh, right," said Denby, with sarcasm. "And how many other times in the dozens of bombings you discussed as a Weatherman did the others go off on their own without you, the clear leader of the Central Committee? How many times? Five, ten, none? How many times?"

"I can't remember that level of detail from almost 50 years ago."

"Oh, please, Ms. Dohrn, you are making my point — your lies are mounting and mounting. You know full well that you were never, ever, cut out of Weatherman decisions, because you were the top dog." Purpose rose to object to Denby's failure to ask a question, but she beat him to it: "I'm sorry, Your Honor. My frustration with the witness is showing. Please allow me withdraw that comment, and ask this simple question:

"Ms. Dohrn, can you tell the jury what you know about the "John Doe" approach to civil lawsuits?"

Dohrn hesitated, thrown off track by the turn in direction. "Uh, yes, that's when you don't know who injured you, but still file a suit for damages within the time provided by the civil statute of limitations. You reserve the right to add the real name of the defendant, should it ever be discovered."

"Right, Ms. Dohrn. And have you ever checked records in the San Francisco courts to see if John Doe, or should we say Jane Doe, suits have been filed by survivors and families from the Park Station bombing?"

Again Dohrn hesitated, showing precisely the caution that Denby hoped the jury would take as calculation. "I may well have. It's prudent to be prepared."

"Indeed. Were you lying this morning when you said you were shocked to learn about the roofing nails in the Townhouse bomb?"

"Absolutely not," responded Dohrn quickly and forcefully.

"Well, isn't it true that only you and Mr. Ayers have maintained the fiction that the Townhouse group was operating on its own? Haven't Machtinger, Wilkerson, Rudd, and Flanagan all written or stated in interviews what I want you to admit now, that the first bombings by the three Weather collectives — Townhouse in New York, you in San Francisco and Berkeley, and Ayers in Detroit and Cleveland — were all intended to be lethal, and that they were indeed coordinated, proposed to the Central Committee for approval? Isn't that right?"

"It's correct that we knew about those particular targets, but not correct that the bombings were intended to be lethal. I knew nothing about the roofing nails. I assumed the bomb would be like the others, simply dynamite, placed where no people would be hurt. That did shock me."

"OK, Ms. Dohrn, I'll grant you that lie, since I can't prove it wrong, but in New York you knew there was a lot of dynamite, and that the target was a dance, so that pigs and imperialists would die, correct?"

"All I knew was that the collective had chosen Fort Dix because it was a place that had been under many protests by anti-war groups that we wanted to support."

Denby erupted in another display of disbelief: "Incredible. How can you make that statement about supporting those groups and conveniently leave out the part where they were non-violent and wanted nothing to do with you? Hadn't they in fact refused to let Weatherman take part in their demonstrations because of your violence?

"But never mind, let's stick to our current business. I'd like to explore for the jury why you and Mr. Ayers created this narrative that you've pitched to filmmakers and book-readers ever since, that you didn't have operational control of the Townhouse collective, and that you in the West and Ayers in the Midwest weren't trying to kill anybody — when you did in fact try to kill police in Berkeley, Park Station, Detroit, and Cleveland.

"So, again, here's a direct question. Did or did you not construct this narrative of out-of-control renegades Terry Robbins and John Jacobs for your own selfish purpose, at first to reduce your chances of being charged for murder or assault from these early bombing, and later to protect your job at a university?"

"Well, you can call it a narrative," replied Dohrn, "but we chose to broadcast what we knew to be the facts about Terry and J. J. operating in violation of policy in order to protect the organization. We realized that the liberal left would help us, fund us, move us around, listen to our analysis, but not if they thought we hurt people. By moving to symbolic bombings, and saying that nobody but the rogues had ever put bystanders at risk, we strengthened our operation. And our operation was morally justifiable, indeed required of us, to end the genocide of five million people in Indochina.

"Sure, we all had an interest in not getting dragged into court. That's one of the reasons we didn't put out communiqués or admit to the first actions, like we usually did during our armed propaganda campaign. But the more important reason was because it would have hurt the organization, too, and not just us as individuals, if we'd been tarred with Terry and J. J.'s brush."

Denby stood mute, by design, so the jury could see her shaking her head at the egotism of the answer: Dohrn was Weather, so what was good for Dohrn was good for Weather. The she mused out loud. "Well, all I can say to that is, 'Let's hear it for James Watson.' If he hadn't figured out DNA, you'd still be lying, saying you knew nothing about lethal bombings, and you'd never have entered the plea that finally gives Brian McDonnell's family some measure of justice."

Purpose rose slowly, as if reluctantly. "Your Honor, I am tired of defense counsel's speeches. Would you kindly strike that entire gratuitous statement, and remind her to ask questions instead?"

Brittain thought about the request and surprised both lawyers by declining to strike. "No, Mr. Purpose, I'm not going to strike. Ms. Dohrn has taken tremendous latitude in her answers, ranging broadly for her own purposes, so I'm going to allow that little bit of editorializing, assuming that it's leading to a question. But, Ms. Denby, after this loquacious witness steps down, let's all try to keep our witnesses and ourselves on track!"

"Yes, Your Honor," said Denby, "I was leading up to this next question, about something Ms. Dohrn and I both know she is still lying about, a lie that could put my client in the death chamber. Ms. Dohrn, you knew about the Weather-cat killings all along, you approved them for J. J., didn't you? Wasn't that your deal with him: he helps with armed propaganda and takes the public fall, but he gets to carry out the assassinations, as long as he helps you set up young Valerius for these killings, so you have someone to trade, just in case Park Station comes back to haunt you?"

"Again, absolutely not. After the Townhouse, the Weathermen never harmed a single person, only property."

"I'm going to get back to your Weather-cat denial, count on it, Ms. Dohrn, because you just went on record saying that you went non-lethal for tactical, not moral reasons, so deniable assassinations should have presented no problem for you. But I just can't let such nonsense about property and not people pass. Now, when a bomb goes off on some property, aren't any people who are close enough to it liable to be hurt?"

"Yes," replied Dohrn. "That's why we always called in warnings. "

"No you didn't, not in Berkeley," snapped back Denby. "And we all know it was Weatherman at Park Station. There was no warning for Brian McDonnell, was there? And not at the Detroit police offices, when Mr. Ayers planted a bomb with Mr. Grathwohl, which fortunately Grathwohl reported in time to the FBI, right?"

Dohrn shook her head strenuously. "Those were all before Townhouse. I said it was after Townhouse that we always called in warnings. The horror of our friends' deaths caused us all to rethink what we were doing. We came up with a new strategy, designed to minimize the risk of any casualties."

"OK, let's take that little fiction, that you were capable of murder, but only until you saw your comrades, Diana Oughton, Teddy Gold, and Terry Robbins, destroy themselves, and then saw your SNCC friends Ralph Featherstone and Che Payne do the same thing three days later on their way to bomb the H. Rap Brown trial. Your claim is that those horrors made you a pacifist. But let's take Pittsburgh, with the police, fire, and security personnel searching the upper floors when you warned about a basement bomb, and barely missing the explosion that destroyed the 29th floor.

"Or take Cambridge, or the Pentagon, AID, IT and T, or any of your other bombings where you sent in a warning. Wasn't it just dumb luck that kept people from being killed there, because a warning doesn't necessarily get to everybody in time, does it, when you don't know where all the people are? Doesn't planting a bomb in a building necessarily say that you consider collateral damage for civilians acceptable in the pursuit of ending a genocidal war?"

"As I said," replied Dohrn, "there's always a risk, but we did our best to minimize it. But doing nothing as America kills, that's violence too."

"So all non-violent forms of protest are 'doing nothing?' I give up. With logic like that, I am embarrassed that you were hired to teach law, although I'm glad your terrorism kept you from getting a license to have the privilege Mr. Purpose and I have of arguing in court. And in fact, that itself is an area that will help establish your continuing support of murder to make a political statement. Tell the jury, please, why you weren't admitted to the New York bar, despite passing the bar exam."

Dohrn responded carefully, unsure about Denby's purpose. "I believe it was because of my criminal record from what I consider political crimes in the Weathermen, from the street demonstrations in 1969 and our armed propaganda."

"You know that's not true. The street-fighting and bail-jumping charges were reduced to misdemeanors with no jail time, and all the bombing charges were dropped because the FBI broke the law in its surveillance. I have the New York Bar Association report right here, and you know what's in it. Again, please tell us why you weren't allowed to be a real lawyer, professor." Denby finally used the title, but with a sneer, to convey to the jury her opinion of Dohrn's appointment.

"Well, the report did mention my refusal to cooperate with a grand jury on a fishing expedition, but it wasn't clear that this was the sole reason for its decision."

"Just any grand jury? You were jailed for seven months in 1982, Ms. Dohrn. Surely you can remember why. Please, tell us what happened."

"OK, I was asked questions about a case I knew nothing about, the Brink's armored car hold-up in Nyack, New York. I was asked to give a writing sample, and to testify about friends, comrades from the May 19 group, who had allegedly been involved on the periphery of the Brink's case, who had killed nobody yet were being tried for murder just because they once had been in the Weather Underground.

"Even though I knew nothing about it, I wasn't going to take part in a charade by the district attorney who was trying to drag Weatherman into an action that took place five years after we disbanded. Two of our comrades are still in prison today, nearly 40 years later, and they didn't kill anybody. They should never have been tried for murder, and I wasn't going to help, like a good German. I stood up for what was right by refusing to cooperate."

"Oh, Ms. Dohrn, thank you," said Denby with acid in her voice. "Thank you for helping the jury understand that the laws of every jurisdiction in America are just plain stupid, that planning, carrying out, and acting as a get-away driver for robbery and murder isn't really robbery and murder. You know full well that the law says it is, so are you arguing something else, that your friends had no moral role in the murder of three people, two police officers and a Brink's guard, just because they didn't actually do the shooting?"

Dohrn cut her losses and sat silent. Denby continued: "Silence, huh? Just like the buttons you and Mr. Ayers wore and also put on your five-year-old son when you refused to testify, right? 'We won't talk.' Remember, Ms. Dohrn, this was far from your friends' first armed action as part of the 'Family' that the all-white May 19 group formed with the Black Liberation Army. They already had a number of armed robberies behind them. And it was far from their first murder. That was the shooting of Brink's guard William Molroney four months before, for no reason, after he'd given up the cash. I ask you again, did your friends play no moral role in the Brink's murders?"

Dohrn still sat silent, cornered for once by someone clearly as smart and as showy as her. Denby decided against asking the judge to demand an answer, and moved to the question she had been setting up with the Brink's dialogue.

"You refused to assist the grand jury, despite having been granted immunity, which was a crime, correct? That's why you went to jail, that's why you were never allowed to become a lawyer. So, let me again ask the questions you refused to answer back then. First, did one of the Brink's defendants have an identification card you had forged, and used at one of your jobs in New York just before coming out from the underground in 1980?"

Dohrn spoke up this time, turning to the judge and saying, "Your Honor, I refuse to answer on the grounds that it may tend to incriminate me. I am invoking my Fifth Amendment rights. I have no immunity on this matter at this point."

Purpose, Denby, and Brittain huddled behind the electronic noise-canceller to work through this latest roadblock. The judge said the witness was correct, the defense counsel asked the prosecutor to offer immunity, but Purpose said, "No way, Your Honor. This witness isn't going to extort anything more from the government. For all I know she had a role in that Brink's case, and I'm not going to fall for any more of her schemes. That's absolutely beyond my pay grade, and given the heartache she's already caused me, I'm not even going to ask."

Denby tried to make the most of her disappointment. "Well, Ms. Dohrn, we're going to have to leave your involvement in the Brink's case behind. That's a case in which, incredibly, you've equated your refusal to help solve a triple-murder of police and guards to the resistance to the murderous Hitler regime by brave Germans, like the officers in the Valkyrie plot and the non-violent White Rose pamphleteers. My Lord.

"But let me ask you just one question about something you yourself have introduced, your proud refusal to help solve the crime. Shouldn't the fact that you took the Fifth because you are still scared of being held liable for these three murders warn the jury that you and political murder are no strangers, that you would see nothing wrong in offing a few pigs with John Jacobs, the assassinations for which you've set up Valerius Shaw?"

"No, counselor, and you're violating my constitutional rights, and you, Your Honor, are letting her do it. You both know full well that the Supreme Court has held that taking the Fifth Amendment cannot be interpreted by a jury to cast doubt on me, and further...."

Judge Brittain smashed the gavel down, stunning the courtroom. "Take the jury out, please," she said with obvious but restrained fury. She waited without expression as the jury filed out. Purpose kept his head down, knowing what was coming and realizing there was no benefit in being seen as the witness' protector during it. Denby also kept her head down, to keep from laughing in delight at the self-destruction of the witness. She only wished the jury had been allowed to see what was coming.

"Ms. Dohrn, I warned you about trying to take over my courtroom. You lectured me in front of a jury from the witness stand. Unbelievable, especially for a lawyer, at the bar or not. You are sentenced to five days for contempt of court, not for invoking your constitutional right in refusing to answer a question, but for trying to address the entire court on the law — on which, as I'll tell the jury when they return, you are in error. It is defendants, and not witnesses, who may not have their motives questioned by attorneys or jurors for invoking the Fifth Amendment.

"You will be taken into custody when you come off the stand today. If you continue as a witness, you will be brought to and from the courtroom by the U.S. Marshall. No, no, no, you may not speak. I don't want to hear a word about this from you, now or ever, in this courtroom. If I do, you will serve for contempt of court until the end of the entire trial. If your lawyer wishes to challenge my decision, it can be done in a brief, submitted to my office." Boom! Down came the gavel again. "Bring the jury back in."

After Brittain's correction of Dohrn's statement, Denby knew not to go anywhere near the Brink's case. It couldn't get any better than a judge slapping down a witness in front of a jury. Instead, she spent the better part of two more days forcing Dohrn to describe in detail her role in the bombings and her frequent interactions by phone with J. J. in their planning. She couldn't shake Dohrn's denial of knowing of J. J.'s connection to the murders, but she did make her look somewhat dense for not having figured it out.

Purpose had had enough of the radicals. He decided not to put on Ayers. Black had already submitted Ayers' statement for the record and reviewed it on the stand, so he could refer to it in his closing argument if he needed it. His final witness wasn't particularly cooperative, but through a grant of immunity would have to help him out. Black's energetic digging in the memory of aging leftists in Swarthmore had finally paid off. She had found Melissa Laurel, the indisputable link between Shaw and Jacobs.

* * *

CHAPTER 20: MARCH 2018 — SWEET MELISSA

"Your Honor, the witness has been granted the broadest possible immunity for her testimony, but I still request permission to approach her as a hostile witness."

Purpose was taking no chances with his final Weather-witness, having been burned by Dohrn and Ayers from the second he'd first heard their names from Imaglio. From the time Black had found her, Melissa Laurel had angrily ducked and weaved and asked that the government just go away from her quiet, happy life as a Methodist minister to a small congregation on the Iowa side of the Quad Cities, in Davenport. Even after getting immunity, her answers in the deposition were pointedly minimalist. By having her declared a hostile witness, Purpose could badger and lead her the way Denby had savaged Dohrn, and force her to answer in full.

"Reverend Laurel, when you were the printer and publisher at the so-called underground press in Swarthmore in the early 1970s, did you do favors for the Weather Underground, pass messages, help keep travelers out of sight, give them money and food, things like that?"

"Yes." Melissa spoke without elaboration, and even without tone, refusing to give any more than she needed to.

"You were visited by John Jacobs, J. J., in June 1970. What did you do to help him?"

"He stayed with me."

"Your Honor, please direct the witness to answer fully, or we'll be here for a year," begged Purpose. It took a few direct instructions from Brittain, but the reluctant the Reverend Melissa Laurel eventually became more forth-coming. Laurel said that she'd helped Jacobs find Val Shaw, despite knowing that J. J. had been expelled from the Weathermen, and that she assumed he and Val were planning their own actions against the war. She testified that the two men had been inseparable in the summer of 1970, hosting at least a dozen shooting sessions attended by Melissa and other local radicals on state land twenty miles from Swarthmore.

"The rifle lessons were for self-defense, if the police chased us down sometime. Everybody knew what happened to Hampton and Clark in Chicago, and we wanted to be able to keep that from happening to us." Melissa denied, though, any knowledge of a trip by Val and J. J. to Boston in October 1970, or any shooting at people by them at all.

"But by that time, weren't you Val Shaw's lover? Wouldn't you know why he wasn't around?" Black had easily established the romance, but couldn't nail down a starting point. Only Purpose, in court, could find out for sure. "I believe we were, by October, but I still knew nothing about a trip to Boston," responded Laurel.

Having made his point, Purpose moved on. "Why did Val Shaw finally drop his stand against student deferments, and ask for a 2-S from his draft board in January 1971? Was that J. J.'s influence, because he wanted Val out, and free to help with political assassinations?"

"J. J. often told Val to take the deferment, so he could continue anti-war work. I don't know if that's what put him over the top. I've already said that I don't know anything about any assassinations." Melissa continued to be careful with her words, but kept away from her earlier one-word answers, so as not to anger the judge like Dohrn, whom she knew was still sitting in jail, finishing her five days for contempt.

"Oh, really?" Purpose walked over to face her, just as Denby had faced off with Dohrn. "When J. J. left town that fall you continued to talk to him on the phone until 1975, didn't you, telling him when Val was going to be traveling for his job as a musician? Wasn't it obvious that bombings and then murders followed, every time you passed that information? You have immu-nity, so please answer fully."

"No, I never thought of the connection, at least not for a couple of years. It wasn't like J. J. had a standing order for me to tell him when Val traveled. It was just that J. J. and I kept in touch, we were friends, and he'd ask me, sort of by-the-by, how Val was doing and where he was playing, like maybe J. J. would go see him if he was in that city. And there were lots of other times that Val went in the limousine and nothing like that happened, so I didn't make anything of it."

"How very convenient for you, Dr. Laurel, to never have been part of a conspiracy to bomb and shoot people. I'm sure your congregation wouldn't like to have an assassin for a minister. Still, you must see my skepticism that for five years your lover, the defendant, never told you what he was doing, and you, with access to all the underground newspapers and all the Weatherman and Weather-cat communiqués, never put it all together with Mr. Shaw's travels that you just happened to share with J. J."

Melissa appeared finally to crack, seeming to forget her resolve to talk as little as possible. She had already thought out what she would have to say to her congregation about her past, and so the well-practiced response came out coherently.

"I wish you people would leave me alone. When the war was raging, yes, I helped hide people I knew were bombing, not because I supported bombing, but because I didn't want to help the government, which was doing its own bombing, far worse than the Weathermen. Today, I'd turn in anybody I knew was planning a bombing, in a heartbeat. Look, it was a crazy time, and I was wrong. I want to be clear about that. I was wrong. I made a mistake, of the heart, for the best of causes, and I repented. I went to divinity school, I became a minister, I counsel people, I try to help them.

"And all this you are trying to pin on me was nearly 50 years ago. I wasn't like Bernardine and Billy and J. J. and all them, back then: I printed, I didn't bomb. And I'm not like them now, still supporting the bombings as justified by the times: as a minister I am committed to non-violent resistance, only, to our imperial adventures and the harm they did in Viet Nam, and then in Central America in the '80s, and that they do today in the Middle East. Becoming violent makes us just like the government we are criticizing."

The judge called for the morning break, and Purpose huddled with his team. They had much of what they had wanted from Laurel: the closeness with J. J., the shooting practice, the advice to drop the draft struggle. They didn't believe a word of her claims of ignorance. She was in on it, from the start, and seduced Shaw to stay close to him, for sure. But they had nothing tangible in a case that already relied more on talk than direct evidence. Purpose decided to drop the combat pose, follow up on the late suspicions she had acknowledged in the immunity negotiations, and then let her go.

"Hello again, Reverend Laurel. I appreciate how hard this is for you, to relive difficult and wrenching decisions from decades ago, and I promise you, I would just as soon not be talking about them either. But to find justice for the horrific murders of six government and private officials, men and women who were brutally denied their dreams, hopes, and families because of the violence you now agree must be renounced, I must ask you about a key factor in this case. And that is the state of mind, from 1970 to 1975, of Valerius Shaw.

"Now, nobody from that time knows his state of mind like you, other than him, and I don't know if the jury is going to hear from him, so I must ask you just a few more questions."

"Objection, objection! Outrageous!" Denby shot up from her seat, at first intending to call for a mistrial, but then catching herself, because as a strategy that needed more thought. Holding the mistrial motion in reserve, she simply asked the judge if she would consider instructing the jury to disregard the prosecutor's implication of guilt, and explaining why that was necessary.

Brittain at first wanted to have the jury taken out while she castigated Purpose, but then figured that the only way to avoid a reversal of a verdict would be to allow the jury to hear her lecture him. She followed an angry dressing-down with a clear instruction to the jury that the Fifth Amendment's protection against even the implication of guilt, which she had denied to a witness, Dohrn, applied iron-clad to defendants. Nothing whatsoever was to be thought about whether or not Mr. Shaw chose to testify.

Purpose apologized profusely to the judge, but only for the possible misinterpretation of his statement about Shaw, not admitting that he had tried to taint the defendant. He had taken a chance in his indirect reference, but he had succeeded in one of his pre-trial goals of making the jury at least think about Shaw's refusal to testify. Then he returned to his final work on Laurel.

"When did you realize there was something suspicious about the connection between Mr. Shaw's trips, Mr. Jacobs' calls, and various bombings and killings?"

Melissa replied: "I can't say for sure. But I do remember becoming worried after the murder of the little girl in Pittsburgh, whenever that was."

"That was June of 1974, Reverend. So, what made you suspicious at that time?"

"Well, there was language in the Nathan Hale communiqué that struck me as similar to something J. J. had said to me not too long before, so I reread it, and then realized there was also stuff just like some of Val's letters to the editor, and it hit me, all of a sudden, that the middle name of his son, the boy I'd been sometimes babysitting, was Hale, although Val never used it. I believed, right then, for the first time, that something strange was going on."

Purpose was almost there. His soft and understanding persona was doing much better than his belligerent one. He asked her, "So, did you go then to Val or to J. J. and simply say, what are you doing, are you involved in these killings?"

"Well, I was sure curious, but I was also feeling cautious, so when J. J. next called, I off-handedly asked him why he didn't just ask Val for his own travel schedule. He was suddenly sharp with me, said he talked to Val all the time, that he didn't know what I was talking about, that he didn't remember asking me anything about his travels. Alarm bells went off. There was something in his voice that gave me a physical tremor of fear, like I'd never felt before.

"Then I remembered that J. J. told me once that some people in the Weather Bureau had threatened others with execution if they tried to leave the group. And he'd said that he agreed, 100 percent, with that point of view. I knew radicals who'd ended up in the Symbionese Liberation Army, and murdered a school superintendent in Oakland for some ideological reason. I knew people who were in the cult with Jim Jones, who told me they'd chanted their willingness to die for him, people who did later die in the Jonestown suicide and massacre of a thousand Bay Area folks. There was craziness out there! Once I got the whiff of murder, after Pittsburgh, given that talk with J. J. about executions for the Weather Bureau, I actually didn't want to know, I just wanted to get away.

"I freaked out. I left Swarthmore almost immediately and broke off all contact with the movement, so nobody could find me. I moved to Vermont, worked quietly under a false name, and didn't make a public peep until Bernardine and Billy were above ground, and the last ones, the most violent, Kathy Boudin, Judy Clark, David Gilbert, Marilyn Buck, were all in jail for the Brink's murders. And I think time has proved I was smart to hide away. If they could justify killing bank guards for the revolution, they could justify killing a possible rat like me, in a heartbeat. Anyway, by the mid-1980s I felt it was safe to get involved in work against the contra war, the war in El Salvador, all that, and I surfaced and went to divinity school."

"One final question, Reverend." With this sudden burst of venom about the violence of the Weathermen, Purpose had more than he could have hoped for. But he had to end on the Weather-cat murders, not the Brink's ones, so he tried one last time to tie the assassinations to Weather's wanton sense of righteousness.

"The implication of your running and hiding is clear to me, and I hope to the jury as well. But I want you to make it clear. You ran because you believed that John Jacobs and Valerius Shaw, both of whom you knew extremely well, were capable, because of ideology, personality, whatever else, of killing a congressman, a general, a diplomat, and others, including you, for the sake of the revolution, is that what you are saying?"

"Well, J. J., maybe, but I wasn't scared of Val. I didn't think that guy could be a killer, and I knew him well, like you said. Mostly I was scared of the Weather Bureau, of Bernardine, she was the brains, the leader, and maybe of Billy, Jeff Jones, Kathy Boudin — those were the people I felt could kill for the revolution. That's why I ran."

Purpose felt his high start to slip away. Where had that come from? Get her off! "Your Honor, I'm done with this witness." And after Denby had Laurel briefly reaffirm this gift, this claim that it was the Weather Bureau, and not Shaw, whose potential for murder put her on the road, the prosecution rested.

* * *

CHAPTER 21: APRIL 2018 — THE DEFENSE

"Val, Selam, we're in far better shape than I thought we'd be by this point. We always knew they'd have the strong suit on the travel times, but Dohrn looked pathetic, opening up our claim that it's a set-up, adding more than reasonable doubt. And thanks to sweet Melissa, the jury thinks she'll kill for the cause. The only question is, will they accept how devious, how complex she and Ayers had to be to set you up, and keep you set up, for nearly 50 years? Can they believe that someone could be so cunning, so perseverant, to keep all the moving parts in line?"

Sharia Denby was sitting in her firm's DC office with Shaw and his wife, sharing coffee on a Saturday morning. She was using the weekend to make her final decisions on defense strategy before trial resumed on Monday. The lawyers the firm had put at her disposal, ranging from ten-year partners to first-year associates, were all in the building, working on closing arguments, just in case she decided not to put on a defense at all.

The firm had long since gone into *pro bono* mode on this one, blowing past the half-million dollars Val and Selam's families had put together, with all their siblings and parents joining them in refinancing homes, cashing in stocks, even parts of their IRA's, with the ten percent penalty. But the partners had decided it would be worth it in publicity — the next troubled tech billionaire would know the firm's name, for sure. It would be even better if Sharia actually won, giving them the sort of O. J. moment that had catapulted Johnnie Cochran's firm to national stature and success, even long after his death.

"Now, here's what I'm thinking for the defense. While I'm tempted to drop it completely, and go straight to the jury with Laurel's fear of the Weathermen in mind, I think there are three holes we still have to fill. First, the jury got too much of me, a lawyer, exposing Dohrn's lies and hypocrisy as the basis for reasonable doubt on whether Val was set up. We're prepared to put on the Berkeley professor whose work kept showing up in the government subpoenas, Vanessa LeBlanc. She's got her ticket and is waiting for the call. I got ahold of her dissertation on this — she was one of the first scholars to strip away the "violent rogue" dodge — and after talking to her during pre-trial, I realized she had a lot of goodies that didn't make it into her work.

"She can catalogue the constant flow of Weather-lies and, more importantly, explain the contempt the lying reveals that Ayers and Dohrn have for the system. If the jury grasps their continuing hope of world revolution, the way they party like it's still 1970, they'll see that for them, it would be all right to murder then, set up a patsy, and keep lying about it now.

"I mean, people with so much belief in their cause, in their superiority, that they kill for it, what makes them different from Val and the other protestors? It's personality. These folks are that small part of society that is prone to being sociopaths. They are the Jonestown types, the ISIS types, the militia that pulled off the Oklahoma City bombing, both the leaders and the followers. They naturally gravitate toward certainty and then extremism, whatever their politics might be. I know Dohrn showed us flashes of it in arguing with me, and with the judge, but I want a clear exposition, so the jury knows that an expert in terrorist groups says they still are one, in their own minds, with no concern for those who openly disagree with them or for collateral damage among bystanders."

Val spoke up. "Well, I have no problem with that. Selam?" His wife shook her head. She had come to some of the strategy sessions, which had required the firm to write memos for the file describing her as Val's agent because of the murky but usually unchallenged grey areas where spousal and lawyer privileges overlapped. Selam then looked straight at her, and added: "Come on Sharia, you didn't call Val down here to mull over witness lists. You know what you're doing, we trust you with that. What's up? There must be something you really need from him."

Denby laughed. "My goodness, Selam, you must be a terror in staff meetings. No foreplay, right down to business? Hey, I'm just clearing my throat, getting to the second and third holes in our case. And yes, I really do need Val's decision on them.

"Watching the jury, I would say that we were wounded by just two things in our hunt for reasonable doubt: why Val switched on the draft, taking a student deferment after Jacobs asked him to be available for violence, and why the Cambridge bomber, Alice Truxton, was so hard to shake, so credible, about seeing you with J. J. in October 1970.

"I mean, Sweet Melissa has you at rifle practice with Jacobs all summer, and then in October, rifle shots get deflected at Huntington's house. I know you weren't in on it, but we don't have any proof. We've searched the microfilms for any ad or listing about you playing in Swarthmore that weekend, but the hippie weekly that would have been most likely for those clubs never made the cut at the public library.

"Now I told you I rarely put a defendant on the stand, but the stakes are pretty high here if we can't fill these holes, and I wonder who could do it other than you. But first, explain the draft thing to me."

"Well, Sharia, on the draft, it's pretty simple," Val responded. "J. J. may have been in my ear that summer, but you notice I didn't take the 2-S then. I did it in January 1971, right after I got the six-month medical deferral. Why? Gee, what had just changed in my life?"

Denby sat without answering, confused. Selam spoke up: "It's not your fault, Sharia. You don't have the family dates in your head. That's just after Nathan's birth, December 20, 1970. Val had a son. He didn't want to leave him, or drag him to Canada. That's not the kind of parent he is."

"Is that true?" Denby turned to Val. "Was this great moral stand of your youth, all this agonizing over the right way to oppose the war, just blown away, just like that?" She snapped her fingers.

"It's funny, Selam and I have never talked about it in much detail, but she's got it perfectly. It happened in a heart-beat — Nat's. I took one look at him as the nurses wheeled him by, that thoughtful little face looking at me. I remember thinking bizarrely that with his puffy cheeks he looked like Winston Churchill pondering a new brand of cigar. Anyway, I just knew, right then, what was right.

"Well, if not right, then clearly more right than the competing, previous right thing of going to jail to try to save the lives of the Vietnamese and the G.I.'s. That's what you learn as an adult, that the real choices aren't between easy and hard, like in the kids' hagiographies I'd read in the elementary school library, like Nixon pretended in his fake agonies, but between two imperfects.

"It was over. I didn't know it until I was on the way home from the induction center, the next month, with a six-month medical deferment, that I just finally decided to decide. I actually sat down that night and wrote a song about it, it was so simple. I still remember the words: 'I'd die like a Gaul in Roman times, that's what I used to say.' And then I riffed off a Dylan line about giving you heart to someone, but keeping your soul. The draft got my heart, but Nat trumped it; my line was 'give a child your soul.' That was my choice, between prison six months later and the long-term student deferment: immediate heroism like Horatius at the bridge, or a life of heroism in being a patient, present father. I knew I'd made the right choice.

"Not to say that it didn't hurt then, and doesn't hurt now. I would respect myself more, and expect others to as well, if I'd hung tough, and gone to prison. I wish I had. It was the right thing, like I said, but just not right enough. Part of me has always wondered, as I knew I would, if I was fooling myself, chickening out and using Nat as an excuse. But so what? Even if it's true, if I chose from subconscious fear, I still did right by him. I felt, not thought, that he needed a father, not a David Harris poster, while I sat in jail, and that was that."

"Well, it's a good tale for a jury," said Denby. "But can anybody else tell it? Who knew?"

"Hmmm...you know, I purposely didn't confide back then in other people, like draft counselors or other resisters. I was just a kid, I knew I was impressionable, and I was too scared that this key decision wouldn't be mine. Only when I was grown, writing some history on the movement, did I find out that only a few thousand kids actually went all the way to jail out of maybe half a million who broke the draft laws, many of whom never even registered. The Army was getting the bodies it needed, and massive prosecution would have just rocked the boat for no reason.

"Of course I'm sure I talked about it with Sally, my first ex-wife, I call her, like the country song, just in case I have to divorce Selam for something. Just joking! Amhara believe in shotgun divorces, not shotgun weddings. But I really can't recall, and born-again Sally and I haven't talked in years; since Nathan finished college, only at his wedding. I do know from what Nathan told me in high school, though, that she doesn't recall a lot of what happened the way I do."

Denby thought about it for half a minute. "Nah, the jury's not going to buy anything from an ex-wife anyway, and we sure don't want the prosecutor going after her, opening up all sorts of worm cans. Probably scare her into the Fifth or the spousal, and then we look as bad as his star witnesses made him look. But maybe we can get the song in, and get somebody who knows your music to talk about it. What about the recording engineer, Coles?"

"Well, I know he thinks I'm not their guy, because he called and told me so when the FBI talked to him. But I didn't know Bill until a couple of years after that decision."

Selam spoke up. "Here's an idea, since all you need to do is plant the seed, not prove the claim. Why not let LeBlanc look through Val's writings, from back then and all the way to now, and when she's testifying about Weather's philosophy you can have her contrast it with Val's, show that Val isn't one of them. Then, you can slip in the draft and birth-dates and have her assess the lyrics of that song as proof of his state of mind. Have her put 'like a Gaul in Roman times' into the context of 'give a child your soul' by not going to prison. That should make the jury see Nathan, and not Jacobs, as the cause of his draft-dodging."

There was a long silence, and then Val laughed. "Well, Sharia, now aren't you glad Selam decided to join us today? Like the old Merle Travis song says, 'If you don't think she's a lot of fun, just ask the man that owns one'!"

"I'm not familiar with Mr. Travis, and I'll leave the sexist lyrics for your revolutionary generation, but thanks, Selam. I do think we might be able to fill that hole with the good professor, and I love the whole concept of the contrasting philosophies. But I'm still stuck on Cambridge, right? Is having you take the stand to deny going there worth the risk of letting Purpose get into your business for as long as he wants? I'm thinking not, especially since we can fill those other two holes."

"I'm thinking not too, Sharia, but not for that reason. I talked about this with Selam for the first time last night, and we agreed that you need to know too. I can't take the stand to say I wasn't there, because I was. I'm sorry to mislead you, but when I told you I was innocent of the charges, I was being cute, on purpose. The charges didn't include the Huntington shooting."

The room was quiet, as Denby sat and thought to herself about that. "Jesus Christ, how could I be so dense? How could I forget the first rule of criminal law, of all law, for that matter? Everybody lies, maybe a little, maybe a lot. Everybody wants to look better to themselves and others than they are. Everybody's a little bit greedy, and able to justify it to themselves. Thank God I didn't put him up there to get torn up and go to jail for what he didn't do because he got caught lying about what he did do. Well, then again, maybe he did do the six murders, maybe he's lying about that too. No point in asking that."

"I sure wish I'd known, Val." Denby let that hang in the air. "So, Nathan's birth did a lot more than turn you into a draft dodger from a draft resister, huh?"

"Sharia, I'm sorry. I'm sorry. I didn't want to admit it to you, to Selam, to anybody. I was just as crazy as all of them, 18 years old and Viet Nam crazy, Fred Hampton crazy, happy to join J. J. in out-Weather-manning the Weathermen. Even shooting at Huntington didn't bring me up short."

"Details, I need to know it all," said Denby.

"Well, it was a surprise that I was the shooter, actually. The plan was always for J. J. to shoot and me to be the backup on this one. Operational security, one of us absent, to preserve the long-term mission if the shooter got caught. But he was busy with the bomb, and I had gotten just as good, maybe better than him, with all that target practice, so he sent me. Hell, maybe that was all part of the set-up, too.

"Anyway, his scouting a few weeks before had missed the storm window, or maybe it had been added. When I saw Huntington in the scope, just 30 yards from my blind across the street, it was like a movie, just like the target practice we'd done with head models, no emotion for me. I was surprised when the window glass shattered and the shot missed.

"We'd practiced on glass, and a perpendicular shot always went straight through, leaving a small hole. I didn't think about it, but fired again. This one missed too, and I realized as I was packing the rifle into the fishing rod bag that there was a storm window there, still hanging, with two holes in it. We figured out later that the stronger material deflected both bullets.

"I walked alleys back to the house we used, and we headed straight out for Swarthmore. I'm sorry to say that I was still on board, almost eager for another chance. But it's true, one look at Nat and I snapped out of it. Seeing such a human life, bursting with potential, it made me literally sick that I had ever tried to end one.

"At least I was smart enough not to argue with J. J. about it. He'd left town, anyway, so I just told Melissa that if she ever talked to him, let him know I was done with politics. He'd know what that meant. Christ, 'ever talked to him'? It was pretty clear from your cross-examination that she was feeding him my schedule once I started playing for Dom, for all those years. All they had to do was keep an eye on me, make sure I wasn't with some witness at the time of these hits."

Denby stopped Val's ramblings. "Shades of Nixon, Val: what did you know and when did you know it? When did you get the connection between Weather-cat and you?"

"When the FBI put it in the indictment, period. Even when Bill Coles emailed me, I could not for the life of me figure out what he was talking about. I know it sounds lame, like Dohrn on the stand claiming she didn't know, but in my case it's true. I was oblivious to all the bombings and murders; I really had put politics behind me, like a bad dream.

"I think I was so disgusted that Americans accepted Nixon's plan to keep the war going with Vietnamese bodies that I even stopped reading the papers. I was taking classes, taking Nat to the playground and the stream, not always thinking about the war all day long. I mean after a while, like everybody, I knew vaguely about some killings they were calling Weather-cat, but I never focused on the cities they were in, never got this whole scheme until the FBI cracked it."

Val stopped and thought. "You know, Melissa's story helps us, but now I'm starting to think that it's bull, all this running from fear once she figured out in 1974 that there was murder in the air. Look, she would have been reprinting all the bombing communiqués, and she worked on organizing anti-war protests out of the religious office at Swarthmore. She would've had to see the connection of the bombing and the murders, with J. J. in on both. Maybe she was in on setting me up too, knowing damn well why J. J. kept asking about my travel schedule."

"Hello! Hate to break it to you, stud," interjected Selam, "but did you ever wonder why a worldly 25-year-old woman would take up with a teenager? It couldn't have been your usual musical magic, the bar room effect of the boy on stage. I'll bet you guys were an item as soon as J. J. brought you over, right? She was a regular Mata Hari for the cause!"

Denby laughed. "Now, now, that was all a long time ago. And as I recall the story, Selam, one look at you and it was all over. Back to business. Let me tell you how I'm leaning on all this. I don't care what Laurel's lying about: she was gold for us for running scared, and we are not introducing any ideas to the contrary. I think I'm going to use the professor to deal with the Weathermen's murderous hearts, paint Val as a pacifist, and immunize us on the draft question. Val, Selam, nobody can ever hear, nobody ever, for your sake and mine, about Cambridge, got it? We're going to ignore Truxton's claim until closing arguments, and then I'll do a little dance around my professional obligation not to lie, and just cast some doubt on her motives."

* * *

CHAPTER 22: APRIL 2018 — THE PROFESSOR

Sharia Denby addressed Judge Brittain: "Your Honor, the defense calls Professor Vanessa LeBlanc as an expert witness, generally on radical activists in the 1960s and 1970s and specifically on the history and the ideology of the Weather Underground."

Purpose sat unhappily at the prosecution table, having lost his battle with Denby over relevance. He'd hoped Val Shaw would be the one explaining the madness of the times, because he apparently still believed in it. Now, Denby's witness would trash Dohrn, and he'd just have to sit and take it. There was no benefit to his case in taking part in a contest of who was more wicked, Dohrn or Shaw. He'd just save his ammunition for summation, to hammer the evidence home again. At least there was a silver lining: the leeway the judge was giving the defense would hamper any appeal.

The prosecutor had been unhappy, actually, since Melissa Laurel had called Dohrn capable of murder and Shaw not. Not that the case was gone, by any means. He still felt that with Alice Truxton's Cambridge I.D. to show pattern and with the solid evidence on motive and means, he could win it. But he'd be happy to listen to an offer. Of course, he couldn't be the one to start that discussion. If Denby came to him, he thought he could get something like five years on conspiracy for aiding Jacobs, two with good behavior. The local D.A.'s probably wouldn't try to follow up. If the feds couldn't get murder, how would they?

Denby, too, thought the prosecution could still well win it, despite the boost Val had gotten from Dohrn's shrinking credibility and Laurel's fear of murderous Weathermen, but she wasn't mulling over whether to approach Purpose. Val had ruled out any plea from the start and had reaffirmed it after his shocking revelation about being the shooter in Cambridge. Of course, if Purpose approached her, that would be a different matter. Then she'd have the whip hand and could maybe come up with a suspended sentence to take back to Val. For now, it looked like both sides were just going to roll the dice.

"Professor LeBlanc, have I paid you or compensated you in any way to be here?"

"No, you haven't," LeBlanc. "Just air fare and hotel. I checked with my university's counsel, and that's the policy she recommended to preserve my scholarly standing." She didn't look much like a scholar, with her stylish dress and the carefully-done red hair cascading over it, but she had a scholar's laser-like focus on whoever was speaking and whatever was being said. "I'm a political scientist and not a partisan in any of these matters, and I told you, as I told Agent McGurk when she interviewed me during the investigation, that it's part of my job to profess, to talk with anybody about any of my findings."

"Well, this certainly is a new experience for me, an expert witness who refuses to be paid. But what if you write a book about this case, perhaps you can make a lot of money, get a movie deal? Perhaps that's why you're here?" Denby wanted to pre-empt any aspersions Purpose might cast.

"Well, Ms. Denby, that would be wonderful, but the meager sales of my academic books, focused on today's authoritarian movements of the left and the right, are typical for most academic works. That tends to make me realistic and hence pessimistic about another one. And as for the movies, well, hope springs eternal, but a very fine if necessarily simplified Weather-drama, *The Company You Keep*, covered much of the same ground as this case, and had less than stellar receipts when it came out six years ago. I'm not sure how much demand there is in America for looking back on this history, or on any history, for that matter!"

"All right, professor, then let's get to the key question. Your reputation as a scholar is attested to by your long list of degrees, publications, grants, memberships, and awards. You have read nearly everything there is to read by and about the Weather Underground, and you have read everything we could find that was written by Professor Shaw, from the 1970s to today.

Based on your expert analysis, please tell the jury who's more likely to have had no moral problem with planning and conducting these six assassinations, the Dohrn-Ayers team, or Professor Shaw? Who has the track record that makes it more likely that they could have resorted to the brutal violence of these politically-motivated crimes?"

"I'm sorry, counselor," started LeBlanc. "I know the court has designated me an 'expert witness' whose opinion the jury should weigh with respect, but it's for the very reason I was so designated, that I'm a scholar, that I must object to answering your question immediately. In academia we don't use the *ad hominem* argument, positively or negatively. Just as I wouldn't let my students reject out of hand a claim because it's made by someone without a degree or with a felony conviction, I wouldn't let them just accept my conclusion simply because I'm credentialed and have never been accused of a crime.

"And I wouldn't want the jury to, either. While you'll see that I've reached a personal conclusion on your question, it's certainly not one of scientific certainty. I'd prefer to describe the issues and the evidence and then my analysis, so the jury can have the same facts available as I do, when they finally answer your question themselves in the jury room. So, let me begin, if I may." LeBlanc turned to the jury and began a lesson, as if she were in a classroom, forming perfect paragraphs, without using a single note. Denby was startled by unexpectedly losing control of the witness, but her preparatory conversations with the professor convinced her that it would all come out right.

"As a political scientist, my task is the same here as when I write about politics: to use primary documents, participants' memories, and others' analyses to assess the evidence for and against theories. And three theories have been presented in this case:

"First, there's the defense theory, which is that Bernardine Dohrn, Bill Ayers, and J. J. Jacobs, having faked to all (except the Weather Bureau) Jacobs' May 1970 expulsion from the Weathermen, formed a tiny cell that planned and carried out the murders. To protect themselves, they engaged in a complex conspiracy to use Shaw's travel schedule and performance times to set up him up to look responsible. The motive for that conspiracy, the defense claims, was to have somebody to trade to the government if Dohrn's role in the Park Station killing was ever revealed.

"Second, there's the Dohrn theory, which admits to the fake expulsion of Jacobs and the formation of the tiny cell, but claims it was done only to facilitate bombings, and that she and the Weather Bureau had no knowledge of the murder plots. In this theory, Jacobs on his own, without Dohrn and Ayers' knowledge, planned and carried out the murders with Shaw.

"Finally, there's the government's theory, which simply claims that Jacobs and Shaw murdered together. Jacobs is dead, so the only issue is Shaw's conduct. The dispute over Dohrn and Ayers' knowledge of or partici-pation in the murder plots is irrelevant to this theory, as are the various roles played by Jacobs and Shaw in the actual murders. The government does not say exactly who did what, but the arguments and evidence it has submitted strongly imply that Jacobs handled planning and scouting while Shaw was the hit-man, following pre-planned instructions after arriving in the various cities for his musical appearances.

"The only case I can identify in which Jacobs possibly even had to be on the scene was the murder of Mr. Gray and his daughter in Pittsburgh, where a sophisticated bomb was attached to a vehicle. Unlike his familiarity and practice with a rifle, there's no record that Shaw knew anything about bomb-making."

Denby began to feel silly, standing there and nodding, so she went back to her seat, and let the professor continue the lesson.

"Central to evaluating these three theories is the ideologies of the partici-pants. I know that defense counsel has asked me who was more likely to be violent, Dohrn and Ayers or Shaw. But violence is simply a tactic, something to use in pursuit of a goal. So, what are their goals? That is the question I focused on.

"By goal, I don't even mean something like 'stop the war' or the broader 'end U.S. support for dictators who cooperate militarily or economically with our imperial plans.' What I mean by goal is, what is the outcome in the United States that will allow those things to happen? And here's where the credibility of the three theories can be best assessed.

"One of the things I discovered in doing the research for my dissertation, and which will be the crucial issue here today, is the importance of ideology. The Weather Bureau had an ideology, a set of beliefs that organized their actions. People who criticized them as rich kids acting out tantrums against their parents, or white kids subordinating themselves to and mimicking black leaders to assuage their racial guilt, may have identified some trees, as the metaphor goes, but they're missing the forest.

"Like most revolutionary groups in history, and like al-Qaeda and other terrorists today for that matter, the Weathermen took pains to explain very clearly why they did what they did. Their reasoning is transparent and logical, and their narrative is consistent. And to be fair to the perspective shared by the Weather Bureau and the defendant, Valerius Shaw, about American imperialism, I note that our government, like most governments with military forces deployed outside their borders, also uses an ideology to justify its actions, also has a simple narrative, and also broadcasts both very clearly.

"America's military narrative has a lot to do with freedom — expanding it, securing it, providing its benefits to other peoples. Like the European imperial narrative that preceded it, a narrative of altruistically passing along the benefits of 'civilization' to Africa, Asia, and the Middle East, it too can cover all manner of sins. And we've seen it used incessantly since the end of World War II, and indeed throughout our history of expansion from east coast colonies to world super-power. The great Russian novelist Leo Tolstoy likened all such narratives, whether presented by rebels or governments, to 'the brushes that go in front of a train to clear the way on the rails; they clear the way of people's moral responsibility'.

"Put plainly, the Weather Bureau was a cult with a powerful leader, Bernardine Dohrn, no different from other religious cults of the time like the Moonies, the Jonestown suicides, the Symbionese Liberation Army that kidnapped Patty Hearst, or the Scientologists. She exhibited complete control of the cult starting in 1968, when she mystified mainstream anti-war activists by declaring that she was a revolutionary communist, with a 'small c,' meaning she wasn't in the Communist Party.

"In 1969 to cement her rule, as a test of loyalty and to accustom her followers to accepting her orders in all realms, she instituted, in a classic cult move, the practice of group sex, of all members, male and female, being sexual partners. Her reign ended in November of 1976, when she had been reduced to having only one backer left, Bill Ayers, and was forced in classic Stalinist style to denounce herself in writing and abdicate to a rival faction led by Clayton van Lydegraf, who had been a 'big c' Communist before she was even born.

"There was an ideology, a set of interlocking, unquestionable beliefs that Dohrn promoted, and which she brilliantly guided her small and ever-dwindling band of converts to adopt, sometimes with lengthy discussions and sometimes with rapid decisions that challenged them on the spot to follow her or desert her. This ideology was expressed consistently as she demonstrated ultimate control over the key events of the Weatherman era: the summer 1969 Chicago convention that saw the writing of the Weatherman statement and the expulsion of the PL faction, the fall 1969 street-fighting of the 'Days of Rage,' the Christmas 1969 war council in Flint, Michigan, that started the bombing campaign, the Mendocino meeting in May 1970 that supposedly expelled J. J. Jacobs and prepared the 'Declaration of War,' the December 1970 'New Morning' statement, the 1974 *Prairie Fire* book, the 1975 *Underground* movie, and the choice of symbolic bombing targets throughout this entire period.

"I've written down my summary of the five-part ideology Dohrn imposed on the Weathermen, and I'd like it put up on the screen so that the jury can read it with me. It has a sequential logic, each piece supporting the one that follows. Direct quotations from the *Underground* interviews in 1975 are shown in the text." Denby had known this was part of the plan, so she snapped on the screen, and LeBlanc began to read.

● It's the system: You say you want to stop the genocidal Viet Nam war or keep there from being similar wars? You can't do that without ending the system of U.S. imperialism as a whole.

● Seize power: But you can't end imperialism without overthrowing the U.S. government, which uses its power to protect its capitalist bosses.

● How to seize power: To overthrow the capitalist U.S. government you need to be Marxist, Leninist, and Castro-ite:

1. Marxist means to reject profit and ownership and adopt social-ism as the economic system. "People, not Rockefellers, made the wealth...Profit is a theft, and the cause of poverty." Communism is the answer, not just economically, but spiritually: it attacks feel-ings of "isolation and atomization."
2. Leninist means to form a leadership group that seizes power and then enforces obedience in the new era.

3. Castro-ite means adopting the *foquismo* strategy for insurgency that Fidel Castro used to defeat the U.S.-backed Batista regime. As explained by Regis Debray in *Revolution in the Revolution?*, attacks by a small vanguard help the population "focus" on the issues and eventually join the rebellion.

● "Armed propaganda" spurs the revolution: In the American context, the Castro model means that the vanguard, Weatherman, radicalizes the masses for revolt not by organizing labor or students or other groups to demand reforms, but by military action that creates chaos and inspires already alienated working class and radical white youth to join in. "The people are backward now, divided by the canny rulers, poisoned and prodded by their fears."

● Bombing educates potential revolutionaries on both the facts and the possibility of success: "We reflect the views of the demonstrators by attacking their target...We wake people up to their possibilities."

● Communiqués show people America's true past, from the people's perspective, and counter the official classist and racist lies: "The reconstruction of history is a battle."

● It's working: The world-wide war against U.S. imperialism is already succeeding, with anti-colonial movements in Indochina, Latin America, and Africa creating Che's "two, three, many Viet Nams." It is also being fought by black Americans through urban riots and radical groups like the Black Panthers and its underground offshoot, the Black Liberation Army, by Hispanic Americans, notably in the FALN Puerto Rican bombing campaign, and by Indians in the American Indian Movement.

● So, white Americans have a moral duty to create a revolution by supporting the "Third World" movements at home and abroad — even if many of them, cautious because of their small-minded nationalism, disagree that conditions are right for a white military campaign in America, and even denounce our actions as "Custeristic" adventurism.

● Messianic white anti-slavery warrior John Brown is our hero and role model, and our newspaper *Osawatomie* is named after the Kansas town where Brown first battled the slavers. His son was murdered and his forces defeated, but he persisted and within four years sparked the civil war that led to black liberation. And today, "It's already happening... subject to the same laws as in the rest of the world...Revolution is becoming more and more likely...We will fight it out in the streets...We foresee a torrent of rebellion and the working class taking power. As Mao said, dreams and toil coincide."

"Now," continued LeBlanc, "this ideology was essentially memorized, believed, and almost physically incorporated through repetition and response by Dohrn and her followers. Deviation wasn't permitted. And it explains everything they did. In this context, the various forms of violence, such as street-fighting, bombing, kidnapping, assassination, these are all tactical questions for a particular time. For example, Dohrn's primary motivation at Mendocino for stopping potentially lethal bombings and starting to call in warnings was her belief that causing casualties undercut Weather's support in the anti-war and youth movements, not a belief that 'any means necessary' was immoral for a morally-necessary revolution.

"Dohrn and Ayers said then, and in their many writings since, in Nixonian fashion, that 'mistakes were made' by the supposedly rogue Townhouse collective. But the context of these writings make it clear that the mistakes they had in mind were bad wiring and not predicting a negative reaction by the left, and not the act of murder. If an assassination campaign could create chaos, fear, and publicity for revolution without being attributed to Weatherman, Dohrn and her adherents would have no moral problem with it. Indeed, even 40 years after the fact, Dohrn wrote this about her bombings: 'The greater crime would be to do nothing, or not enough.' So actually, the Weathermen actually would have had a moral problem not taking on an untraceable assassination campaign.

"In summary, I can only conclude that both the government and the defense have theories that are possible, while the Dohrn theory, that Jacobs successfully hid the assassinations from her despite being in the core Weather cell, isn't consistent with the organization's highly-developed ideology and its history. It's also not credible in light of her own exceptional intelligence and awareness, which she demonstrated repeatedly in crisis after crisis. If by chance J. J. Jacobs was free-lancing in assassinations and attacking Weatherman in communiqués, and you can see why I dismiss that chance as minimal, everything we know about her makes it highly likely that Bernardine Dohrn would've made it her business to figure it out the very first time, and not after five years."

* * *

Denby was pleased with the professor's first day on the stand. The jurors had actually paid attention to her complex lesson. They may not have absorbed much of the detail, but they would remember that whoever had perpetrated the actual violence, Dohrn would have been controlling it. That was all she had wanted out of the day. LeBlanc had just one more point to make about Dohrn, she told Denby before court the next morning, before turning to Shaw.

"Professor, you focused on Ms. Dohrn's propensity to violence yesterday. I hope today you'll contrast that with the defendant's." Denby knew her only role would be to start LeBlanc up, because she seemed to know where she wanted to go.

"Well, counselor, I focused primarily on Ms. Dohrn's ideology, because it explains her attitude toward violence as a tactic. And I'll get to Professor Shaw's ideology and what it implies about violence. But first I would like to explore the question of the Weathermen's credibility, again within the context of ideology." LeBlanc turned to the jury and resumed her seminar.

"You see, just as violence is a tactic that serves the Weather ideology, so is lying. They lie both to protect themselves and their viability for the struggle, and to create a narrative that inspires new recruits. Remember? 'Reconstruction of history is a battle'? And they wage the battle constantly. As Winston Churchill said when explaining why history would treat Prime Minister Chamberlain harshly, they know the outcome because they write the history.

"Dohrn claimed in 1970 that John Jacobs was a rogue in the Townhouse plans, and only after 48 years, testifying in court under the threat of a trial for murder, did she admit that she knew his target. Now we have her new claim that J. J. was a rogue in the assassination plans, not just acting on his own but tricking the Weather Bureau about it. The historical record did not support the previous rogue claim, and it does not support this one. As you recall from my testimony yesterday, if J. J. was up to something, it's my judgment that the Weather Bureau certainly knew of it, and likely approved or ordered it.

"But a lie in this case to protect the organization and its members would be nothing new. The members of the Weather Bureau became practiced and convincing liars, successfully fashioning consistent stories about identities for their entire ten years underground. Famed journalist Sy Hersh told the *Washington Post* reporters Woodward and Bernstein, as they discussed Nixon's staff during the Watergate scandal, that 'I know these people. The abiding characteristic of this administration is that they lie.' It's the same with these Weathermen.

"For example, consider Dohrn's lies about not just big things, like the Park Station killing or the 'rogue' Townhouse collective's lethal plans, but the little things, like still claiming today that she and Ayers did not use children as 'beards' to case bombing sites. Or claiming that her 'Dig it!' tribute at Flint to Charles Manson's followers for sticking a fork into murdered white 'pigs' was just a neutral commentary on the media's obsession with the case. In fact, the entire theme of the Flint conference was a tribute to violence like Manson's, to anybody who attacked the rich or the police, even 'white pig babies.' Many is the time Dohrn was reported to have held up four fingers in the humorous 'fork' salute, at Flint and in later years, while underground. But her lies help keep her viable as a leftist political figure, so she lies.

"One of the things that Weather lies about, despite decades of celebrating and advocating violence, is their own violence, and that of their black heroes. Consider Kathy Boudin in the *Underground* film complaining of the holding of 'beautiful Ruchell McGee in prison on a trumped-up crime.' Black Panther McGee was photographed holding a shotgun that is taped to the neck of a judge in the Jonathan Jackson kidnapping right before the judge's head was blown off. Why not just admit he was a warrior?

"Ayers and Dohrn still repeat, in a book in 2009, the long-discredited lie that 27 Black Panthers were killed by police in 1969. Panther lawyer Charles Garry's actual claim was 28 killed in 1968 and 1969, but during a 1971 investigation by journalist Edward Epstein that was quickly reduced to ten, because the police had nothing to do with 18 of them: domestic disputes, crime, and political rivalry, including a torture-murder by the Panthers themselves. And of the remaining ten cases, all but three were killed after attacking police, almost all of them during armed robberies in which the police had no idea they were Panthers.

"Only the Hampton-Clark killings came during a police initiative, a raid based on accurate reports of a cache of illegal weapons, and the third police killing, of 17-year-old Bobby Hutton, came after the Panthers initiated a shoot-out as they monitored a police patrol. Why not just say that the Panthers were at war, and claimed the right to violence, but came out on the losing end in three cases? Because the lie helps justify the revolution.

"Consider Kathy Boudin's laughably obvious lies when she's trying to show parole boards, unsuccessfully in 2001 and finally successfully in 2003, that she had been just a confused kid angry at injustice and didn't have a violent bone in her body when she was in the Townhouse collective, aged 26, or was taking part in armed robberies of Brink's trucks, aged 38. Let me read you what she said about her ignorance of the Townhouse plans:

> And I was staying overnight at this house, it was like a movement house. It was a place where people were having discussions, talking about the work that they were doing. And I was taking a shower the next morning and the house collapses around me, essentially. And I subsequently learned that people had been actually making a bomb in the basement of that house. And people were killed. The people that were killed were not people that I knew...

"Of course, Boudin did not just happen to wander by a bomb-making factory to find a place to sleep. She was a member of the collective, approved the plan, and knew those killed, intimately.

"And of her six years in Weatherman she said: 'Other people built bombs during that time...My work was not doing violent work, but organizing conferences and educating people...I was never involved in violence directly.' This from someone who was with Weather from beginning to way past the end, from the first street fights to the last bomb, and beyond, from someone whose collective at Flint called itself the Fork.

"In the 1981 Brink's robbery by the Family, a coalition of the Black Liberation Army, or BLA, and Boudin's white May 19 successor to Weatherman, two policemen and a guard were murdered. Boudin served as the 'beard', a white woman whose presence in the cab of a get-away U-Haul truck would lead police to think the truck wasn't connected to the armed robbery that had just been committed by the black men hiding in the body of the truck. And the beard worked: when an officer at a road-block forced her out of the cab of the truck with a shotgun, she convinced him she wasn't connected to the crime and asked another policeman, 'Tell him to put the gun back.' The first officer did just that, right before the five armed robbers rolled up the back door and burst out shooting, killing two policemen.

"Again Boudin feigned ignorance before the parole board, testifying that her husband had asked her to come to a meeting with a stranger, who then asked them to drive the vehicle:

> I don't really know what the Black Liberation Army is...I don't know who jumped in the truck...I was able to put [the possibility of casualties] out of my mind because I was so desperate to be able to do something useful [for oppressed people]...I had not been around guns, was not involved in it, I saw myself as not even involved in the robbery in a certain way, because I didn't have a relationship to it. I saw myself as waiting in a parking lot, essentially, to pick people up.

"In fact, Boudin had used her above-ground job to help find get-away cars for previous Family armed robberies. Far from not knowing what the BLA was, her connection with it went back to its founding. The Townhouse collective had fire-bombed the home of the judge trying 21 New York Panthers, who became the nucleus of the BLA. The May 19 group took part in the prison raid that broke out BLA leader and long-time cop-hunter Joanne Chesimard, known as Assata Shakur. Boudin may even have named her son Chesa to honor Shakur, just like Ayers and Dohrn, who raised Chesa while his mother was in prison, named their own son after Zayd Shakur, Chesimard's partner in cop-hunting and in the unplanned shoot-out where he died and she was convicted of murder.

"So, this consistent subordination of truth to narrative is as problematic for a historian as the self-celebratory histories of the American foreign policy elite that the Weathermen so heavily and, in my opinion, rightly criticize.

"Now let me contrast that with what I have concluded about the ideology, propensity for violence, and credibility of the Weathermen with that of Professor Shaw.

"The surprising thing here is that you can't really say, reading young draft resister Valerius Shaw or even today's Professor Shaw, that he even has an ideology, some consistent explanation of why things are the way they are, and how they should be changed. Oh, he has always agreed with the Weathermen to a T on their first point of ideology, that specific wars are part of a system of Imperialism, that Viet Nam, in a dig at liberal anti-war activists, was no 'mistake' but rather inevitable and typical. And the United States role in the Third World still troubles him, pains him, defines him.

"Weatherman Jeff Jones said in 1975: 'We have a job: to explain what imperialism is.' Well, Shaw still has that job, and like Weatherman, he takes part in the battle to reconstruct history — although he skips the attention-getting bombings and goes straight to the communiqué. But he clearly rejects the rest of their ideology, the parts that led them to reject American culture and voting, and try to overthrow the government by force.

"The most recent article Professor Shaw published, right before his arrest, reads almost like the newspaper ad he took out in 1970 in opposition to the draft. He took issue with an editorial that warned 'if we get in a war, Trump will be a dangerous leader,' and listed the many countries of combat in a war we are already in, the one that he, and to be fair, the Pentagon too, calls 'the Long War' for control of the Muslim world. But when it comes to why those wars are always going on, why we have what he (and indeed many scholars, some of them not opposed to America's global role) refers to as imperialism, and how to stop it? He proposes nothing beyond the need to confront the self-congratulation in our culture and our history, from the elite down to the plebes, of our military role in the world, the claim that the good we do that justifies our 'temporary' support for dictators who cooperate with our deployments.

"That's why in the article Shaw attacks the Navy's TV ads that intone, 'America's Navy, a global force for good,' as an example of the last refuge of imperial scoundrels: the claim that our military deployments and expenditures are an altruistic gift to world stability. He also attacks the elite version of the same claim, a recent paean to power by Robert Kaplan arguing that without our dominance of the battlefield at sea there would be no 'liberal maritime order.' Instead, Shaw sees a straight line to today from Admiral Perry entering Tokyo Bay in 1853 and forcing trade on our terms. He calls America not the world's policeman, a friendly cop on the beat, but a mafia enforcer of self-interested rule.

"He then criticizes the Marines' ads that show them as a global humanitarian organization, racing toward chaos to drive out bad guys and bring relief to huddled refugees, rather than as the paid muscle that keeps our friendly dictators, the real bad guys, in power. He describes an ROTC sign on the Vanderbilt campus that says "Global reach starts with community outreach" as it urges young officers to wear their uniforms while taking part in community efforts, like bringing gifts to poor children. Shaw writes: 'Truer words were never spoken.'

"But while he agrees with Weather on the fact of imperialism and on how it is marketed at home, he buys none of Weather's ideology about Marxism, Leninism, and Castro-ism. In fact, he rejects each of these big three clearly and often. Shaw's a capitalist, a 'small d' democrat, and a vicious opponent of dictators, be they leftist or rightist. He argues that lots of powerful non-capitalist countries have become imperialist, so the notion that capitalism is the culprit in U.S. imperialism is wrong. He argues that lots of cultures where individualism and materialism are celebrated have not become imperialistic, and that nations as expansionist and racist as we have been have not gone on to become imperialist, so the notion that our culture is inherently imperialist is also wrong.

"During the Viet Nam war Shaw really doesn't say much of anything about why we invaded, neither the economic or cultural explanations. He's just sad and angry and feeling guilty and he wants the war to end. As a loner, he isn't exposed to the intense discussion and criticism and self-criticism that the Weathermen were. He doesn't develop a coherent ideology. And it's pretty much the same today. The statistician in him sees the world as too complicated, the causes too varied, for simple theories he calls bivariate, in which just one main variable drives the outcome.

"And because he's barren on ideology, the question of violence does indeed take on an importance to Shaw that it does not for the Weathermen. He may agree with them that Presidents Johnson and Nixon in the 1960s and Clinton and Obama more recently are leading criminal organizations, cults that convince soldiers to commit massive violence to preserve U.S. rule over other countries. But he doesn't think, as the Weathermen did, that this means that counter-violence is justified or even a duty. You can see him explore this question of violence in one of his songs: "Roman Times."

"The title is about an empire with which the singer has been battling, but the song is actually a surrender, a withdrawal from the battle. Ms. Denby asked me to evaluate it because it might indicate that family matters, and not John Jacobs' plans, led Valerius to change his mind and take a student deferment. Well, that was obvious, but what interested me more was what the words also revealed about Shaw's thoughts on violence as a political tactic. So I'd like to play it, and have you read the words as we go."

Denby finally had something to do: she set up the portable record player she had borrowed from a jazz-obsessed friend and ran a cord from the output jack to the court speakers. As the jury watched, she carefully slid Shaw's 1973 LP out of its cover. While the song played, she showed the lyrics on the courtroom screen.

"Now," said LeBlanc as the song died away, "what the singer 'used to say' was that he would 'die like a Gaul in Roman times,' suicidally taking on the powerful forces of the empire rather than bargaining with it. But now, with the birth of his son, he sees a higher duty to 'run away' and take care of him. Going to prison for the principle of draft resistance is what has dominated Shaw's thinking since he turned 18, but he says he'll give it up for his son's benefit, and in fact that is precisely what he does, right after his son's birth. But dying like a Gaul also means killing as many invaders as possible, and Shaw is giving up any propensity to such violence at the same time."

"Here Shaw resolved the problem of being the 'Good German' that the Weathermen constantly rail about, and that he has traced, in his own writings, to his parents' admonitions when he was a child and young teenager. Shaw threw the term back in his parents' face when he is drafted, to be sure, but being a parent makes him see the complex meaning of the admonition, the recognition that it's tough for the Germans who want to preserve their

families. Resistance in Germany meant not just exclusion from social benefits, like schooling and jobs, but imprisonment and perhaps death, for parents and children alike. All occupied countries learn this lesson, and there's
no right answer.

"Opponents of Nazi rule, whether Jewish or Christian, from France to
Poland, faced an extreme version of Shaw's choice between doing the right
thing for their people, their country — which is resistance — or doing the
right thing for their family — which is keeping your head down. Of course,
speaking up, let alone acting, against the American government in 1970 was
nowhere near as dangerous as speaking up against Hitler in 1933, let alone in
1938 when it was ruinous or 1942 when it was suicidal, but the point is that
everybody had to make calculations. Heroes endangered their families and
could see very little reward, very little impact on fascist rule.

"When Bernardine Dohrn is saying 'Christmas-time is an obscenity' in
1970 because of the continuing imperialism abroad, such as the war in Viet
Nam or the murder of Fred Hampton at home, and castigates families who
celebrate it, Valerius Shaw is collating hand-made picture books as presents
for his new son. It doesn't look to me like he's planning on scouting for a
rebel army's attacks, like the first Nathan Hale, and like Dohrn. It looks like
he's planning on sticking around with his new Nathan Hale.

"I have to see meaning in Shaw naming his son for a hero of the revolution
that created the American government and Dohrn naming her son for a hero
of the revolution that wanted to overthrow it. By analysis she develops an
ideology that says only revolution can remedy America's illness, but Shaw
seems to have an unanalyzed faith, perhaps rooted in his historian mother's
own ideology, that it can be reformed, that you can reach the American people because there is goodness in so many of them. Violence is the outcome of
Dohrn's decision, non-violence is the outcome of Shaw's.

"Again, on balance, without certainty but with confidence, I think that
the defense's theory is made more believable by the historical evidence than
the government's. It's more likely that Jacobs set Shaw up than that he convinced Shaw to become a killer."

* * *

Purpose certainly didn't want to engage LeBlanc in a discussion of dates and speeches, and from his perspective the less anybody said about Dohrn and Ayers and their bizarre beliefs, the better. His best hope, he thought, was to produce some skepticism within the jury about the professor's logic in using a song to clear Val of murderous intent.

"Professor LeBlanc, thank you for educating us all here these past couple of days. I now know more about the ins and outs of radical politics than I ever thought possible. And I do hope your appearance here helps the sales of any book you write on this case, that's for sure. You never can tell which one will hit the big time! I mean, remember *The Hunt for Red October*, or *Harry Potter*, or even your fellow professor, Allan Bloom, and his unexpected success with *The Closing of the American Mind.*

"But your testimony is all just speculation, isn't it? The jury surely noticed that I never once objected to your speculation on the state of mind of people you've never met, because there was nothing factual to object to. So let's leave the academic exercise behind. The issue is not which of these aging radicals is more believable: the issue is the evidence. Valerius Shaw is on trial in a federal court for three brutal murders, and there are another three for which he'll be held accountable in state courts. You don't, do you, know for a fact that he is innocent of these charges, do you?"

"No, I don't," responded LeBlanc, ignoring Denby's pleading look for her to qualify her admission, and restate some of the evidence for her conclusions.

"And you do know that if Valerius Shaw played any role in the conspir-acy with Jacobs, even if he weren't the actual angel of death, the hands-on killer in each instance, that makes him guilty of capital murder under federal law, if he had any knowledge before-hand, for any of the murders?"

"I have no idea if that's true. I am not a lawyer."

"Well, trust me, it is," snarled Purpose, "and I am sure the judge will so instruct the jury." He moved quickly to his next question, before the judge would rebuke him for making reference to her positions. "Now let's look at the defense theory, which you call more likely, because of the various actors' political backgrounds than the government's theory. And let's assume with the defense that Shaw was innocent of these crimes. Just how likely is it, in your expert opinion as a historian, that Shaw could go to a city for one or two nights, six times in five years, have a political murder take place while he was there, and that's seven times if you add in the documented case of Professor Huntington, have the communiqués be signed by a group sharing his son's name, and not start to think he was somehow connected to it? Is that believable?"

"I can't speak for the defendant's awareness of these things, and I'm not even sure of the relevance of the question," said LeBlanc.

Purpose caustically hammered LeBlanc, desperate to crack her air of rea-son and moderation. "The relevance, professor, is that you're painting a pic-ture of a non-violent, good-hearted reformist young critic of the government, yet we have no record of any government entity, any police force, receiving word from Shaw of his suspicions. We know he'd met with John Jacobs. If he'd turned him down, as the defense claims, because he opposed violence, wouldn't he have tried to stop Jacobs when he finally figured out that he was killing people?"

The hammering failed. "Oh, well, that I can answer. You simply wouldn't believe how many hundreds of people there were during the Weathermen's ten years underground who opposed them, who thought they were wrong, dangerous, violent, intolerant, and just plain really crazy, but still helped hide them and move them, without a peep to the police. If this was Professor Shaw's crime, it would actually fit the mood of the times. Incredibly, the FBI files I've reviewed show not one case of an anti-war person providing information that helped the FBI."

Purpose jumped on LeBlanc's claim: "Ah, but you told us earlier that this resistance to cooperation with the authorities was in part due to the successful ruse of the Weather Bureau claiming that the Townhouse leaders were rogues, and that the rest of them never intended to hurt anyone. Shaw wouldn't have had that excuse, would he, if he'd figured out that Jacobs was killing people?"

"That's a good point, if in fact Shaw knew it all," replied the professor, now drawing furious looks from Denby.

The prosecutor decided it was a good time to move on, after at least a tiny victory. "Now, I want to go back to your testimony about Mr. Shaw's song for his son, Nathan Hale Shaw, and what it might reveal about his decision to stay in play for J. J. Jacobs' plots and the Nathan Hale Brigade, as Ms. Laurel, an eye-witness, not a professor 50 years later, told us.

"You said that *Roman Times* revealed somebody willing to leave behind an all-consuming, deeply-believed struggle, whether its tools were combat or draft resistance, and trade it in for a peaceful family life. Now, to me, that's quite a stretch, quite an unjustified conclusion, from one song. But let me go along with your belief that a song of Mr. Shaw's can clarify his thinking about political violence. Let me just play you and the jury another one, and you'll see what I mean.

"If it please the court, I would like to introduce a recording of the defendant singing one of his compositions, *American girl, American man.* This recording was provided to the FBI by the Birchmere music club in Alexandria, Virginia, which has saved the tapes from its 'sound-board' since 1970, in the hope, frequently met, that artists will decide to release a 'Live at the Birchmere' cut on one of their albums. The sound-board is the console you often see at the back of a concert hall, which takes all the microphones on stage and mixes them into what comes out of the speakers for the crowd, and then saves the mix as a matter of course.

"This recording is from February 14, 1975, the night of the murder of Daniel Parker, the head of America's agency that provides relief supplies to poor people overseas. Most likely murdered, I might remind us all, with the same gun that Alice Truxton says was used by the defendant to try to kill Professor Huntington in Cambridge, at the start of his assassination spree, in 1970."

Denby thought about objecting, but then realized that Purpose was probably conflating and conjecturing a simple tale from Truxton's more complex testimony precisely because it was objectionable, and he wanted a battle over it, with all the repetition of facts it would entail. She kept quiet, figuring that the less the jury heard about Cambridge, the better — especially now that Val's confession would create ethical problems for her if she discredited the allegation. Just leave it as a mysterious detail, she decided, a referendum on the credibility of an admitted bomber.

Purpose submitted the copyright papers for the song, which were from 1974, and an affidavit from the recording engineer, Coles, stating that Shaw had written the song and recorded a demo tape of it that year. Then he had the Birchmere recording played while the words were scrolled on a large screen for the jury to read.

"Professor, you're an expert on the political history of the 1970s right? Can you tell the jury who the 'American boy, American man' in this song was, and why he's 'standing in the courtroom, with your gun in your hand'?"

"That would probably be Jonathan Jackson, the younger brother of Black Panther George Jackson, a well-known prison author, an armed robber who was indicted for murdering guards. George was also the subject of a top-selling song by Bob Dylan. Jonathan Jackson invaded a California courthouse and seized a judge and other hostages, whom he wanted to trade for his brother's freedom. While driving out of the complex he was killed along with the judge and two of prisoners who had joined the escape attempt."

"Thank you, professor. Now, the 'gun in your hand' in this song of tribute was a sawed-off shotgun, that was then taped to the neck of Judge Harold Haley — I always want to honor the real names of the real people these so-called humanitarians sacrificed — and it was used to blow his head off. This song glorifies the revolutionary murder of a judge, a 'pig' to Mr. Shaw and his friends, a pig who enforces the laws for what he considers an evil empire."

As soon as Purpose attributed the word "pig" to Val, he started whispering fiercely to Denby. "Never, never, never. That's one of the reasons I hated the Weathermen."

"Objection, objection, Your Honor," interjected Denby. "This is really too much. Counsel has clearly been reading the defendant's writings, which indeed do label American foreign policy as an 'evil empire.' Now, such labeling isn't a crime, not under our first amendment right of freedom of speech, and in fact, Professor LeBlanc already told the jury that it's a widely held analysis throughout the world and indeed in American academic circles. She testified that even scholars who support America's global reach characterize it as an empire in the sense that this word is used in the study of history.

"But precisely because counsel has read my client's pieces, he knows full well that Professor Shaw has never used the Weathermen's favorite word, pig, to describe anybody, not a judge, not a police officer, not a congressman who supported the Vietnam war, not a general, not a State Department official, nobody. In fact, he was and is disgusted by that word and the contempt for people it reveals, and it was one of the reasons he rejected the advances of the Weathermen in 1970. Mr. Purpose's willful and knowing breach of the truth is a violation of court rules, of his own professional oaths. It's a most serious matter, and I urge Your Honor to review it fully."

"Is counsel suggesting that I consider contempt charges against Mr. Purpose?" Judge Brittain glared at Denby, who had ignored her specific instruction to the lawyers never to broach the issue of contempt, which was her prerogative alone. "Because once we get into contempt charges, I am sure Mr. Purpose will have similar objections to what you just did before the jury, willfully and knowingly yourself, trying to testify in place of Professor Shaw in your objection."

"Of course not, Your Honor," replied Denby, although both of them knew full well that this was exactly what she'd been suggesting. "I merely would like you to instruct the jury to disregard any implication in Mr. Purpose's question that my client ever joined his witness, Ms. Dohrn, in calling police, soldiers, government officials, judges, and all white people who weren't in their little cult, and even the white fetuses of women who were in her cult, pigs."

Purpose could see that he was getting the worst of the ongoing discus- sion of his effort to dirty up Val's shoes, so he brought it to a close. "It was my mistake your honor. I misspoke. I didn't intend to include Mr. Shaw in the list of his fellow revolutionaries who were calling others 'pigs,' and I with- draw that error." He couldn't resist a final stab, though: "Frankly, I don't know if he did, or if he didn't. I assumed they all used the same jargon."

"The jury has heard Mr. Purpose's apology, and it will disregard any inference that the defendant used the term 'pig' and indeed disregard Ms. Denby's characterization of Professor Dohrn's use of the term that hasn't been supported by previous testimony. Continue, please."

"All right," said Purpose, "Professor, we were at the part where I was going to ask you about this song that talks about 'your gun in your hand,' a gun used to kidnap and assassinate Judge Haley. You say that one song, the Roman one, from 1971, is pacifist, and tends to clear Mr. Shaw of murderous intent. But if you can reach that conclusion, wouldn't you agree that this song, which he wrote well after his son's birth and was still singing in 1975, is violent and tends to implicate Mr. Shaw in murderous intent?"

"Not at all, not at all," responded LeBlanc. "I'm not a music critic, and the Valerius songs are just part of the puzzle that led me to differentiate his written statements from those of the Weathermen on the moral issue of using violence to stop the war in Viet Nam, or disrupt what he, and they, considered to be the system that led us to support the dictators in South Viet Nam and other countries. And as I indicated earlier to Ms. Denby, it's beyond my ability to translate this written rejection of violence into the state of Professor Shaw's heart, or to predict his actions. You seem to think that I somehow 'cleared' Valerius Shaw, but I did no such thing. I am not qualified to have an opinion about the legal questions this trial asks.

"That being said, I would like to answer your question. Now, I've never heard this song before today — it's not on his album. But I will say, looking over the words that are still displayed there, that it strikes me on the surface as being more commentary than advocacy. It seems to be equating Jonathan Jackson's feelings of being trapped by life with those of the clearly less polit- ical girl. So I would say that I don't agree with you that these words glorify Jackson or advocate what he did. 'You only loved your brother, and you had to set him free.' That sounds like someone who is trapped by their own feel-ings, not the author's."

"Come on, professor, 'all of you are a part of me'? You don't see sympathy, the sort of sympathy that justifies an action, in the 'equating' you found? If shooting a judge is equated with washing the dishes, you don't think the writer at least accepts them both as reasonable actions? Your Honor, I have no further questions, no more interest in the speculation of this witness, who has strayed so far from her expertise in political science in trying to clear a murderer."

* * *

Epilogue: June 2018, Chicago

What is patriotism for a citizen of America, that sprawling, gargantuan, 'loose, baggy monster,' cultural generator to the world and mecca for foreign talent and drive, land of the globalist and the nativist, the proud sophisticate and the proud know-nothing, land of the hidebound and the creative, land of the celebrated homebody with a 50-year-old watch fob and the celebrated mobile entrepreneur, that schizophrenic liberal empire, slave-holding and continent-grabbing venerator of freedom and mutual respect, neocolonial vessel of human rights, arming dictators while talking democracy and believing in both, a Fox of hatreds and a Hedgehog of tolerance, the bull elephant in the china shop and the cooling china saucer of modern times in so many spheres?

Is patriotism a primal group pride in military action? Is it the tingle of electricity, the pop of joy, the warmth of collaboration your body feels when America demonstrates its dearly-purchased, historically unparalleled ability to rain deadly Special Forces or cruise missiles on uncooperative wogs, half a world away? When a European Jew hugs you because your father's generation liberated Auschwitz (even though it didn't — thank the evil Soviet Stalinists for that)? When you see college students out in droves on their six a.m. ROTC training runs, or police and firefighters suited up for another day of readiness to sacrifice themselves for strangers?

Don't tread on me. We'll put a boot in your ass, it's the American way. Don't mess with Texas. Marines — first to fight, last to leave. We don't start fights, but we finish them. Say what you mean, mean what you say. Slow to anger, hard to stop. Strong and silent. Speak softly and carry a big stick.

Or is patriotism a pride in thought, in culture, in the drive to create and the perseverance to succeed? Is it the tingle, the pop, the warmth you feel when foreigners praise Cooper, Whitman, Twain, Hughes, DuBois, Penniman and Price, Goodman and Coltrane, Ford and Gates, Duane and Greg, or Walker and Grisham, when a sixteen-year-old Chinese exchange student tells you he chose Thomas as his "English" name because he always admired Thomas Jefferson for the Declaration of Independence and the Virginia Statute for Religious Freedom — even if you are a Hamiltonian in the great dispute over the 10th Amendment? (Perhaps a subject of Her Britannic Majesty would feel the same way with another Chinese student who, truly, took the name Thomas because he's always loved Thomas the Tank Engine.)

But patriotism can also be a pride, an identification, a communion with those whose creative thought led them inescapably to radical, even at times military action against the motherland itself, to correct it, to hold it to its claimed values, to make it lovable rather than leave it ugly. Without the rebels, the fundamental yang to the yin of self-celebration and sclerotic convention, there is also no America. Is there not a thrill of respect, if not always a nod of agreement, when you think of the deeds of the violent warriors of conscience Nat Turner and John Brown, the peaceful warriors of conscience Jeannette Rankin and Robert Browne, Bob Moses' Mississippi martyrs Chaney, Goodman, and Schwerner, Black Panthers Fred Hampton and Bobby Seale, and yes, young, foul-mouthed, glazed-eye certain Bernardine Dohrn and Billy Ayers and their tiny Weather Underground?

"What am I doing in jail? What are you doing out there?" (Henry David Thoreau, 1846) "We must name that system. We must name it, describe it, analyze, understand it, and change it." (SDS president Paul Potter, 1965) "I could never again raise my voice against the violence of the oppressed in the ghettos without first having spoken clearly to the greatest purveyor of violence in the world today: my own government." (Martin Luther King Jr., 1967) "I'm going to read a declaration of a state of war." (Bernardine Dohrn, 1970)

* * *

Dohrn and Ayers, in their mid-70s, no longer young but maybe, in the natural calm of time, as Dylan sang, younger than that now, sit together on the "L" as it rattles south to Hyde Park on a Saturday night. They're riding back from a fund-raising dinner in the Loop for a "climate change" march on Washington, the sort of march they would have attacked back in the day, storming the stage to denounce collaboration and compromise with politicians and celebrities who want to reform the system rather than overthrow it — indeed to denounce any environmental movement as a naïve, self-centered draining of energy away from the anti-imperialist movement.

Bernie and Billy are no longer foul-mouthed, but they are just as glazed-eye certain that imperialism flows from the American character and that its crimes justify Malcolm X's "any means necessary" to stop them, as glazed-eye certain as the architects and worker bees of American exceptionalism are that it too flows from the American character, and that its benefits justify any means necessary to expand its reach.

Still dressed in the '60s uniform of loose jeans and work shirt, but with the modern addition of high-arched Nike running shoes and Patagonia vests, the couple sits listening to music — the Jefferson Airplane, "Volunteers of America," in fact — while they share the ear buds of an iPhone 7+. "Look what's happenin', out in the streets: got a revolution, got to revolution. Hey, I'm marchin' down the street: got a revolution, got to revolution."

A hooded figure walks slowly up the car, and stops in front of Bill and Bernardine, peering at the subway map on the wall behind them. They don't look up, and pretend to talk only to each other as they converse with Melissa.

"Hey, girl, that was mighty fine work," whispers Bernardine. "I'd give you the biggest hug, but let's assume the FBI is pissed and still watching. Hell, after Snowden showed our paranoia was mild, you can almost guarantee somebody's groovin' along to the Airplane with us right now! So keep your head focused on that map. *La lucha continua.*"

"*A luta continua,* indeed. I was glad to help. But I gotta say, I couldn't figure out what you were going for. I just did my lines like you wrote them. Didn't you want Shaw to go down?"

"No, no need for that, and there was no need for you to know," answers Ayers. "You did better on stage as the clueless, angry, bourgeois preacher. We gave them Shaw with one hand — and Bernardine did enough in court so they couldn't accuse her of violating her deal on San Francisco — and then you came in as the other hand, to muddy the waters and get him off.

"Our plan was perfect. Nobody knows what hit 'em, not Shaw, not his lawyer, not the Fibbies...although they think long and hard about these things, and probably will eventually get it. Nothing they can do about it then, though. See, we didn't want to help them put anybody in prison, in the end, certainly not somebody who still rants in public against the empire. Your little boyfriend sure still keeps the faith, doesn't he? And besides, J. J. never told us, and we never asked — maybe Shaw really was his side-kick. Best as I can recall, the only one J. J. asked us for help on was Pittsburgh, the bombing. The others, who knows?"

Bernardine chimes in: "And as for the great negotiator, dumb-ass Trump, we left him holding the bag. I'm free for Park Station and there's still no convictions for Weather-cat. No wonder he went bankrupt so many times! And didn't you love the sister's comeback on the government about his Jonathan Jackson song, in the closing arguments? That alone was worth the price of admission.

"Advocate violence in a song? Hell, he's sung Pretty Polly gets stabbed in the heart, and her heart's blood did flow; the Knoxville Girl gets grabbed by her golden curls, and dragged around and round, and thrown into the river that flows through Knoxville town; Staggerlee shoots Billy over a Stetson hat and tells him, 'God'll take care of your children, I'll take care of your wife'; Shotgun Slade wipes out the work crew trying to put the choo-choo across his land; Johnny Cash shoots that deputy down, just like Pretty Boy Floyd... It's all just good fun. No advocacy there!

"Anyway, dear, I hope the publicity doesn't mess you up with your congregation in Iowa. Come the revolution, we can always make you Minister of Religion, though! We'll need at least one believer around to placate the medievals."

The figure in the hood chuckles. "Rose, I can keep operational security too: you never knew it back then, but I was in the religion department at Swarthmore just to get access to all their resources, credibility, and useful fools. It was great place to hide and recruit. It's always been a cover, my religious nonsense, a great way to make a living, and I could care less now that I have another way. Hey, if they fire me, they'll probably be another bunch of kumbaya liberals who want to make a statement by having me 'come by there.' And if not, well, I assume that's the second half?"

"We're the next stop," says Bernardine. "Have a great life."

As the train slows for 51st Street, the two graying warriors stand and brush past Melissa, leaving a shoulder bag on the floor in front of their seats. She remains standing, checking the map once more as if uncertain of her stop. But she is very certain, certain that the $200,000 in the bag, along with the initial payment, will make for an extremely soft landing wherever she alights. She played that right, she laughs to herself. She would've done it for free. She's a disciplined revolutionary. The Central Committee asks, the Central Committee receives. But, hey, even the players get played sometime.

She'd done her research: she knew the pay-off wouldn't put much of a dent in the burgeoning estate of William G. Ayers, Billy's dad, who ran Illinois power giant Commonwealth Edison for 36 years. His estate was adjudicated after Congress had agreed to a proposal by George W. Bush to double the floor for exemptions from "death taxes" while maintaining the "step up in basis" that eliminates any capital gains tax on inherited stocks, like Ayers' holdings in Exelon, Com-Ed's parent company.

America. Land of opportunity, land of no consequences, where the ruling class passes its fortunes along to its kids even as they rail against income equality, even if they say, like young Billy Ayers, "Bring the revolution home, kill your parents, that's where it's really at."

America. No punishment for any of her foreign crimes because, just like Valerius Shaw, she hasn't been proven guilty beyond a reasonable doubt.

America. Land of the perpetual bipartisan empire, arming feudal, oil-friendly Saudi sheiks from Roosevelt's day to Trump's with every president's reign in between, as the convenient excuses of state congratulated by court scribes morphed from anti-fascism to anti-communism to economic stability to democracy and lately to anti-terrorism and blocking China, which would supposedly, magically take over our rule if we decided to leave other countries' politics alone, and somehow constrain human dignity even more.

America. Where good people cheer for camouflage uniforms on baseball players but don't know the history of the people who've felt the crush of the empire maintained by the real uniforms: the Vietnamese patriots, the Guatemalan peasants, the Salvadoran priests, the Bahraini marchers, the Somali refugees, the writers, workers, teachers, and others who every day get on the wrong side of the global network of friendly thugs our government arms, trains, and funds.

America, where a memorial wall honors 58,000 invaders of Viet Nam, Cambodia, and Laos, and not the millions in those countries who died as a result of the invasion — and yes, it was "no mistake." As Bobby Kennedy said in 1961, before the war got too hot, "We've got twenty Viet Nams a day to handle." Now it's up to a hundred, countries in which it's our empire and not their citizens that chooses the government. Weatherman elder Mark Rudd says that after decades of activism, from protest to violence and back again, "I still don't what to do with this knowledge." Are any of us any closer than he is to figuring that out? Now that's a patriotic question, one Valerius would like.

* * *

Non-Disclaimer

Like *War and Peace* (I always wanted to write that phrase), this book is neither purely novel nor history, but rather "what the author wished and was able to express," in this case about patriotism in the imperial America of my lifetime. I use some real people as characters, because they are unique historical partisans on the questions being raised. Tolstoy couldn't have used a fictional French or Russian emperor in telling the story of 1812. Similarly, Bernardine Dohrn and Donald Trump need to play themselves in my fiction about the America I've lived through.

Indeed, this book has a lot more real than fictional characters. So "any resemblance to actual persons, living or dead, or actual events is purely" purposeful, not the usual accidental. If someone is somewhere doing or saying something in this book, I have done my best to make it accurate if it happened, and reasonable if it didn't.

The real characters include members of the Weather Underground and other groups that were at war with the United States from the late 1960s into the early 1980s, and a lot of public figures from those times. The real characters also include public figures from more recent times, as well as, just for fun, musicians and club owners who interact with my traveling musician. To help the reader keep them straight, I provide below a scorecard of all the players, real and fictional.

The real characters use dialogue, take actions, and issue statements that are consistent, in my opinion, with their histories. Except for the bombings, it's all fictitious, but to me, believable, based on these characters' histories and their own voices in writings, interviews, and public appearances. As the book makes clear, the Weathermen have taken credit for all of the bombings except the one at Park Station in San Francisco.

Among the real characters are two, Congressman Felix Hébert and Administrator of the Agency for International Development Daniel Parker, who most definitely did not die in the manner described in the book. Again, as noted, all of the assassinations in the book are fictional. However, the Weather Underground did actually bomb all of these people's places of employment as described, and in such a way that could well have killed them. The aspersions to Representative Hébert for possibly partaking in the Louisiana sport of bribery are cast by a fictional FBI agent, and I have no basis for endorsing them. Similarly, Sally Parker was a noted hostess, but her tastes are my invention.

Some of my scenes rely heavily on facts and concepts contained in the numerous memoirs by and books on the Weathermen. Among them I found historian Arthur Eckstein's book on the Weather Underground and the FBI, *Bad Moon Rising*, the most invaluable and credible. But my interpretations are not his.

Unlike in *War and Peace* (there, did it again!), some of my characters are still alive. This presents some legal and ethical issues. It is not my intention to libel people when I make up actions and dialogue for them, or have other characters or the narrator describe them and their actions and beliefs. I believe I am playing fairly with them, attributing words and actions that are reasonable fictions, based on the facts of their lives.

The primary legal and ethical question here is: Is it fair for me to have an admitted criminal thinking about committing, and perhaps committing, another crime? (The book leaves much of who actually does what in suspense.) Specifically, can people who advocated killing "pigs" — a catch-all word meaning cops, soldiers, and their managerial class in the capitalist empire, and indeed anybody, even close allies, who wouldn't walk their latest party line, and who admitted to planning and carrying out bombings where those pigs worked, be considered libeled when they are portrayed fictionally as pondering and perhaps committing assassinations of said pigs?

For me, no. Perhaps some litigious, pig-hating, real-world characters will disagree with their fictional portrayal. But since the surviving Weathermen and I both love to read Dylan like the Torah, Dante, or Shakespeare to find inspiration for the choices we make, let me remind them that Zimmy wrote, "to live outside the law, you must be honest." You chose to be "outlaws of Amerika," Castro in your own land. You reached for the golden ring of the overthrow of the government. History will absolve you too, as it always eventually does. *Tout comprendre, tout pardonner.* So respect your decision, as I do, even as I disagreed with it then and now, and be like Fidel when he was tried for the attack on the Moncada Barracks. Don't keep obscuring the truth with cause-serving and self-serving lies to the public or to your parole board.

Like Iran–Contra plotter Ollie North, when you failed and were brought before the bar, you chose to use the laws of a system you held in contempt to avoid punishment. Fine with me. Hey, I'm not pure. I used the draft laws I railed against to beat the draft. I've never regretted it, or begrudged anybody else's attempt to avoid having to kill or be killed in an immoral invasion. Al Gore's nonsense about going to Viet Nam as an Army journalist to save a working class Tennessee kid from combat is just that. But you be honest, too. Ask yourself: are not the conversations and plans and the fictional assassinations in this book consistent with your beliefs, then and perhaps now?

In some way, even the fictional characters in this book are real people, being composites of the many folks I've met in my suddenly lengthy life. As is the case with the songs and sounds of Valerius, the traveling musician, all my work is derivative. Tolstoy's dictum was to write what you know (Trifecta!). Well, I know these folks. At least I did until I started writing and they took over, making my fingers tap out things I hadn't thought of before.

* * *

LIST OF CHARACTERS (appearing or referred to)

The Anti-Imperialists

Fictional Characters

Valerius "Val" Shaw: college student and musician, and then Vanderbilt professor

Sally: Shaw's "first ex-wife"

Nathan "Nat" Hale Shaw: their son

Shaw's mother: a Swarthmore professor of American History

Shaw's father: a lawyer

Jonah Shaw: Shaw's brother

Selam Dibaba: Shaw's second wife

Art Thomas: Shaw's roommate at the University of Chicago

Max: Shaw's dorm adviser, U of C

Thad Leslie: member of the U of C Students for a Democratic Society

Julia: a Pittsburgh waitress and college student

Alice Truxton: Cambridge Weather Underground member

Melissa Laurel: Swarthmore radical publisher and Weather supporter

Real Characters

Members of the Weather Underground, at war with the United States:

● Bernardine Dohrn née Ohrnstein a.k.a Rose Bridges, Bill Ayers, Howie Machtinger, Eleanor Raskin née Stein, Jeff Jones, John "J. J." Jacobs, David Gilbert, Mark Rudd, Cathy Wilkerson, Kathy Boudin, Diane Donghi, Linda

Evans, Judy Clark, Ron Fliegelman, Diana Oughton, Terry Robbins, Teddy Gold, Brian Flanagan, Clayton van Lydegrafe

Members of other anti-government groups:

● Susan Saxe, Kathy Power, Sam Melville né Goodman, Jane Alpert, Marilyn Buck, Joanne Chesimard a.k.a Assata Shakur and Zayd Shakur of the Black Liberation Army, Ralph Featherstone and Che Payne of the Student Non-Violent Coordinating Committee, Patty Hearst, Black Panthers Fred Hampton, Mark Clark, Erica Huggins, Alex Rackley, Bobby Seale, George Jackson, Ruchell McGee, and Huey P. Newton

Communist Party leader Angela Davis and her bodyguard Jonathan Jackson

Vietnamese revolutionary leader and president Ho Chi Minh

Cuban revolutionary leader and president Fidel Castro

Argentinian revolutionary Che Guevara

French revolutionary theorist Régis Debray

Murderous cult leaders Charles Manson, Jim Jones, and Donald "Cinque" DeFreeze

SDS activists Tom Hayden and Bruce Dancis

Weather supporter Dennis Cunningham and his daughter Melia Ellis

Informant Larry Grathwohl

Martin Luther King Jr. né Michael

Malcolm X né Little

Movement attorneys Charles Garry and William Kunstler

MIT professor Noam Chomsky

Singers Eartha Kitt and Joan Baez, and Baez's husband, draft resister David Harris

Abbie Hoffman, leader of the Yippies

Anti-war Senator Charles Goodell

Julius and Ethel Rosenberg, executed Soviet spies

Bob Dylan né Zimmerman

The Imperialists

Fictional characters

Mar'Shae "Black" McGurk: FBI agent

Jerry Cummings: her supervisor

Fox Grier: FBI agent

Tony Tritt: San Francisco police chief

Salvatore Imaglio: assistant attorney general

George Hemmings: U.S. Army major general

Lucy Van Oss: director of the MIT Center for International Studies

Roosevelt Gray: Gulf Oil executive

Halim Gray, his wife, and Mary Gray, their daughter

Victor Iglesias: International Telephone and Telegraph executive

James Purpose: federal prosecutor for the District of Columbia

Real Characters

President Donald Trump

His adviser Steve Bannon

Commentators Sean Hannity and Paul Harvey

Attorneys General Jefferson Sessions, John Mitchell, John Ashcroft, and Robert Kennedy

FBI Directors James Comey, J. Edgar Hoover, and Clarence Kelly

FBI deputy director Mark Felt a.k.a Deep Throat

National Football League Commissioner Roger Goodell

"Chicago Eight" Judge Julius Hoffman

Presidents Dwight Eisenhower, John Kennedy, Lyndon Johnson, Richard Nixon, Bill Clinton, and Barack Obama

National Security Advisors McGeorge Bundy and Henry Kissinger

Nancy Kissinger, Henry's wife

Assistant Secretary of State William Bundy

Secretary of Defense and World Bank president Robert McNamara

Harvard political scientists Samuel P. Huntington and Carl Kaysen

U.S. Army Generals William Westmoreland and Bruce Palmer

San Francisco police sergeant Brian V. McDonnell

San Francisco police officer Robert Fogarty

Louisiana Congressman Felix Hébert

MIT Center for International Studies administrators and fellows Max Millikan, Walt Rostow, Lincoln Bloomfield, and William Kaufmann

Viet Nam counter-insurgency planners Edward Lansdale and Daniel Ellsberg

IT&T president Harold Geneen

Administrator of the Agency for International Development Daniel Parker

Sally Parker, his wife, and Geoff Parker, their son

Chase Manhattan Bank and Council on Foreign Relations president David Rockefeller

Governor Nelson Rockefeller, his brother

Senator Joseph Biden

Court historians Michael Mandelbaum, Robert Kaplan, and Niall Ferguson

Classicist Allan Bloom

Neutral Parties

Fictional Characters

Dominic LoPinto: booking agent

Rachel: a Harvard student

Bill Coles: recording engineer and producer

Harold Middles: Bill Ayers' original lawyer

Sharia Denby: Shaw's trial lawyer

Judge Anne Brittain

Vanessa LeBlanc: Berkeley political scientist

Real Characters

University of Chicago professor Theodore "Ted" Lowi

Yale president Kingman Brewster

Supreme Court Justices Neil Gorsuch and Clarence Thomas

Marin County judge Harold Haley

Nation of Islam leader Louis Farrakhan

War reporter Neil Sheehan

Greg Craig, Shaw's original lawyer

Judge Lance Ito

Brink's Guard William Molroney

Musicians:

• Eagles, Aztec Two-step, Emmy Lou Harris, Harold Betters, the Seldom Scene, Smokey Robinson, Donovan, Orleans, Chris Smither, John Bailey, Pete Townsend, Tom Waits, Jackson Browne, Curtis Mayfield, Bonnie Raitt, the Beatles, James Burton, Gram Parsons, Ralph McTell, Bill Monroe,

Gerry and the Pacemakers, Ralph Stanley, Merle Haggard, Tompall Glaser, Waylon Jennings, B. B. King, Amédé Ardoin, Mick Jagger, Robbie Robertson, Willie Nelson, Rodney Crowell, Shel Silverstein, Conway Twitty né Jenkins, Loretta Lynn, Merle Travis, Jefferson Airplane

Non-musicians: The Monkees and Beatles-breaker Yoko Ono

Producers George Martin and Glyn Johns

Historians Kai Bird and Arthur Eckstein

Writer Bryan Burrough

Cornell University president and physics professor Dale Corson

Commenting on the Townhouse explosion: Phil Ochs and Dustin Hoffman

Pittsburgh club owners Will Shiner and Gus Greenlee

Washington, DC, Cellar Door promoter Jack Boyle

Bethesda, Maryland, Red Fox Inn owner Bobby Edwards

Arlandria, Virginia, Birchmere restaurant owner Gary Oelze

"I.Q." researcher Arthur Jensen

Journalist Edward Epstein

* * *

Printed in the United States
By Bookmasters